Burning Rock

"A novel"

Mingo Twain

By Mingo Twain

Acknowledgments

I could never pen enough words to express my gratitude to Bonnie Mastenbrook. Her support has been unending. I could never have finished the book without her help.

A special thanks to a true friend, Randy Smith, for his input. Randy has talent beyond measure and if he ever decides to write books himself, I feel certain they will all be best sellers.

Dr. Jonah Womack. Thank you for your encouragement and support.

Cover design by Reata Strickland. Thank you, Reata, for all your time and patience.

Preface

Jake Roberts was a poor country boy growing up in the Appalachian Mountains. Unable to gain acceptance from his cruel unloving mother, he had no self-esteem. His problems escalated when a worthless stepfather entered his life. Searching for someone to bond with, he paired up with the new neighbor kid, Ryan Tyler, who was outgoing and daring. The two unsupervised boys soon found themselves involved in a host of criminal activity.

As they grew older, their bond grew stronger, making them inseparable. It's one wild adventure after another, as Ryan's leadership, uncanny ability to read people, and desire to be rich, lands the two in the middle of an organized gambling ring. As disaster strikes the tables are turned. Ryan then has to depend on Jake, if they are to survive.

Prologue

The room was dim, lit only by the amber-colored lights from overhead. As they laid me on my back and strapped my legs and arms to the table, a million-and-one thoughts and emotions flowed through my head. Why the table, why the straps, was this necessary? I had been gone a long time and many laws had changed, but how could they keep me for so long? What about an attorney, how could they deny me a lawyer, and my rights, did I no longer have rights?

They have accused me of murdering ten people, including my best friend - hiding undercover for years, then concocting a preposterous story to cover my tracks. After more than a week of interrogation by a criminal task force, including agents from the FBI, they've found nothing to disprove my story. I passed three lie detector tests, and suffered through hours on end of physiological evaluation.

They're frustrated because I've not broken down and agreed with them. They keep asking me about 'The girl'. Someone saw us together before I went to the police. I came to the police for help, but they immediately arrested me, so I decided to tell them nothing about her. I dare not even think of her name, afraid that they can somehow pull it out of my mind. Since they continue asking about her whereabouts, I assume she got away, and went to see the woman in Virginia. I pray she got there safely, if so I might get help soon.

How far will they go before I finally break down, and confess? I'm innocent though. I can't confess to something I didn't do. Why won't they listen to the truth, isn't that what they want?

Sometimes things happen that you can't explain. You know what took place, but the "why" and "how" just don't make sense - and then no one believes you. "You have no proof, no evidence to corroborate your story," is what the police keep saying over, and over again. I even took them back to the site, and explained how I'd escaped. I thought that hard evidence would change their mind, but the scene had changed! I was beginning to doubt myself. Perhaps I would awaken and find I'd been in a coma and this was all a dream.

Dr. Roget might be my last chance. I have faith that his examination will prove I still have my sanity. The great Dr. Roget, a renowned hypnotist for the CIA out of Langley. He had just entered the room. If I pass his test, will I be a free man? They have no evidence, and the judge will have no choice but to set me free, or will they put me away in a mental institution? All I can do is tell the truth, and I know while under hypnosis, I'll do just that.

A nurse carted in a metal rack containing several IV bags. She stuck my arm and began to make the connections with the tubes.

"What's all this for?" I asked. "I thought you were just going to hypnotize me doc! And being tied down wasn't what I expected."

Dr. Roget had explained in our briefing that he would put me into a deep sleep. Then he'd ask me questions, in order to find out where I'd been and what I had done. I was expecting him to wave a watch in front of my eyes and tell me I was getting sleepy. Nothing, however, was ever mentioned about the need for an IV.

"The IV is to make sure you don't dehydrate; you will be talking a lot," explained Dr. Roget.

"Come on, doc, you want me to be up front and honest, so why don't you do so the same?"

"Very well, Jake. The IV is for hydration, but it also contains sodium pentothal, the "Truth Serum" --- plus an experimental drug, but you need not be concerned about that. You've told everyone here quite a wild tale. I want to hear your story, the true story, so I'll have you start at the beginning."

As Doctor Roget was talking, the nurse turned the butterfly valve, and I saw the liquid begin to flow down the tubing.

"Wait a minute!" I said. "I have some questions."

Dr. Roget said something, but I couldn't make out the words. The light in the room started dimming, and I could only hear a low tone ringing in my ears. I felt like my mind was separating from my body and being carried away somewhere for examination, as if to go to another room perhaps, behind closed doors, where it would tell everything about my life, everything, both the good and evil I'd done.

Chapter 1

I was nine years old. It was the first dead body I'd ever seen. My granny hit her head on the sidewalk after suffering a massive heart attack and falling off our front porch. I was at school and didn't know what had happened until I got off the bus and saw a crowd of people at our house.

We lived in Lynco Hollow. It was just another Appalachian Mountains coal camp, like so many others. My momma, two sisters, Bernice and Janet, and I, lived with Granny in her house. We hadn't always lived with her. When I was four years old, my daddy was killed in a roof fall inside the Lynco No.7 Mine. Up until then, we lived in a house owned by the coal company. Momma said they made us move out after Daddy's funeral, so we moved in with Granny. Now she was dead too.

I don't remember daddy, but from looking at pictures, I know what he looked like. Momma said he named me Jake after his grandpa, who was a known horse thief. I think she was kidding about that.

Momma grew up in Indiana. She never liked living here in the mountains. She said she felt closed in by the mountains, and she especially didn't like being close to a coal mine. She said the whole place stank and was sooty. Granny was from Indiana too, but I never knew how she and Momma ended up here in Lynco. I'd heard it was because of, Jim Cooper. Jim and Granny ran a beer joint for a while, in Matheny, a few miles east of Oceana. Momma worked there, and that's where she met my daddy.

Granny liked my sisters, but she didn't like me. I don't recall her ever saying a kind word to me, but curse words came easy for her, and she never held back, always calling me bad names. I don't know what happened in her life to make her so mean. Whatever it was, she passed it down to Momma because she's even meaner. I sometimes wished I'd not been born, or wished that Momma had given me up for adoption. I wondered why Momma would have children if she didn't like them. As far back as I could remember Momma was always looking for any excuse to make fun of me or hit me, often both.

I found a few of the curse words I'd heard granny say in the dictionary. Most of the words weren't there though. She must have made them up, but whether they were real words or not, the way she used them got the point across.

Granny's house looked exactly like all the others in the neighborhood, except it was yellow instead of white, and the front porch was underpinned. All the houses in Lynco belonged to the coal company until they shut down their three big mines back in 1965.

The houses weren't really worth much, but the mine owners put a high price on them. Many of the houses were traded to the miners in exchange for their pensions. What houses the miners didn't buy were sold to anyone else interested. Momma didn't know for sure, but she thought Jim Cooper had bought several of the houses, and got them very cheap. He then traded this one to Granny for her half of the beer joint.

The wake was held at Granny's house. Lots of people coming through that I didn't know, and it was strange seeing Granny laying inside a casket in the living room.

Granny was proud of how her house looked and there were rules you followed, one of which was not eating in the living room. You had to either eat in the dining room or on the porch, but never in the living room. The night of her wake the dining room was full of food dishes people from the church, and the community had brought in. Some of the people there were eating in the living room. If Granny knew, she'd be mad as heck. Although she was mean she was still my granny, and it upset me, those people weren't showing respect.

I told one woman she was spilling crumbs onto the floor. Before I could say another word, Momma was on me like a cat and busted my rear, then made me stand with my nose in the corner. It embarrassed me that all those people watched me get a whipping.

Back then there used to be a lot of traveling preachers who would come through the area for revivals and such. Granny would always put them up at our house, for as long as they stayed in the community. I thought it was strange, Granny being half owner of a beer joint while boarding preachers at her house. I guess if they didn't stay with us, they'd have to stay in the hotel up in town. Staying in the hotel would have been my choice. I had always wanted to do that.

13

The three-story hotel was the tallest building I'd ever laid eyes on. The name of the hotel was 'The Mountain Lair'. It had a set of circular steps in front, which you had to climb in order to enter the narrow but long hotel building which ran down the alley. On the left corner of the main floor was a large picture window with writing on the glass that read 'Restaurant'. The windows in the guest rooms were the crank out kind and there were no screens in most of them. The curtains were always hanging out the windows, fluttering in the wind. The hotel was a mysterious place, and I had always wanted to go inside and explore the rooms and corridors. I couldn't understand who stayed there though. It wasn't as if our town was booming and had a need for a hotel.

Maybe those preachers didn't stay at the hotel, knowing they'd miss getting Granny's home cooking if they did. Her delicious fried apple pies were known about all over town. Her fried chicken and white gravy with mashed potatoes and green beans was a meal nobody could turn down. Granny knew the best way to fix it all. If she'd opened a restaurant instead of a beer joint, we would have gotten rich.

One of the preachers who used to come and stay with us was there at the wake. He was a short thin man with a long face. I remembered him mostly because he was always so loud when he talked. I guessed that helped him as a preacher, old folks didn't have a problem hearing him.

I heard Momma talk about him to her friend, Joyce Lambert, one time. "That man must have learned how to whisper in a saw mill," she said. Joyce laughed for so long that I became tickled just from hearing her laughing, and I almost peed in my pants.

The preacher was wearing a black suit with a white shirt and one of those funny ties that looked like two or three long shoelaces hanging from around his neck. To me,

14

he looked more like one of those undertakers you see on the TV westerns.

I hated standing in the corner with my nose against the wall. I'd turn my head and body to the side, so I could watch people. I knew if Momma saw me doing that the punishment would be worse than before. Two girls from school were there and saw me get a whipping, and now they were giggling from across the room. They were both pretty, Italian girls with long black hair. There were many Italians living in Lynco. When the mining camps were constructed, it attracted a lot of immigrants. The mining companies liked the Italians, mainly because they were hard workers and many of them were skilled stonemasons.

The mountainous terrain around Lynco made for a great place to play but a harsh place to live. No matter which way you turned the terrain was the same - a mountainside, then the valley floor consisting of a road, railroad, creek, and then another hillside. When the mines opened, most of the good land went for building the coal preparation plant and coal storage yard. The remaining flat land was along the creek bank. That's where most of the houses were built, and many of them get flooded when the spring rains come.

After Granny was buried Momma tried to find a job, but there weren't any. She got a few food stamps and some commodity cheese, but that wasn't enough to support all four of us. Momma took some handouts from friends and relatives, but she knew that wouldn't last. I overheard Momma talking to our neighbor Louise one evening. She said she'd found out that Granny didn't own the house. She said it belonged to the bank. Granny had taken out a mortgage. She missed several payments, and owed more on the house than it was worth. Momma said unless her luck changed we may have to move.

Although we were poor, it really didn't seem like it. Nobody else in our neighborhood seemed to have any more than we did. There was a family of ten living across the creek in an old wood shack that looked like it had originally been a horse stall. It had wood floors though. The boards ran vertically on the outside had large gaps. Even though they had papered the walls with newspaper, at night when they had lights on it shone through.

I was scared. What was going to happen to us? Would we lose our house? Where would we live if that happened? Would we end up like the family across the creek? I had many questions and no one I could ask.

Momma started dating a man named Bob Crump. He worked for an insurance company in Welch, about an hour drive from us. I think he spent more time drinking than selling insurance. I don't know what Momma saw in that man. To me, he was just somebody else for her to take care of. He did give her some money, which helped us out, but when he was around, she treated him like a king, and treated my sisters and me as if we were dirt. I wasn't allowed in the house when Crump was there, unless the weather was bad. Momma told me to get outside and out of her sight.

Secretly, we called him "Crump the Grump." Momma wouldn't let us call him anything other than Mr. Crump. If she'd heard us call him "Crump the Grump," well, I'll just say we wouldn't have been able to sit down for a few weeks.

The one good thing, if there was one, was that with Crump being around it looked as if we could remain living in Granny's house. He worked out some sort of deal with the bank. I could tell it was a big relief to Momma. I suppose every thorn has its rose.

Momma had a wringer washer and a big rinse tub on the back porch that had belonged to Granny. I had to fill the washer and tub using buckets carried from the spigot located halfway down the side of the house. Mrs. Simmons from across the street came over one evening. She and

Momma were sitting on the porch whispering. I had filled the washer and was supposed to be getting water for the rinse tub. Instead, I was under the porch eavesdropping, and could hear every word they said.

I found out Momma was going to have another baby. I knew that wasn't right, Momma wasn't married. Soon everybody in Lynco would be talking about it. If Mrs. Simmons knew, everybody would know. Momma said she was worried how it was going to look. She said, "All I need is another damn baby to take care of." Momma having another baby worried me, but not nearly as much as when she told Mrs. Simmons that Crump was going to be moving in with us.

If Crump was around and Momma wasn't, he'd hiss at me, like an ole alley cat. He never missed a chance to tell me I was a lazy boy and needed some chores to keep my mind from drifting off in the wrong direction. Imagine that, Crump, the lazy boned bottom dweller telling me I was lazy.

I'd thought about running away from home a couple of times, and once I really did. I was going to live under a cliff that overhung a sandbar down by the river. I went there with a sack of crackers and a jar of apple butter. When it started getting dark, I got scared and came back.

A couple of weeks after I'd heard Momma and Mrs. Simmons talking, my sisters and I were sent to my aunt's house in Huff Creek to spend a few days. We'd been there a few times before, and I'd always enjoyed it. I had several cousins and we played tag, and, "kick the can." We played all day and late into the evening. My uncle was a Foreman for a large coal mining company. That meant they lived in a big company house. It must have had ten to twelve rooms, and there was a bathroom both upstairs and downstairs.

I knew why we'd been sent there. Momma and Crump had gone down to Pearisburg, Virginia to get married then went off on a honeymoon somewhere. In Pearisburg, you could get married and not have to wait on a blood test. I guess they got in a hurry and wanted hitched before Momma's belly started getting big.

After the honeymoon, Crump moved his things into our house. It was as bad as I had expected. Crump's drinking and smoking were bad enough, but he and Momma fussed a lot, and then she'd take her frustration out on us kids. I just kept my distance and tried to be invisible when I could.

Momma told us her last name was now Crump, but we could keep the name Roberts if we wanted to. I didn't have to hear it twice. I was a Roberts. It would have been fighting words if somebody had called me Jake Crump.

I didn't think it was right, me having to mow grass once Crump moved in. All he did around the house was put beer in the refrigerator. He told me mowing the grass would be one of my many chores. I rolled my eyes at him and he backslapped me with an open hand. After he did that Momma took a belt to me, and I didn't think she'd ever stop hitting me. I didn't complain after that, I just did as I was told.

There was an old storage building behind Granny's house. One of my uncles stopped by one day to pick up some things he had stored there. He found a gasoline powered lawnmower. It was buried beneath a pile of roofing shingles left over from when the house was re-roofed years ago. He tinkered with it for a while and it started. He told Momma he didn't need it and left it for me to use.

Until then, the mower I had to use was one of the old spiral blade types with a cylinder that turned as you pushed. The blades were dull, and I had to go over the same area two to three times. That was a lot of work, so having a powered lawnmower was going to be great. Crump said he'd show me one time how to crank the

18

gasoline powered lawnmower. After that, he said I'd have to maintain it myself or go back to mowing grass the old way. I was only nine years old, and knew nothing about engines.

The house next door was empty. It had been remodeled at some point and was a nicer than our house. It had crank out aluminum framed windows, and aluminum siding. The grass in the yard was overgrown. Weeds grew up alongside the house and sidewalk, which made the place seem spooky. The windows were dusty because of the dirt road where we lived. It was impossible to look inside except when I'd take the bottom of my shirt and wipe the window off.

I had nightmares occasionally. In some of the dreams, I was inside the vacant house and saw bodies lying on the floor covered in blood, and their heads were cut off. Other times there were ghosts flying around while dragging long chains. I think Crump was the reason I had the bad dreams. Ever since he'd moved in, I stayed on edge and was nervous most of the time.

Despite the nightmares, there was a big wooden swing on the covered porch of that house, so during daylight hours I'd go over to there to swing. I'd peer through the windows to make sure the ghosts and dead bodies weren't actually there. Then I'd sit in the swing for hours. That old swing was a safe haven for me, to get away from Crump and Momma.

Seemed I was just a snotty nosed kid who could do nothing right, and it was worse with Crump living with us. I would have gone and lived with my aunt and uncle in Huff Creek if Momma would have suggested it. I don't even know if they would have wanted me though, Momma said I wasn't good for anything. Sitting in that swing for hours, I could be somebody. Most often, I'd pretend I was a jet fighter pilot or a spaceship commander.

19

If there was a bright side to life those days, I was getting older and could be outside more, not under Momma's feet. I could go to the house next door and spend hours without anybody missing me.

Chapter 2

It was my birthday, June 5th.1978. School was out for the summer, and I was thankful. I was eleven years old, and to celebrate, I slept in a bit longer than normal. What awakened me was the heat. The upstairs of the house was a big open space. There was a small landing at the top of the stairs, which was located mid-way down the length of the house. From there, the room opened to the left and to the right. A grown up could stand in the middle of the room but not on the sides because of the angled roofline.

Bernice and Janet slept upstairs in a regular sized bed at one end of the room. I slept on an old army barracks spring framed bed positioned against the opposite wall. It didn't take the sun long to heat the roof in the summer, making the upstairs temperature feel like the inside of an oven. There was a window at each end of the house. Like everybody else in the neighborhood, we had slider screens you could pop in and out of an open window. We put the screens in late each evening to let the night breeze blow through and cool the room off enough to allow us to sleep.

Cars going by during the day threw up a suspended cloud of dust. It would migrate into the house, so each morning one of us had the job of taking the screen out and closing the window. We kids had that chore a week at a time, and it was marked on a calendar at the top of the stairs. There wasn't much traffic at night. That, plus dampness in the night air made it possible to keep the window open without the dust coming inside.

That day Janet had already gotten up and closed the window, causing the upstairs to heat up faster. She'd forgotten to close the window a few weeks back and dust got in the house, covering all the bedding Momma had just washed. Janet got a hard beating for that and Momma had her wash all the bed linens again. She also had to clean the house and Momma grounded her for two weeks. After that Bernice, Janet, and me made a pact, we'd cover for one another. The first person up closed the window.

I don't know why Momma always reacted first by giving us a whipping before finding out the facts. She never spent any time playing games with us kids, or even just sitting and talking. There just didn't seem to be any fun in her life.

I could smell oatmeal cooking and a growing boy like me never missed a meal. I got dressed, wearing only a pair of cut-off shorts. In the hot summer that's all boys wore, just shorts and no shirt, except the Sullivan kid who lived down on River Street. The kid was light-skinned so his momma always made him wear a t-shirt and a baseball cap when he was outside.

I went downstairs and found Momma was in the kitchen cutting up rhubarb to make a pie. I liked rhubarb pie, but unless you use a ton of sugar, it would be too sour to eat. I was hoping she was going to wish me a happy birthday, but that morning she had nothing at all to say. I knew better than to ask if I was going to get a birthday cake or a present, it had never happened before. I didn't expect this birthday to be any different.

Chapter 3

Four months into her pregnancy, Momma miscarried and lost her baby. After that, I thought she would be sad and want us kids to be around by her side. Instead, she seemed to be meaner than she was before, so I'd tried to be invisible, and stay out of her way. I felt sorry for Momma. I knew her heart had to hurt from losing the baby, but her actions never indicated that. I thought she must cry about it at night when she was alone, and no one was around. A few times after she lost the baby, I'd tried giving her a hug, but she didn't want anything to do with that. She'd smack me away with a backhand. I just wished

I knew what would make her happy. Then I could try to fix things for her.

I guess her losing the baby may have been a blessing in some ways. Just as she had told Mrs. Simmons, she had enough kids as it was. Besides, the new kid might have looked like ole Crump.

Janet normally made oatmeal in the morning to feed us kids. I got a bowl from the cabinet and took the pot off the stove to dish the oatmeal out. What remained in the pot was as thick as molasses in the dead of winter, but I knew better than to complain. Anytime you complained about food Momma would just say, "Eat it or go hungry, I don't care."

I sat at the kitchen table, quietly gulping down the thick goo, then went back to the sink and washed my bowl and spoon. After that I headed toward the back door to go play outside, but Momma grabbed the back of my neck as I was about to open the door.

"Not so fast young man!" She said in a gruff manner.

I hated when she said things like that, and in that tone. It always meant I had to do some chore. Sure enough, that time was no different.

"Get your skinny ass out there in the garden, and pull those weeds from the corn and tomatoes. You were told to do that yesterday, and if I have to tell you again I'm going to set your ass on fire!" Then she shoved me out the screen door and onto the porch.

I knew not to say anything sassy, roll my eyes, or give any sort of body language about my displeasure. If there's one thing you didn't want, it was for Momma to give you a whipping in the summer time, because she used a switch from a forsythia bush. A forsythia bush was the equivalent of a leather whip with bone fragments, similar to what they used in biblical days. Boy, did it hurt and leave welts.

When Momma gave you a switching, it consisted of her swinging the switch in all directions like a mad person, while you stood in place dancing and screaming. Wearing only a pair of shorts and no shirt meant there was a lot of exposed skin. She'd hit your legs, back, arms, and head. No part of your body was sacred or spared. All you could do was stand in place dancing. If you ran, it was going to be double bad when she caught you, and she'd always catch you.

I hated working in the garden more than any chore I had to do. The corn leaves would scratch my arms and legs, and bugs would fly at my face. It was always hot when I had to work in the garden. Pulling weeds by hand was stupid, and hard, and it didn't seem to me the corn was having any problems because of them being there. I never understood why we didn't just let the weeds grow. Those were thoughts I knew I'd better keep inside. Never would I say anything about it to Momma.

I wanted a drink of water before heading into the garden. The oatmeal I'd eaten was still hung in my throat, and I was thirsty. I looked through the screen door, back into the house. I saw that Momma had left the kitchen. I carefully opened the door trying not to make it squeak then went to the kitchen sink. I knew better than to dirty a drinking glass, so I cupped my hand under the faucet and slurped down a good bit of water.

I heard Momma coming so I scurried back out of the kitchen, eased the screen door open, and was careful not to let it slam shut. The door gave out that ole familiar sound, the screech of a screen door opening or closing. I knew Momma heard it. She didn't say anything, but I knew I'd hear about it later.

I jumped off the porch while in the same motion grabbing my sneakers, then slid under the porch to put them on. My sneakers had to last until school started back, and I knew I wasn't supposed to wear them while working in the garden. Knowing I was taking a chance on getting a beating, I ignored all logic and slipped the shoes onto my feet. Maybe that's why Momma didn't like me. I was always breaking her rules.

I didn't mind going bare footed, except in the garden. The ground was always damp, and I didn't like getting dirt between my toes. Besides there were lots of bugs and sticker weeds that irritated my feet.

I hurried along just pulling the big weeds and letting the little ones go. If you've ever pulled weeds, you know that the small ones won't come out easily when you yank on them. You can never get the roots out, the weeds break off. I knew I'd be sent back out there in a few days anyway, the weeds grew three times faster than the corn.

When I was finished, I looked at my shoes. The brown dirt from the garden had covered both shoes. I had to do something quick. There was a box of rags and an old toothbrush on the back porch. I knew I'd better get my shoes cleaned before Momma saw them in that condition, otherwise I'd be in a world of hurt.

As I came out of the garden and headed toward the back porch, I heard a commotion from the other side of our house. It was coming from the house next door, the vacant house, where I liked to play and get away from Momma and Crump. As I rounded the corner, I saw a moving van in the front and two men in uniforms carrying things inside. That wasn't good. I was in a state of shock. Without any kind of notice, I was losing my secret get away place.

I walked over to the fence line, made of old wooden posts spaced about eight feet apart, with three strands of barbed wire stretched between the posts. Tall weeds and grass were tangled into the barbed wire. It formed a walled barrier, which I hid behind while watching the movers. Aside from the men carrying large furniture pieces, there were other people around. A man and woman were there carrying in small boxes, and they were giving instructions to the two men in uniforms.

I saw a boy carrying in a table lamp with no shade attached. He was about my size. I became very interested. A new kid was moving in next door. That took some of the sting out of losing my secret hiding place.

The coal camp where we lived had at least a dozen boys my age to play with, but most lived down on the west end. Another kid on my end of the camp would mean evening things a bit. A couple of the kids who lived on the far end of the camp decided a while back that Lynco would be split, east side and west side. After that when we played baseball or other games, you had to be on the team according to the side of the camp you lived on, and my end didn't have as many boys.

What about a bicycle? Did this kid have a bicycle? Could he even ride one? It didn't take long to answer those questions. As soon as the boy returned from putting the lamp in the house, I heard one of the men inside the truck say, "Here you go, Ryan," as he pushed a bicycle down the ramp.

This boy didn't have just any old bicycle. It was the coolest piece of machinery I'd ever seen. It was a twenty-inch boys bicycle with an extend fork on the front to give it a chopper look, and Oh Wow - the bicycle had a banana seat! It was yellow and had black stripes going across it, giving a tiger skin look.

The boy took off on the bicycle, heading down the dirt road in my direction. I was standing by the fence about thirty-five feet back from the corner, so he never saw me. He had the front wheel off the ground as he pedaled, at least until the bike went a little left, hitting a pothole in the road, throwing him a bit sideways. He quickly adjusted though and continued down the road. He also made what I thought was a very good siren noise.

I didn't have a bicycle, or at least not one to claim as my own. Janet had a twenty-six-inch girls bicycle. Although it was officially hers, all of us kids shared the bike. Lucky for me, the girls didn't like riding, so most of the time I was the one doing all the cycling.

In the beginning, the rule was that I'd have to ask my sisters if they were going to ride the bike. If they said no, then I could take off riding. I suppose the reason for the rule was because once I took off out of the yard, I'd be gone for an hour or more, not giving anyone else a chance to ride.

I watched this kid as he went completely out of sight, just past the old sawmill. That's where the road takes a slight curve, but after that, it's a straight shot all the way to the end of the camp down at the one-lane bridge. I stood there for a minute watching then I could see him heading back.

I moved forward to the corner fence post, and the kid spotted me. He came barreling down the road. Just before he got to me, he slammed down on the pedal with his right foot, locking the brake and sliding to a stop. It produced a little screech from the rear tire.

The rear tire was wider than the one on the front, resembling a racecar slick. It's hard to get a screech from a bicycle tire on a dirt road, but that bicycle did. I was already hoping this boy would be my friend, and someday he might even let me ride his bike.

The boy was a little shorter than I was. He had a more stocky build. He was most certainly my age. I had a buzz cut, just as most the other boys in the bottom. I could only think of one other kid with a different haircut. It was Ted, who lived by the car wash. He had a flattop. I liked Ted's flattop, it made him look mean and tough. Flattops must have cost a little more when you got a haircut because Momma told me 'no' every time I had asked for one. Anyway, this kid had a different haircut. His hair was long

29

and combed over to the side. Aside from that he looked normal, and I was sure he'd fit in.

As the bike came to a halt, a small dust cloud followed. The boy jumped off the bike and came over with his right arm extended, wanting to shake hands. He did it the way you would expect 'The Lone Ranger' to do as he rode up to a stranger and dismounted his horse. This kid seemed bold and unafraid of anything.

"Hi, I'm Ryan, Ryan Tyler," he said.

We shook hands, and I introduced myself in a similar manner.

"I'm Jacob, Jacob Roberts, but everybody calls me Jake."

Ryan seemed different. It wasn't different because of the way he looked. His demeanor is what was different. I was a little tall for my age, and skinny. Ryan was what I would call big boned, not fat by any means, just a tad on the stocky side. The attitude, the demeanor, that's what set him apart. I was backward, shy, and often unsure of myself. Ryan, on the other hand appeared to be bold, forward, and held his head high with confidence. We talked for a long time. It was an instant bonding of a friendship.

Ryan told me his mom and dad had bought the house. They were moving from a place called Coal City, over in Raleigh County. It sounded a lot like Lynco, just another coal mining camp.

I didn't mention to Ryan about the dead bodies that might be inside the house his folks were buying. If they were actually there, he'd know soon enough. I still couldn't help but believe there were people dead in the closets or buried beneath the house. I'd let those thoughts occupy my mind for so long I believed they were true.

I'd never heard of Coal City, but I had heard of Raleigh County. I could pick it out on a map just by its shape, and I knew it bordered Wyoming County, where I lived. I liked the name Raleigh. It made me think of the picture of that pirate looking man on the pack of cigarettes.

Ryan said Coal City was about an hour ride in the car. He said their house had burned down two months ago, and they'd been living with relatives. I asked where they'd gotten all that stuff they were carrying into the house, and that bicycle. He said it was all new, that his daddy had fire insurance, and it paid for everything.

As far as I knew, we never had any kind of insurance on our house. I wondered if Crump had taken out a policy. That wasn't likely, unless his name was listed as the sole beneficiary.

Ryan's dad was a coal miner like my daddy had been. His dad was what they called a 'Boss Man', which meant he was responsible for a bunch of other men and told them what to do. Being the boss meant you received better pay than the other workers did. It wasn't an easy or pleasant job by any stretch of the imagination though. It was a lot of responsibility. If the boss didn't see that the men produced a lot of product, they were replaced quickly, with no warning. Bosses also worked every Saturday and most Sundays.

Ryan had a brother named William. He was older and had already left home. Ryan called himself a 'mis-conception'. He said his mom and dad made a mistake when they were old, but it was the best mistake they'd ever made. We both laughed over the joke he'd made.

Momma was outside on the porch looking my way then she yelled at me to come to her. I told Ryan I had to go. I was walking toward Momma when it hit me, my shoes! I had no way of hiding them from her, but it didn't matter, she'd already seen the dirt on my sneakers, that's why she was calling to me.

Momma didn't use a switch to beat me. She used my shoes. She made me take them off then she looked them over. Holding one in each hand, she beat me with them. She fiercely swung back and forth mostly hitting my face and back.

For the next couple of days, my face was swollen, and my left eye was black and blue. Even though it was summer, I had to wear a T-shirt for a while to hide the bruises on my back. Momma said I had to tell my friends I'd gotten in a fight. If I said otherwise, she'd beat me again. I think Ryan saw Momma whipping me that day. He never asked anything about it, and I never mentioned it.

Ryan, being the only kid at home, got more and better toys, plus a spending allowance. I wasn't envious though, I felt sad for Ryan that he didn't have sisters or brothers to play with when it was too cold to go outside. Then again, sisters were just people you had to fight with over everything, so I suppose Ryan had the better situation. Besides, his momma never beat him for anything he did, and he didn't have to do chores except take out the garbage.

As summer lingered, Ryan and I got to know one another. We quickly became best of friends. I loved those long summer days. The sun came up early, and by eight o'clock would burn the fog off the river and mountains. Then it would get hot, and the sound of jar flies and a host of other insects, birds, and chattering squirrels jumping from tree to tree would fill the air.

We played with the other boys in Lynco Hollow, riding bicycles, playing tag, and baseball. Ryan had a ton of comic books. He also received a few magazines each month. He gave me his magazines after he'd read them. One of the magazines was about outdoors and survival skills, and another was about science and making useful gadgets from things lying around your house.

Ryan had already set a goal for his life, to be rich and famous. I think he liked the famous part more than the being rich part. Me, I had never thought much about money. I had wants but never gave any thought about being rich. Having a caring family would have meant more to me than all the riches in the world. I knew that wasn't going to happen, but having Ryan around took some of the sting out of that. He and I became best of friends.

Ryan and I started tinkering with electricity and chemistry. We'd read about how people could invent things in their basement, start a business, and then become millionaires. We never received a severe shock, nor were we blown up by one of our homemade bombs, but it's a wonder we didn't. I don't remember where we got the baking soda, shotgun shells, and other items, but it seems there was always something around for us to play with that would burn, ignite, or explode.

I had to be careful Momma didn't know what we were doing. If she found out, I'd be sent to Prunty Town. She threatened on several occasions to send me there. I didn't know where Prunty Town was, but I knew it was far away, and it was a prison for young boys. Adults were always talking about kids being sent off to Prunty Town and never being heard from again.

Ryan had a natural talent. He was good at reading people. He was bright, but a tiny bit on the arrogant side, although he was only like that to others, he never ever talked down to me. He liked playing games where he could gamble. With his ability to read people, he had the upper hand that they didn't know about. To him, it wasn't as much what he won as it was the satisfaction of knowing he had beaten you at something.

Sometimes six to eight of us boys in the camp would gather at someone's house and play games. More often than not, it would be at Daniel's house since both his parents worked and were gone during the day. Ryan would get bored with board games and want to play poker. There were at least two or three of the boys always agreeable to playing for money.

The few nickels I was able to earn I wasn't about to lose in a poker game, so I just watched. Ryan got a nice allowance from his dad, so he always had a few dollars in his pocket to gamble away. He was good to me and always shared when he won. He'd buy us both a soda pop after his poker games, and we'd bang the bottles together as he'd say 'bottoms up'. Ryan called me his bodyguard even though he was a better fighter than I was. Ryan was good for my self-esteem. He included me in everything, and made me feel like I was somebody.

Since I never played in the poker game, Ryan would have me hold his money until he needed it. At the end of the day, he'd give me a couple of dimes or a quarter. Ryan didn't feel sorry for me because I was poor, I was his friend, and he liked sharing the wealth with me. He would always say he was paying me for the protection I provided.

I'd watch as Ryan played cards. No matter what the card game, he would win a few hands then purposely lose a few hands. After that, he'd sucker the others into playing an all-or-nothing hand, which somehow he always won.

Only once did I see him lose. The other times he'd clean the other players out, then we'd get on our bikes and head to Jim Stepp's store for a cold root beer and a bag of peanuts. That became so commonplace that ole Jim Stepp would see us pull up on our bicycles, and by the time we'd be in the store, he'd be popping the tops off the root beer.

We'd sit out front of the store and drink our soda while Ryan would talk about how he suckered those boys out of their money. He got better and better as time went on, but it got to the point if he was going to play poker it had to be somewhere other than Lynco. Everyone there knew better than to get into a poker game with Ryan Tyler.

Chapter 4

One of our favorite things was cutting the base of wild grapevines that grew high in the trees on a mountainside. We'd swing on them, soaring out into the air. It wasn't uncommon to swing out a hundred feet or more above the ground. Whenever we'd cut a new vine, we'd take turns being the first one to swing, testing the vine, to ensure it would hold our weight. Several times the vines broke sending us flying to the ground. I suppose hitting the ground and sliding on the steep slope instead of hitting flat ground is all that saved us.

My dad's brother, Jesse, lived in Kentucky. He came by to visit for a few days once. He wanted to see the old home-place, as he called it. Jesse didn't stay at our house. I think it was because he didn't like Crump, so he stayed at the hotel in town. The old log cabin he and my dad grew up in was up a hollow where no one lived anymore. It was called Big Reedy Creek. He was going to hike there and see if anything was left of the old place. He asked if I'd like to go, and I was excited. Momma said 'no', but Uncle Jesse insisted, and she finally gave in.

We hiked into this big, deep hollow that lay a couple of miles down the river from Lynco. The hollow started in an area along a big bend in the river. There was some nice flat land on both sides of the river at that spot but not a house anywhere. The bend in the river backed up water there during heavy rains and caused flooding, making the land unsuitable for building. There was an old swinging bridge there, which you had to cross to enter the hollow. The main structure of the bridge consisted of double steel pole supports on both sides of the river. The poles held steel cables that stretched across the water. Wood planks were connected to the steel cables, forming a walkway. Many of the planks were rotten and several had fallen away, creating a treacherous crossing.

Starting at the river, Big Reedy Creek hollow was almost three miles deep. It was a beautiful setting of high lofty hills on both sides of the valley. The woods were teeming with wildlife. A meandering brook with crystal-clear water flowed through the middle of the hollow. Several smaller hollows branched off, each providing Big Reedy with tributary streams.

The valley floor was up to a quarter mile across at its widest point. In the few areas where the valley was narrow, the swift moving stream had cut deep ravines, but in the wider areas the stream meandered and moved slowly, trickling over the worn stones. It was a woodland paradise with an abundance of large hardwood trees. The beautiful lush meadows made it tempting to lie down in the tall fragrant grass and gaze dreamingly at the clouds floating by above.

I asked Uncle Jesse, why there wasn't any mining there. Everywhere I knew of with a hollow that big there was a coal mine present. He explained it to me. There weren't any coal seams present, because of a large geological fault that ran up the hollow. He said when he was as a boy, he witnessed gas well drillers try and drill that land, but the ground was so faulted it would hang their bits up and they never once got a good hole started, and they soon gave up.

We found the remains of the cabin where Uncle Jesse, my dad, and their sister grew up. Now it was nothing more than a few old rotten logs tossed about, but you could still see where the foundation had been. Uncle Jesse said Big Reedy contained about twenty houses back in the 1930s. Not a soul lived there now. In a few grown-up areas along the creek you could see a few remaining boards of an old house or two. Along the creek bank in places were the remains of where people had discarded their garbage. Several decades of leaves and weeds now covered everything.

We dug through one of the old trash piles, over the hillside from where their cabin had been. He found the remains of an old shoe and part of an old toy car. Uncle Jesse stood there for a while. I could see a tear in the corner of his eye. I didn't know what to do. Every time I'd ever tried being a comfort to an adult, it had gotten me kicked, hit, or beaten. I decided it was best to just remain quiet and let him ponder on whatever it was he was remembering. After several minutes, we continued on our way.

At the head of the long hollow, the valley widened. There it was filled with stately beech trees. The towering trees filled the valley, and their large sprawling limbs were a temptation to any boy who liked to climb. The biggest beech stood near the left hillside and shadowed a small rock outcrop.

The outcrop had an overhang of ten feet or more across, and was about seven feet in height underneath, forming a shallow cave. Uncle Jesse explained to me that the first settlers in the area discovered the cave and often camped there. There were mysterious writings on the cave wall, consisting of strange symbols.

Legend was that Indian hunters camped there a lot and wrote in their language about hunting adventures in the area. Uncle Jesse said the rock formation produced heat and even on the coldest winter day snow wouldn't stick to it, thus it had always been known as Burning Rock.

It was a great outing, and I truly enjoyed being with Uncle Jesse. He treated me well and didn't mind talking with me. He let me ask him questions, and not once did he call me stupid. Secretly, I was hoping he would ask Momma if I could go live with him.

After the trip with Uncle Jesse, Ryan and I started going to Big Reedy to play. We would go there and spend all day playing in the creek or pretend we were pioneers discovering a new territory, exploring an unknown land. We looked for Indian artifacts but never found any.

Digging into some of the old garbage piles where houses had been we did find a few old elixir bottles. I took the bottles home and was going to start a collection. I put them on the windowsill upstairs. One night when I went upstairs to go to bed, I saw they were gone and accused Bernice of taking them. She told me Crump had been upstairs and had seen them. A short time after that Momma came up and got them, and threw them all away. It made me mad. They were nice bottles and not hurting anything. After that, I started hiding things from Momma. I knew it wasn't right, but I did it anyway.

Ryan once found an Indian head penny in Big Reedy. We were on our way home that day walking along the railroad tracks when a train approached. Ryan placed the penny on the tracks and let the train run over it. It flattened the penny out to the thickness of a sheet of paper and about the diameter of a golf ball. I thought that was a crazy thing to do, the old penny was likely worth a lot of money, but it wasn't mine so there was no use fussing about it.

The beech trees at Burning Rock became our favorite place to play. The clear stream flowing on the opposite side of the beech grove was full of fish, and we often tried our luck spear fishing with spears we'd made from tree limbs. We were only successful in jabbing a fish once or twice and never speared one large enough to eat.

The beech trees had big sprawling limbs around their entire circumference. The limbs began about five feet off the ground and every three to four feet up another cluster of limbs would start, continuing all the way to the top. The trees were easy to climb and provided a nice canopy, which was why there was little to no undergrowth on the ground.

Ryan had a hunting knife he had gotten from a mail-order catalog. It was a nice knife, with a barbed section half way back on the top side, a leather case, and a whetstone compartment on the front of the sheath. I didn't have a hunting knife, but instead I had an honest-to-goodness bayonet from WWII. The case was old and looked to be homemade, but it served its purpose. I found it when Momma had me clean out the root cellar.

Momma had several older brothers who had served in the war and one of them must have left the bayonet there years ago. I kept the bayonet hidden except when Ryan and I were ready to head off into the mountains to play. Momma would have wrung my neck for having such a thing.

One of the old beech trees had somebody's initials and a date carved into the bark. It was a deep carving, and the bark had grown around the letters. The letters could still be made out clearly though. The initials were, RLW. A date was carved in the tree below the initials. December 10, 1928. Ryan and I thought that was cool, so we carved our own initials and date into the tree also.

The largest beech stood right beside Burning Rock. It's huge, perfectly spaced limbs, made it our favorite tree to climb. I climbed to the top and estimated it to be sixty feet above the ground. I could see over the canopy of most other trees and get a good look at the valley for about a quarter mile downstream. I didn't go up that high very often. The treetop limbs were small, bending over when I put my full weight on them.

We were playing in the beech grove one day when Ryan had the urge to go off by himself, for what we called a 'power dump'. Our toilet paper consisted of a handful of wide leaves. We were always careful about where we pulled our britches down because poison ivy was prevalent in those hills.

While he went off to do his business, I climbed the big beech tree to the third set of limbs. I straddled a limb then pulled out my bayonet. In big deep letters, I carved into the trunk 'Welcome to Burning Rock'.

Ryan returned shortly and climbed into the tree. He approved of the carving and said he needed to make an official statement. He climbed to the very top of the tree. While holding on to the tree top with his left hand, he pointed down the hollow with his right hand and yelled out, "I hereby christen this tree, and the place called Burning Rock. Tis the official and protected territory of Ryan and Jake, til death do us part."

Ryan was about to continue his funny speech but a gust of wind went by, causing the treetop to sway, and he nearly fell out of the tree. He comically scurried back down the tree laughing, all the while making a sound like Shrimp on the Three Stooges. I laughed at him until my sides hurt.

Never once did we see another soul while playing in the beech grove. That's the way we liked it. It was the ultimate get-away. The only sounds there were those made by nature. Although every now and then when the wind blew just right, you could hear the whistle from a train in the distance.

Reading Ryan's magazines, I taught myself what I could about curing meats and trapping wild game. The mountains were full of wild berries and nuts, and I can't think of a one I didn't try eating except for a buckeye. I'd read they were poisonous to humans, so I left them for the squirrels to tend to.

I knew someday I'd be old enough to live by myself and not have to be around Crump and Momma. I kept hoping though that Momma would mellow out and we could all be a big happy family. Until then, I wanted to continue spending time with Ryan; he was adventurous and daring. I felt free when we were out doing things together.

It seemed like every day Crump got meaner, which made Momma meaner as well. I got the attitude, that if I was going to be accused of getting into trouble every time I was out, I might as well make it true. Ryan's folks never checked on him to see what he was doing, so we lived footloose and fancy free. The two of us, being unsupervised, started getting into things we shouldn't have.

Chapter 5

It was a hot and humid summer evening. Ryan and I had been sitting on the railroad tracks, waiting until dusk turned to night. The surroundings were dim, lit only by a quarter-moon that had just cleared the hilltops in the eastern sky.

I moved across the yard quickly, then hunkered down as I slid along the side of Jimmy Prichard's house. Just as I was getting ready to snatch a carton of empty soda bottles off his back porch, I heard someone whistle. It was Ryan. He was still on the railroad tracks about thirty yards away, acting as the lookout.

I dashed under the open porch just as Jimmy opened the door and came outside. A lot of junk was stored beneath the porch, so I didn't have a lot of room to hide. As luck would have it, Jimmy sat down on the edge of the porch, dangling his feet just inches from my nose.

I sat there quietly while Jimmy smoked a cigarette. I could smell the smoke, and as he flicked his ashes, some of them landed on my face. My heart was pounding out of my chest. It was all I could do to stay still and not move. Finally, he got up and went back inside.

As soon as I heard the back door close, I grabbed two of the four cartons sitting just a few feet from where Jimmy had been perched and took off running. My adrenaline was pumping heavily throughout my body as I dashed off toward the tracks where Ryan was still waiting.

We only got two cents per bottle, trading them in at the Lynco company store. Ryan was sixteen, and I was fifteen. People in the coal camp were catching on to their bottles missing so that was our final attempt at stealing soda pop bottles. The risk far outweighed the profit. Still, it was more for the thrill than the money we got for the bottles. Ryan's gambling winnings in one day far exceeded all the bottles we could steal in a month or more.

Two weeks later, we rode our bicycles to town early one evening just before dark. We'd been making plans after scoping out the new sporting goods store on the upper end of Oceana. We rode beside the railroad tracks, which ran along the hillside and across the river from the town. With no roads or houses there, we wouldn't be spotted.

The new store was right beside the tracks and a short distance off the highway. There weren't any other buildings close by, and the only streetlight was near the highway. It didn't shed a lot of light on the building.

Our best approach was from the side of the building bordering the railroad. That's where it was the darkest. We waited until it was good and dark then put our plan into action. We ditched the bicycles in the weeds alongside the tracks and crept down the bank to the side of the building.

The store had only been open a month, and I could still smell the fresh paint on the cinder blocks. A set of metal doors used for deliveries, was on the side of the building where we were. Ryan pulled on the doors but neither would open; they were locked. I tried prying open the doors using a screwdriver I'd brought, but that didn't work. We went to the back of the building where there was a small window, about fourteen inches by twenty inches. It looked large enough to crawl through, but it was nearly seven feet off the ground.

There was a pile of wooden pallets stored further down the side of the building. We stacked them up to create a platform, getting us close enough to reach the window. I thought I'd have to break the glass, but the latch wasn't closed. The window opened as soon as I put pressure against it. As I peered inside, I saw a dim light glowing near the sales counter. It was coming from a light on the telephone. The rest of the building was dark.

Having planned this out, Ryan and I both had penlight flashlights with us. We'd gone to the company store the day before and each stolen a penlight, batteries, and a pair of cotton jersey gloves, so we wouldn't leave fingerprints.

I put my head through the window and looked down the inside wall. I didn't see anything hanging or stored there. It was unobstructed all the way to the floor. I crawled through the window headfirst. Ryan helped lower me in, first holding my legs then my feet as I went further inside, sliding down the wall. I still couldn't reach the floor so Ryan had to let me go.

I dropped onto the floor hitting hands first, and rolled forward. My feet landed on a magazine rack knocking it over. It clanged loudly as it bounced around on the floor, while scattering magazines in all directions. I froze in place. My heart was in my throat trying to pound its way out. After a few seconds, seeming more like hours, I relaxed.

As cars on the highway passed a slight curve in the road, their headlights shone inside the store. One had just gone by, the light hitting me directly in the face. I quickly dashed behind the sales counter as I saw another car approaching from a distance.

"Are you OK?" Ryan whispered from the window above.

"I think so," I said.

"See if the back door will open."

I crawled through the customer area then through the doorway opening leading to the storage area. I pushed on the door handle, nothing. I hit the handle of the second door, and it swung open. Ryan was waiting outside the door. He quickly came inside also dropping to his hands and knees.

We didn't tarry long once Ryan was inside. We split up and began taking whatever we could find that wasn't tied down. Ryan brought two pillowcases for us to fill with the loot. The pillowcases were an excellent idea, except they were white and easy to see.

I opened the door of the display case where the pocketknives were located and raked them all into the pillowcase. Next, I tossed in some expensive fishing lures. Ryan grabbed some compasses out of the display as well as some hunting riflescopes and range finders. After that we were just grabbing anything we could find to fill the sacks.

The gun racks were locked, but it didn't matter. Rifles were too big to carry. I opened a sliding door behind and underneath the sales counter and saw some handguns lying there.

"Ryan, come get a load of this!" I said in a loud whisper.

He scurried over to the counter and immediately grabbed a 25 caliber, pistol.

"Awesome, my brother has one of these." He said.

About that time several more cars passed, immersing the building with light.

"We better get the heck out of here, just in case there was a silent alarm." Ryan said.

I grabbed a big handgun sitting on the shelf and tossed it into the sack. We crawled across the floor until we reached the storage area then opened the door and crawled through. Once outside the door, we stood up then gently closed the door behind us. We ran across the paved lot, through the weeds and back up the incline to the railroad tracks where we'd ditched the bicycles.

We sat in the darkness on one of the rails and caught our breath, then gave each other a high-five before mounting the bicycles to head back toward home. A hundred yards down the tracks from our location the railroad crossed the highway, and immediately after that was a railroad trestle which spanned the river. If we made it across the trestle without being seen, we were scot-free. After that, it was complete darkness, just a dark set of rails running along the edge of a mountainside, all the way to Lynco Hollow.

We looked left and right along the highway, waiting until there wasn't any traffic approaching. After wrapping the pillowcases around the handlebars, we quickly pushed the bicycles across the highway and onto the trestle.

The trestle was about a hundred and fifty feet long and curved to the right. The curved trestle also banked slightly, with the left rail elevated above the right one. The slight elevation difference created a balance problem for us, and the wooden ties weren't spaced evenly, making it an even more treacherous crossing, especially at night.

Not very far onto the trestle, we had to stop and dig the penlights out of our pockets. It was too dark we couldn't see the wooden ties. A mishap here meant a fall to the rocks in the shallow river some seventy-five feet below. Ryan was in front. I kept bumping his rear wheel as we hurried across in single file.

"Dang it, you're going to knock me off this bridge if you don't stop," Ryan said, whispering loudly.

I didn't reply. Cars were approaching the railroad crossing, now behind us, and I was certain we'd be spotted. I mistakenly bumped him again, this time my front tire hit his rear tire and fender, causing Ryan and his bicycle to lunge forward.

"You're going to kill us both!" Ryan's voice was now becoming angry.

Before we cleared the trestle, I slightly bumped him twice more.

There was a small clearing just past the end of the trestle. We lifted the bicycles across the rails, pushed them into the clearing, then in synchronized motion; we collapsed to the ground. After a few heavy sighs, we began to laugh. As we lay on our backs for a long time, we allowed our heart beats to return to normal.

It was a three-mile trek down the tracks before reaching the mouth of Lynco Hollow. Due to the darkness and the narrow path beside the tracks covered in large cut stone, it was impossible to ride without wrecking. We had to push the bicycles all the way to Lynco. Along our way, we talked about the loot. We couldn't keep it all. Our purpose was to sell the loot. We just didn't know how to go about it yet.

I had an old army cot in the shed behind our house. I frequently slept out there, unless the temperature was below freezing. I'd cleaned and organized the shed, and hung all the yard tools, to create some personal space. In doing so, I'd found a place to hide things from Momma and my sisters. I didn't have to worry about Crump he never came out to the shed, that's where tools were kept. Ole Crump the Grump wasn't about to do any work.

Ryan's dad was working afternoon shifts at the mine. His momma didn't care if he was out all night or not. She hardly ever spoke to him anymore it seemed. She would normally fall asleep in her recliner with the TV blaring until Ryan's dad came home around two o'clock in the morning. Then she'd get up and go to bed, never looking in Ryan's room to see if he was even there.

When we got to the shed, it was 11:30 p.m. We parked the bicycles against the shed then went inside. I reached up and screwed the light bulb into the open socket overhead so we could see. I turned the wooden door latch to lock the door from the inside.

I rolled out some foam rubber strips on top of the old workbench constructed from rough-cut lumber. I'd found the rolls of foam rubber when I cleaned out the shed. They were long enough to form a nice cushioned bed, which Ryan was going to sleep on that night.

Ryan and I had already agreed to each keep the pistol we'd stolen. We'd also decided to each keep one of the knives, then try to sell the rest. I dumped my bag on the foam rubber and the big handgun dropped onto the table. Both of us said "wow." My heart was beating fast again. We examined the gun, looked it all over, but we were careful not to point it at one another.

It was a 44 magnum, revolver with a nine-inch barrel. The big gun looked like a cannon. I opened the cylinder and saw it was loaded with six hollow point bullets. Ryan picked up the 25 auto, and we looked it over. It had small white pearl grips, and the frame was stainless steel. When he broke the barrel down, two shells were inside. The gun easily fit in the palm of his hand. It could easily be concealed, unlike the pistol I'd stolen.

We flipped a coin to see who'd pick a knife first. There was never a doubt Ryan would win the toss. He picked a nice bone handled knife then I did the same.

Ryan had an older cousin who lived in Holden, in Logan County. His cousin was a deputy sheriff, but not an honest one by any means. Ryan had plans to give him a call and see if he was interested in the loot we had to sell. I wasn't keen on that idea, him being a police officer.

After looking over the rest of the stolen goods and talking for a while, we went to bed. I slept on the cot, and Ryan slept on top of the foam rubber on the workbench. The next morning we were up early and Ryan headed home. I put the pillowcases with our loot beneath the bench and covered them with the foam rubber pads.

I went in the house, hoping there wouldn't be any questions about where I'd been, or if I'd heard about a store being robbed. Thank goodness, it was life as normal. Janet and Bernice were fighting over who was going to have use of the bathroom next.

With a house of five people and only one bathroom, it was constant bickering about bathroom time. The girls were always fighting. Often it was one accusing the other of being in their make-up. I thanked the good Lord I was a boy. I could pee behind the shed and skip all that mess of the bathroom.

Ryan and I had already decided we'd better lay low for a while. We'd not go into town, unless absolutely necessary. Ryan waited until his mom was taking a bath that afternoon before using their phone to call his cousin in Holden. He knew he'd never live to see his next birthday if his mom or dad found out about our robbery.

Ryan's cousin was curious about what we had to sell so he agreed to meet us the next day. I was uneasy and suggested we try some other means to get rid of the stolen property. I couldn't see how something good could come from trying to sell stolen goods to a police officer. Besides, it could be a set up. Ryan kept trying to reassure me that it was okay.

Chapter 6

We met Ryan's cousin down the dirt road leading to Old McDonald branch, about two miles south of Lynco. The road ran along the river, far from any houses, and seldom did a car ever come by. There was a wide spot in the road about a quarter mile after leaving the highway. It was a lover's lane where people would go parking.

You had to be careful where you stepped around that place, used condoms littered the ground. A big river birch tree stood at the edge of the wide spot in the road of this ungodly fornication site. We appropriately named it 'The Rubber Tree.' We rode our bicycles to the meeting place but didn't use the pillowcases this time for carrying the loot. Ryan had everything in his backpack, knowing it wouldn't draw any attention.

Ryan's cousin drove up alone in a black sedan.
You could tell it was some sort of unmarked police car.
His name was Larry. Ryan had told me about Larry, and
that he had a twin named Barry. Larry and Barry Tyler
were both Logan County Deputies.

Ryan, told me Larry and Barry had been to his
house on many occasions when they lived in Coal City.
They visited often when Ryan's older brother William was
still living at home. Ryan had never mentioned the cousins
before yesterday. I was still very uneasy about this
meeting. I was trusting Ryan not to steer us wrong. He
knew the history of Larry and some of the things he and
William had done. He was relying on that as a sign Larry
would buy what we had to sell.

Larry stood well over six feet tall, broad at the
shoulders, and a stocky build. My guess was that he was
around twenty-five years of age. Cop or no cop, he didn't
look like anybody you'd want to tangle with. I'm sure
there are men in a jail somewhere who would testify to that.
As he was getting out of the car, he had a disgusted look on
his face. I'm sure what he saw were two snotty-nosed punk
kids running around on bicycles, and thinking he'd driven
all this way for nothing.

"How are you doing Larry?" Ryan said.

"What the hell you boys been into?"

"Nothing really," Ryan replied.

"Sure," he said slowly. "Alright, I hope this is
going to be worth my trip. What you got for me to look
at?"

Ryan placed the backpack on the hood of the car
and unzipped it, revealing the goods inside. Larry placed
both his big hands inside the pack and pulled out some of
the individually packed fishing lures, and a few of the bone
handled knives, still in the original boxes. Ryan was
standing beside Larry, and I was a few paces behind them,
ready to run if needed.

"Damn, these are some nice knives, how many are there?" Larry asked.

Ryan and I had already counted the knives several times and knew there were thirty-two. We'd also written down the price of each item before taking the sales price sticker off. All together, the retail value of everything was just over nineteen-hundred dollars.

"Thirty-five knives, plus the lures, scopes, and other stuff," Ryan said.

I wondered why Ryan had just lied to Larry. Surely, he knew the man would count the knives then he'd be back looking for us.

"Alright, I guess you want to sell this stuff, right? How much do you want?" Larry asked, as he intently looked everything over.

I could tell Ryan was becoming a bit nervous himself, which was unusual. Ryan was always cool as a cucumber no matter what the circumstances were.

"Nine-hundred dollars," Ryan blurted out.

"Well, I'll tell you what, it takes a while to get rid of things like this, even though knives and such are popular with the boys back home. I'll give you two-hundred smackers. It's about the best I can do."

"Shit Larry, It's worth a ton more than that." Ryan said in a smart-aleck tone.

"You watch your mouth around me boy. I've got an idea where this stuff came from, and I've a mind to haul both your asses in." Larry said loudly.

That was it. I knew Ryan had crossed the line. Meeting Larry was a bad idea!

"I'm sorry, Cousin Larry, but I lost a five-hundred dollar bet to a boy at school, and he's a senior. If I don't pay up by next Tuesday, I'm in a world of hurt."

That was another lie. I couldn't believe Ryan was playing these games with his cousin, especially since he had just mentioned taking us to jail.

"I'll tell you what I'll do Ryan, you being kin folk and all. I'll give you three-hundred, but not a dime more."

Larry had a big fat wallet, one of those on a chain. He whipped it out of his pocket then removed three crisp new one-hundred-dollar bills and handed them to Ryan. I could see that Larry's wallet was packed full of money, likely all big bills. Deputy Sheriffs don't make a lot of money, so I wondered what all Larry was doing on the side to have a wad of bills like that.

"It appears to me that you boys have entered into a life of crime. That's going to lead you down the road to nowhere," Larry said. "I've already heard about your gambling Ryan. Gambling and stealing will either get you killed or put in prison, so you best heed to my words and find something else to keep yourself occupied. Are you hearing me loud and clear Ryan?"

"Yes sir!"

"Alright then."

Larry picked up the pack and started walking toward the back of the car.

"Ryan, I'm taking it your daddy and momma don't know about any of this so you best not let them know we've talked, much less met. Be sure though to tell your brother, I said hello."

Larry threw the backpack in the trunk as he was talking to us. He then opened the car door, got in and drove off. Ryan and I both let out a sigh of relief. I didn't say a word, and neither did Ryan. We waited until the dust from Larry's car settled, then got on our bicycles and sat there in the middle of the road a few more minutes.

Ryan pulled out his wallet, took out a fifty-dollar bill, and handed it to me, along with one of the bills he'd gotten from Larry. He put the remaining one-hundred-dollar bills in his wallet, stuck it in his back pants pocket and we rode home.

My mind replayed the brief meeting with Larry as we rode along. I had one-hundred and fifty dollars in my pocket. It was more money than I'd ever had in my entire life combined. It was bittersweet though. At that moment, I felt like I'd just been robbed by a cop.

At the dinner table that evening Crump was telling Momma about the break-in up in town at the new sporting goods store. I thought my heart was going to jump out of my chest. I had to put on a poker face, just as Ryan had been teaching me. I could tell my face was red. Fortunately, no one was paying attention to me. Momma said that store had just opened up a few weeks back and was curious to know what happened. Break-ins and robberies of any type were uncommon where we lived, so news of such a thing was big and traveled fast.

Crump said he had stopped to get some cigarettes and had run into Caleb McAllister, the town's chief of police. McAllister had said whoever broke in the store did ten-thousand dollars of damage and stole nearly thirty-thousand dollars of sporting goods, almost wiping the place out. *He's a bare face liar,* I thought. I wanted to scream that out, but I kept on eating and acting as if I wasn't even paying attention to what they were discussing.

Crump continued and said that McAllister thought it was related to a series of store break-ins over in Raleigh County, but Crump said he disagreed with him. Crump figured it was a set up to collect insurance money. Boy, that was a sigh of relief to me, knowing Ryan, and I weren't suspects. About that time, Bernice asked if someone would pass the mashed potatoes without saying "please" and it got Momma off the robbery talk.

"Ain't none of you damn kids got any manners?" She screamed out.

Momma slung a spoon full of mashed potatoes from the bowl, across the table, and onto Bernice's plate. The potatoes splattered and covered Bernice's blouse. She started to get up from the table. I could see she was also welling up as if she was going to cry.

"You cry and I'll whip your ass from now 'til dark!" Momma said, still screaming. "Now eat those damn potatoes, and I dare you to leave a bite."

It was quiet during the rest of dinner. No one else said a word.

Later that evening I was sitting out on the front porch thinking. Thinking was something I'd found myself doing too often those days.

What about the people who owned the store? Would they turn in a bunch of stuff to the insurance company that wasn't stolen? They'd get more money from the insurance company than what we'd taken, which was fraud. Then Larry practically stole the stuff from Ryan and me, which was a crime also. I just didn't know what the name of it was called. Ryan and I, being the real bandits, got the short end of the stick. *If we ever decide to do another robbery stunt, we'd better come up with a better game plan.*

Chapter 7

The next day was Saturday. At breakfast, Momma
said we were going to Welch with her and Crump to see his
insurance office. She also wanted to do some shopping for
back-to-school, and wanted us kids there. She told me I
needed a new pair of shoes, and since I was making money
by mowing grass for a few of the neighbors, I could make
that purchase myself.

"Can't I stay home? Heck, I don't want to see
Crump's office," I said.

Momma reached across the table and hit me with
her fist, nearly knocking me out of my chair.

"If you ever call him Crump again, you better hope
I don't hear it. It's Mister Crump to you son, and heavy on

the Mister! You better get some respect in your thick skull, or else I'll beat it into you, Jacob!"

Momma got up from the table and left the room. I wiped my lip, and it was bleeding. Bernice and Janet snickered and made faces at me. Then Bernice sarcastically whispered, "Who's your daddy, Jacob Crump?" I wanted to do her the same way Momma had just done me. Instead, I got up from the table and stormed off.

I had no desire to go anywhere with Crump, but this was going to be my first trip out of Wyoming County, so I was excited. I was sitting on the porch waiting for Momma and Crump to get ready when Bernice informed me that Janet wasn't going. She had graduated high school in the spring and had been making plans to move away.

Her friend, Martha, had some relatives in Hickory, North Carolina, including an aunt who lived alone. The aunt said they could move in with her. There was a good probability of her getting a job in one of the furniture factories in the Hickory area. I would have expected Momma to object, but instead she seemed to think it was a great idea, said it was one less mouth to feed.

I jumped off the porch and headed toward the car. I saw Ryan coming out of his house. He and I had planned to go up Big Reedy that day and shoot our new guns. I ran over to his house and told him my situation. He said he would get with me that evening when I got back home.

It was about an hour drive to Welch. I didn't see anything out of the car window that looked much different from Lynco or Oceana, until we got to Pineville. We drove past the courthouse. It was a huge stone building with big columns in the front, sitting high on the hillside above the road, making it look even bigger. Pineville appeared smaller than Oceana, having only a Main Street that ran a quarter-mile, then a back street that brings you back out of town.

Crump made the full circle. We stopped briefly to peak out the window at Castle Rock, a large butte formation situated alongside the riverbank. It was about a hundred and fifty feet high and maybe forty feet across. Steps circled the rock all the way to the top and there was a flat area on the peak. I saw a few people up there sitting on a bench. I wanted to get out and climb to the top, but Crump said we didn't have time to stop.

When we got to Welch, we stopped at Crump's office first. It wasn't big and fancy like I had imagined, instead it was small and dirty. The walls were dark wood paneling, and the only thing hanging was the last year's calendar from The Bank of Baileysville. Old newspapers were stacked in uneven piles along the window in front.

Crump's desk was covered in papers and three half-filled coffee cups. The coffee cups had made dark rings on the papers they were sitting on. An ashtray stand was beside Crump's desk. The entire room smelled like stale cigarette smoke. The ashtray stand had a metal pedestal, and the top was red and black plaid material, with a chrome ashtray that contained two chrome birds that looked like crows, one on each side. The crows were looking into the ashtray with their beaks open. A partly smoked cigarette with a white filter was stuck in one of the bird's beak and had lipstick on the butt. As far as I knew, Crump didn't wear lipstick, so I wondered who had smoked it.

We didn't stay long at Crump's office. I could tell he didn't like us being there. The answering machine on his desk had a red light blinking. He told us all to go get in the car, and he'd be there soon as he checked to see who had called.

Welch was a big city, bustling with traffic, a multitude of tall buildings, and a multitude of stores. Crump parked the car, got out, and put some coins in the parking meter. I peered out the window for quite some time, just looking up at the tall buildings and counting how many stories each one had. The tallest one had twelve.

We shopped at several big department stores and a five-and-dime. After Momma found a pair of penny-loafers that fit me perfectly, she allowed me to roam about by myself. At least the shoes were on sale. That was a blessing since I had to buy them with my own money.

Crump put two dimes in the parking meter giving us two hours to shop. I carried a wristwatch with a broken band in my pocket. Momma made me look at it to see that it matched the time on her own watch then told me to be back at the car in an hour and fifteen minutes. She said the meter had already been running for at least 30 minutes. Bernice didn't mind staying with Momma because they were going to look at dresses and all that nonsense. I didn't have a clue where Crump had disappeared to, nor did I care.

The stores were enormous, and I had to keep a map in my head about where I was and which direction I'd gone, otherwise I'd get lost.

Back home I'd put my hundred-dollar bill in a peanut butter jar and hid it in the shed. I had some more money in the jar as well, but had the fifty-dollar bill in my pocket that I'd gotten from Ryan the day we met Larry down at the Rubber Tree.

Ever since school was out for the summer, I'd been mowing grass for five people. I'd also been helping Micah Taylor dig a ditch. He bought a vacant lot down on North Street across from the church. Since it was swampy ground, he was going to put in drainage ditches filled with seepage pipe and gravel. Digging those ditches was hard work, but he was paying me two dollars an hour, which was more than the minimum wage of a dollar-sixty-five. By having my own money, I had a few things now that I wanted and life was getting better.

There was a Montgomery Ward store across the street from where Crump had parked the car. It had a sporting goods section in the rear of the store. Until then, all I'd known about these big-name stores was from catalogs. In the middle of the sporting good's section was a sales counter with a glass front. Some handguns and riflescopes were in the display.

Working behind the counter was a timid looking boy about my age. He was tall and skinny like me but wore black-rimmed glasses and had blonde hair. There weren't any customers around at the moment so he was busy using glass cleaner and a rag, cleaning the glass cases. I walked up and asked him if they sold pistol shells.

"You mean ammo?" He said.

He had a sissy sounding voice, and it was raspy as he talked.

"Yes, ammo," I replied, with a smart-aleck tone.

He pointed to the shelf behind me that I'd just walked past. I turned to look. It was unreal. There must have been a thousand boxes of any cartridge size ever made. They were sitting on long shelves that ran from floor to ceiling. I turned back and asked the boy if you had to be a certain age to buy ammo in McDowell County.

"I don't think so," he said, shrugging his shoulders. I went to the shelf and immediately found the section where 44 magnum shells were stored. There were several varieties and brands. I selected a box of 44 magnum wad cutters, not even knowing what that meant. I took a quick look around to make sure Crump wasn't there and then placed the box on the counter. The clerk rang them up and I handed him the fifty-dollar bill.

"Ooh oh wee, let's hope we have change," he said with his squeaky voice.

It bothered me hearing a boy or man talk like that, it just wasn't right. He raised the cash register drawer, revealing tens and twenties laying there along with a few personal checks, so he was able to make change of my fifty.

He put the box of shells in a small paper bag and handed it to me. I asked if he had a larger bag, and he handed me a large shopping bag with a rope handle. I dropped the smaller bag in the larger one, folded the top over, and headed back through the store. I bought a quarter pound of maple nut goodies at the candy counter on my way out of the store and put them in the big bag. That way if anyone asked what I had I could pull out the candy. The candy was fresh and smelled extraordinarily good. I didn't know if I could keep from eating it all, before we started home.

I left the store and went back to the car. Crump was sitting behind the wheel reading a magazine. I stood on the sidewalk a short distance behind the car leaning against a building until Momma, and Bernice showed up. Then we all got in the car and drove home. During the ride back home all the chatter was about the stores and the sales. I was never asked by anyone what was in the bag.

Chapter 8

On Sunday afternoon, Ryan and I headed into Big Reedy Creek. It had rained heavily on Saturday night, and the river was running high and almost out of its banks. Both of us were uneasy about crossing the swinging bridge. Those old boards were making it a more treacherous crossing each trip.

Falling into the rushing waters below would surely mean you'd be swept away to your death. We took our time holding tightly to the wire ropes. Each step caused the bridge to swing back and forth. Finally, we reached the other side and wiped the sweat from our hands and brow.

We had the pillowcases with us that we'd used in the store break-in but this time they were for a different purpose. On our way there, we'd stopped at the gas station and loaded the sacks with empty oilcans from the dumpster, knowing they'd make good targets. We also found some throwaway soda bottles to put into the sacks.

Ryan's brother William had been home on Friday, and Ryan had showed him the 25 auto. He went to Hatfield's Hardware in Oceana and bought two boxes of shells for Ryan. William didn't appear to be concerned about what we had done. William told Ryan about a time when he, along with his cousins Larry and Barry, broke into a feed and hardware store in Holden.

Ryan told his brother about how Larry had swindled us, by only giving us three-hundred dollars for all the knives and stuff. William said he was going to have a talk with Larry about that.

We didn't go very far up Big Reedy that day. We were too excited about shooting the guns. Someone long ago had chiseled out six holes in a big flat rock sitting along the creek to hold blocks of salt for cattle to lick on. A tree had fallen across the now swollen creek there, making it the idea place to put the oilcans and soda bottles.

From the creek bank, we reached out, careful not to fall into the water, and put a soda bottle and two oilcans on the tree. Then we marched off twenty paces, which was about where the salt lick was located, figuring it to be about fifty feet.

Ryan went first. He got out the 25 auto and held it at arm's length with one hand, squinted and pulled the trigger. When the gun fired, it had a report like a 22 rifle, just a little louder. Nothing moved on top of the log. He squeezed off another shot with the same result. Ryan broke the barrel down to reload and told me to take a shot with my gun. I removed the 44 magnum from an old dishtowel I'd wrapped it in to protect it from scratches. I was

64

nervous. I'd never shot a pistol before, and certainly not a big one. I had read in a book how to hold it and how to stand.

With my feet shoulder-width apart and holding the pistol with both hands, I took aim and squeezed the trigger. I was ready for some recoil but nothing like that! I stumbled backwards and almost fell. The report sounded like a bomb exploding, and fire shot five feet or more from the end of the barrel. As I regained my balance, I saw Ryan hunkered down, holding his ears. I looked and the oilcan I had aimed at was lying across the creek on the opposite bank from us.

"Holy Crap!" Ryan exclaimed, as he stood back up, removing his hands from his ears.

My adrenaline was flowing, and I felt big.

"That was powerful," I shouted.

"Take another shot," Ryan said, as he moved further back and behind me.

I took aim at the soda bottle, and squeezed the trigger, more prepared now for the hard recoil. The gun roared as before, and fire belched out the end of the barrel. I stumbled back again, but quickly regained my balance. The glass bottle exploded into a thousand pieces.

"You're a natural. A gosh dang natural," Ryan said. "And that cannon is out of this world."

It took a few minutes for my ears to stop ringing then I asked Ryan if he wanted to shoot the gun. He accepted. He had already seen the recoil produced from the gun when it's fired. He stiffened his body, as he got ready to shoot. He pulled the trigger and fired off a shot. The recoil sent Ryan stumbling back and falling to the ground.

"Good goolie loolie," Ryan exclaimed, as he stood back up, brushing the dirt from his pants.

We looked, and the oilcan was still sitting on the log. I told Ryan to take another shot, which he did. That time he didn't fall, but he stumbled backwards a good ten feet. It was the same result. He'd missed the target.

I enjoyed watching the fire shoot from the gun barrel, and hearing the loud explosion that followed as the bullet broke through the sound barrier. It made me feel big and powerful to have such a weapon.

I took the 44 magnum and shot again, this time even further back from the target. The remaining oilcan lifted off the log, going high into the air, then tumbled back down, landing in the stream.

"Alright!" Ryan said. "Here, now try my gun, smart aleck."

We placed more bottles and cans on the fallen tree. I took the 25 auto and pointed it at the oilcan then squeezed off a round. There was only the slightest recoil. I looked closely. The can was unmolested.

"Dang it," I said.

"Try it again," Ryan said encouragingly.

I did, taking careful aim that time, then squeezed off the second round. It was the same result the oilcan was untouched. We tried shooting the 25 auto at closer distances, but neither of us could hit a target. Ryan got within ten feet and fired at a soda bottle. The bullet hit the tree just below the bottle causing bark to fly up, making the bottle unsteady. It teetered for a couple of seconds then tipped over, falling into the water. We laughed until our sides hurt.

We shot half the box of 44 shells I had bought, shooting at cans from fifty to a hundred feet away. Ryan only hit one out of ten, but I never missed once. It was the best feeling I'd ever had about anything.

"Hot damn you're good, that settles it. You're my bodyguard from here on out," Ryan said.

We stayed out of town for the next week, hanging out mostly on the railroad tracks behind our houses. Well into the second week after we had robbed the store, I got the itch to spend some of my money. I wanted a holster for my prized possession, the 44 magnum. I walked the railroad tracks to town, wanting to avoid the highway. It was stupid thinking back on it, but I walked to the store that Ryan and I had broken into. When I got to the store, I went straight inside.

There was only one man working the store. He was busy with two customers at the counter looking through a gun catalog. I didn't recognize the two men or the store clerk. The clerk was a big man, not extremely tall but broad at the shoulders and muscular. He was wearing a camouflage shirt and hat. I couldn't help notice his thick handlebar mustache, and his face was leathered. He looked like he'd spent a lot of time in the sun. As I entered the store, he asked if he could help me. I told him I was just looking, so he turned his attention back to the two men and the catalog.

I took a good look around the store and thought how different it appeared in daylight. It was as if I'd never been there before. There weren't any roped off areas or taped windows as you'd expect to see after a crime took place. Instead, it looked as normal as any other store. The store building still had that faint hint of fresh paint smell, bringing back memories of the night we broke into the place.

I walked over to the left back corner. There on the wall was a display of fifteen to twenty leather holsters. Some had belts, and some in plastic bags were sold as the holster only. There was a shoulder harness and holster like the cops use hanging there. It wasn't a belt holster. Instead, it was a shoulder holster. It appeared large enough to hold the 44 magnum.

I took it off the peg hook and looked it over. It was made of nice quality leather. There was a padded area where it fits against your side underneath your arm. I liked the smell of leather and couldn't help but put it close to my nose and take a whiff. It had a price tag attached, $23.95. That was a lot of money, much more than I had anticipated spending, still, I really liked it.

I took the holster to the counter. The clerk turned aside from chatting with the two men and gave me his full attention. I asked if he could take any less for the harness and holster.

"What in the world does a boy your age want with something like this?" He asked.

It wasn't a question presented with suspicion it was more from curiosity. I told him it was going to be a birthday gift for my dad, but I really couldn't afford that much.

It bothered me to be blurting out a lie like that, but lately I'd found myself doing it more and more. Ryan lied a lot and it never seemed to bother him, but I always felt bad when I lied. It was becoming a habit, and I knew I had to be more conscious about what I was saying. I didn't ever want to be comfortable with lying.

The store clerk seemed touched that I would buy my dad such a nice gift. I was surprised at his reaction, figured he would be gruff and stern, wanting to stand his ground on the price.

"Let me see what I can do," he said.

He looked in the catalog rack sitting on the counter then got his calculator out.

"How about twenty dollars, including tax?" He asked.

"Great," I said, and pulled out two tens from my wallet, handing them to him.

He put the holster in a large paper sack that had the name of the store printed on it, plus some sort of logo. He then asked if I needed a receipt.

"Yes please, just in case it doesn't fit Dad's gun."

There I was lying again. I wasn't doing so well winning that inner battle.

"Just bring it back in good shape within thirty days if it doesn't work out," he replied.

He then went back to the conversation with the two men, who were still deep in thought while looking at the catalog. I went out the door and walked off to the side of the building. I figured he might be wondering why I was on foot and not with somebody in a car. My heart was pounding in my chest, something else that seemed to be happening quite often.

The holster fit the gun perfectly. Out in the shed, I put the harness on and adjusted the straps so it would be snug but not too tight. I placed the gun inside the holster and practiced drawing it out several times. I didn't have the gun loaded. If there was one thing I knew, it was that you never played with a loaded gun. A few times, I drew the gun out and dropped to one knee into a firing position, pulling the trigger, shooting at an imaginary target.

I put on a lightweight jacket and looked into the mirror of an old dresser stored in the shed. I turned in every direction. I couldn't tell that I was carrying a gun. It was perfectly concealed.

Having the gun made me feel powerful and in control, and I liked that feeling. I started carrying the gun with me anywhere Ryan and I went unless it was too hot to put a jacket over my shirt. The weather didn't matter to Ryan. He carried the 25 auto in his hip pocket at all times. All he could possibly do would be to scare the heck out of somebody with that gun. It wasn't as though you could use it to shoot anybody at a distance further than arm's reach.

Chapter 9

A few weeks later school started back. The high school had a chess team. They practiced in the library during lunch. The coach wanted Ryan to play on the team, but he had no interest. On occasion, he would go to the library and play against the best players, winning every time.

The chess team coach had tried more than once to get Ryan to join, but he didn't want to be tied to the team. He only wanted to play when he felt like it, and besides, they wouldn't let him bet on the games.

Even though chess is a slow moving game, it was fun to watch Ryan play. He kept several moves in his head. His opponent would carefully study the board and after much debate make a move. Ryan didn't ever study the playing field. He stared at the person he was playing, making them nervous. Just like playing poker, he had multiple ways to intimidate his opponents. They'd give up or make a stupid mistake.

Several of us boys from Lynco gathered in the hall one afternoon shortly after lunch. Most of the teachers were in the lounge smoking cigarettes. There was always one teacher though who had the dreaded duty of 'hall patrol'. That particular day, it was Mr. Belcher.

The school was a long two-story building with a stairway on each end. The top and bottom floors were identical, consisting of the stairways and a long hall on each floor. Classrooms branched off on both sides of the hallways. We were on the bottom floor. Ryan spotted Mr. Belcher heading for the stairs on the far end of the hall. There was a fire alarm bell located midway down the hall on both floors.

"Watch this!" Ryan said.

The halls were full of kids on lunch recess so there was good cover for what Ryan was about to do. He went over and yanked on the fire alarm chain. Ryan let it ring for a few seconds then let it go as he walked back in our direction. He passed us by and kept on going, heading for the stairway on the far end. Ryan had his upper body all stiff like, walking like a robot. He had everyone in the hallway laughing.

Mr. Belcher came running out of the opposite end stairway and proceeded to the bell to catch the culprit. He knew there wasn't a fire - it was some punk kid playing a game. By that time, Ryan was on the second floor. The fire alarm up there was located directly above the one on the bottom floor, and now it was blaring away. Belcher took off, back toward the stairs he had just come from. Before Belcher had reached the stairway, Ryan had reappeared downstairs. We all were still laughing heartily.

Ryan passed us by again, grabbed the downstairs alarm, and let it scream out another four to five seconds. Again, he walked our way, passed us, and disappeared into the far end stairway. He had just cleared the entrance when Belcher reappeared from the stairway on the opposite end of the building.

With a frustrating look on his face, Belcher stopped and put both hands on his waist then raised them above his head, as if he wanted to cry out "Why Me!" No sooner had Belcher raised his arms the upstairs alarm was sounding off again. We all laughed.

Belcher came over to where all of us boys were standing and got behind us.

"Say a word and I'll have you all expelled from school," he said.

As expected, here came Ryan darting from the stairway, heading back toward the downstairs bell. I stepped out from the crowd just as Ryan was getting to me, put out my left arm to stop him, and pointed with the other hand toward Belcher. Ryan was too caught up in the moment. He jetted around me and continued down the hallway.

"NO RYAN, DON'T," I shouted, but it was too late.

Ryan gave the chain a yank. The bell was sounding, and I could have sworn it was two to three times louder than ever before. He quickly turned around to get our nod of approval.

Belcher had stepped up behind Ryan. He was standing there with his arms crossed and head slightly tilted to the side. As Ryan turned he was staring Belcher right in the eye. I don't know why Ryan did it, but his next action was hilarious to us boys watching. He reached out his right

72

hand, and with his index finger extended, he touched Belcher on the shoulder and said, "Tag, you're it."

Ryan received a three-day suspension for that stunt. For a while, he thought he was going to be thrown out of school. The principal gave him a big speech about violations of the fire code and how they were going to get the Fire Marshall involved. That was just a scare tactic because it never happened. Ryan had to take a letter home from the principal for his mom or dad to sign. I signed the letter that evening as Mrs. Tyler. Ryan never told his mom or dad.

The next three days Ryan got dressed as if he was going to school but instead of coming to the bus stop for a ride to school, he went down the railroad tracks and into Big Reedy to spend the day. He spent all three days up at the beech grove. That was 100% better than being in school. It made me wish I'd been the one ringing the fire alarm.

The third day of Ryan's suspension, he met me getting off the bus from school and was all excited. He told me that morning after the bus left, he had headed down river and up into Big Reedy to spend the day. There were two vans parked at the swinging bridge when he got there. When he got to Burning Rock, six strange men were there. He questioned them to see what was going on.

They were a team of scientists from some university in London, England. Someone here in the United States had contacted them about Burning Rock and had sent photographs of the writings on the rock. They had come to study the writings. Ryan said they were there all day making measurements, using paintbrushes to brush dirt away, and taking a multitude of photographs.

Ryan watched the men work. They told him a bunch of stuff about ancient writings, but he didn't understand any of it. I was concerned these men might want to turn Burning Rock into an archeological dig site

73

and ruin the entire place. I wasn't nearly as excited about this news as Ryan was.

We talked and decided it was best not to broadcast what he had witnessed. Even if the scientists never returned, half the town would want to go there and peek at the writings and ruin our getaway spot in the beech grove.

We hung out at the gas station down at the mouth of Lynco Hollow a lot. There was always a group of adults hanging around there as well, talking about politics, and discussing local events. Not once was there news about the scientists mentioned, and as far as we knew, no one ever took a hike up Big Reedy to check out Burning Rock, which was fine with us.

Chapter **10**

After Ryan returned to school, he didn't get into any more trouble, at least not at school. It was Ryan's senior year. He had to make sure he didn't get anything bad put on his permanent record. That wouldn't look good to the people at Carter University.

Ryan applied to attend the University in Roanoke Virginia. He was accepted. The university had only existed for twenty years but already had become a prestigious business college.

Acceptance into Carter was difficult for a non-resident of Virginia. Ryan had not only been accepted, they told him if he had good grades after his first year at school, it was likely he'd be given a fully scholarship. He was going to study finance, and was excited about getting out of Lynco.

Ryan would be the first person in his family to attend college. His parents were excited and proud of him. I was excited for Ryan as well. I just didn't want to see him go away.

It was good seeing his mom and dad happy and proud of him. It made me wonder, would Momma be proud of me if I were to be accepted into college somewhere?

Ryan's birthday was October, first. It was a Saturday, and his brother William was coming home for the weekend. That morning Ryan and I were in his dad's garage just hanging out. William pulled in driving his black 68 Mustang. I'd seen him driving that car before. William's wife and two kids were behind him. She was driving a new Lincoln Continental.

William saw us in the garage and came over to talk. Ryan asked William when he'd gotten the big fancy car. William said he'd had it about two weeks. Ryan then asked why he had brought both cars. William had a big grin on his face and wanted to say something. Ryan and I both were clueless about what was going on.

"I was going to wait until Dad got out of bed, but I may as well tell you now. I'm giving you the Mustang as a birthday present," William said. "Now you'll have a set of wheels to drive to college."

Ryan's mouth dropped open and so did mine. Neither of us could talk. William thought that was funny and laughed.

"There's one catch to this deal though," William said. "You have to pay for your own insurance."

For the first time ever, I saw tears in Ryan's eyes. Ryan always had himself together no matter what the circumstance, but this hit him hard. It was unexpected and touched him deeply. He gave William a hug and told him he didn't know what to say, except thank you. William said we needed to go inside and talk more. I told Ryan and William this was a family affair. I was going to run along, but would catch up with them later. They went into the house, and I headed over to the shed. I was as happy as Ryan was. We could now put our bicycles out to pasture - we had wheels!

Chapter 11

Having a car gave Ryan and me a new kind of freedom. We could now get places faster, and we could go greater distances.

The days were getting cooler, and the nights were cold. I didn't complain because it gave me an excuse to wear a jacket, and underneath, I had the 44 magnum. Ryan carried the 25 auto in his back pocket no matter where we went. Anytime he was out in his car, he wanted me to tag along, which was fine. I liked being there as his sidekick.

Ryan's love for gambling kept growing. I suppose he had an addiction, but if there's an upside to that, Ryan never lost. He might only win a dollar, but he never left a game a loser.

One of the seniors at school invited Ryan to a poker game coming up on Saturday in the community of Ravencliff. Having a car made it possible to go places like that. Ravencliff was about fifteen miles from Lynco.

We arrived at the location where the game was to take place around one o'clock in the afternoon. It was a cold day for October. The sky was dark gray, and a light snow was falling.

The place we were at wasn't exactly your upscale gambling parlor. It was an old auto body shop with a three bay garage. The outside of the building was constructed from rough-cut lumber, which had weathered over many years.

There were several junk cars parked outside of the garage. There was also a variety of car parts strewn about, giving the place the appearance of a junk yard. Smoke was billowing out of a smokestack protruding from the rusted tin roof and the smell of burning coal filled the air.

I wasn't comfortable being there. Before we got out of the car, I checked the pistol to ensure it was fully loaded. We went inside and the first thing I noticed was a haze of cigarette smoke hanging in the air. Twelve people were playing cards at three tables sitting in the center bay.

All the people playing cards were teenage boys. Two men who were standing by the coal stove warming their hands. I couldn't tell their ages. They had long beards, and their clothes were dirty. They seemed out of place. I told Ryan that we'd better keep an eye on those two.

I didn't see the boy from our school at the game, and I didn't recognize anyone else. I figured these boys must go to Glen Rogers High School, a few miles up the road from where we were.

Ryan introduced himself to the crowd, and soon he was sitting at a table shuffling the playing cards. Nothing exciting happened, so after watching a few hands of poker I went back outside to get some fresh air. Most of the time when a poker game was going on there were others around not playing, just like me. The card players never seemed to mind as long as you weren't in their space or trying to help someone cheat.

One of the men who had been standing at the stove came outside and struck up a conversation with me. He looked a bit rough around the edges, but he was actually just a good ole country boy. He had a jar of home brewed moonshine and asked if I'd like a drink. I wasn't interested, but to keep from embarrassing myself, and looking like a wimp; I turned the jar up and took a large gulp. It wasn't bad. I expected it to burn like fire going down, but it was smooth as water. A few seconds later, my guts were on fire, and I became very light headed.

The man who gave me the booze laughed loud then went back inside. I went to the car, now covered in about an inch of snow and began scooping it up. I almost cleared all the snow off the car hood, eating it, hoping it would put the fire out in my stomach.

I finally started getting some relief, and my senses were returning. I went back inside to see how Ryan was doing with his game. Another hour went by before Ryan got tired and decided to leave. The cigarette smoke was burning his eyes as well as mine. That's one problem with poker games, a lot of people smoke. Ryan won nearly eighty dollars. He thanked everyone for a great time then we headed out the door.

The other rough looking man, the one who had been standing at the stove when we first went in, followed us outside. I put my hand inside my jacket and was holding it near my gun, anticipating trouble was about to begin.

When we got to our car, the man was still only a few paces behind us.

"You fellers be interested in a gun?" He said.

Ryan and I both turned around. The man stopped in his tracks, and appeared to be frightened.

"A gun?" Ryan replied.

"Yep"

"What kind of gun you got?" Ryan asked.

He motioned us over to a pick-up truck. I was concerned about that situation and looked all around, making sure there weren't more people out there hiding behind cars, ready to ambush us. We walked over to the truck. The man opened the truck door, removed a Smith and Wesson 38 special pistol from the glove compartment, and showed it to us.

"It's a bit hot to touch if you know what I mean," he said.

"What do you want for it?" Ryan replied.

"I don't rightly know," the man exclaimed. "I just need to get all I can fer it."

Ryan took the 25 auto out of his hip pocket and a twenty-dollar bill from his wallet. He held his hands out with his palms up. The pistol was in one palm and the money in the other. "Here…it's a good trade," Ryan said.

The man surprisingly agreed to the deal. He took the 25 auto and the money from Ryan and handed him the 38 special. Ryan looked the gun over, opened the cylinder, and took the shells out.

"I've seen you before," Ryan said, knowing he'd never laid eyes on the man. "If I find out this gun has a broken firing pin, or don't shoot good, my bodyguard here will be coming back to look for you. Show him your piece, Jake." I couldn't believe Ryan was playing this thing up. I wanted to get the heck out of there, but I played along. I whipped the 44 magnum out and held it across my body, revealing the size of the big handgun.

"Holy shit," the man said. "Mister, I ain't lookin fer no troubles, I's can dame guarantee ya that there's a good pistol, I stole it from my brother-in-law who shoots a lot."

The temperature had dropped. It was much colder than when we had arrived a few hours prior. Still, I detected a few beads of sweat rolling down the side of his face as he stood there. I put the pistol back in the holster, and we walked back to the car.

Ryan had never driven on roads that were snow covered before, and he punched the gas too hard as we took off. We went into a half spin as we sped out of the parking lot and onto the highway. We weren't trying to be showboats, but I'm sure it looked that way. After Ryan was on the highway and back in control of the car, he looked over at me and smiled. "Now maybe when we go shooting I can hit the friggin target," he said.

The next day Ryan asked me to go to a card game with him up at Hatcher, just outside of Oceana. Momma was on the phone when I went to ask for permission to go out. Crump was sitting in the recliner drinking a can of beer and detected I wanted to speak with her.

"Your momma's busy boy, what the hell do you want now?"

"Nothing, I was just wondering if I could go up to town with Ryan."

"I don't give a rat's ass where you go boy, long as you're away from here."

I hurried out of the house and to the shed to get my gun. The snow had stopped sometime during the night, and the sun was out. It was warm enough to begin melting the snow that had accumulated on the cars and grass. The temperature inside the unheated shed was colder than the air outside. As I strapped the gun on, I could feel the cold from the metal penetrating my side, even though the leather holster.

The poker game was going to be at Darrell Haven's barbershop. Darrell had been in the same location cutting hair for over fifty years, and everybody in town knew him. He was a jolly likeable man. I'd been there many times in the past getting my haircut. I didn't recall ever being in his barbershop that he wasn't laughing and telling jokes.

Before going to the barbershop, Ryan drove down to the Rubber Tree. The place where we'd met Larry to sell him the items we'd stolen from the sporting goods store. Ryan wanted to shoot the 38. It gave me an opportunity to shoot the 44 magnum as well.

Someone had thrown out a few beer cans, which we gathered. We set them on some rocks down by the river then walked back toward the car. I shot four times and hit three cans. Ryan asked me to shoot the 38 special first, said he was afraid it might blow up in his face.

"So I'm the guinea pig huh?" I said. "I guess I'm expendable. I'm..."

Ryan stopped me. "Just shut up and shoot, I want to see if you can hit a target before I try."

It was a well-made firearm, and it fit my hand nicely. I held the gun out with one hand extended. I took aim and pulled the trigger. There was a good bit of recoil, but nothing like the 44 magnum. The beer can went tumbling through the air and landed in the river. I didn't say another word, I just handed the gun over to Ryan. He stuck his tongue out at me as he took the gun from my hand.

Ryan aimed the 38 special and squeezed the trigger. The gun went off, and one of the beer cans went flying through the air. Ryan yelled like a wild man.

"Well, who'd ever thunk it!" I said. "You hit it the first time."

Ryan laughed. "Yeah I did, but that wasn't the one I was shooting at!"

We didn't continue shooting; we were both laughing too hard. It was about time for the game to start, so we left. We were still laughing in the car, all the way to town.

The door to the barbershop was locked when we got there. We could see through the Venetian blinds that people were inside moving about. I was guessing the blinds being closed were in order to hide the gambling activity from passersby. We were within the city limits, and the police had to know what was going on. I determined, they either didn't care or were getting some sort of kickback.

Darrell peered from behind the shade that covered the door. He then unlocked the door and let us in. As we entered, I first noticed that unlike the poker game yesterday at Ravencliff, Ryan and I, were the only teenagers in the place. Everyone else in the barbershop was a senior citizen.

"Well, a couple of young whipper-snappers. Come on in," Darrell said.

Greetings were exchanged then Ryan sat down to play cards. I was the only one not playing that day, but no one seemed to mind.

Those men weren't prepared for Ryan. He was on top of his game that afternoon. After only thirty minutes had passed, Ryan had won over four-hundred dollars. It was like taking candy from a baby. The men started grumbling, and one became upset and said it would be a good idea for us to go home. Darrell didn't put up with any trouble. He told them all to calm down then he smiled at Ryan and me and said he would show us to the door.

Darrell walked outside with us and told Ryan he would like it if he'd stop by the shop the next evening. He said he needed to chat with him a bit. Ryan agreed, and we left. I told Ryan on the way home, as I had many times, how interesting it was to watch him play. Ryan liked it when I bragged on him, he always sat there smiling and taking it all in.

"It doesn't look as if you'll have any trouble making your insurance payment now," I said.

"As I've always told you Jake, I'm going to make it big someday," Ryan said, still grinning.

Ryan took his car to school each day. I rode with him instead of riding the bus. After school on Monday, we stopped at the barbershop to see Darrell. Business was slow that evening. Darrell didn't have any customers when we arrived. He was sitting in one of the barbers chairs smoking a cigar. We went in and sat down. Darrell didn't have any jokes to tell that day. He was all business.

"I watched you closely yesterday, and I'd already heard some things about you, Mr. Tyler." Darrell said, in a calm and pleasant voice. "Son, I've played poker nearly all of my life. I've played in too many high-stakes games to remember. You could say I've played with the best of them and not be wrong." Darrell took a puff from his cigar then continued. "You're damn good boy, a natural. If you discipline yourself, and don't get too cocky, you could win a lot of money with the talent you have."

Darrell took another puff from the cigar and looked at me, then back to Ryan.

"Who's your friend?" As if, he didn't know me. I could tell Darrell was joking now. "He's my bodyguard," Ryan said.

Darrell laughed loudly and went into a coughing spell.

"Damn cigars," he said.

When Darrell stopped coughing, he sat there for at least two minutes, looking at Ryan, and not saying a word. It was getting weird, and I was feeling uncomfortable. I know Ryan was too. After nearly another minute of silence, Ryan started rising up out of his chair to leave, and I was following his lead.

"Sit down a minute," Darrell said.

Ryan and I both sat back down.

Darrell began talking again but in a firmer voice.

"That game yesterday was something my friends and I do nearly every Sunday afternoon. Sometimes, like yesterday, we get a call asking if a stranger can join in, and normally we accommodate them. We don't play for a lot of money, so the boys get upset if someone raises the stakes. You did that yesterday quite charmingly, and they didn't even notice for a long time. That takes talent. Do you like money, Ryan?"

"Yes sir."

Darrell could tell Ryan and I couldn't make sense of what he was trying to say, so he started over.

"OK, I'll cut to the chase. Ryan, have you ever heard of a club called 'A Gentleman's Wager'?"

"No sir," Ryan replied.

Darrell's face became very stern he raised his eyebrows.

"Well, I'm going to tell you all about it son, for two reasons. One, because you have a special talent, and if anybody I've ever seen could win a lot of money at the game we call poker, you are it. Two, I'm going to tell you about it because if you and your pistol toting friend here don't get your asses off the streets and grow up, the both of you are going to end up dead at a young age."

I was shocked, and could tell Ryan was also.

"That's right. I know the two of you run around with guns on you, stealing, and playing in two-bit poker games. Sooner or later there will be trouble, and not the kind you can easily get out of."

It was as if Darrell knew everything Ryan and I had ever done, and he wanted us to stop before we got hurt. He was speaking from concern. He wasn't chastising us. It was strange, but somehow comforting. I wondered if that was what a caring parent acted like.

Darrell had our undivided attention. He leaned forward and looked directly into Ryan's eyes.

"Gambling is an addiction son, and you've been bitten, so it's highly likely you won't ever stop. That being said, I don't think there's a cure for you. Perhaps I can steer you somewhere that you won't end up on the wrong end of a gun. I can get you started with 'A Gentleman's Wager', so as least you'll be safe."

Darrell leaned back in his chair as he continued.

"'A Gentleman's Wager' is a group of individuals who play cards, just like you and me. They have strict rules though - its organized poker, and - No guns, no knives, no weapons of any kind. They run background checks on you periodically to ensure you are financially stable and to see if you've had a run-in with the law. There are different levels of membership going from one, the lowest, to ten, the highest. The levels of membership give you prestige and also determine the monetary limits of the games you play in."

Darrell got out of his chair and paced the floor as he continued talking.

"The club has been around for over two hundred years. The club got its start in Europe and now covers several countries throughout North America, Europe, and Asia. Let me sum it up for you Ryan. You can play cards and gamble with this group of people, and not have to worry about trouble of any sort. With 'A Gentleman's Wager,' there is no trouble, period. Before each game begins to play, the money to be wagered is collected and secured with a local administrator, either in cash or by electronic means. There is an initial background check, a five-hundred dollar initiation fee, and an annual due, also dependent on the level you are playing in. Oh, and in case you're wondering, the fees and dues are to provide security and bribe the police."

Darrell was smiling.

Ryan seemed interested until the end part about the fees and such.

"Sorry Mr. Havens, I don't want anybody to tell me when I can and can't play, or charge me to play."

"Don't worry about the fees, Ryan. I'll gladly pay the fees for you. As soon as you win a fortune, you can pay me back. In the club, you don't have to play any certain number of games. You play when you want to. There isn't a minimum or maximum number of games. It's good advice kid. You can bank on the words of this old man."

"I'm interested, but I'd like to hear more about this club before making a decision," Ryan said.

"Come see me again on Wednesday evening at 6:30 p.m. Oh, and your bodyguard can go to the games if you join, he just can't go inside and play. One more thing, he also can't bring his little friend hidden under his jacket."

When we got back to Ryan's house, we sat in the car for a long time talking about all Darrell had told us. I was bothered that Darrell knew about my gun, and that we had been stealing. I told Ryan I doubted that Darrell was just a good guesser. If he knew, who else did? Darrell was right too. We had to get away from crime. Sooner, or later poker games in back alleys or auto repair shops were going to be big trouble.

I thought Darrell had a good idea but at the same time, I was worried that Ryan might join that club. If he did, I likely wouldn't be running with him as much, and I didn't like the thought of that. What would I do when Ryan was always gone to some poker game? He wasn't just my best friend. He was my only friend.

I didn't go with Ryan when he went back to talk with Darrell. After the meeting, Ryan came back excited. He had taken Darrell up on his offer to pay if Ryan joined. It looked as if in a few weeks Ryan Tyler would be a full-fledged member, if he could pass their background check. Ryan was hoping he could make money in organized gambling games, but he was more excited about making some connections. He told me that was the ladder to success, who you knew.

After the initiation and background check, Ryan started going to weekend poker games at various places around Wyoming county, as well as Mercer and Boone counties. He was placed in the club at level one.

I didn't understand all their rules, and there seemed to be a lot of them. In level one, Ryan's bets were limited to a total of one-hundred dollars per hand. That way, a player with a bank full of money couldn't put the other players out of the game by wagering an enormous amount at one time.

The first game Ryan went to he had approval for five-hundred dollars. That was only the limit he could lose, he could win more than that. He came back with over a thousand dollars in winnings and was elated. He was starting to live his dream of getting rich without having to work.

I couldn't believe so much money was changing hands in a single game. Just a couple of years ago, we were cashing in two-cent soda pop bottles, now Ryan was walking around with hundreds of dollars in his pockets. He had just turned eighteen a few months back and was already richer than most of the coal miners living around us.

Darrell mentored Ryan for several months and introduced him to many of the important people who controlled the local gambling. I went with Ryan on a few of his weekend outings of 'poker galore' as I called it.

Normally, the games lasted only a couple of hours. It didn't bother me, not being allowed inside the area where the poker was being played. On most occasions, there were other people around not playing as well. I tried making friends, but people around the gambling joints were standoffish and hardly spoke to me.

The variety of people in the club was interesting. Lawyers, doctors, politicians, police officers. No wonder it was a safe place to gamble and not have trouble with players or the law; the law was there. Ryan played several times in the town of Mullens at a judge's house. I liked going there. It was a huge house, and he had a pool table. While Ryan played cards, I played pool with the judge's teenage son.

By the middle of May, just before Ryan graduated from high school, he'd been in 'A Gentleman's Wager' for only a few months, but had moved up to level three. This level allowed bets of up to one-thousand dollars per hand. Ryan was making money every weekend and had already bought a topnotch stereo system for the car as well as lots of new clothes and shoes.

Darrell missed Ryan's first game at level three but was going to meet him at the game to be played the following Saturday. Darrell, himself, had never moved past level five, and that was after many years with the club.

I was planning to ride along with Ryan but Momma was upset with me. I was grounded. I'd cleaned and polished Crump's dress shoes as I was told to do, but I'd forgotten and left them on the back porch. A dog came by sometime during the night and chewed the left one nearly in two, and the right one was missing. I was grounded for two weeks, and she took a belt to me. I was seventeen but still cried like a baby.

I had to stand in front of Crump while she whipped me. Additionally, I had to give him fifty dollars of my hard-earned money for a new pair of shoes. I also had to apologize to him. Having to give my money to Crump was hard. Getting a whipping by my momma, being almost a fully-grown man was harder. Momma showed no love or compassion toward me. I kept fooling myself, thinking that deep down she cares at least a little bit. The fact that she didn't care hurt worse than the beatings.

For the first time since Ryan began playing cards with 'A Gentleman's Wager', he lost. He only lost thirty-five dollars, which by now wasn't much to Ryan. Losing is what bothered him. He said it was because I wasn't there. He said I was his lucky rabbit's foot. Ryan had played on other occasions without me present, and won money, so that wasn't true. I told him what had happened with the shoes. It made Ryan mad. I told him not to be, that was just the way life was at my house. I'd never told anyone about the spankings and belt whippings before.

After telling Ryan I felt ashamed for doing so, it was a family matter. Even though he was my best friend, and we didn't hide things from each other, it was something private, and I shouldn't have told.

I don't know if losing on Saturday upset Ryan, or if it was what I'd told him about Momma, but on Sunday, he didn't go to the poker game he had scheduled. It was the first time since he had joined the club that he didn't play on both days of the weekend.

On that Sunday afternoon, I was sitting on the back porch steps when Ryan came by to visit, carrying the Sunday newspaper with him. Ryan's mom and dad got the newspaper delivered to their house, and Ryan normally read it cover to cover. I wasn't interested in reading. Besides, we didn't get the paper.

"You need to read this," Ryan said.

The front page of the newspaper showed a picture of Burning Rock. The article beneath the picture was about the scientists from England that Ryan had spoken to during the time he was, suspended from school. It explained the writings, called 'petroglyph writings', and said they weren't written by Indians. It was an old Irish language called 'Fogom'. It had been written on the rocks, many hundreds of years before Columbus discovered America. They were able to decipher the meaning of the symbols written on the wall.

It read, "*The earth opened her mouth and we came forth to a new world. The sun rises again in the east and sets in the west, and we rejoice in her warmth. This month of Nina, in the year of our Lord Jesus 305 Anno Domini.*"

"This means what I'd heard about the Vikings coming to America before Columbus must be true," I said. "And, there were other Europeans here as well! Holy Cow!"

"I bet they don't change the history books at school," Ryan said.

"Why not?"

"It's all about money. They have a lot of money tied up in the Columbus theory."

We talked about the newspaper article and hoped it didn't get a lot of attention and ruin the beech grove, by thousands of visitors going there. When the scientists arrived, some time back, it never made the newspaper, now the entire state knew about it.

Chapter 12

It was early February the following year, my last semester of my senior year in high school. Over the last few days, there had been snow flurries but no amount of snow accumulation. The nights had only been slightly below freezing so for February in West Virginia it wasn't bad weather.

Ryan was in his first year of college and hadn't been home since Christmas break. He had told me how well he was doing. He spoke about some of the poker games he'd been in with 'The Club', as he now called it. He'd also met a rich family in the area and was getting to know the people. He was going to take a part-time job with them, and said it would help move his career forward.

I was lost not having Ryan around to do things with me. I'd been spending a lot more time in the mountains trying to learn some trapping skills, but with little luck.

For the last two weeks, I'd been talking to a nice girl at school, Valerie Toler. She was in the lunchroom one day, and I was sitting across the table admiring her beauty when she looked up and caught me watching her. It embarrassed me and she sensed my backward shyness.

She approached me in the hall the next day and started talking to me. Her voice was pleasant. I could have stood there for hours just listening to her talk. It was awkward talking to her at first. I wasn't used to being around a girl who wanted to talk to me, but it didn't take long for my anxiety to fade away.

We began talking in the hall before school each morning before classes, during lunch, and while waiting for the buses after school. She was a year younger. She was sixteen, and her strict parents didn't let her date. It wouldn't have mattered anyway since I didn't have a car.

On Friday, Valerie told me she had talked to her mom and dad the night before and asked if it would be okay for me to come to her house, and they agreed. Then she asked if I'd like to come Saturday evening to watch television with her. "Sure," I said.

Valerie lived in Kopperston, a small mining community north of Oceana. It has two coal camps, the upper and lower camp, stretching out a couple of miles along a fast-moving creek. She lived in the lower camp, which was a good nine-mile hike from Lynco Hollow. I didn't take my gun, knowing I couldn't keep my jacket on in Valerie's house.

On that winter day, it was dark by five o'clock, and once the sun had gone down it got cold quickly. When I got to Valerie's, it was a little past six o'clock. I was glad to finally arrive and get inside a warm house. I'd hitched a ride for more than half the way there, but had to walk the remainder of the way.

Her parents checked me out immediately, asking plenty of questions. I was expecting some questions, but still felt very uncomfortable. They liked it that I had manners and said my parents must have taught me well. It made me wonder where I got good manners from, it certainly wasn't from Momma or Crump.

Valerie was an only child, and her parents were very protective. Although at the time, I wished they weren't so protective. I still admired that they were though. It was a nice visit. We sat in the living room with the television on, but didn't pay much attention to what was showing. We were more interested in talking and looking at each other.

I left Valerie's house just after nine that evening. I could tell her parents were getting a little restless with me being there for so long. She walked out on the front porch with me, and as I was saying goodnight, she kissed me. I'd never been kissed before. She was pressed against me, and I could feel the warmth of her body, smell her perfume, and she used her tongue to touch mine, sending a wild sensation through my entire body.

She said goodnight, then hurried back inside. I stood there for a few seconds and savored the moment. Not only had I never been kissed before, my first one was a French kiss. My heart was light and although the night air had already begun to cool my skin, I felt warm and fuzzy inside. I was thinking how I could approach Valerie on Monday to ask if she would go steady with me. It was going to be perfect, and nothing was going to mess it up.

There wasn't a lot of traffic on the highway, so I expected to do a lot of walking. There wasn't much of a chance of hitching a ride that time of night, especially since a light snow was starting to fall. I was feeling good though after such a pleasant evening and didn't care about the weather. I think I was falling in love. Could that even be possible? Did I know what love was?

A mile south of Valerie's house, I was walking by the Little League Baseball field. I saw a car parked there. It seemed out of place. It was an older model Chrysler Imperial, and it was a convertible. I noticed it sitting there when I was on my way to Valerie's house. I had made a mental note to check it out on the way home.

The only convertible I'd ever seen in our town was a VW Beetle. The Imperial had Ohio tags so I suspected it must be someone visiting, or perhaps passing through and the car had broken down. The only light in that area was from a street light fifty yards away. Even in the dim light, I could tell the car had nice chrome hubcaps.

Earlier in the summer, Ryan and I had stolen two hubcaps from a 69 Cadillac and sold them to Jacky Shubert, a junk dealer, in Bear Branch. Everyone knew Jacky. He was a very likeable man. He had a large garage with a couple of acres of junk cars in the back surrounded by a high fence and razor wire.

Everyone knew Jacky would buy anything if he thought he could sell it for a profit. He didn't care if it was stolen or not, he never asked questions. He'd given us fifteen dollars for the two hubcaps, which was a good profit for less than five minutes work.

The Imperial had chrome spoke hubcaps, which would net a good sum of money. I carried a short-handled regular tip screwdriver in my jacket pocket at all times, just for occasions such as that. I looked around at the houses close by and then looked up and down the road to make sure no cars were coming. I dropped down low and went around the car popping the hubcaps off one by one. In less than a minute, I had all four of them stacked together and was on my way.

There was a dirt road about two-hundred yards further down, where a bridge crossed the creek, leading to a natural gas pumping station. My plan was to cross the bridge, which was about thirty feet or so from bank to bank, and find a place to hide the hubcaps. I'd devise a way to get back later to pick them up.

I was nearing the bridge when I caught a glimpse of light from behind me. I turned back, and two cars were approaching from up the highway. I stepped over the guardrail then scooted down the embankment toward the creek and hunkered down, waiting for them to pass.

Just as both cars got to my location, they stopped suddenly. Simultaneously, a man got out of the passenger side of each car. In the next instant, spotlights were shining in my face. I couldn't see anything except the lights in my face, and the blue lights now flashing atop the cars.

It was the cops. I was caught red handed!

"Hands above your head, punk, and don't even think about running!" One of them yelled out.

At that moment, all the strength I had in me left. I couldn't have run if I'd wanted. Besides, the only place to go would have been the icy, rapid moving creek, just a few feet below. I held both hands high in the air. I could tell from the reflection that one of the spotlights was shining on the four neatly stacked hubcaps lying at my feet.

"Come up out of there!" One of the officers yelled.

I blurted out that I needed my hands to climb back up the embankment, and don't ask why, but for some reason I said something to the effect of "I don't have a gun." I don't recall climbing up the embankment or stepping over the guardrail. My next memory was while being bent forward over the hood of a police car while being handcuffed.

The hood of the car was hot from the idling engine. Someone was pressing my face hard against the metal, and my cheek was absorbing the heat. My nose felt runny, like when you have a cold, but the taste in my mouth indicated it was blood.

I thought about how it is in movies, cops being nice and taking you downtown for questioning, but that wasn't what I was experiencing. I had a feeling things were going to get worse, and that the night had only begun. One of the cruisers belonged to the State Police, the other to the County Sheriff's department.

They put me in the back seat of the county car. I sat there while the four officers stood outside talking. I couldn't make out what was being said. The police radio in the county cruiser was blaring with a female talking.

She had a high-pitched voice with a thick country accent. The distortion from the speaker was horrible and hurt my ears. I didn't know how anyone could ever understand what she was saying. All I could decipher was an occasional, "Ten-fer, I copy."

After a few minutes, I heard doors shut. The blue lights of the State Trooper cruiser went off next. The car moved away, speeding down the highway. The two county deputies climbed into the car and sat down. I noticed they didn't buckle up.

The driver was a big fat cop. He breathed heavily, and even from the back seat, I could smell his cheap cologne. The smell filled the air and made me nauseated.

The other deputy was tall and skinny. I noticed that he had a shaved head, and I could see a large tattoo on the left side of his neck. I thought again of television shows, where there is always a fat cop and a skinny cop assigned together. It must be some sort of code they followed. Hollywood could have used these two as their models.

The deputies acted as if I wasn't there. They were involved in a conversation and never addressed me sitting in their backseat. Finally, the big cop put the car in gear and we started down the road.

We had only gone a short distance when they pulled into a gas station. The car seemed to drift off the road and stopped next to the gas pumps. The gas station wasn't open, but the lights on the awning overhead were on providing good light in the car. The handcuffs were hurting my wrist, but I didn't think it would be a good idea to say anything.

The fat cop turned the radio down to where it was barely audible. I was grateful that I didn't have to continue listening to that chatter. Next, he turned the car off. My heart sank, I knew something was about to happen.

Both cops were looking straight ahead out the windshield, still acting as if they had forgotten I was there. The skinny cop opened a can of smokeless tobacco. I couldn't see it, but I could smell the aroma of wintergreen when he removed the lid. His raised his hand to his mouth, making the motion of putting the tobacco inside his lower lip. He snapped the lid back on then spit out the partially rolled down window.

Still looking straight out the windshield he began to speak. "We ran your ID Roberts. Ya know what we got ya fer?"

The tobacco in his lip caused his speech to sound muffled. Still, I clearly understood what he had said. I didn't speak. Although he had asked a question, it wasn't presented as a question. Instead, it was more of a statement.

"Those hubcaps are the least of yer worries son. What'd ya do with that there dozer ya went and stole yesterday up in Crany?" He asked.

This time he was asking a question. I was greatly alarmed about what he had said, and reacted quickly, like a kid who'd been caught with his hand in the cookie jar.

"What on earth are you talking about?" I yelled out.

The words had just left my mouth when the fat cop flung open his door and got out of the car. He opened the back door, reached in, and hit me across the upper left arm with his nightstick. Severe pain instantly radiated up my arm and into my left shoulder. I moaned loudly, almost screaming. He had a stern look as he pointed the stick at me.

"Don't play no games or give us any sass, just answer the damn question, and your answer best be the right one!"

He was breathing hard and his horrid breath was hitting me directly in the face. He continued looking at me with a determined face. He moved forward and was half-way into the car. I thought he was going to climb right on top of me. The skinny cop turned his head to the left and looked around at me from the side of the headrest.

"The cotton pickin Caterpillar D9L bulldozer boy, the big yeller one you's a riding on yesterday. What the HELL did ya do wit it?"

I was sitting straight in the seat with my head turned sideways and pulled back a bit so I could see both men in my vision. I was wincing in pain as my arm was feeling like it was broken.

"Mister, I'm telling you the truth, I don't even know where Crany is, and I surely don't know anything about a bulldozer," I said with a muttered voice.

The big cop swung his club and hit my arm again, this time a little below where the first blow had landed. I screamed that time. The pain was worse than from the first blow. He drew back his arm again, so I leaned toward the passenger side of the car attempting to get farther away from the blow I was about to receive. I heard a cracking sound as the stick hit my head. A sharp pain penetrated from the impact point throughout my entire skull then I blacked out.

When I regained consciousness, it took a few seconds before my eyes adjusted. My arm was throbbing something awful, and I could tell there was some swelling on my head behind the left ear. I was lying in the seat, handcuffs holding my arms behind me, and my head resting against the passenger-side door.

I raised my head slightly, enough to see through the window. Lights were shining and illuminating a large building up above the road. I recognized the structure. I was looking at the county courthouse.

I could feel the car climb the steep hill then turn right before we leveled off in a parking lot behind the courthouse. The car stopped. Again, it was the fat cop, who got out and opened the back door. He reached in with both hands, placing one on my leg and the other on the back of my neck. He jerked me out of the car in one motion.

"Come on cock sucka, you're home now," he said, grunting heavily.

The sudden movement caused my arm to start throbbing. Severe pain was radiating through my head. The cold night air penetrated my skin and for the first time since hiding behind the guardrail, I realized I wasn't wearing my jacket anymore. The fresh air entered my nostrils and rejuvenated me somewhat.

As my feet hit the ground and I stood erect, not knowing if my legs were going to support me. I wobbled for a second and fell back against the car then tried to regain my balance. I had no energy. If the cop had intended to lead me to a cliff and throw me off, I couldn't have resisted. He took his right hand and grabbed the back of my shirt, leading me toward the building.

Still holding my shirt, lifting me partly off the ground as we walked, he led me to a small room that smelled heavily of a pine based cleaner. The room was small and contained only a table and two chairs. The fat cop slung me face forward over the edge of the table and removed the handcuffs.

"Sit," he said then walked out of the room.

I moved my arms back and forth in every direction, trying to get them moving again. It hurt moving my left arm, but I knew that unless it was broken, I needed to get some circulation going, so I tolerated the self-inflicted pain. I sat down, placed my head against my right arm on top of the table, and let my left arm dangle by my side.

A female deputy came into the room wearing the same style uniform as the two cops that brought me in were wearing. She looked to be in her 40's, and the color of her hair was bright orange. Although not obese, she had very large hips, causing her stride to appear out of kilter. I elevated my head enough to watch her movement as she sat down across from me.

"What the hell happened to you?" She said, after taking a long look at me.

I hadn't noticed, until now, that the skinny cop was standing at the door, and he answered the woman, drawing each word out slowly.

"We _ caught _ him _ stealing _ hubcaps _ from _ a _ car."

I could tell his voice irritated the female cop, as it did me.

"He _ tried _ to _ git _ away _ and _ he _ stumbled _ over _ a _ guardrail, and _ slide _ down _ an _ embankment _ into _ the _ creek."

The fat cop walked back into the room and had a big smirk on his face.

"Yeah, the damn fool, wonder he hadn't broken his neck!" He added.

They chuckled then turned and left. I didn't see them again. The female deputy left also. She returned in a few minutes with a hot wet cloth and wiped my face, head, and neck. She left again and came back with a cold can of Pepsi, popping the top as she entered the doorway and approached the table. She sat the soda pop on the table.

"I thought you could use this," she said, then left the room again.

I started to use my left arm to pick up the drink. When I started to move my arm, the pain was too bad, so I used my right hand. I gulped down three-fourths of the can in one swallow. The Pepsi was cold and stung my throat going down. I could feel it enter my empty stomach. At that moment, I thought it was the best tasting drink I'd ever had.

I again started moving my left arm a bit in a small circular fashion. It was painful but bearable. I felt certain nothing was broken, but I knew it was going to be a long-time healing. I gently touched the back of my head where the nightstick had struck. A knot had risen, and it felt to be the size of a golf ball. I could feel a small cut near the bottom of the knot, and it burned when I touched that area.

My senses started kicking back in and my concern wasn't so much about my wounds as it was about what they were going to do with me. They apparently thought I had stolen a bulldozer, and if they pinned that on me, I was doomed and would be in prison most of my life. I just knew those cops had made up a report and would claim I had confessed to stealing the dozer.

Then there was Momma finding out. How would she react? Even if I didn't go to prison, I knew I'd be grounded for the rest of my life. Then I thought about Valerie. She'd never speak to me again, and even if she did, her parents would find out about this and wouldn't allow us to date. What a mess I'd made!

The door opened again. An older officer, perhaps in his mid-fifties came in carrying a large white telephone with a speaker attachment. He plugged it into a phone jack on the wall beside the table. I concluded it was so people outside the room could listen to what we were saying, also to make a recording. He had a manila folder under his arm with a bunch of papers stuffed inside, many of which were sticking out.

The officer didn't tell me his name. He didn't have on a nametag, just like the two cops that brought me in, and the female cop. I was thinking it must be police protocol to keep their identity secret, no one wanted me to know their name.

It was easy to detect he really didn't care much about what he was doing, just get the eight hours in and go home was the attitude I picked up on. He was wearing a white long-sleeve shirt. As he sat down, his sleeves rose a bit, and I could see his watch. It was almost three in the morning. He opened the folder and peered over the top of his glasses, making eye contact with me for the first time.

"Alright, let's get this over with," he said.

"Get what over with?" I replied.

"Is your telephone number 555-9003?"

"Yes sir," I said.

He punched a button on the side of the phone, placing it in speaker mode. I could hear the dial tone then he began making the call.

"I want you to hear every word of this; and by the way, this is being recorded," he said, still looking over his glasses.

The phone at our house began ringing. It rang seven or eight times, but no one answered. Our home telephone was on a party line, so I was surprised that one of the neighbors didn't answer. Finally, a sleepy gruff voice answered the telephone.

"Who the hell is it?"

It was Crump.

"This is Officer Matson of the Southern Region Joint Task Force." He announced with a strong voice.

He went on for nearly five minutes telling Crump about the hubcaps and how crime in our area had been on the rise. He said the officers had seen me early in the evening, and that I was a suspect in other criminal activities as well. He went on to say the police had set up a stakeout. He said that I'd been apprehended shortly after a struggle with four police officers.

He mentioned nothing about the missing bulldozer, which I thought was odd. I later found out some boys out in the mountains riding dirt bikes had stolen the bulldozer. It had been parked at a surface mine site. The boys had been able to get the bulldozer started then went joy riding on it. Not knowing much about the controls, they drove it into a large tailings pond where it sank out of sight.

About two minutes into the call, I could hear Momma in the background. Crump was feeding her the news as officer Matson blurted it all out. Crump sounded like a mocking bird, repeating every sentence, but the jerk also added a lot of emphasis and drama.

I wasn't prepared for Matson's next words.

"We've spoken to the owner of the car, and he doesn't want to press charges, so you can come and pick up your son."

I was ecstatic. They were going to set me free. Crump repeated what he had said to Momma, and I could hear the two of them mumbling in the background.

"Officer," it was Momma's voice now on the telephone.

"What if I don't come and pick him up, then what?"

"Ah hmm, well Mrs. Crump, if you don't pick him up, then we will hold him for forty-eight hours. After that, the judge will likely declare him a threat to the community, since he won't be under control of a legal guardian. He'll have no choice but to send your son to the juvenile detention center in Pruntytown. It will be for a minimum of thirty days and up to a maximum of six months. It all depends on the judge."

Oh Lord, I thought. Pruntytown!

"Leave his skinny little ass in jail," Momma responded then hung up the phone.

I wasn't crying audibly, but tears were streaming down my face. Officer Matson didn't react to any of that. He unplugged the phone, wrapped the cord around it, stuffed the folder back up under his arm, and left the room.

Shortly afterward, another officer came in and handcuffed me, led me out of the room, and down a series of hallways. We stopped in front of a large room that had bars across the entire front. A door, also made of bars stood situated in the middle of the room. He opened the door, took off the cuffs, pushed me into the cell, and closed the door behind me. He never spoke a word to me during the entire ordeal.

I was in a holding tank. There were ten to twelve others in there as well, lying along the walls' sleeping. There weren't any pads or pillows, just an empty room with nothing to rest on. Everyone was using their arm for a pillow or just lying flat on their back, stretched out on the concrete floor.

An open toilet and sink were in the far-right corner, but I didn't see any hand towels or toilet tissue. My body was aching and I was exhausted, but it was my heart hurting the most. I lay down in an open area along the wall and was thinking about how Momma had abandoned me just for attempting to steal some hubcaps. After a little while, I fell asleep.

It was mid-afternoon the next day. I was still in the holding cell. Except for two boys, all the other men and boys in the cell had been released. No additional prisoners were brought in. The two remaining didn't speak to me so I kept silent, thinking that was the best thing to do.

We hadn't received any food or water in the holding tank, and I was starving. I was at the sink splashing cold water on the back of my head, hoping to ease the throbbing. I heard someone enter the cell area. I looked up and saw a police officer with a ring of keys turning the lock to the cell door.

"Roberts, let's go," he said.

I was elated and thankful. She had reconsidered. Momma was here to pick me up. I wasn't looking forward to the lecture and likely was going to get a good beating. Still, I'd be free, and not heading to Pruntytown.

The officer handed me my jacket and wallet, then lead me through the maze of hallways. I put the jacket on as we walked and quickly looked inside the wallet. My driver license was there but the forty dollars that had been inside was missing. I placed the wallet in my back pocket and kept moving. He led me to a waiting area located in the front of the building. He unlocked a glass door then held it back while motioning me to step through.

"You're free to go," he said.

Momma wasn't there as I had been expecting. Instead, it was Ryan! He had a smile on his face as he walked up and gave me a hug.

"I bet you're hungry," he said.

We shot out the front door and climbed into his car. As we took off out of the parking lot, Ryan said he would take me to the 'King of Rock' Drive-In. It was located at the end of Main Street in Pineville, just a couple of blocks down from the courthouse. We pulled in and a young girl quickly showed up at the window with a pencil and notepad. Ryan ordered for the two of us.

"Two BBQ's with slaw, two orders of cheese fries, and two chocolate shakes," he said.

"They took all my money. I can't pay for that," I said to Ryan.

"Don't worry about it Jake, I've got everything covered."

We sat there talking about what had taken place. I asked Ryan how he found me and how he even knew I was in jail. He explained that word travels fast in a small community and that Mrs. Conley, who was on our party line, had been eavesdropping on the phone last night. She in turn called Ryan's mom, who in turn called him at the university.

"I couldn't let you rot in jail or be sent off to Pruntytown," he said.

The food arrived. I was starving and Ryan laughed as he watched me eat. He said it appeared that I inhaled the BBQ.

"Well, what now?" Ryan asked, once we were through with our milkshakes.

I told him I needed to call Momma. He dug in his pocket and pulled out a quarter, handed it to me, and pointed to a telephone booth across the street. Ryan followed me over to the phone, wanting to lend me moral support. I dropped the quarter in, got a dial tone, and called home. It rang twice then Bernice answered.

"Bernice, this is Jake."

She didn't ask me how I was, all she said was "hold on."

Momma got on the phone. Her voice was rough and loud.

"I'm all ears," she screamed out.

"Momma, I'm sorry," I said.

"Sorry ain't good enough you bastard! You've embarrassed me and disgraced our fine family. I hope they keep you in jail until you rot!"

"Momma, I'm out now, and I want to come home."

"Well I don't know how in hell you got out, but you ain't got a home mister. You can come by and pick up your clothes if you want, I'll have them waiting for you." Then she slammed the telephone receiver down.

She had been loud enough that Ryan had heard both sides of the conversation.

"I'm sorry Jake, I really am."

"What am I supposed to do now, Ryan?"

108

Tears were showing up again even though I was trying to hold them back.

"You and I have been friends for a long-time Jake, and we've been through hell and high water. It's always been us taking care of each other with no help from anybody, and now ain't any different," Ryan stated. "You can come live with me. We'll survive just like we always have, and heck man, it'll be better than ever."

I asked Ryan if he would take me to Lynco, so I could get my things. I wasn't worried about the clothes I didn't have many. I was however, concern about the 44 magnum stashed away in the shed. If the wrong person, like Crump or Momma, found it and contacted the police, I'd be in a worse mess. I'm sure if they ran the serial number on the gun I'd be back in jail again, and who knows what I'd be charged with. If that happened, I don't think Ryan or anyone else would be able to bail me out of jail.

We headed west toward Oceana. When we reached Lynco, Ryan turned up the hollow toward home. I had a lump in my throat as big as the one on the back of my head. As we pulled in front of the house, I saw clothing strewn about the front yard. The temperature had dropped and sleet was falling, covering the clothes in a thin layer of ice.

Ryan and I got out of the car. He opened the trunk as I went through the gate and began picking up my belongings. Tears were streaming down my face again. I couldn't bear to raise my head to see if anyone was watching from our house, or the neighbors.

Ryan helped me gather my clothes and place them in the trunk of the Mustang. He closed the trunk and told me he was going on over to his moms to visit, and I needed to come along. I said I'd be right there, but first I needed to go out to the shed and get a few more things. He got in the car, and started it. Once he put the car in reverse, he backed up to his mom and dad's house.

I walked back into the yard and started around the side of the house toward the shed. Momma raised the dining-room window, just as I was passing by.

"You got your stinking clothes, now get the hell off this property, and don't let me ever see your ugly, lying, stealing face again!" She screamed out.

I looked up at her, tears now streaming down both sides of my face.

"Ok Momma....I love you."

She slammed the window down. Immediately she was gone from sight. I ran to the shed. I didn't try to gather up anything but the gun, which was wrapped in an old towel, the holster, and an old cigar box with my money. I ran back out the door, went to Ryan's car, got in the passenger side, and closed the door.

I shoved the gun underneath the seat then just sat there. I didn't want to go inside Ryan's house. I needed to just sit there and cry. It wasn't long before the windows were fogged over, and I couldn't see outside.

I was numb from the inside out and was playing the last twenty-four hours continuously in my head. What about school, I was a senior and wanted to graduate. I wanted to see Valerie one more time. I wanted to stay here and live at home. Even though home life wasn't good, it was familiar. It scared me to think about the future, or if I even had one.

Ryan opened the driver's door and got in. He started the car and let it run for a few minutes until the defroster cleared the windshield. He'd shown me today what it meant to have a best friend, a genuine friend who cared and would be there for me in a time of need.

He put the car in gear and we drove away toward Roanoke. I was leaving my home, familiar surroundings, everything I had ever known. It was the lowest point of my life.

Burning Rock

Act Two

Chapter 13

When we got to Roanoke, Ryan drove me around campus. The college wasn't as big as I had imagined it to be. There were no dormitories so Ryan had an apartment on the west side of town about two miles off campus.

The apartment consisted of half of the third floor of an old four-story house. It was situated on a hillside. You had to climb forty steps even before getting to the porch on the main level, then all of the steps going on up to the third floor. It didn't matter to me, if it had been a dungeon. I would have swam across a moat to get to there, just to have a place to stay until I could figure things out.

The apartment had two bedrooms but only one bed. Before leaving Lynco, Ryan had put a large box in the back seat. It contained an air mattress and a few other odds, and ends. I put the air mattress in the spare room to sleep on, at least temporarily. We'd also stopped at a store on the way to his place and bought a toothbrush, deodorant, and other items I'd need to get me started.

My mind kept going back to all that had happened. My world as I knew it had fallen apart in a short time span. I had made a big mistake trying to steal those hubcaps. I had so many regrets and wished I could have gone back and done things differently. Thinking about all that made me sad.

I was scared of stepping out into this unfamiliar place. Although I was with Ryan, and I knew we were going to have a good time together, I had an empty feeling inside.

My arm and head hurt, but those were superficial wounds. My heart is what hurt the most. I kept trying to pull myself together. I needed to think positive. I had a chance now to start fresh, have the freedom to come and go without somebody beating me with a switch or belt. I could be my own man and make my own way. I knew if I applied myself, this could turn out to be a good thing. I could find a job, and maybe I could even save up enough money to buy a car.

Ryan and I talked about how to get things situated for me, and clear up the mess I had made. I had enough credits to graduate high school without attending the remainder of the spring semester. Ryan was going to let me take his car back to the high school and get all the paper work completed.

Over the next week, I went to nearly every place of business I could find, trying to find a decent job. The answer was always the same. I didn't have a high school diploma so no one would hire me. No one seemed to care when I explained I was a good worker and could keep my nose clean. They all turned me away, not willing to giving me a chance. After being turned down so many times, I was getting angry and bitter. I asked one man what it would change by me having a stupid diploma in my hand!

Ryan kept telling me I only needed a part-time job. He said all I needed was to have a job as a cover. He had something planned for us, and money wasn't going to be a problem. I figured he wanted to drag me into the poker scene, but he knew I couldn't win at that game.

Ryan was the hustler, and a good one. For as long as I'd known him, he'd said that he wasn't going to work for a living. His plan was to let everybody else work and provide for him. I always thought Ryan could do just as he had planned, but where did I fit into that? I couldn't depend on him all my life.

On Saturday, I was going to go with Ryan to a card game in Lynchburg at a fancy estate. Everyone was required to wear a suit, and I didn't have one. Ryan took me to a store and had me fitted for a suit. It was dark blue with light blue pin stripes. The woman working at the store said it made me look older and distinguished.

"Imagine that," I said.

The suit after taxes cost a hundred and eighty dollars. Ryan handed the woman two crisp new one-hundred dollar bills and told her to keep the change. When we got to the car, I told Ryan I didn't know what to say, and I didn't know when I could pay him back. He said I wasn't supposed to pay him back. It was a gift for going to the game with him that evening.

I knew Ryan had moved up in 'The Club' but he was doing better than I had imagined apparently. Ryan wasn't one to boast about how much money he had though. He was quick to flaunt himself, as well as his money in a card game, but never out in public places, and he knew he didn't need to impress me.

When we got to the house, there was an entrance gate and a guard shack. The attendant must have known Ryan. He looked in the car and greeted Ryan as Mr. Tyler before waving us through. I was impressed. Ryan had been making some connections here, and had done so in a short time span.

The house was huge. It had big columns in the front, and there was a circular driveway with a water fountain in the middle of the front lawn. The grounds looked as if they had been manicured. I was way out of my element, but Ryan seemed to fit right in, and acted as if he owned the place.

I knew the owners had to be super rich. They had people who parked the cars, people who took your coat, people carrying silver platters with food, and drinks. It was unlike anything I'd ever seen before. As we entered the house, I saw it was full of people, I estimated a hundred or more.

Ryan knew twenty or more of the people there. I thought again about how odd that was. He'd only lived in this area a few months but already knew many of the people at the party. It had to be acquaintances from the gambling club.

After a few introductions, Ryan told me to just mingle, see if I could get to know a few people on my own. He headed off to one of the rooms upstairs where a poker game was going on.

After Ryan left, I walked around the house looking at all the fine furniture. I could tell the paintings on the wall were originals. I was fascinated with the artwork. I envied someone who possessed the talent to create such beauty. I walked along all the walls looking at the art.

It wasn't long before an older woman came up to me and started talking. I surmised she was in her fifties, yet still quite attractive. She had a great figure. Her hair was nicely styled, and her green eyes would grab the attention of any man. She had a glass of wine in her hand, and I could tell it wasn't her first one for the evening. She was tipsy and was giggly like a teenage girl.

"I don't think I know you young man," she said.

"I've never been here before," I replied.

"I see. Did you come alone or with a friend?"

"I came with Ryan Tyler."

"Oh yes, Ryan Tyler. Richard is quite fond of him, says he has potential."

I didn't know who Richard was, but I was guessing that this was Richard's house, and she was his wife. She kept staring at me for what seemed like an hour, when, in fact, it was mere seconds. I couldn't help but stare back into those beautiful eyes. I tried to collect myself, and felt embarrassed. She sensed me being uncomfortable. She also sensed my vulnerability, and decided to play with that.

She came closer, still holding her wine glass, and laid her free hand on my shoulder. She detected me tensing up. I could tell she liked that, and it made her feel like she had power over me. She put her lips up to my ear. I thought she was going to whisper something to me. Instead, I felt her wet tongue inside my ear making a circular motion. She gently bit my ear lobe, and it sent chills down my spine. Even my toes tingled.

I was frozen in place. I couldn't decide if I needed walk off, or just stand there until she was finished. She moved around in front of me and rubbed her breast against my chest.

"The house is full right now, but I want to see you later tonight," she said.

I felt ridiculous, and my face was blood red. I didn't know if others were watching. I couldn't think of what to say or how to say it.

"Ma'am, I'm with Ryan and I don't have a car, so I can't stay later," I said in a voice that must have sounded like a small child speaking.

She laughed and kissed me on the cheek and then took a step back.

"Oh my God, you're a virgin," she said.

Now my face felt very red, and my palms felt sweaty. She laughed lightly, and grinned. "Baby, don't you worry. It may not be tonight, but soon I'll turn you from a boy into a man." She then turned and walked off.

After that, I walked out to the back of the house where there was a heated swimming pool. I was hoping to avoid another encounter with the woman. I sat in a lounge chair for a long time watching a group of young kids swimming. I didn't go back inside the house until Ryan came looking for me some time later.

On the way home I told Ryan what had happened. He thought it was funny and asked why I didn't take her into a bathroom somewhere and screw her.

"Gee whiz Ryan. You took me to a place I didn't fit in. It was full of people I didn't know, and you say I should have screwed her in a bathroom?"

"Calm down," Ryan said, as he laughed. "What did she look like anyway?"

I told him. He laughed again while slapping his knee.

"That's Richard Newton's wife," Ryan said.

"She mentioned Richard," I replied. "She said he was fond of you, and that you had potential."

"Well, I'll be damned," Ryan, remarked.

"She and Richard own that place don't they?" I asked.

"Yes they do, and right now the two of us are working for them."

"What do you mean?"

"You'll see soon enough, just trust me."

Ryan drove a few miles down the road, until we were on the riverfront. He pulled up to a row of shanties and stopped.

"Get into the driver's seat, I'll be right back," he said.

"Wait a minute Ryan, what are you doing?"

He had already shut the door and was moving behind the car, then disappeared into one of the shacks. I moved into the driver's seat.

Ryan was gone less than five minutes then he reappeared. He opened the passenger side door and got in, holding a one foot by one foot cubed cardboard box. There was a label on the top written in an oriental language.

"What's that?"

"Just drive, I'll give you directions," he said.

I was a bit perturbed. I placed the car in drive and pulled onto the highway.

"Listen Ryan, I don't know what it is you're getting us into, but listen to me for a few seconds. I am forever grateful for all you've done for me, but I am not going to go to jail over some drugs. Drugs or whatever else is in that dang box. I want to go to college and graduate and get a decent job, and raise a family."

"Stop the car right now," Ryan said.

I did. I stopped the car in the middle of the street. Ryan was perplexed, thinking I was going to pull off the road before stopping. He held up both his hands, in a gesture to make me stop talking and listen to him.

"Listen to me, Jake!" Ryan was talking fast and with a lot of emotion. "I've made some great contacts for us, and those contacts have powerful political connections. With that being said, you need to trust me. We WON'T go to jail. I don't know what's in the box, and I don't care what's in the box. We are going to get rid of it in a few more miles….and dang it we'll NEVER know what's in the box. The thing is Jake, its safe. Don't ask me how I know it's safe, but believe me; it is safe!"

A string of cars had now pulled in behind us and several drivers were blowing their horns.

"Safe or not, we don't need all this attention, so drive!" Ryan said.

I put the car back into gear and we went on. It got deathly quiet in the car other than Ryan's occasional directions he gave me until we arrived at a Chinese restaurant. I stopped the car then looked over at Ryan.

"You're right, man. I have to trust you. I'm sorry for getting upset, I just don't like surprises like this."

"Wait here," he said. Ryan got out of the car with the box and went into the restaurant.

A few minutes later, he was back at the car. He asked if he could drive home, so I slid across the seat. He got into the driver's seat, and we took off down the road. I was silent, not knowing what to expect next. Ryan put his hand inside his suit jacket pocket. He then pulled out a white envelope and handed it to me.

"This is your cut for that delivery we just made," he said.

Ryan looked straight ahead at the road as I opened the envelope. My eyes got big, and my head jerked back slightly as I looked inside and saw a stack of one-hundred-dollar bills. I took them out and counted. It was a thousand dollars.

I sat there for a moment looking at the money, feeling it, letting it shuffle through my fingers. I'd never seen that much money at one time.

"I got the same amount you did," Ryan said.

Ryan saw my expression of disbelief. He tried again to assure me it wasn't drugs, but I could tell he didn't have a clue if it was or not.

"What do you really think was in the package?" I asked.

"It could have been Cuban cigars, or it could have been government secrets; I don't know, but it was a hell of a lot of money we made for less than an hour's work. Oh, by the way, I made another three-thousand dollars tonight at the card game."

"Gosh dang Ryan, we're both rich," I said, as I shook my head in amazement.

It's strange how quick money can change a person. I went from being upset and scared to being elated and joyous, just by seeing all those bills stacked inside the envelope. I knew there was more money to be made here. Having money meant having power, and Ryan had fallen into something good. I needed money to survive but had to be careful that I didn't let it control me.

The following day we sat on the balcony of the apartment and talked about the previous night. I had mixed feelings and expressed them to Ryan. I wanted to go back home and make arrangements so I could get my diploma. After that, I wanted to come here and look for a job again. "You still won't have your diploma for a few months," Ryan said. "Why don't we form a pact and work together for the Newtons? Give it three months Jake, then if it isn't working out for you walk away. I'll not say another word"

"The money is great, Ryan, and it's very tempting. The thing is that ordeal with the Wyoming County deputies took a few years off my life, Ryan. I'm scared, and I don't want to spend my life behind bars."

"All I'm saying is for you to think about the envelope I handed you last night. Jake, you couldn't get a job in this town and make that much money in three months. I promise you, we aren't going to be moving drugs, and the Newton's are powerful people and will protect us, I've got Richard's word on that."

"You're awful sure about somebody you hardly know, Ryan. Just what do you even know about this man, Mr. Newton?"

"Well, he owns 132 banks, has four ocean front condominium buildings in Myrtle Beach, owns a casino in

New Jersey, owns seven golf courses, and - I know his wife wants to screw you!"

We both burst out laughing.

"Well, Ryan, next time I might let her take me into a bathroom and have her way with me!"

"I'm going to stay in school and get my college degree," Ryan said. "But, I'm going to be working some for Mr. Newton as well. He's mentoring me on how to conduct business deals. The jobs I do for him will be selective. He and I have already discussed that. I'm going to continue trying to work my way up in 'The Club'. Newton, by the way, happens to be a level ten member.

You can go to college too, Jake. In the meantime, if you decide you want to work with me, I promise, no surprises like last night. From now on, if you're doing something illegal with me, you'll have full knowledge of what you're getting into.

Chapter 14

The following week I made the trip to Oceana and met with the school principal, Mr. McKinney. He told me he'd heard about my trouble. He also heard that the two deputies who roughed me up had been fired by the Sheriff.

I wondered if they had gotten into other trouble. Perhaps the female deputy, after seeing my condition, had filed a report, setting off an investigation. It didn't matter, I was happy to hear they weren't patrolling the highways anymore. Mr. McKinney also said he'd spoken to Momma.

"Did she say anything about me coming back home to live?" I asked with enthusiasm.

I knew I sounded desperate, but I was surprised to hear he and Momma had spoken. I wanted to hear what had taken place. Perhaps she had asked him if he knew how to contact me, maybe she wanted to talk.

"No, Jake, I'm sorry," he replied. He hesitated before continuing. "I don't want to lie to you. She said if you showed up here I should make up some charges and have you thrown in jail. Maybe she'll have a change of heart someday, but for now I'd stay away from here."

My heart sank. I had grown up in this town, and it was my home. I already missed running in the hills, and all the good times playing in Big Reedy. Most of all I missed my family. I didn't care about making lots of money and being rich and famous. All I really wanted was to be loved, and have a good family life. I lowered my head, and tears welled up in my eyes. I know Mr. McKinney felt awkward, and I didn't have a right to burden him with my trouble.

I pulled myself together and thanked him for his time. As I was leaving, I asked him about graduation, when it would be, rehearsal and all.

He shook his head in sorrow.

"I'm sorry, Jake. Not with all that has gone on. The board won't allow me to let you walk the aisle with the other students. I'll have to mail you your diploma."

I stopped and stood there for a few seconds before responding.

"Mr. McKinney, I know you don't make the rules. I appreciate you taking time out of your busy schedule to meet with me. I also want to apologize for the position I've put you in. Although I have no desire to be rich or famous, someday I will be, and I'll give back to the school and community that I love so dearly. Kids do bad things sometimes, sir, but that doesn't mean you toss them out like dirty bath water. Please pass that message on to the Board of Education for me."

I walked out, got in Ryan's car, and drove back to Roanoke. I took, Mr. McKinney's, advice. I didn't attempt to go see Momma.

That meeting changed me. People were too fast to throw others away when they've done something wrong. No one ever seems to want to step in and find out what that person's issues are and how they could help. Instead, they just wad them up and throw them away, like a piece of used paper. I'd been painted as a thug. No one was ever going to think of me as anything but a thug. So why shouldn't I become a thug?

I never looked for a job again, part-time or full time. I applied to Carter University. I was accepted into their pre-law program. I decided I wanted to be a lawyer for people who'd been handed a bad deal. I'd represent those that had never been given a chance. Yes, I was going to be a lawyer, and I was going to be a dang good one. I thought that I might even open a law office in Oceana one day.

I worked alongside Ryan, doing deeds for Mr. Newton. He liked Ryan, and took him under his wing, mentoring to him about running his businesses. It pleased Mr. Newton that Ryan was studying finance and doing well.

Mrs. Newton took a liking to me. Her interest in me wasn't like the first time we met. When she was intoxicated and wanted to have sex with me while Ryan was with Mr. Newton playing cards. She liked my manners. She said I had a heart, cared about people, and that I would go a long way in life if I let my heart lead me. Her interest in me was from genuine care. She even told me once I was her adopted son. I liked that, it made me feel like I was part of a real family.

Chapter 15

I completed a full semester at Carter University and had gotten all "A's" on my finals exams. I was feeling good about life. Ryan and I were working week-ends for the Newtons doing a variety of jobs, not just package deliveries.

I found out the Newtons had other couriers in the past, but now it was just Ryan and me. Loyalty and trust were the keys to moving up in their business. Through the eyes of Mrs. Newton's, I was making it by leaps, and bounds. If it was a job involving Ryan, it was always Mr. Newton giving the instructions, but if it was just me, Mrs. Newton was always my contact.

It was Wednesday, December 30th. Ryan's brother had called and said he was home in Lynco visiting his parents. He wanted Ryan to come home for New Year's. School was out for semester break, and the Newtons were in Hawaii for the holidays. I was hoping they would have invited me to go, as they did some of their other staff, but it never happened. I knew I was still the new kid on the block and would have to keep working my way up if I expected benefits like that.

I'd gotten in contact with Janet just before Christmas. My intentions were to visit her in North Carolina. She was happy I called, and we talked for nearly three hours. She told me she wasn't going to be home during the holidays; she was getting married. She sounded happier than I'd ever heard her be. She and her fiancée were flying to the Florida Keys, with plans on getting married there and staying two weeks on their honeymoon.

Janet had been in contact with Momma and Bernice. I was hungry to hear news from home. She informed me that back in July, Bernice moved to Huff Creek to live with our aunt and uncle.

Crump, had tried to rape her one day while Momma wasn't home. She was upstairs folding laundry when he sneaked up behind her and threw her on the bed. He was able to get all her clothes off, but she escaped. She ran over to Mrs. Simmons house naked. She stayed with Mrs. Simmons until Momma came home then went back over to the house.

She told Momma what had happened. All she got for that was Momma whipping her and putting bruises on her face. Momma said Bernice made the story up for attention. Momma told Bernice she had shed bad light on her good name, just as I had done. Bernice called our uncle the next day. He came immediately and took her back to his house to live. She said Momma never said a word, even seemed happy to see her go.

126

She also said that in September, Momma went to Welch one day to have a surprise lunch with Crump. She found him in the back of his office having sex with another woman. When Momma found the two of them together, she went ape crazy. The woman ran out of Crump's office, and onto the busy highway, stark naked. Before it was all over, Momma beat Crump with one of the woman's high-heel shoes. She put his left eye out with the heel, bit part of his ear off, and kicked him until he was almost dead.

The police arrested Momma but Crump wouldn't press charges, so she got off. He did bankrupt her however. Crump somehow got the house in Lynco put in his name. He kicked Momma out of her own house. Janet said she'd heard Momma moved back to Indiana and was living with a truck driver she'd met. She had also heard that Crump had sold our house.

Part of me wanted to laugh because Momma had gotten some of her own medicine, but I didn't. I was sad deep inside. I was sad for Momma because I knew all too well, what it felt like to be thrown away. I wouldn't wish that kind of hurt on the devil himself.

Ryan persisted that I go home with him and stay with his family over the New Year's holiday. I didn't really want to go. I didn't want to see my old house with someone else living there, but finally I decided to go.

Ryan's brother, William, was in visiting, along with his wife and two small girls. He'd brought a large box of fireworks he'd purchased in Tennessee. About a half-hour before midnight on New Year's Eve, the entire family went outside to watch the fireworks go off.

William went to the middle of the street to set off the high-flying booming fireworks. It was cold outside, clear skies with temperatures hovering around twenty degrees. No one complained about the temperature until after the grand finale then it seemed everyone was suddenly cold. We were all tired and the kids were cranky, so we all went to bed.

While we were outside, I kept looking over at my old house. I could see there were different window treatments, but aside from that, everything looked the same. It appeared that the people who had moved in weren't home. The house was dark inside. I thought about Momma, and how she must feel. She'd lost Granny's house and had to move away. I hoped she was okay and happy wherever she was.

On New Year's Day, William, Ryan and I, were out back tinkering in Mr. Tyler's workshop. We were putting together a wood lathe that Ryan had gotten his dad as a Christmas present. A black car pulled into the Tyler's driveway. It looked like an undercover police car. Two men who looked identical and wearing identical clothing stepped out of the car. Both men were wearing sunglasses. I knew it had to be Larry and Barry, Ryan's cousins from Holden.

William went out to talk with them but Ryan and I stayed inside, warming ourselves by the wood stove. After fifteen minutes or more, we decided to put our coats on and go outside. We wanted to find out what was going on.

The men were getting ready to leave as we walked toward the car. Larry threw his hand up to Ryan and me as he was getting back into the car.

"Hey dudes, how ya doing!" He said. "Oh, William, you can bring your little brother and his buddy too if you want, the more the merrier."

After Larry and Barry left, we all went back to the workshop.

"What was that all about?" Ryan asked.

"You boys want to have some fun tonight?" William asked.

"Doing what?" Ryan replied.

William held his head slightly elevated and had a bit of a smirk on his face.

"Going to a cockfight," he said, as he clapped his hands together.

"A cockfight!" I exclaimed.

"That's right."

I'd heard of cock fighting but didn't know a thing about it.

"Okay William, spit it all out," Ryan said.

William started explaining. "Larry and Barry are security for a cock-fighting ring over in Gilbert. I used to go to these things all the time when we were growing up. We had to stop because there was always trouble. Cockfighting is illegal but the cops are in on it now. They're paid to keep trouble down. Larry and Barry are providing security and want us to come tonight. It'll be tons of fun. I'm feeling lucky and think I can win a lot of money."

"I don't know," Ryan said. College is going well, and I have a good job. I don't want to take a chance on screwing that up. We could even be shot by some redneck. Anything could happen.

"So when did you start wearing panties?" William fired back. "Besides, when did you ever pass up a chance to bet on something? Larry and Barry will have our backs, so don't worry. You don't have to gamble if you don't want to. Just watch me, and enjoy watching those silly rednecks. I'm going to take all those redneck's money."

"Alright then," Ryan said. "But, you know I'll be the one taking all the rednecks money."

William left the shop and went back into the house. Ryan and I talked about the cockfight for a long time. I didn't want to go. I would have rather gone back to Virginia and spent a quiet evening, eating popcorn and watching television. Ryan convinced me that William would never take us if he thought it was going to be a bad scene. He tried to convince me that if Larry and Barry were there for protection, there was no way things could get out of hand?"

"I'm still not so sure, Ryan, but if I were to go, we'd need to take our guns, just in case."

"Jacob Roberts, I'm surprised at you. You pretend to be a tough gangster one second and the next it appears to me; you're the one wearing the panties around here. So, what's your answer, yes or no?"

I punched Ryan in the arm then he kicked me in the shin and took off running.

Chapter **16**

Ryan and I got our guns out of the Mustang around four in the afternoon. We each cleaned our gun and loaded the cylinder. I strapped on the holster, placed the gun inside, and put my jacket on.

It was New Year's Day. By five that evening it had already gotten dark. William, knowing the way, and being the most experienced driver, took the wheel. We rode the Mustang. Ryan's new stereo was jamming the entire trip, until we turned off the main highway at Gilbert.

William was familiar with the area and knew exactly where to go. He'd gone to a cockfight at that location once many years ago. After we left the main road, we traveled nearly two miles on a one-lane dirt road along a creek. There, the road became curvy, with several switchbacks. It wound back and forth toward the top of a mountain.

The road was deserted, which was a good thing. There wasn't a place to pull over to let a car pass if we'd met one. Looking out the window of the car, I could see that from the edge of the road it was a straight drop-off of several hundred feet. If we went over, the only thing to stop us from going all the way to the bottom were a few white poplar trees, nothing more.

As we approached the top of the mountain, I spotted lights ahead. The light was coming from a large wooden shack, where the cockfights were to take place.

There was ample parking in the knee-high grass in front of the shack. Forty or more cars and trucks were already parked there. They weren't parked in any given direction or order, everyone had parked where they pleased.

After stopping the car, William looked at Ryan, then around to me.

"I know you cowboys got your weapons, but you can't be packing inside this place. Leave your guns in the car," he said.

Ryan placed his 38 in the glove compartment. I was in the back seat. I took my jacket off in order to remove the shoulder harness then put the gun beneath the passenger seat. I was careful not to point it at anyone while doing so.

As we were getting out of the car, both Larry and Barry were walking up to greet us. They had on light gray matching uniforms with baseball caps that sported the word "Security" in bold block letters.

"Bout damn time ya got here!" Larry said as he embraced William.

Barry gave William a high-five as Larry moved out of the way. Ryan and I were getting out on the opposite side of the car. Larry came over and shook our hands, greeting us as if we'd been best friends all our lives. Larry seemed different and once I got a whiff of him, I knew why. He reeked of alcohol and marijuana.

Barry led the way as we walked up the slope to the entrance of the shack. As we went inside, the smell of animals mixed with cigarette smoke immediately filled my nostrils. The place was even bigger than it looked from the outside, and was teeming with activity.

People were moving about greeting each other, smoking, and drinking straight from their liquor bottles. A series of speakers were set around the shack and bluegrass music was playing. The harmonic distortion from the speakers was bad. As the music blared loudly, I had a hard time distinguishing between a fiddle and a guitar, but it didn't seem to bother anyone else.

As we moved further inside I saw the ring where the fights were to take place. The floor inside the shack was dirt and covered in straw. The twenty-foot diameter ring was inset a foot below the floor. Two-inch steel poles were driven into the ground around the ring perimeter on six-foot spacing.

The tops of the poles were about four feet above the floor. Two strands of wire rope, one a foot off the floor and another near the top of the poles, stretched around the ring. There was an opening a few feet wide on opposite sides of the ring. In the back of the shack, the wall was lined with a hundred or more cages, all filled with roosters. They were singing their war cry, adding to the noise in the place.

The music stopped and people immediately started closing in toward the ring ropes, indicating the fights were about to begin. William, Ryan, and I moved in as well, trying to get a good view of the activities about to take place.

The three of us were the only people in what I considered normal dress, aside from Larry, Barry, and a few other security people, all in uniforms. Everyone else was wearing dirty farm clothing, mostly bibbed coveralls, and cowboy boots. Nearly all the men had long untrimmed beards, were chewing tobacco, and spitting in the floor.

Those men there looked as if they lived hard. They all had stern leathered faces. Not a single man was smiling. It was a rough looking crowd. We were outsiders here, and we were being given plenty of unfriendly looks.

A man entered the ring with a microphone. He welcomed everyone, and began rattling off rules. His accent along with the bad sound system made it difficult to understand his words. When he was finished, I didn't have a clue what he had actually said. It must have started the games though. Two men went to the cages in the back. Each grabbed a rooster from their box.

A whistle was blown. The two roosters held by their owners at the opposite openings of the ring were turned loose. The roosters strutted around for a few seconds and then ran toward each other. As soon as they met, it became a tangled whirlwind. Both roosters were jumping in the air and throwing punches, hoping to land the razor sharp spurs on their opponent and slice them apart.

I didn't know roosters could make so many sounds. Both were taking death-defying blows, to all parts of their bodies. They called out sounds indicating satisfaction for the one throwing the punch and agony for the recipient.

The crowd was going wild, using their arms as if to throw jabs at the roosters. It was mass confusion with everyone whooping and hollering. The activity of those men watching two birds fight to the death was both comical and frightening.

Finally, one of the roosters flopped over near the opposite end of the ring from where we were watching. The rooster lying on the ground was dead. The winner, while badly hurt itself, paced around the ring like a boxer after a victorious fight, strutting before the crowd.

There were both cheers and jeers when the fight was over. The man with the microphone was also the moneyman, the one who took the bets. He began handing out money to the winners. I wondered how he knew how to distribute the money. He didn't have a list or anyone helping him. There must have been three to four dozen different wagers. His ability to keep that straight was more interesting to me than seeing the roosters fight.

After he was finished distributing the money, another man, who must have been his partner, grabbed the microphone. He entered the ring to announce the next fight and to let the bets begin. I could only assume this man had the same ability to remember all the bets. He went around the ring in a counter-clockwise direction, collecting all the bets for the next fight, not writing any of it down.

I pulled out a ten-dollar bill and put it in his hand betting on 'The Distiller' whoever that was. All the bird owners had nicknames. It was a blind bet, but Ryan was betting on 'The Distiller' so I felt it was a safe bet.

Once all bets had been placed, two more men went to the cages and removed roosters. When they returned to the ring, the owner's names were announced once more. 'The Distiller' was on our left. He was an ordinary looking man, mid-fifties, had a dirty face, and was wearing coveralls. He blended in nicely with the crowd.

On the opposite side of the ring, there was a monster of a man called 'Sled Track'. He was six feet eight inches tall and as broad a man at the shoulders as I'd ever seen. He had a muscular build, and small squinting eyes. He was without a doubt the meanest looking man in the entire shack. I knew he was someone I'd never want to tangle with.

The whistle blew. Immediately the owners released their roosters. Instead of doing a little strut first, as the previous roosters had done, they went straight toward each other. The two birds, equipped with their blades of death, met like two football linemen colliding at a goal-line stance. Feathers were flying as they tangled and began throwing punches with those razor sharp spurs.

I found myself caught up in the action and was hollering like the rest of the crowd. Suddenly, the rooster belonging to the big man went down, but that didn't stop the other rooster from continuing to throw blows. 'The Distiller' jumped into the ring, now with long cuffed leather gloves on, and grabbed his rooster. 'Sled Track' came into the ring next, grabbed the downed rooster, and saw it was still breathing. Someone handed him a lit cigarette. He took a long drag, grabbed the bird, turned it over, and began blowing smoke into the rooster's hind end.

I didn't realize this was one of the rules of the game. I also didn't know blowing smoke into a wounded rooster's butt would revive it for a short time so it could continue fighting. It's like a fighter being down on an eight count and getting back up. I'd never seen anything like that before, and it was all I could do to keep from laughing.

Although I was able to contain myself, Ryan couldn't. He let out a laugh that came from deep inside. We may have been okay if he had stopped at that, but then he pointed at the big man blowing into the rooster's rear and continued laughing. The crowed quieted quickly, too quickly. Ryan had turned to William and in a loud voice said, "Look at the Jolly Green Giant blowing smoke up that chicken's ass!"

The big man crossed the ring and went out the opposite side. He continued on, coming toward Ryan. He moved swiftly for such a big man, and it caught the entire crowd off guard. The man got to Ryan and stopped, looking down on him.

"I've burped boys bigger than you," he said.

I suppose Ryan thought a fight was inevitable. In a single motion, taking everyone by surprise, Ryan shoved his left hand into the man's throat, while at the same time placing his right leg behind the giant. Ryan's left thumb went right into his Adam's apple as he shoved the man back, causing him to trip over Ryan's right foot, falling to the ground. Like a cat leaping on its prey, Ryan was on top of the man before he hit the dirt floor and had already delivered a left and right hand punch to the man's nose and mouth.

William and I leaped forward at the same time, having the intent of delivering our own blows to the man before he had a chance to recover and do damage to Ryan. No sooner had I started forward my motion was stopped. Two men, one on each side of me, grabbed my arms. A third man came around with his fist, landing a solid blow into my mid-section. They let go, and I went down to the floor as fast as the big man had when Ryan tripped him.

The blow knocked all the air out of me. I felt as if I were going to throw up and pass out at the same time. I lost my bearings for a few seconds. Finally, I was able started breathing again. I tried to get up, but a large open hand pressed my head downward then rubbed my face into the nasty smelling dirt floor.

The next thing I remember was Larry grabbing me by the back of my shirt and jerking me to my feet. Barry and the rest of the security guards were in action stopping the fight before it went any further.

When I looked around, I was expecting to see Ryan with half his face missing. Instead, he was unscathed. He was standing a few feet to my left. One of the security guards had him restrained. Two men were helping the giant, Sled Track, up off the floor. He had blood dripping out of his nose. His right eye had a nasty cut over it, which was bleeding profusely.

Sled Track wiped his lip, and looked at the fresh blood on his fingers. His face was contorted, and I could see fire glowing from his good eye. He didn't realize his other eye was bleeding at the time. It shocked him once he saw the blood otherwise the entire security force in the place couldn't have kept him off Ryan.

Two men stepped in with a rag and a stool. They sat the big man down, and started tending to the cut over his eye. Suddenly, he rose up off the stool and began moving toward us. Larry pulled his gun and cocked the action in one motion. He placed it against the front of the big man's forehead. That stopped his motion, and he sat back down. Larry immediately withdrew the weapon and placed it back in his holster. Several of the big man's friends had moved toward us and the security people were trying to push them back.

"That's enough!" Larry said in a loud voice demanding attention. The crowd got quiet.

"The fight is over! Strata, do you owe these men any money?" Larry said.

Strata must have been the announcer's name. He walked over to us. I noticed his face was blood red and tobacco juice was running out of the corner of his mouth and down his straggly beard. He was giving us a look that could kill. He gave Ryan and William each a wad of money, then shoved a twenty-dollar bill into my shirt pocket. All I cared about at that moment was getting out of the place alive, and I wasn't sure that was going to happen.

"Okay everybody, the fights over. Sled Track, you're out of here for tonight - and these three gentlemen, I'll see them to their car - they won't ever be back." Larry announced.

Larry, Barry, and one of the other security guards each grabbed one of our arms, leading us out of the building as they walked us to the car. Larry was in the lead, holding William's arm. He was fussing at William as we walked, but I couldn't make out what he was saying. I was still recovering from the blow I'd taken and was concentrating on my own well-being. Whatever Larry was saying, I knew it had to be something about Ryan, why he couldn't behave himself, and the trouble we'd caused him tonight.

William got into the driver's seat. Ryan held the passenger's seat forward. I crawled into the back then he got in. We backed out of the parking space. Larry was at the driver's side window, walking alongside the moving car, and giving William instructions.

"Get your ass out of here, William. Those rednecks in there are mostly all related and they'll be looking for more trouble. I'll call you tomorrow."

Larry slapped the top of the car. William maneuvered the car through the tall grass and onto the dirt road. Once we started driving off that mountain, I felt like a large weight had been lifted off me.

As we came down the curvy road off the mountain, Ryan was cursing and ranting about how he put ole Goliath in his place. I wasn't saying a word. I was still shaking from what had taken place. My insides were still aching from the blow I'd taken. I kept feeling my ribs wondering if any of them had been broken.

As we neared the bottom of the mountain and started along the creek, I looked back through the rear glass. I saw headlights from a car coming down the mountain from above, moving at a fast pace. I told William and suggested he speed up. William said it was probably Larry or Barry seeing that we got off the mountain safely, but that he'd speed up, just in case.

As soon as we hit the paved road, William had the car in first gear and punched the gas pedal hard. The car fishtailed a bit as a shower of mud was thrown into the air by the tires spinning on the pavement. Where we exited the dirt road onto the highway, there was a long straight stretch. As the straight road was ending, and we were starting into a curve, I looked back again. I saw that the car coming off the mountain had gotten to the highway, and was coming in our direction.

Within two miles, we entered a long curve in the road that ran along a big bend in the Guyandotte River. William was certain now that the car quickly approaching us from the rear wasn't Larry or Barry. We entered a stretch of road containing one of the few passing zones on the highway. William said he was going to slow down and let them pass.

The car behind us came closer. I looked back just in time to see a fireball erupt just outside the window of the passenger side of the car. Within a second the back glass of our car shattered, then fell into the back of the car as one big heap of broken glass.

William instantly dropped to a lower gear and sped up, hoping to put some distance between us and the other car. At the end of the river bend, the road separated from the river as it curved slightly. There it started up a long hollow before climbing another mountain with lots of curves in the road to negotiate. I knew if we got to the curves, we should be in a position where someone shooting at us would have a hard time hitting their target.

Another ball of fire came from behind us. Although it wasn't a direct hit, a couple of pellets came through the now open back window, and hit William in his right shoulder. If it wasn't clear before, it was now, they were shooting at us with a sawed-off shotgun.

The pellets didn't have much impact and didn't penetrate William's jacket. Still, they delivered a sting. He lurched forward while cursing the people in the car. We were already going nearly seventy miles an hour on the dark, narrow highway. If William tried going any faster, we were sure to wreck.

I wasn't about to just sit there useless and die from either a car wreck or a gunshot wound. I reached beneath the passenger seat and pulled out the 44 magnum. I cocked the hammer back and readied myself. I got to the best firing position I could get into, considering I was in the back seat of a speeding car on a curvy road.

Both cars moving made it impossible to aim precisely. I pointed toward the front of the car behind us, aimed as best I could, and squeezed the trigger. The gun firing inside the car roared like a bomb exploding, and fire from the muzzle appeared as it if extended to the car trailing behind us. The driver's side headlight of the car chasing us instantly got dark.

William wasn't ready for the explosive sound of the gun being fired. He jerked the steering wheel violently and almost put us into a spin. It flung me across the car and into the back seat door on the driver's side.

"Son of a bitch!" William screamed out. I didn't know if he was referring to the 44 magnum being discharged or having nearly wrecked us.

I pushed myself away from the door in order to recover my balance and get back into a sitting position. As I was doing so, another shot was fired from the car behind us. None of us was hit, but the sound of buckshot hitting the car was a clear indicator the car behind us was still within range for the shotgun to be effective, and they weren't backing off.

I pulled the hammer back again on the single-action pistol and raised up to get a view of the car behind us. I could make out the shape of the car better now with only one headlight shining into my eyes. I aimed at the driver's side of the windshield and pulled the trigger.

I was temporarily blinded by the muzzle flash of my big gun being discharged so close to my eyes. Still, I could see the car behind us weave just a little. Suddenly, the car trailing us made a quick right turn, ran off the road and down over a steep embankment. "You got em!" William cried out, as he peered into the rearview mirror, now cracked after being hit by buckshot.

William stopped the car and said he wanted to go back. We were somewhere around half-way up the mountain and there was nowhere to turn. He maneuvered the car back and forth until it was turned around then headed back the direction we had come.

When we got back to where I'd fired the last shot, it was clear to see where the car had left the highway. Tire marks were present across the road and in the dirt along the side of the road, then disappeared over the hillside. William got out of the car, walked over to the side of the road, and looked down the embankment. He reported he could see the car. It was at least a hundred feet or more over the hillside and turned on its side up against a tree.

Ryan yelled that a car was approaching from down the road. We didn't stick around to see if anyone was hurt in the wreck. William jumped back in, turned the car back around then headed back up the mountain. Our fear was that the car approaching belonged to more of Sled Track's friends. We put some distance between us and the other car. William never let up, speeding all the way back to Lynco.

We sat in the driveway at Ryan's house for a long time. At first, no one spoke a word then William and Ryan started talking about our adventure and the adrenaline rush. The adrenaline in my body had left after the last shot I fired. I may have killed someone. My thoughts bounced back and forth from the guilt of thinking I'd killed the people in that car, to what would happen next and if I would be going to jail.

The excitement waned as the night wore on and we all got sleepy. We went in the house and went to bed. I slept that night, but it was a restless sleep. I dreamed someone was chasing me, and I couldn't run. Early the next morning Ryan was banging on the bedroom door.

"Jake, are you in there?"

"Yeah, what's going on?"

I was afraid he was going to tell me the cops were looking for us.

"Come on out to the workshop, William's wife fixed us all a big breakfast and we're going to eat out there and talk."

"Okay, give me just a few minutes."

I laid there for a few more minutes then started to get out of the bed. I fell onto the floor. I was sore from the top of my legs to my throat. It was all from that gigantic blow I'd taken in the mid-section. I never saw the man who threw the punch, but he must have been as big and brawny as the man Ryan had sent tumbling to the ground. I pulled myself up and sat down. While putting on my clothes and feeling my ribs again, I kept wondering if something inside me was broken.

Ryan and William motioned me to the back of the garage where a card table was set up. William's wife, Clarissa, cooked a breakfast of eggs, bacon, homemade buttermilk biscuits, hash brown potatoes, and fried apples. Until then, I hadn't realized I was hungry.

I thought about how it was when I was living next door. Momma never cooked breakfast for us unless it was oatmeal. I sat down and gorged myself as if I'd never eaten a breakfast like that before. William watched as I ate and was amazed at my appetite.

After we finished eating, we talked a bit about the events of last night then went out to look at the car. The back end of the car was a mess. Both taillights were broken. The trunk, as well as the top, had a hundred or so pit marks made by pellets from the shotgun. The back glass was shattered and laying on the window ledge behind the rear seat. Ryan shook his head and was all but in tears. The car was his pride and joy, now it looked as if it had gone through a war zone.

William suggested we clean the garage out and move the car inside, out of sight, before people started driving by and asking questions. William told Ryan to find an auto body repair man. One who would not only fix the car but also keep his mouth shut about the bullet holes. Ryan already knew who that would be.

Larry Stanley lived just down the street from our apartment in Roanoke. He was about our age but already had a good reputation for being an excellent auto body man. He'd graduated from vocational school in auto repair a couple of years back and had opened his own shop in town. Ryan said that Larry owed him some money from a poker game. He would use that as a bribe to keep his mouth shut.

Around noon, we were still in the garage. Two Logan County Sheriff's deputy patrol cars pulled into the driveway. It was Larry and Barry. They were dressed in their deputy uniforms. We all went out to meet them. I was hanging back as we walked. My heart was pumping around two hundred beats a minute.

Larry sat down on the hood of his cruiser and placed his feet on the bumper. Barry leaned on the fender beside of Larry with his arms crossed. We stood in front of Larry as he began telling us what kind of trouble we'd made for ourselves. My knees were shaking and the big breakfast I'd eaten earlier was now churning inside my sore stomach.

"I'd like to think you boys drove straight home last night without any trouble" Larry said. "I don't rightly much figure that's the case though."

Larry had pulled a toothpick out of his pocket and put it in the corner of his mouth while he was talking. His country accent grew worse with the toothpick dangling there.

"They found a wrecked car this morning on Horsepen Mountain. It went over da hill and damn near hit bottom fer it got caught on a tree. Turns out there were two brothers of the ole boy Ryan whipped up on last night in that car."

Ryan started to talk. Larry tilted his head down and to the side as he threw his left hand out, indicating he wasn't through talking, and we needed to listen.

"I ain't here to play now boys, so ya'll be quiet and be damn sure to hear what all I's got to say," Larry said. "Now that car is totaled, and the two boys are near death."

Near death. That means I didn't kill the driver!

"They had to use the 'jaws of life' to git that boy on the passenger side out of the car. He's got some pretty nasty cuts on his face and both legs broke, but he mite make it. The driver though, he ain't in too good a shape. He's got a ruptured spleen, broken back, head injuries, and it appears he took a large caliber bullet to his right shoulder. He's also gonna loose his right arm, that's if he's lucky enough to live."

Larry stopped talking and sat there, staring us down. None of us said a word. The silence was painful. I just wished he'd get to the point, then I could decide whether or not to stretch out my arms for the handcuffs or take off running. I knew I could outrun both of them, but where would I go? How would I survive as a fugitive?

Larry was still staring us down when Barry pitched in. His speech was every bit as bad as Larry's was, if not worse. I found myself watching his mouth as the words seemed to force their way out of his lips.

"They found er large bullet hole in da headlite. Hit went straight through and exited da fender leavin a big ole hole – ."

Larry's face had turned blood red. He interrupted his brother.

"Damn it boys, you created a mess that I don't know how to git ya out of. Nobody at that cockfight knows we's kin, as fer as I know. And, I don't think anyone remembered ya from years back William. So here's da deal. Most of those ole boys are either kin, good friends, or neighbors. They got a hard-on fer you three and they's aiming to come lookin fer ya. I suggest ya stay the hell out of Mingo County, and git rid of that car. At least paint hit a different color. Better yet, why don't you two turds git in it and head back to Virginia and don't come back. I'll do what I can to cover yer tracks on my end, but I ain't promising ya nuttin. And, if one of them ole boys dies; well lets jest say that it mite change everything."

I was hearing Larry's words and trying to comprehend. I hadn't thought about those men from last night hunting me down. I could hide from them in Virginia, possibly. At the same time, I was hearing good news. It appeared Larry wasn't going to be taking me to jail. Not only that, but Larry was going to try covering things up for us.

I just hoped the man in the wreck didn't die. I didn't want to have that on my conscience. I was smart enough to know though, if he did die ole Larry and Barry wouldn't have my back.

Larry slid off the car hood and moved toward the driver's door of the cruiser. Barry quickly went to his cruiser and got inside. As soon as the door had shut, he had the engine started, backed out of the driveway, and sped down the hollow. Larry opened the door to his car and stood there looking back at the three of us. I'm sure to him; we looked like three whipped puppy dogs who had lost our mother.

Larry shook his head. "William, I love you as much as I love my brother Barry. But, your damn little brother and his punk friend ain't nothing but pure bred trouble."

Larry then looked at Ryan and me.

"Ya'll think I ripped ya off on those knives a few years back. Well now were even. If I ever lay eyes on you two again, it mite be to put your asses in the slammer. I've done all I care to do fer ya."

Larry got in his cruiser. Just like, Barry, he started the engine as the door was closing shut. He spun back out of the driveway without even looking to see if a car was coming, shifted into drive, and sped off.

I knew I needed to disappear for a long time while things cooled off. Ryan and I would be in Virginia, so I was sure those men from the cock fights weren't going to find us. We just had to figure out a way to keep out of trouble, and somehow I knew that would be difficult - trouble seemed to follow us.

Ryan and I headed back to Roanoke that afternoon. William kept the rest of the family distracted while we exited the garage with the damaged car and drove out of sight. As far as I know, none of them saw the car or ever learned about our adventure.

On the way back, I talked Ryan into stopping in Huff Creek briefly and let me visit with Bernice. It was good to see her, and she seemed happy. She liked living with our aunt and uncle and said she loved being a part of a real family.

She knew the story about Momma. She knew about the house, the fight with Crump, and everything. Bernice said she didn't care about the house, and Momma got what she deserved. I told her to try and not let the bitterness eat at her. I told her that retaining hard feelings toward Momma would only make her miserable and wouldn't do a thing to Momma. I knew though that it would take a long time for her to get past what had happened.

147

When we got back to Roanoke, Ryan took the car to Larry Stanley for repair. After Larry took a close look at the amount of damage done to the care, he determined the repair bill would be more than the vehicle's value, especially with the high mileage on the car.

Ryan went to a car lot the next day and traded it for a new pickup truck. He didn't get much trade value because of the Mustang's condition, and he had to make up a story about how the car had been shot up. Ryan's love affair with the Mustang made it difficult for him to let it go. It was the only tangible thing I could think of that Ryan was ever been attached to.

Several months later, I made a few calls and found out the two men in the car wreck lived, and were out of the hospital. It had been weighing on my mind, and I had to know if they had survived.

The one with the broken legs was a diabetic. He had some complications during recovery and lost both legs from the knees down. The other man lost his right arm, and after getting out of the hospital, he had a severe stroke. It greatly affected his speech and use of his left arm. I felt bad for the men, knowing I was the one who caused the wreck. Even though their intentions that night were to kill us, I still felt my action had resulted in their lives forever being changed.

Chapter 17

Over the next two years, Ryan and I made hundreds of deliveries for Mr. Newton. We became his first choice for doing his secret work, and not once was there ever any trouble. We were trusted as his couriers and if ever questioned by the police, we knew there was to be no connection to Mr. Newton. In return, we were well paid. He was a powerful man, with powerful connections, leading all the way to the White House.

I never knew what we were delivering. Sometimes, it was a container as large as a fifteen-gallon drum, while other times just an envelope. Our pay was beyond imagination, so we never asked questions. Trust was the main thing. He trusted Ryan and me, and in return, we trusted him and respected him.

We stayed in the same apartment, although we could have easily bought a nice house and lived a lavish lifestyle. I was paying my own way, bought a good used car, and was putting money in the bank. All the while, I was in school and getting a college education.

I was interested in the discipline I was studying, and my grades were nearly always A's. In high school, I never applied myself and just scraped by, willingly accepting bad grades. Now I had some direction in my life and it made a world of difference.

We both liked the apartment and didn't want to live anywhere else. The apartment was comfortable, and the rent was cheap. Ryan's goal in life hadn't changed. He wanted to get rich and let everyone else do the work. He wanted to move up higher in the club. He risked a lot in those card games. He knew he could make a fortune or lose everything he had. He loved the thrill and lived for the moment.

Making money wasn't the thrill to Ryan it was the chase, the excitement. He often said he wanted to win ten million dollars, then he would retire and just take it easy the rest of his life. We both knew that was a lie, he could never quit.

I never had sex with Mrs. Newton. Ryan and I were at their house often, and although she would flirt with me at times, she knew I respected her as well as Mr. Newton. I would never betray either of them in any way, form, or fashion. She trusted me and knew I was dedicated and loyal. I can't say the same about Ryan. He respected Mr. Newton also, but only from a business standpoint. Many times, Ryan was alone with Mrs. Newton in her bedroom. He repeated the words that Mrs. Newton had said to me when she and I had first met. She took him from being a boy to being a man.

On one occasion, Mr. and Mrs. Newton were vacationing at a resort in South Carolina. They invited Ryan and me to join them for a week, and we accepted. They asked us to play a round of golf with them one day. I had learned to play the game but wasn't a very good golfer.

On the thirteenth hole, Mrs. Newton hit her ball near some trees close to the next fairway. A man playing the other fairway hit a ball, and it landed very close to Mrs. Newton's ball. She was about to hit her ball when the man approached her. He was built like a professional football player and had a 'bad boy' attitude. He told her she was about to hit his ball and to leave it the hell alone and get the f... out of his way. I was close by, and my temper flared. I took a five-iron and with a half-swing laid it up the side of his head. The man fell backward and hit the ground.

"I believe you owe this lady an apology, or would you rather you and I continue this round of golf?" I said, while standing over him.

The man held his hands close to his face and flinched, as if he was waiting for me to hit him again.

"I'm sorry lady; I made a bad mistake," he said with a wimpy voice.

Mrs. Newton hit her ball, and we continued our play as if nothing had happened.

When we got to the next tee box, all the men had teed off and were heading back to our carts. Mr. Newton hadn't spoken about the incident. Suddenly, he spoke rather loudly, saying I may have overreacted a bit.

Mrs. Newton was sitting there, in her and Richard's golf cart, and heard what Richard had said.

"He's a man among men, and I'm grateful someone had the guts to stand up to a big bully," Mrs. Newton replied. "Richard, whatever you're paying this fine young man isn't enough."

She sped off toward the women's tee boxes, leaving Mr. Newton standing there holding his golf club. He began walking toward the women's tees as Ryan and I slowly followed in our cart.

Chapter **18**

It was the middle of May after my junior year in college. Ryan had just graduated and accepted a job working full-time for Mr. Newton as a finance manager for a group of his banks. I didn't have a clue about what his duties were, but he wasn't getting any blisters on his hands. We were still running packages for Mr. Newton on the weekends. For the last ten months, all the jobs he'd given us were for delivery in New Jersey. I was going to be working full-time for Mr. Newton during summer break from school. Once school started back, I was also expecting to pick up some jobs during the weekdays, as he needed me.

It became somewhat of a routine. Every Friday around two in the afternoon, I would pick up a van in Lynchburg, Virginia, to use for the delivery. Usually, it had a logo on the side for some small business or a utility company. Ryan would drive another van, identical to the one I would be driving.

Most trips we'd deliver the vans to a warehouse, pick up a car, then go to Mr. Newton's casino where a room would be reserved for us in the casino hotel. On Saturday, I would hang out in the casino, and Ryan would be off in a poker game with 'The Club'. On Sunday, we would drive home.

We didn't get paid cash on the spot anymore. The money was delivered to our apartment once we got back from the job we were doing. Mr. Newton expected us to do our banking with his banks, with which we had no problem; they paid good interest, and they were FDIC insured.

On June 20th, we made a delivery as usual and there weren't any problems. Ryan and I ate a nice surf and turf dinner in the casino restaurant. We then spent the night in our usual penthouse suites. Life was good. All the luxury anyone could ever ask for, it was great. Fine food, good wine, Cuban cigars, and plenty of beauty queens everywhere you looked.

Ryan didn't have a sanctioned poker game that Saturday as was normal. Something had happened and the man who was hosting the game canceled. Ryan wasn't about to gamble in the casino; he knew the odds, and he knew he couldn't beat the house. His many talents didn't help him at all in a casino setting.

Ryan had some friends from college that lived in New Jersey. He called one of those friends to see if he'd be interested in meeting for dinner. The friend told him about a big poker game that was going on and invited Ryan to come play. He agreed, thinking it was a good idea. I was angry with Ryan and reminded him it would be breaking one of Mr. Newton's rules. I told him if Newton found out we'd be in a heap of trouble, and besides, he didn't know those people, and it could be a setup; anything could happen.

Ryan was always the coolheaded one and always calmed me down. He said I was always overcautious and needed to chill out once, in a while. He promised if I went with him that he would only stay an hour tops, then we would come back to the casino strip and catch a good comedy show. I reluctantly agreed and went along.

As it turned out, we were given directions to a house located in a nice gated community, which eased my tension. I was expecting some hood where we would have to fight our way out. At least we followed one of Mr. Newton's rules; neither of us carried a firearm.

There were a dozen or so cars at the house when we arrived. A big party was going on inside. I told Ryan I wasn't going in. I would sit outside until he came out. Ryan frowned, but knew there wasn't much use trying to talk me into going inside.

After more than two hours, Ryan finally reappeared. I was furious, as he expected I would be. I had been pacing the parking area in front of the house, watching a host of people come and go from the party.

Ryan had been drinking, which was uncommon for him during a poker game. That was another rule he'd never broken. It wasn't Newton's rule he'd broken. It was Ryan's own personal rule - never drink, when playing poker. It was a sure-fire way for him to make a mistake and lose the shirt off his back. Ryan knew that when he drank he became loose lipped and that always spelled trouble. It was odd that he had broken his own rule this time. I was wondering if something was bothering him.

"You drive and I'll drive," he said, as he threw me the car keys.

Although Ryan didn't appear to be drunk by any means, it didn't make sense what he had said.

"Are you drunk or what?" I asked.

"No, I'm not drunk," he replied, while laughing loudly. "What I said was you drive and I'll drive. You drive this new Corvette, I won it tonight!"

My mouth dropped open. I didn't know how to react, and several things were going through my head. The first thing being some big dude with a big gun was going to come busting out of the house and kill us both, just for looking at his car. Ryan could tell I was confused and thinking the worst.

"It's alright," he said. "I won this car fair and square in a double or nothing, do-or-die hand. The car is mine. The owner is upset a bit, but he'll be fine. He actually belongs to 'The Club', just became a member. He has my address. He's going to send me the title in the mail on Monday. It appears he may not go very far in 'The Club', unless his luck changes."

I was unsure about this deal, and ill at Ryan. I stood there looking at him with my arms crossed and a look of disapproval on my face.

"Listen, it's OK, Jake, here take the dang keys. You drive the Corvette."

I wanted nothing more than to get out of that place and get back to the casino. I took the keys, jumped in the Corvette and zoomed off, leaving Ryan still standing in the driveway.

I was testing the car as I drove down the freeway. It was powerful, a finely tuned machine. I liked the way the car handled and was considering talking to Ryan about selling it to me once we got back to Roanoke. I turned on the radio, and an old disco song was playing. I was singing along and didn't realize I was ten to fifteen miles per hour over the speed limit until I saw the car with blue lights flashing. It was quickly closing in behind me.

I turned the radio off, pulled off the road, and stopped. The police car pulled in behind me and parked. It was getting dark, so he left his headlights on as well as the flashing blue lights on top of the cruiser. I had never been pulled over before so I started to get out of the car, not realizing you aren't supposed to do that. I opened the door to step out. I looked back and saw that the police officer had his cruiser door open. He was standing behind the door with his gun drawn, pointed right at me.

"Drop to your knees and put both hands in the air," he screamed.

I stood up straight, shocked by what I had just heard.

"Do it now!" The officer said.

I dropped to my knees and held my hands high. Another cruiser came sliding in and parked on a forty-five degree angle in front of me, blocking the Corvette from being moved.

The first police officer came up to me. He told me to lay forward with my face down, and my arms spread out.

"Hey, I know I was speeding, but I wasn't going that fast, what's with all this?" I exclaimed.

"Shut up," the officer said.

The second cop was out of his car now. He put his right knee in my back and slapped a handcuff on my left wrist, and then pulled my arms together and connected the remaining open cuff on my right wrist before thoroughly searching me.

They stood me up bent me over the hood of the Corvette. That brought back memories of a few years back, and I knew, just like that long cold February night in West Virginia, this was going to be a long night as well.

"Officer, can I speak?"

"Yeah, you can speak. Tell us your life history, PUNK!" He replied, with a strong New Jersey accent.

"I don't have a story, except I was driving too fast and thought I was going to get a speeding ticket."

"Un-frigging believable," he said.

They put me in the back of a squad car and took me to their precinct. I was a bit more educated now and had an idea about what to say or not to say. Just as before, they led me into an interrogation room, only this time; there were two police officers in suits sitting at the table waiting for me. They gave me a donut and some coffee. How ironic I thought - donuts and police. I don't like coffee but I was hungry and ate the donut once they removed the handcuffs.

They started asking questions, and I answered each one politely. They were simple questions, like where do live, and how old are you.

"Am I being charged with something?" I asked.

The two officers looked at each other and smiled.

"Are you being charged with something?" The one on my left said sarcastically.

I looked into his eyes, waiting for him to feed me information. I kept waiting, but they didn't appear ready to volunteer information.

"Ok, what am I being held here for?" I said.

The officer on the right finally spoke.

"Alright, we have you for speeding, reckless driving, driving a vehicle without proper registration, and the biggie - grand theft auto!"

My head jerked back in amazement, and my eyes got bigger.

"What are you talking about?" I said, in a tone that displayed disgust. "All I was doing was driving my friend's Corvette back to the Casino Newton where my room is, and yes, I was speeding, but I didn't steal the dang car!"

"Is that right?" The officer on the right said. "You stole that car this morning, and you've been joy riding in it all afternoon."

I quickly surmised my situation. They think I stole the Corvette, and they think I've been driving it all afternoon. Mr. Newton can't be involved in this, and neither can Ryan. I was in a real pickle! I knew the hotel cameras would have me coming out of the parking lot with Ryan around five-thirty. That should negate the riding around all afternoon business. How do I get out of the fact I was driving the car? It was apparent to me now. Ryan won a car, but the car he won was stolen. That's why the man he won it from didn't put up a fight or even give a crap about us taking his car. Dang, I was in a world of trouble!

"Officer, I'd like to call my attorney," I said. "I have nothing more to say."

They took me to fingerprinting, to booking then placed me in a cell for two hours. After that, I was allowed to make a call. Ryan could contact a lawyer and get me some help. I called his hotel room and lucky for me; he was there. He was beside himself, not knowing what had happened to me. He had taken a different route back to the hotel, thinking I was ahead of him.

I asked Ryan if he would contact Mr. Newton, he'd know what to do. Ryan said he would. He also said this might get him fired or thrown out of the club, or both. Then he realized how that sounded and apologized to me over, and over. He kept saying he should have driven the Corvette.

"No, you shouldn't have driven the Corvette. You should have never been there period!" I said.

Ryan made the call to Mr. Newton and by Sunday afternoon, I was out on bond. Mr. Newton or Ryan didn't come to get me out of jail. It was Mrs. Newton. After my release into her custody, she told me she would have to take me to her room and chain me to her bed, so I wouldn't escape. I didn't know if she was joking or not.

Mrs. Newton took me back to the casino, and we ate dinner. She didn't tie me to a bed or even invite me to her room. After dinner, she went to her room, stating she had to make a few calls on my behalf.

On Monday morning, I met Mrs. Newton in the casino restaurant for breakfast.

"I was on the phone for a quite some time last night, and even though it was Sunday, I was able to get you the best attorney in the State of New Jersey," she said.

I didn't know what to say, but I think she could see the gratitude on my face.

"It's going to be alright, Jake," she said. "I'm going to personally see you are taken care of."

I wasn't feeling as optimistic as she was.

"Mrs. Newton, are you aware of what happened?"

"Yes, Ryan told Richard and me all about the poker game, how you didn't want to go, and about telling you to drive the Corvette. He was afraid Richard was going to fire him."

The look on her face suddenly changed. It was stern, and she had an intense look in her eyes.

"I run this outfit you've been working for Jake Roberts, not Mr. Newton."

I was shocked! If that was the case, she kept it well hidden. Her words caused me to think back to meetings, and jobs Ryan and I had done for the family. I would have never guessed it was Mrs. Newton running the show. Still, I had no doubt about what she was telling me.

"I am very appreciative of you keeping silent about why you and Ryan were here in Jersey, and for taking the fall for Ryan for this mess he created," she said, smiling. "As I told you, Jake, I will see to it you are taken care of. You are loyal and true to me, and I shall be the same."

Mrs. Newton told me she had to go back to Virginia and was going to leave. She handed me a thick envelope, keys to a rental car, and a note with the address of the attorney. She said I had an appointment to see the attorney at ten that morning. She left the restaurant, and I sat there for a while pondering over all she had told me. So it was Mrs. Newton, who ran the show, I'll be a son of a gun, imagine that.

I looked inside the envelope and saw it was full of fifty and one-hundred-dollar bills.

The address of the attorney was smack in the middle of town amid all the high-rises. I never liked city driving, and I was nervous that the police might be following me. I had to try to shake off the paranoia.

When I got to the attorney's office, his secretary rang him, and he was there right away. He led me to his office and started talking to me as if we had been friends all our lives. He said his name was Randy Smith. He appeared to be well mannered. He had an air about him that demanded respect.

Mr. Smith sat in his chair for a few minutes and rattled off things he already knew about me. He had obtained quite a bit of information in a short time. It showed me that he was a worker, and he'd been doing some real homework.

"Jake," he said. "I was on the phone with Mrs. Newton just prior to your arrival. A few minutes before that, I was on the phone with Judge Kraus, and before that, with the prosecuting attorney. I'm going to lay it on the line son; it's not that bad, but it's also not good.

I felt a lump in my throat, and my heart started beating faster as he continued. "Judge Kraus says he is sick and tired of car thieves in this state. He says that car thefts are rampant here in New Jersey, and he has the power to do something about it. You being from out of state don't help matters much. The judge wants to make an example out of you."

"I didn't steal the car, why won't anyone listen to me? It's all a big mistake!"

"Just calm down Jacob and let me finish. Now you and I both know you didn't steal the car, but to Judge Kraus, you did, and he isn't going to hear otherwise. H e thinks you're guilty and that's all that matters. It's a bit prejudice but its reality."

I stood up from my chair. "It doesn't sound as if you think I'm innocent, and I came here thinking you were on my side and were going to help me!" I flopped back down in the chair. Smith could tell I was angry and getting more frustrated by the minute.

"I spoke with the prosecuting attorney. He is willing to cut a deal." Smith said.

"What do you mean cut a deal? I'll be found innocent because they don't have a thing that proves I stole that car."

"Shut up for a minute, Mr. Roberts, and let me explain something to you. So you think you want to go to trial? Let me see here; you were driving the car, and it wasn't yours. You were speeding. You didn't have a registration nor were you able to tell the police who the rightful owner was, because you didn't know. So tell me, Mr. Roberts, just what do you think a jury is going to do, let you off scot free on your good looks and your kind words?" Smith was fuming and flustered. "You're screwed Jake, I don't know how else to put it do you. I'll help you with this to the best of my ability, but my friend, YOU'RE SCREWED!"

The room was silent for a minute before Smith spoke again. "Jake, you have no prior arrest record. Although you did have some trouble in West Virginia, a few years back - for stealing! You aren't part of some gang, you have good grades in college, and Mrs. Newton is the key, she can get you a minimum sentence."

I collapsed back in the chair. "Mr. Smith, I don't want to go to jail. Oh Lord, please help me."

"The judge wants to make you an example, as I've already said. I can't change his mind.

Shane Kraus is the toughest judge in New Jersey. That means seven to ten years Jake. I've spoken with the prosecuting attorney, who happens to know Mrs. Newton quite well. He is willing to recommend to the judge you get one year, if you agree, otherwise we'll be in court. And, if we are in court Jake, I don't have a good way to defend you."

I sat there for a few minutes, stunned. How did I get to this point? Why has this happened to me? I had two choices and neither of them good because both meant going to jail.

"Mr. Smith, I guess for being a fool I'm about to lose an entire year of my life." I said in a voice so low it was barely audible.

I signed a plea bargain, and Smith took it to the prosecuting attorney's office the following day. The two of them talked then went to see the judge. It wasn't fair. Regardless, I wasn't going to rat Ryan out and I'd made a pledge to protect the Newton's, and I was going to stick to my word no matter what.

The judge wasn't willing to take a sentence reduced to only twelve months. After a lot of arguing, the judge said he would accept seventeen months and nothing less. I wasn't there, but Smith agreed to the seventeen months. Little did I know; the agreement I had signed gave the judge authority to put me in jail for any length of time he felt was appropriate, as long as it was less than the maximum sentence.

I was angry when I got the news. It was a done deal, and I couldn't change it. I blamed Smith. I felt like he'd misled me, and it was going to cost me five additional months of my life. I hated lawyers even though I was studying to be one. I was angry. I was also worried. What else had Smith done that I hadn't agreed to? How would I survive in prison? Just when it seemed my life was getting good, this had to happen.

Chapter 19

Mrs. Newton did take care of me. She came back to New Jersey and went with Mr. Smith when he saw the judge again. They say money can't buy happiness, but it sure carries a lot of weight. Mrs. Newton asked the judge to put me in a minimum-security prison where politicians and white-collar criminals are incarcerated. He agreed to that if I would start my sentence immediately. He said there was an opening at the prison, and he wanted me off the street now.

The prison was just outside of Princeton. I was dreading being locked up. I feared being someone's sex slave or having to join a gang and get my body covered in tattoos.

When I arrived at the prison, I saw there was a fence around the compound but no razor wire. I also saw tennis courts and a swimming pool. I was handcuffed while riding in an unmarked van. As soon as we entered the compound, one of the two officers accompanying me took the cuffs off and led me to the warden's office.

For nearly two hours, I sat while the warden talked. He told me all about the facility and the amenities it had to offer, and warned me about my behavior. He said I was blessed to be there but the least little screw up, and I'd be transferred to a maximum-security lock-up. He also said my sentence would be extended. The warden said it was easy to escape, but asked why I would want to leave a country club setting and take a chance on being shot.

After the meeting with the warden was over, a guard led me to my cell. I had a nice cell to myself. It had a full-size bed, a desk, and a television. The warden was right these weren't bad quarters.

I was required to work each day for five hours. Since I was the new inmate, I was given kitchen duty. I had to help prepare meals for everyone. It was hard for me to believe that I was in prison and had access to knives and all sorts of weapons.

There were no gangs, but everyone hated me. To them, I was just a hillbilly hick from West Virginia and didn't deserve to be in their prison. I'd not served in any office, nor was I established in the business community. I didn't fit into their mold. All the inmates shunned me, which was fine. I didn't think any of them could hold a decent conversation anyway. I liked being alone. It gave me more time to think. The downside was I had too much time to think.

Visitors were allowed on weekends. On the first Saturday, Ryan came to visit me. It wasn't like on television where we had to talk on a phone through a thick glass window with a cop listening with every word. We were allowed to sit in a lounge for two hours drinking sodas and eating pastries.

Ryan told me that Mr. Newton was very upset with him and wanted to fire him. The only reason he didn't, was Mrs. Newton wouldn't let him.

"Did you know that Mrs. Newton actually is the one who runs everything, not Mr. Newton?" He said.

"Yes, Mrs. Newton told me that."

"I couldn't believe it," Ryan said.

Ryan got a serious look on his face. For one of the few times since I'd known Ryan Tyler, he looked at me with genuine tears in his eyes.

"Jake. I don't even know what to say. It would have been so easy for you to rat me out, and to tell the police. Instead, you said nothing about the poker game. You also didn't mention how you got the Corvette. You've taken the fall for something that was one hundred percent my fault. I'm going to make it up to you, please believe that."

"It's hard, Ryan. I can't deny that, it's very hard, but it is what it is. I want to think if the shoe was on the other foot you would do the same for me."

Ryan continued his weekly visits, and once I got a visit from Mr. and Mrs. Newton. I felt like they were family. They let me know that once I got out of prison, they wanted me to come back to work for them. I felt like I had grown so much and was appreciative for what they had done for me. Being in prison wasn't their fault, and they easily could have turned their backs on me. I told them that as soon as I got out of prison, I'd come to see them.

The time went by slowly. I was antsy about getting back to the outside. I wanted to start a new life, free of crime. I was hoping Mrs. Newton could find something for me that paid decent money and didn't involve moving unidentified packages. When she told me to come and see her as soon as I got out, I knew she meant what she said.

With less than two months before my release, Ryan didn't come to visit on Saturday. I was hurt, and didn't understand. Was he injured? Was he upset with me? I was stuck in there, not knowing much about the outside world aside from the national news on television. I looked forward to Saturdays when Ryan would visit. I could relate to Ryan. We share common interest, unlike the inmates. I was hurt, then angry. I felt betrayed.

Why would Ryan suddenly not come see me? I was close to getting out of that joint. The following Saturday was the same, no Ryan. I was beginning to worry that something had happened to him. Ryan was prone to finding trouble so anything could have happened.

Thomas Bailey was in the cell next to me. He was a studious sort of man, always reading the newspaper from cover to cover. He would talk for hours on end about the stock market and what he felt were good investments. Although he had only been there for a few weeks, we had become friends. He didn't play the silly games the others there played. It didn't matter to him where I had come from or how I'd gotten there.

Thomas knocked on the wall one afternoon after he had been reading the paper.

"Hey, didn't you tell me you were from Roanoke, Virginia?'

"I'm not from there, but I live there," I replied.

"Didn't you say your friend's name is Ryan Tyler?"

My heart sank. Oh God, he was reading an obituary. Was it a car wreck? Could it have been a plane crash? I knew Ryan was dead.

I was scared to hear what Thomas was about to tell me, but at the same time it was agony not knowing. I just wished he'd blurt out the news so I could hear what had happened.

"Yeah, his name is Ryan Tyler, why?"

"Well, according to the paper he won the damn lottery. He won $19 million dollars, the lucky bastard."

"What!"

"Yeah, says '*Roanoke man, Ryan Tyler, bought the winning ticket for the multi-state lottery at the Jack-n-Jill convenient store on Hart Street. He matched all five numbers plus the powerball, winning the twenty-fifth largest jackpot in the game's history, and the second person from Virginia to ever win.*' Goes on to say that Tyler elected to take a one-time cash payoff of $11.4 million."

"Don't go shittin me Bailey," I said.

Bailey reached the paper around the bars from his cell to mine.

"Well hell, read it yourself Roberts."

I grabbed the paper. *Could this be real? Could this be the same Ryan Tyler?* My mind was racing in twenty different directions. It had to be Ryan. I read the article three times. I knew where the convenience store was located. Ryan and I had delivered packages there on several occasions. Holy cow!

I sat down to read the article for the fourth time and noticed the newspaper was over a week old. That was why Ryan hadn't been here, but why didn't he contact me to let me know. Was he going to contact me? Surely there was a valid reason, we were best of friends. Now he was rich, just as he had always wanted to be.

I lay on the bed for a long time trying to imagine how all this could have taken place, and where Ryan was right now. I also thought about how Ryan had reached his goal in life to have ten million dollars. He could quit gambling now, and settle down forever to enjoy the finer things in life. I remember telling him he would never stop. I wondered which of us would be right.

The rest of that week, I kept thinking I heard a guard call my name saying that I had a visitor, but it was my brain playing tricks on me. Special visits were allowed on weekdays if the warden permitted, and surely, he would let Ryan see me.

On Saturday, I was excited, because I knew Ryan would be there to visit me. It was almost four in the afternoon and visitation was nearly over, still no Ryan.

My heart sank, and I was feeling low. Then a guard came to my cell and said I had a phone call. No visitor he said, but a phone call. As the guard led me to the visitor area where the phones are located, he seemed to move extra slow. I wanted to push him along, speed him up. It seemed like an eternity getting there, and I was afraid no one would be on the line when I got to the phone.

Finally, we got to the phone, and I picked up the receiver. It was Ryan. I was elated! He told me all about the legal mess of getting his money, how he had bought the ticket by letting the computer pick, when in the past he had never done so, he had always picked the numbers himself. We both laughed at that knowing how lucky he'd always been.

Ryan went on to say he had met with the Newton's and discussed things with them. Ryan was going to end employment with them as soon as he cleared up a project that he was helping them with in Florida, to buy a resort near Orlando. The deal was closing the next week.

Ryan said he had sent several messages to the prison, to inform me about what had happened. The messages were to let me know he was stuck in Florida on the final project for Mr. Newton. I told him I never got the messages.

"The woman who took the messages didn't seem very enthusiastic about taking them," Ryan said.

My time was nearly up, but the guard knew I hadn't had a visitor in a few weeks. He was a nice man, and he told me he'd give me another ten minutes. Ryan and I went on talking, and he told me he wouldn't be able to make it up here for the remaining three weeks I had to serve.

He asked me to get a passport as soon as I got out and join him in Europe. He was going on a two-month vacation to Europe and wanted me to catch up with him. He said he had a few poker games lined up in Europe. That's when I reminded him of his goal, to quit after he won ten million dollars.

"Oh yeah, I forgot about that," he chuckled.

I told Ryan I needed to go see Mrs. Newton first then I would think about joining him. He insisted I get the passport. I asked him to find out if a felon could even get a passport. He said he'd research it for me but was sure I could. Besides, I was going to serve my full sentence, and that should count for something. If not he suggested Mrs. Newton, she could make things happen when no one else could.

"I want you to work for me Jake," he said. "I'll pay you more than you could ever dream of earning with the Newtons, and all you have to do is nothing!"

The guard came over to me, informing me I had to hang up the telephone. I told Ryan I had to go.

"Go to our bank in Roanoke when you get back home, and ask for Mr. Boylen," Ryan said. Then he hung up the phone.

Chapter 20

Before I could be released from prison, I had to meet again with the warden. I think he talked longer as I was about to exit the prison than he did when I arrived. I didn't understand all the details but he said that since I served my full term there was no probation period. That was great, I wouldn't have to come back to meet with a parole officer. I told the warden I had nothing against the great State of New Jersey.

"However, make no mistake about it I wouldn't be back," I said.

He laughed and said he understood.

My driver's license had expired while I was in prison so the warden was able to get me a temporary New

Jersey license that would suffice until I got a new one in Virginia. He said it wasn't too much of a problem since I had been in the state long enough to become a resident, then he laughed again.

I rented a car and headed straight for Virginia. It felt wonderful being on the open road, and it felt great being free again. The prison had been all one could ever hope for if you had to be incarcerated, but there was nothing like freedom. I felt like a caged animal that had been set free.

When I got back to Roanoke, I went to the apartment. I found the key Ryan had hidden for me. I didn't think we'd be living there much longer, but for the time I'd spent there the memories were mostly pleasant ones. I went inside and all the things in my room were just as I had left them seventeen months ago, except for a layer of household dust.

It was late in the evening so I went to the market for a few things, then came back to the apartment and sat on the balcony until the sun went down. It was late December and even with extra clothing the chill in the air went to my bones.

I had plan to drive over to see Mrs. Newton the next morning. I wanted to run by the bank before doing so, and see this Mr. Boylen, whom Ryan had asked me to visit.

When I got to the bank, the teller directed me to the second floor, room 202. I had been in that bank many times and never realized there was a second floor. When I got to the top of the stairs, there was a receptionist. She was very polite. She asked who I had come to see. I told her and she rang Mr. Boylen.

An older man who looked to be near retirement age approached me with his hand extended. Although he was about my height and weight, he looked much more muscular than I was. It was hard for me to get a good grasp as I shook his large strong hand. I wasn't that kind of hand from a banker who sits at a desk most of the day. His face was red, indicating he'd, either, stayed too long in a tanning bed, or he'd recently taken a tropical vacation.

"I've been expecting you, I'm Ed Boylen," he said.

He led me to his office, which was quite large. The walls were decorated with what appeared to be original oil paintings. They reminded me of the ones in the Newtons house. I wondered how well Mr. Boylen knew the Newtons.

"Have a seat and let me go to the vault and get a package for you."

He left for a few minutes then returned with a sealed manila envelope.

"I know about the contents," he said. "Go ahead, open it up, then I can answer any questions you may have."

He was giddy and excited as he watched me open the envelope. There were three things inside the envelope. One was a letter from a local GM dealership. It said I was to come to their lot and pick out the car or truck of my choice. I sat there staring at it for a moment. It was very touching. I was excited, yet a bit in denial about it being real. Mr. Boylen sat across from me at his desk smiling the entire time. He was watching a grown man open a Christmas package all wide eyed like a six year old.

The second thing in the package was a standard white envelope bulging from its contents. I opened it and found a bundle of one-hundred dollar bills and a brochure from Charlotte International Airport. There was also a note from Ryan and a list of telephone numbers. His instructions were to purchase a ticket to Europe. I was to call him, find out what city he would be in, and go there. He wanted me there in five days, January, third.

The third item in the envelope was a sealed letter from the bank. I broke the seal and opened the letter. It stated that one-million dollars, was being held in a trust for me. It was payable after I had fulfilled the request made by

174

the other two items, picking out the car, and getting on a plane to Europe to meet Ryan. I read the letter three times aloud, and was starting to read it a fourth time when Boylen broke my concentration. I was trying to comprehend everything. I thought I was dreaming.

Mr. Boylen handed me a key to a safe deposit box. He said I could deposit the trust note there and once I got back from my vacation all I had to do was come see him and collect the money.

Boylen even brought up the passport. He said that Mrs. Newton had been in contact with him and had obtained a letter from the President of the United States to allow me to get a passport. He showed me the letter. I was impressed with the letterhead and it had the president's signature. I know she had to pull some strings, to have done that. Boylen told me they had a department there in the bank where I could get the passport. He called ahead to ensure I was taken care of promptly.

Mrs. Newton must have pulled more strings. There was no waiting period. I left the bank with a passport in my hand. I went and sat in the rental car for a while thinking. The last few days had seemed like a dream, none of it had really taken hold of me, I was still expecting to awaken and be in my jail cell.

Mrs. Newton wasn't home when I arrived at her house, but she had been expecting me and had left me a note to come back at six o'clock, stating there'd be dinner and a party afterward.

I went to the automobile dealership and picked out a four-wheel drive GMC pickup truck. It wasn't the most expensive one they had on the lot nor did it have any fancy gadgets. It was candy apple red and had a standard transmission. It was wonderful, and something I'd always dreamed of having.

That evening, twenty guests were seated at the Newton's table for dinner. I was placed at the head of the table and a toast was made on my behalf, although I wasn't sure for what reason. Mr. Newton stood up and gave a speech about me, saying many boastful things that weren't true. I was embarrassed and blushed continuously. Still, I savored the moment and had a great evening.

Mrs. Newton spoke to me after dinner, saying she knew what Ryan had done for me at the bank. She suggested that I go join my friend in Europe and live life up for a while. She asked if I had gotten the passport and I said I had. Mrs. Newton said that the president owed her a few favors. She said that if he had been in office when I got into trouble with the Corvette, she would have been able to get me pardoned.

She also said if I ever got bored and wanted a good job she would provide one for me. Mrs. Newton then told me I needed to go back to the bank again tomorrow and check my account. She had added an additional three hundred-thousand dollars in my account as a compensatory gift for the jail time I'd served.

"You left the Newton name out of that disaster. Although I can't give you back nearly a year and a half, I can make your future more comfortable," she said.

Mrs. Newton walked away, then went and got plastered. She said she was losing both of the true men in her life and felt a good one coming on. I sat and watched people mingle for a few hours then left. Mrs. Newton didn't approach me about a trip to the bathroom to ravish me, but that night if she had, I would have gone.

Chapter 21

I had a difficult time getting in contact with Ryan. He'd been traveling from city to city and country to country. Finally, I was able to track him down in Paris. He told me to get a flight to London. The telephone connection was bad but I was able to confirm that he would meet me in England. I was to fly first class and he would make the rest of the arrangements.

The flight from Charlotte, North Carolina to London was ten hours and twenty minutes. I didn't like thinking that most of that flight was over water. I suppose that it didn't matter if a plane went down on land or in water. However, if I had any chance of surviving the initial crash, I didn't want it to be in the ocean, where I would drown, or be eaten by sharks.

As I boarded the wide body jet, the flight attendant looked at my boarding pass and motioned for me to go left into first class. I'd only flown two other times before, both being on the Newton's private plane, and I'd always had my gun.

With no weapon, I felt half-dressed, and insecure. I don't know why I felt that way. Since I'd gotten out of prison, I was afraid to carry a gun and had left it hidden in the apartment. The last thing I needed was to be pulled over by the police and they find out I had an unregistered gun on me and no conceal carry permit.

I was nearly the last passenger to board and I couldn't help notice the plane was only three-quarters full. I'd heard on the news that airlines were struggling to fill international flights because of so much terrorist activity worldwide over the last few months. It seemed to me the whole world had gone nuts, nothing seemed normal anymore. I moved along the aisle to my seat, located next to a window as I had requested.

I enjoyed looking out and seeing the earth below, wondering who lived there and what their lives were like. I'm sure their lives were for the most part ordinary, just like mine. After giving that more thought, I doubted their lives were like mine.

My life had been a roller coaster for a long time, and was far from normal. Since Ryan hit the lottery, my life had already changed again. Now it was going to be a smooth ride instead of a roller coaster. I was on a jumbo jet leaving behind all the things that were familiar. It wasn't the first time I had left everything familiar behind, but this time it was on a much broader scale.

Although Ryan hadn't said it, I knew the reason he wanted to meet me in London. It was because of a big poker game. He liked me being with him when he played. He also felt guilty about me spending time in jail, so I expected he was going to do something special.

I didn't mind going to his poker games. It had been a while since I'd seen my highly gifted friend in action doing his thing, and it would be good to join up with him again for some laughs. I was certain we'd also have some time to talk about old times as well as the future. I knew Ryan wouldn't quit playing cards, and now I could only imagine the high stakes games he'd be playing in.

As I peered through the window, we were over water and above the clouds. As I stared out at the clouds below, my mind drifted. I was out of prison and feeling good. In the last few weeks, I'd gone from feeling sorry for myself, sitting in a jail cell thinking no one cared about me, to having my friend back and being a millionaire.

Jake Roberts a millionaire. That just hadn't sunk in yet. What will I do with that kind of money? My plans were to first visit Janet and Bernice when I got back to see if they needed anything. After that, I could tour the country for a few months. I was certain I'd be bored by then and want to go back to work for Mrs. Newton.

The plane landed safely and pulled into terminal one at Heathrow. I didn't like airports, the breakneck speed, running to get from place to place and having to fight the crowds. Security guards gave me the creeps too. They look at you with evil eyes, waiting for you to do something stupid so they can plant your face into the concrete floor just for fun. I'd been there before, and didn't want to experience it again.

I'm sure there are plenty of good cops out there, I'd just never found one yet. Then again, if I hadn't been involved in criminal activity, I suppose I wouldn't have to worry so much. Cops had never done anything to me while I was doing right, only when I was doing something bad.

During the flight, I had spoken briefly with a very nice looking English woman who sat across the aisle from me. She was curious, and kept asking me questions. I didn't tell her I'd just gotten out of prison and went to a bank to discover I was a millionaire - as if she'd believe such a story anyway. She told me she loved my accent and it didn't matter to her what I said, as long as I was saying something.

After we landed and stood to exit the plane, she handed me her business card and told me to call her if I found some time. She said she would show me around London town. As I put my hand out to take the card, she leaned into me and planted a kiss on my cheek. She smelled as pretty as she looked. I instantly blushed, which seemed to make her want to tease me more. She blew me another kiss then walked away. I could see her firm buttocks through her tight skirt.

I was hoping that was just the beginning of how life would be during my trip to Great Britain, all pleasure and plenty of it. I thought that perhaps after spending some time with Ryan, I could give the woman a call and take her up on her offer.

I stood there, caught up in the moment, until the passenger behind me said, "how about moving it buddy the broad's gone now."

As I walked down the ramp and onto the tarmac, I took a deep breath, hoping to take in the smell of the old country. Instead, all I got in my nostrils was half burned jet fuel that sent me into a coughing spell.

I picked the pace up and entered the building in more of a hurry than I should have. I tripped over a briefcase some idiot had set down while talking to a flight attendant, and nearly fell face first. I recovered nicely and blended back in with the crowd before too many people noticed. It was something I would have enjoyed seeing, and likely would have laughed at, if I hadn't been the one who had tripped.

As we walked along the narrow corridor into the terminal, the space opened up. It revealed thousands of people moving in all directions, boarding planes, exiting planes, heading for the food courts, or the rest rooms. It was a mad house, and although I liked to people watch, I was antsy. I didn't know where to go or how to find Ryan. I was hoping he'd be there to find me. I tried following the others from my flight, hoping they would lead me to the baggage claim area.

I felt a hand touch my shoulder and thought some weirdo was already hitting me up for a quarter. As I turned, I saw an older man about my size. He had thick graying eyebrows and a thick push-broom mustache. He was dressed in a black suit with a jacket like chauffeurs wear, and a chauffeur's hat.

"Excuse me," he said. "You must be Sir Roberts."

"Sir Roberts," I said, with a voice that screamed with sarcasm.

"Sir," he replied, with his forehead wrinkled, not understanding what I had said.

I realized I was as out of place there as a fish out of water. My accent was going to be hard for people to understand. I didn't know the customs. I also didn't know how those people would react to my sense of humor.

"Yes, I'm Roberts, who are you?"

"I'm Johnson, Sir."

"Johnson. Dang, that's a good ole American name."

"I see, Sir."

"No, seriously, that's a common name in America."

Johnson cleared his throat. "Come along sir, I'll take you to the car, it is waiting."

"Wait a minute, Johnson. I've got to find my luggage first."

"That's been arranged for you, Sir."

"What do you mean it's been arranged? I just arrived and nobody here has a clue what my bags look like."

"Trust me Sir, your bags will be gathered and not a bloody one will be lost."

Now I detected a bit of sarcasm in ole Johnson's voice, and with a good thick English accent.

"You're alright, Johnson. I'm going to enjoy your company."

We started down the corridor and I asked Johnson if he was going to take me to see Ryan Tyler.

"Those are my instructions Sir. It's a long ride to South Hampton and we shall stop for a bit of lunch along the way."

I decided it was best not to mess too much with Johnson for now. He knew how to get me out of this place. I was as lost as a ball in high weeds.

I jokingly thought that the car would to be a Bentley, with a driver named James. Instead, it was a 1970 Rolls Royce Silver Shadow and the driver was my friend Johnson. The car appeared to be in good condition, but I couldn't help notice it was dusty as if it had been driven on a dirt road somewhere. In the movies there was always someone with a white hanky wiping specks of dust off the car when the passenger arrived, this car was far from that.

"Do you own this car Johnson?"

"I do, Sir."

"I've never seen a Rolls Royce before Johnson, how much is it worth?"

"The original retail was fifteen-thousand-five-hundred pounds, sir."

I was quickly finding that many things were different there in England. I knew those folks spoke English. I just didn't see how we could speak the same language and it sound so different. I didn't want to come on as being too much of a smart-aleck but I was so tempted to say "Fifteen-thousand-five-hundred-pounds of what?"

Johnson opened the door for me to climb into the limo. I'd just gotten off a nearly eleven-hour flight and needed to stand. I told Johnson I'd just stand there until the bags arrived. Johnson didn't respond. He just stood there all stiff like, holding the door open. Finally, two men with a large flat cart approached us with my two bags onboard. Johnson went around and opened the trunk. I climbed into the car. I heard the trunk close then Johnson opened the driver's side door and got in.

The steering wheel was on the right and all the controls appeared to all be out of kilter. I really didn't see how he could drive that thing, but Johnson soon proved to be quite a driver. I was amazed at his ability to negotiate the London traffic.

The car zoomed in and out of traffic as we left the airport and entered the freeway. We were on M25. As best I could tell, highways in England that started with an M were the equivalent of an interstate back home. With a five-hour time difference, I calculated it was around noon in London.

I told Johnson I was extremely hungry and asked if we could stop for some food. I was hoping for a place that served breakfast food, but at that moment, anything would do. Johnson said we would be stopping for tea in Basingstoke, about an hour drive. I had gotten some peanuts on the plane and still had some in my pocket. I munched on them, hoping they would hold me over until we got some real food.

When we got to the town of Basingstoke, the first thing I saw as we left the M highway was an American fast food joint. I most certainly was hoping that wasn't where Johnson was going to stop. Not that I was against fast food, but I was ready for something different, this was England for crying aloud. Johnson slowed the car down and I'll be gosh dang if he didn't pull into the drive-through lane of the fast food place. I don't know if he always drove that way or if he was messing with my head. He kept going straight through the fast food restaurant parking lot and into an alleyway behind the restaurant.

We pulled directly in front of a small cafe called 'The Bassett Hound'. I chuckled and asked Johnson if they served hot dogs. For the first time since we'd met, Johnson produced a smile then laughed very loud.

"If you are in agreement to eat here, I do rather fancy the place. It has ordinary victuals but they are extraordinarily pleasing to the palate." He said, looking at me through the rear view mirror.

"Johnson, ole chap, I'll take your word for it, let's eat."

The Bassett Hound wasn't anything fancy inside, but it was clean and reminded me of a 1950's style diner. They served everything on the menu all day, including breakfast. I ordered what they called the 'coup and sty'. I could have come up with a much better name for a ham and egg platter, but it was good food and I was grateful to get some real country cooking.

Johnson ordered some weird burger that had BBQ sauce, bacon, and a fried hotdog wiener on top that was split down the middle. It wasn't at all appealing to me but Johnson seemed to enjoy it.

He had his napkin stuffed into the top of his shirt and he held the burger way out in front of his body with his neck stretched out. I suppose that was to prevent getting the BBQ sauce on his suit. Holding the burger firmly with both hands he rotated it slightly each time he took a bite, as if it was on a lathe being whittled down. We ate and Johnson took care of the tab. We got back into the car for another hour of riding before reaching South Hampton.

When we got to South Hampton, Johnson pulled up to the Green Lantern Hotel next to Mayflower Park. I recognized that it was a Georgian style building. He said that it had been there since the 1750's. They had added onto the hotel several times in the back, but the front and lobby were still original. The hotel sat in the old section of South Hampton, perched on a small rise, giving a spectacular view of the waterfront.

The artwork and the stonework were outstanding. Johnson told me that Queen Victoria herself had stayed there on numerous occasions. Although I'd heard of Queen Victoria, I didn't have a clue what time-period she lived in. It meant much more to Johnson than to me, but still it was nice to know royalty had slept here.

Johnson stopped the car in front of the hotel, got out, removed my bags from the trunk, and sat them on the brick sidewalk. I walked to the back of the car to thank him and present a tip, but he held his hands up.

"Not necessary, sir, everything has already been taken care of."

A bellman came over to us with a cart and loaded the bags. I reached out to shake Johnson's hand. I could tell from his face that it was a peculiar thing to him. He extended his hand reluctantly. After we shook hand's he got in the car and drove off.

The bellman was a tall kid. He looked to be in his late teens, at best. He had an ear-to-ear smile that spoke to you saying, "I've got a great personality." I was feeling good and wanted to play with the bellman a bit, just for fun.

"This way, sir," he remarked.

"What's yer name?" I replied, in a good ole hillbilly accent.

He stopped the cart as if he couldn't do two things at one time, turned to me and said with a heavy British accent "Laroy, sir."

"Leroy."

"No, it's Laroy, sir."

"Well, Leroy, I'm Jake. And you don't have to call me sir."

"Yes sir."

I was a bit tired or else I would've played with ole Laroy a bit more. He must have attended the same personally school Johnson attended. He wasn't going to be much fun. I followed him down a long corridor to an elevator. We stepped on and went to the fourteenth floor. We got off the elevator, turned right, and stopped at room 1406. There was a note taped to the door that said, "See me in room 1400 at 4:00 p.m., Ryan."

I smiled, and thought, *Ryan, has done well making all these arrangements. He must have something big planned.* Laroy opened the door, took the bags inside, and sat them down. He turned and looked at me with his big smile.

"Will there be anything else, sir?"

"No sir, oh, but a tip, wait just a minute," as I reached for my wallet.

"It's been taken care of, sir," Laroy said, still smiling, as he turned and left.

The suite was huge. It had a living room with a large circular couch, bar, regular size refrigerator, large screen television, dining area, kitchen, and separate bedroom. The bedroom was huge also, king size bed, sofa, three chairs, another large screen television, and a pool table of all things. I'd never seen a pool table in a bedroom and it made me wonder if it was a common thing in Great Britain.

There was a large bathroom in the main living area and another off the bedroom. I didn't count the telephones but there must have been a dozen or more. Overall, the suite was more like a small apartment than a hotel room. The bedroom and living room both had large glass windows that gave a fantastic view of the waterfront. I stood there for a few minutes, watching the boats and ships going up and down the waterway.

I looked at my watch and realized I was still on US Eastern Time, so I set it for the current time in England. I had some time to kill before meeting Ryan. I stretched out on the bed for a bit, then unpacked my bags and took a nice warm shower.

When I got to Ryan's room, I knocked several times, but got no answer. As I started back toward my room, the elevator door opened and Ryan stepped out. We greeted each other with a hug and a pat on the back. It was good to see a friendly familiar face. We walked back toward Ryan's room and went inside.

"These are quite some arrangements you have made Ryan. Something big must be up," I said.

"What do you think is up?"

"It's got to be a poker game, that's why I'm here. I'm you're lucky rabbit's foot," I said, while laughing.

Ryan reared his head back, also laughing.

"POKER GAME," he said loudly. "Sit down, and let me tell you about it."

I could tell Ryan was about to bust inside if he didn't get the information out.

"It's a level ten game, Jake."

"Say again, Ryan."

"I said, it's a level ten game, and I'm playing."

"Good grief, Ryan, that's the top of the tier, and a million dollar game if I remember the rules correctly."

"That's right," he said. "I've got more money than I can ever spend, and I've been lucky all my life. I wanted nothing more than to get to this place, and here I am."

He was excited beyond measure. I leaned back while looking at Ryan.

"Just think Ryan, an ole country boy from West Virginia who started out stealing soda pop bottles grew up to hit a multi-state lottery. Now you're in England to play in a poker game where millions of dollars will change hands."

Ryan was shaking his head in agreement and excitement. We went out and sat on the balcony off his living room. The air was crisp but the view was fantastic and we stayed for a long time talking and taking in the site. It was wonderful being in the presence of my good friend once again.

The next morning we had breakfast in one of the three hotel restaurants. I felt out of place again. I was too much of a country boy to feel comfortable in those surroundings. Ryan, on the other hand, was where he wanted to be. The casino in New Jersey was bigger than this place, but nowhere near as fancy.

We sat down at the table and I quickly determined there were too many dishes, forks, spoons, and cups sitting there for the two of us. Cloth napkins, I'd only used them when dining at the Newton's house. I hoped no one was expecting me to tuck it over the top button on my shirt. Having men in white suits stand behind me, watching while I ate, also made me nervous.

Every time I put my fork down a man in a white suit grabbed it and put a clean one down in its place. I'm an elbows on the table, slurp up my food kind of man. I didn't like anyone touching my plate or utensils until I was through eating. If momma had been there, she'd slapped their hands and given them a good cursing.

The restaurant was nearly full. Everyone was wearing expensive clothing and talking in proper British English. They all held their teacups with the end of two fingers as if they didn't want to get dirty from the cup. I whispered over to Ryan while we were waiting for our food.

"Ryan, we are new money, this is old money. We aren't ever going to fit in with this crowd."

"That's part of my strategy," he said. "I don't want to fit into this crowd. I want them to think I'm ignorant and uneducated. This is just practice. I detest these arrogant people! When we get to the game, I'll put on the same show. It'll make 'em cocky, and they'll think I can't possibly win then WHAM, I'll put it to 'em. We'll smoke their twelve-dollar cigars and drink their twenty-five year old scotch, all the while displaying our backward hillbilly manners. It'll annoy the crap out of them, and you know what else, Jake? When they're annoyed, they aren't on top of their game. I want them to think they are better than I am. I want them to feel more in control, and smarter. I'm going to either clean them out or go home broke."

I knew Ryan meant what he said. He figured this was a chance to rub elbows with the cream of the crop. If he lost, he would never be able to recover enough money to play in this league again. If he won, they'd find a way to push him out because he wasn't of the same breed as them; he knew that.

Ryan said he wanted me to be there, said we'd always be a team and that I brought him luck. He went on to say I was his friend, his best friend, and he wanted me to be there because of that most of all.

"I have a lot to make up to you, Jake. We've only begun to live my friend. We may go home and have to dig into our stash to live, but even at that, it'll be a better life than we've ever known."

Ryan looked at me. I could tell he was reading my thoughts just from the expression on my face. He was an expert at that. He laughed loud enough to where others were now looking toward our table.

"Oh yeah, I got a stash at home, buddy, we don't have to worry if I have a bad night. That won't happen though. I've been in Europe for a few weeks and I've been to Italy, Spain, France, and Portugal. So far - let me think now. Yes, so far, I've won over four-hundred-thousand dollars. Damn, I love this Jake, I just love this."

We finished breakfast then went shopping in a clothing store inside the hotel. The attire for the game that evening was dressy casual and we needed the proper clothes. Ryan told the clerk we were going to a very high-level business meeting but wanted to appear as though we had just left the clubhouse. Ryan was acting goofy and using a good hillbilly accent. It was still part of his act for the upcoming poker game. I hoped he knew what he was doing. As always, I was the cautious one.

The bill for our clothing was more than we paid for six month's rent on the apartment in Roanoke. I didn't like the pants they sold. All of them contained a high percentage of wool. I knew they were going to make me itch and was afraid I'd be walking around scratching everything from my ankles to my crotch. Then I'd be the one putting on a show!

A Rolls Royce limo picked us up in front of the hotel at 4:30 P.M. Unlike Johnson's older car, this one was pristine. The driver opened the door for Ryan and me to step in. We were ready to take a ride in style. The inside of the car was indescribable. Made from the finest materials and everything was plush. It even had a bar. The driver took us down to the waterfront and then a couple miles downstream to Pier 26.

The area was full of large yachts that resembled ships more than yachts. There were two security officers standing at the end of the pier. When we got to their position, they asked for our identification, and announced we would have to be searched for weapons. One of them had a guest list and I saw our names were on it.

After conducting the search, the security officers directed us to walk out the pier a hundred yards or more, where we saw two more security guards standing. We walked down the pier. As we approached the guards, they motioned for us to turn right, and walk down Pier 27. It was another long pier, and ran perpendicular to the one we'd just walked.

On Pier 27, we walked alongside a huge yacht, a football field or more in length. When we got near the bow end of the ship, a walkway was in place leading from the pier to the main deck of the yacht. At the bottom of the walkway, we met a stately looking older man dressed in a twill suit jacket and hat.

"Welcome friends, you must be Sir Tyler and Sir Roberts."

The 'sir' think was starting to wear on my nerves. No one said it with any degree of sincerity, so to me, it was useless saying it in the context in which it was being spoken.

The man spoke with a different accent than anyone I'd met in Great Britain thus far. I was guessing that he was Irish.

We followed the man up the ramp and onto the yacht's main deck. Ryan and I were both impressed. Up until the time that the limo driver dropped Ryan and I off we'd both been thinking the poker game would take place in a private backroom of a restaurant. We never dreamed about it being on a magnificent ship such as this.

It wasn't an ordinary yacht. It was as large as a passenger ship, and appeared to have been constructed of the finest materials available. I don't know why we never thought of the poker game being played on a big yacht. After all, we were in South Hampton. It was only fitting.

The man could tell we were awestruck. He asked if we would like a quick tour of the main deck and some information about the yacht before he took us to meet the other guests.

"There's ample time," he said.

"Yes!" We replied in unison.

"I'm Anthony Nichols, captain of this vessel," he said, while shaking our hands. "You are now aboard the super yacht 'The Enrapture', which means 'to fill with great pleasure'. She was built in Denmark by Weiss Shipping, LTD., for a businessperson in Yemen. After seven years of use, the yacht was sold to the owner of an Egyptian oil company. Three years ago, it was sold to Viscount Tucker, whom you will meet shortly. Viscount Tucker purchased the vessel, mainly for use by his dear wife."

"What kind of name is Viscount?" Ryan asked.

"Viscount is a title, not a name, sir. It is the rank of nobility falling just short of an Earl. The owner of the yacht is Viscount Shelton Scott Tucker."

Ryan didn't ask any more questions and neither did I. We didn't know what in the heck Nichols was saying. Captain Nichols continued talking as we all started walking down the deck to make a loop around the superstructure.

"The ships length is 258 feet and presently ranks number seventy-one in the top one-hundred super yachts of the world. Her present value is ninety-nine million pounds, or sixty-four million American dollars using the current exchange rate. That is if my math skills serve me correctly. She has a steel hull and a displacement of two-thousand four-hundred-thirty short tons. The main deck is teak wood and has two spacious sun pads. There is a wet bar and large oval hot tub aft. A kidney shaped pool and wet bar forward; all with ample seating, dedicated showers, and toilet facilities."

Nichols tour was a bit more than expected. Once he got started, he wouldn't stop. I could tell he was very proud of the ship he was in command of.

"The main deck has a beauty salon center, game room, and a full workout gym. There is also a stateroom, where your poker game will begin shortly. The open stateroom has a full service bar, large dining area, enough space for a dance floor, a grand piano, and an orchestra pit. This deck also includes the owner's office."

It was like listening to one of those guides on a tour bus. The captain was set on giving us every detail about the ship.

"The upper deck of the superstructure is dedicated to the spacious wheelhouse with map room, navigation room, and captain's quarters located aft."

I liked that word 'aft'. I was quite sure it meant in the back or stern end of the boat. I wasn't used to that kind of talk, but I liked it, and I liked the Captain's accent.

"The first deck below contains twelve guest suites with all amenities, galley, large wine cellar, food storage area, movie theatre, and an inset bay containing a thirty-two foot tender with twin three-hundred horsepower gasoline engines."

I had to interrupt the captain briefly, to ask what a tender was.

"Ahh, I'm glad you asked," the captain said. "A tender is a….I'll try to use terms you Yanks might understand. It is like a large speedboat of sorts. It's a water vessel, which can be placed in the water by a crane and then used for trips taken ashore. It proves to be most useful in small ports where the waters are too shallow to dock the large yacht."

I thanked the captain, and he continued. I don't know why he couldn't have just said it was a big speedboat that could be placed in the water to go places the yacht couldn't go. Ryan nudged me and said I shouldn't ask any more questions or the captain would never shut up.

"The second deck below houses a staff of up to twenty-four, and also contains the laundry area, machine shop, and electrical control room. The third and bottom floor contains the engine room with twin 2,400 horsepower engines and two electric generators, both capable of producing 370 kilowatts of electricity. The fuel tanks are located in the bottom deck with a capacity of 100,000 gallons of diesel fuel giving the ship a range of 8,000 nautical miles. The cruising speed is eighteen knots with a maximum speed of twenty-four knots."

At that point, we were back at the ramp where the tour began. Ryan and I were both glad. The tour had turned out to be a bit more than expected. I liked knowing about the yacht but wasn't planning to buy one anytime soon. You could easily tell that Captain Nichols was proud of the yacht, knew every minute detail about the ship, and was eager to share that information with anyone willing to listen. Ryan seemed amused, but was more interested in the poker game and getting the show started.

"You're really fond of this ship, aren't you," I said to the Captain.

"Ah yes, lad, she's a mighty fine ship she is, and I'm very proud to be her captain. Nevertheless, me's sad to say she is about to set sail on her final voyage with me at the helm. Viscount Tucker has sold her. The day after tomorrow we set sail for Hawaii to deliver her to a new owner."

"It isn't any of my business, but if Mr. Tucker bought it for his wife to use, then why is he selling it?"

"He needs the capital, mate. He's expanding his distillery business into India, and needs the cash to build a new plant."

"I've often wondered what it would be like to take a cruise. I bet it would be great on a ship like this," I added.

"Don't give up hope, maybe I'll win enough to buy us one," Ryan said.

I laughed, thinking Ryan was kidding, but the look on his face told me he was serious.

Chapter 22

The three of us entered the stateroom. Everything in the room said 'first-class'. There was a large dining area with a mahogany floor, which stepped down to the left. It contained a table that seated fourteen people, and to the side was an orchestra pit. It could seat six to eight people with instruments. A beautiful grand piano was sitting just outside of the orchestra pit. A man dressed in a tuxedo was setting at the piano playing rather good elevator music.

Ryan and I were the last guests to enter the room. Several others were already there socializing. A tall slender man with yellow hair, who I guessed to be in his early seventies, approached us. He was holding both a fat cigar and a wine glass in his left hand. He reached out his right hand to greet us.

"Ah, gentlemen, welcome aboard 'The Enrapture'. I trust that tonight you will fill yourself with great pleasure. I'm the owner of this fine vessel and your host for this evening. My name is Viscount Shelton Tucker."

Mr. Tucker had the air of a man who got what he wanted. He carried himself with confidence and class. He had a distinguishable feature though that made him stand out, and it was hard to ignore. It was his large teeth. They were huge, and looked like something that would have been on display in a museum. I couldn't help but stare at the pearly white dentures and wonder how all those teeth fit in his mouth. They made the man look comical.

Tucker led us to the bar.

"Gentlemen, order your favorite spirit, help yourself to the hors d' oeuvres, and mingle. We shall start the game in about thirty minutes," Tucker said.

He then walked off to spend time with his other guests. The bar area was as big as any you would expect to see in a restaurant. Fat Cuban cigars were stacked on a silver platter sitting on top of the bar. There was also a huge arrangement of fine appetizers, including caviar.

Ryan picked up a cigar and lit it from a scented candle burning on the bar. He looked out of place and I couldn't help but chuckle.

"What?" He said.

"Ryan, my friend, that cigar hanging from your mouth….it just….it's funny. We are just as good as these people Ryan, but we are far outclassed. I hope you know what you are doing."

Ryan tilted his head back and blew smoke into the air.

"Jake, I know what I'm doing, believe me. Oh, and there's something I didn't tell you."

I had a concerned look on my face. Ryan knew I hated surprises, especially at a time and place such as this.

"Ryan, please, don't go messing with me now, you know I'm nervous about this. If something happens, I don't have a gun, and we'd have to swim to get away from here."

"Calm down, everything is alright."

"What is it then?"

"Tonight's game, I have to pay fifty percent of anything I lose, but I get thirty percent of anything I win," he said smiling.

"I don't understand. What are you talking about man?"

"I'm playing with Newton's money, he couldn't be here. That's how I got in the game. I'm taking his place. He thinks I can win money for him here, so I'm playing with money he had to put up front."

I still didn't fully understand, but there was no more time, Tucker wanted everyone gathered around the card table set up near the bar.

After everyone had gathered around the table, Tucker welcomed everyone and told each player where they would sit. There were five people playing. Aside from the players, there was the piano player, the bartender, Captain Nichols, and myself in the room.

The captain and I were getting ready to go outside since the game was about to start. That was normally the rule, no one in the room but the players and guards. I didn't see any security guards. Yet I knew they would be around somewhere. They had to be nearby in a high stakes game like this.

Tucker motioned to the captain and me and asked us to wait a minute. He then said it would be okay tonight for us to remain in the room if we wished, we'd just have to sit at the bar. I was pleased with that arrangement. It would be interesting to see how high rollers played poker.

Everyone sat down but Mr. Tucker, he remained standing. As he smiled at everyone with those huge teeth, I thought of a good cartoon. The cartoon would be Tucker sitting at the table playing cards with a talking-horse. The caption would say, "I came to win my teeth back."

I knew without a doubt Ryan had noticed Tucker's teeth as well. I could only hope he'd be like me and keep his thoughts to himself.

Tucker said wanted to introduce the players, and he began to his left.

"First, we have retired General Eugene White of the Canadian Royal Air Force. He currently resides in Montreal where he works part-time as a consultant for Nero Aerospace."

Tucker went on for several minutes going into much detail about each person there. Finally, he got to Ryan.

"To my right is Mr. Ryan Tyler. Mr. Tyler is here tonight because a friend of mine, as well as a friend of most of you here, could not join us this evening. That being Mr. Richard Newton."

The things Ryan had told me earlier were starting to make a little sense now. Newton knew all these people. He had played poker with them before. That's how Ryan got set up to play in the game, only he was playing with Newton's money on a commission deal. *What faith Mr. Newton must have in Ryan to let him do this, playing with millions of dollars.* I was worried, Ryan was red faced and looking nervous as Tucker went on about him.

"Mr. Tyler is new to our level of play, although I know he has a special gift, a gift of winning, so we all better be on guard." The others at the table laughed loudly. Ryan laughed also but I could tell it was a forced laugh. Then Tucker, continued.

"Mr. Tyler doesn't have much of a track record with "A Gentleman's Wager" but he did win a lottery game in the United States recently. Merely through an act of luck,

198

and not skill, I'm certain. Nonetheless he now sits in our midst."

I thought Tucker was through because he paused, but then he went on. "Uh, one more thing, Mr. Tyler has brought his friend Jake Roberts, who is sitting at the bar. Mr. Roberts just completed a lengthy jail sentence for a crime perpetrated by Mr. Tyler, thus displaying great friendship and character on Mr. Robert's part. It's nice to know at least one of them has such qualities"

Oh my Lord, what was going on? Ryan looked surprised by Tucker's revelation as well. Everyone else at the table seemed confused also and alarmed that Tucker was doing this. It was as if he wanted to start a fight. I didn't know what Tucker was trying to do, and I could tell Ryan didn't know either. I knew Ryan Tyler was as unpredictable as anyone you'd ever meet so I was holding my breath, hoping he would remain calm.

You could cut the air with a knife and I knew if Tucker didn't shut up, trouble was certain. This must be part of Tucker's plan, to rattle Ryan. Ryan looked up at Tucker and all he could get out was, "But, how did you - ," Tucker cut him off.

"Ah, at last, Ryan, there are no secrets. I hope you did your homework on us as thoroughly as we have you. It's all part of the strategy. I trust that you DO have a strategy!"

All the men at the table, except Ryan, laughed.

I could tell by the look on Ryan's face, this wasn't what he was expecting. It wasn't a part of his strategy and he had not done his homework. He knew nothing about these men aside from what he was now learning. Ryan's strategy was to act like an ignorant hillbilly to throw these men off their game, but it wasn't going to work.

They were better at this than he was, and he had grossly underestimated them. Now Ryan was the one on defense. Tucker went on talking, while Ryan sat there quietly, with a look of concern on his face.

"And then of course there is myself," Tucker stated, boldly. "I do welcome each of you here and I'm certain we will all have a pleasant evening. For those of you who do not know, I own three gin distilleries here in Great Britain, and two in France.

I'm sad to say I recently sold my fine yacht you are aboard in order to provide some of the capital needed to build a new distillery in Cabal, India. India is a country with a rapidly expanding economy, and the millions of people there have a taste for the delightfully refreshing beverage called gin, which I plan to provide in order to satisfy their thirst."

At last, it appeared Tucker was through with his speech. Ryan was sitting there looking like a student who had been called to the principal's office.

"Now, let's make sure everyone knows the rules for tonight's game," Tucker said, as he sat down.

Tucker pulled out a small leather bound book from his coat pocket. It was a codebook developed by 'A Gentleman's Wager'. I didn't know they had such a book, but then again it only made sense. He then motioned the bartender who made a telephone call. Almost immediately two men came into the room and sat down on the far end away from everyone. They both had slicked back hair and hard faces. They were the guards.

As the game began, there was chatter by all the players so I couldn't hear everything that was being said. I did hear Tucker say, "ante up, fifty thousand."

I told Captain Nichols I thought that level ten was a minimum of one-million dollars on the ante.

"Oh no, lad, not to start the game off, but it'll get to that, ye can count on it."

Even though hundreds of thousands of dollars were exchanging hands each round on the table, not being a poker player, I was quickly getting bored. Captain Nichols and I sat at the bar talking to one another and the bartender. We kept our voices low, so we wouldn't disturb the poker players. Occasionally there was an outburst at the table. Someone would curse or shout, or both.

The game had been going on for about thirty minutes when I looked back at the table. Ryan appeared to be relaxed and enjoying the game, so I knew it was going well for him. I was still concerned though, Tucker had embarrassed Ryan, and I was fearful he would retaliate somehow. Perhaps knowing he was using Mr. Newton's money would keep him from making a scene before we could get out of that place.

After two hours, one of the players was out of money. I didn't recall his name, but I remembered he owned some gold mines in South Africa. The man came over to the bar and sat beside me, but didn't say anything. From his actions, it appeared losing a lot of money wasn't a big deal to him. You'd think he had just lost ten dollars instead of ten million. The game went on for another hour. Then, at the same time, two of the other players were out, leaving only Tucker and Ryan to play.

Tucker gave Ryan an evil look.

"Well, my friend, you have done better than I expected. If my calculation is right, of the fifty-million set aside by the players for tonight's game, you presently hold twenty-eight million and I hold twenty-two."

I did some quick math in my head, let me see, if you deduct the ten million Ryan started with, that leaves eighteen-million. Thirty-percent of that - good grief, in less than three hours Ryan had made 5.4 million dollars. My mind was struggling to comprehend such numbers. These men in a few hours gambled away enough money to support a third world country for a year or more.

"Let's call it a night my friend. The game isn't the same with only two players," Tucker said.

I was surprised Tucker wanted to quit. It seemed his goal was to throw Ryan off, even before the poker game got started. Perhaps during the evening, Tucker had discovered Ryan was whipping his butt and he couldn't do anything about it. Maybe he wanted to get out while the getting was good.

Ryan was staring Tucker down then suddenly he turned back to look at me, and winked. My heart skipped a beat, I knew Ryan was about to do something serious. I didn't know what, I only knew trouble was about to start. Ryan turned back to look at Tucker.

"I'd like to make a proposal."

"And what do you propose, Mr. Tyler?" Tucker said, as he was looking at his chips.

"You say this ship is sailing for Hawaii the day after tomorrow?"

"That's right. Captain Nichols will have the ship ready to set sail with my wife and two sons. They want to take the final cruise on 'The Enrapture'. But, I've promised them as soon as things in India get moving I'll purchase a much larger and more luxurious yacht as their play toy." His voice displayed cockiness and arrogance. "Perhaps you will have such a ship one day Mr. Tyler, if your luck can hold up that long."

The two men looked intently at one another. In a short time period, they had learned to detest one another. The two security guards had moved closer to the table. They were getting in place, just in case Tucker needed them. I was hoping this would end so we could get the heck out of Dodge. I'd been there rubbing elbows with those haughty people long enough.

"So, once again Mr. Tyler, what is your big proposal?" Tucker said, still talking sarcastically. It was as if to entertain his friends as much to look down his nose at Ryan.

"I propose we play one more hand, a game of my choice. If I lose, I give you one-million dollars. If you lose, my buddy Jake and I get to go on that cruise, all expenses paid, and I mean everything we might need!"

Tucker laughed heartily while at the same time shaking his head back in forth with a body language that said no way. Then he looked at Ryan, all the while still smiling, and showing those enormous teeth.

"You're out of your mind, Tyler. My wife set sail on this ship with the likes of you two? That's damn good entertainment, thank you for the good laugh, now let's call it a night."

Tucker started to rise up from the table.

"What are you CHICKEN? You scared of losing? Are you CHICKEN SHIT, old man?"

I didn't understand why Ryan was doing this. He'd just won more money in an evening then most men will earn in a lifetime. We needed to just walk out the door and not look back. Nothing good was going to come from this.

Tucker sat back down.

"What did you say to me, boy?"

Ryan's words had angered Tucker. He was someone unaccustomed to being insulted. He was a powerful man and wasn't about to let some punk with new money come in here on his turf and talk to him that way.

Ryan was looking back at Tucker as sternly as Tucker was looking at him.

"Why don't you put your money where your big mouth is, Tucker, or better yet, put your money where your teeth are?" I'll up that wager to two-million dollars."

I should have known better than to think Ryan could pass up taking a shot at Tucker's teeth. The other three players plus Captain Nichols and me were sitting at the bar watching these two men ready to get into a fistfight. Everyone was fearful of stepping in at that point. We didn't know if saying something would helpful or make matters worse.

The bartender was standing motionless behind the bar. The piano player had stopped playing and was sitting on the stool looking toward the poker table. The guards were both directly across the table from the two angry men but standing motionless, waiting for a tip from Tucker to throw us overboard. I knew we were mere seconds from that happening.

Ryan was embarrassing Tucker in front of his friends and employees. Tucker had started the game by trashing Ryan, now he was turning the tide. Two grown men sat there in a face-off, neither wanting to give in, both accustomed to winning and getting their way.

"Alright, Tyler, you're saying two-million dollars if I win, and if I lose, you and your friend go on the cruise, all expenses paid. You're talking about being on this yacht with my family, Tyler. Messing with a man's family is something you don't do....so, if you expect me to give in and play your little game, I will, but it's going to cost you. How big are your balls, Tyler? Since you like playing for high stakes and living so dangerously why don't you make it five-million dollars and I'm in. And of course, you can name the game."

"You've got a deal," Ryan said without hesitating.

I thought I'd fall out of my chair. What had gotten into Ryan Tyler's hard thick skull? This wasn't some child's board game where at the end you pick up the pieces and the play money goes back in the box. It was real life and real money.

Ryan was a loose cannon and totally out of control. At some point in life, he had to learn that when someone insults you, the thing to do is walk away. I didn't give a rat's hind-end about going on a cruise with Tucker's family. Why would Ryan want to go on a long cruise with this jerk's wife and sons? Nothing good could come out of that. Besides, for two or three thousand dollars we could take the best cruise offered anywhere in the world.

Ryan stood up and just as proud as a peacock spreading its wings he opened both arms and turned to us at the bar.

"Gentlemen, come close and witness this event. That is, if my friend and great host here, DISCOUNT Tucker doesn't mind."

Ryan turned back to Tucker, who was still sitting. It was as if Ryan expected a nod of approval, which wasn't going to happen. Ryan's voice was that of a first class smart-aleck and I didn't like what he was doing. He could be a jerk sometimes but he was putting on a real display tonight, and it was too much. Tucker was pretty much like Ryan, except he had lots of old money.

Ryan was trying to prove he was not only just as good at this old rich tycoon, but superior. Neither of them had displayed what the poker club was supposed to be. They both left the 'Gentleman's' part out of 'A Gentleman's Wager'.

"Sit down and let's play your game, then I'll have you escorted off my ship." Tucker said. "Mr. Tyler, this club forms a safety net for those of us who like to play poker and place wagers, sometimes low, often times high. It was set up as a club for men among men, gentlemen among gentlemen. You have not presented yourself in such a fashion here this evening. No matter who wins this hand we are about to play, I will speak with Mr. Newton tomorrow about your behavior and, I'm going to also recommend that you be removed from this organization. Now, let's play your game. Name your poison."

Surprisingly Ryan didn't have a retort. He looked over at Captain Nichols.

"Why don't we let you deal, Captain, you look like an HONEST man."

"This too, is highly unusual, but I'll go along, Tucker said. "What game do you propose?"

"Five card no-peak, deuce's wild," Ryan said.

"A game for children," Tucker said. "I'm surprised you would pick a game which doesn't require at least a small amount of skill."

Captain Nichols shuffled the deck and dealt five cards face down to each player. The object of the game was for one player to turn over a card then the opponent turn over his card or cards until he can beat the card turned up by the first player. Once the opponent is able to trump the first card turned up, the play goes back to the first player, and so on until one person is out of cards and a winner is declared.

Tucker was trying to recompose himself and get back into his, gentleman mode.

"You go first, Mr. Tyler."

Ryan was sweating but Tucker wasn't. Ryan was without a doubt the one with everything to lose. Perhaps his temper had waned enough for him to realize what a position he had created for himself. Getting into a level ten game had been Ryan's dream. He had done so then blown away his chances of ever doing it again. If Ryan lost, it would be five-million dollars down the tubes. If Tucker lost, his biggest concern was informing his wife that two additional passengers would be on the cruise.

Ryan flipped over the first card.

"The jack of diamonds," Captain Nichols announced.

Now it was Tucker's turn. He turned over his first card.

"The 9 of diamonds."

Tucker would have to play a second card. His 9 didn't trump Ryan's, Jack. He turned over his second card.

"The 9 of diamonds - ace of clubs."

Tucker then had the best hand. Ryan slowly turned over his next card as Nichols called the cards out.

"The jack of diamonds - ace of spades."

Ryan smiled. His cards now beat what Tucker had on the table. It was back to Tucker again to play a card.

"The 9 of diamonds - ace of clubs - 2 of spades."

Tucker had turned over a wild card and now had a pair of nines, beating Ryan's hand.

"Shit," Ryan exclaimed.

Sweat was visibly clear all over Ryan's face. He turned to me and asked me to find something to wipe his face. I took one of the cloth napkins from the bar and handed it to him. He wiped his face then the palms of his hands. My own palms were wet as well.

Ryan slowly turned over his next card.

"The jack of diamonds - ace of spades - ace of diamonds," Nichols blared out.

Ryan blew a puff of air from his lips, indicating a sigh of relief. His pair of aces with a jack high beat Tucker's pair of aces with a 9 high.

Tucker without hesitation reached down and flipped his next card, all the while staring at Ryan, and enjoying seeing him sweat.

Nichols made the announcement. "The 9 of diamonds - ace of clubs - 2 of spades - 5 of hearts."

It wasn't enough to beat Ryan's hand. Now Tucker had to turn over his last card. It wasn't a time when you could hear a pin drop. There was plenty of noise as everyone standing around the table rubbed their hands across their pants, trying to remove the sweat, and everyone, even the security guards, were breathing heavily.

Tucker turned his last card over.

"The 9 of diamonds - ace of clubs - 2 of spades - 5 of hearts - and 9 of clubs."

Tucker had trumped Ryan's cards. He had three of a kind, three 9's with an ace high.

"Damn it!" Ryan shouted out as he reared back in his chair.

Ryan had two cards left. He didn't want to prolong the drama and the misery. He flipped his next card over.

"The jack of diamonds - ace of spades - ace of diamonds - 7 of spades." Nichols called out.

It wasn't enough. Ryan would need his last card in order to beat Tucker's hand.

The two players looked at each other intently. My knees were feeling a little weak and I wanted to either sit down in one of the empty chairs or just walk away and not know what happened next.

Ryan put his right thumb on the corner of the face down card, as if it would break if not handled gently. A stream of sweat was rolling down his face and dripping onto the table.

Ryan flipped the card over. Nichols didn't have to announce anything, Ryan's action and the card on the table told the story. It was the 2 of hearts

Ryan's last card was a wild card. He'd won with three aces trumping Tucker's three nines.

Ryan jumped up from the chair and turned sideways, looking over his left shoulder at Tucker. He leaned forward with both of his arms up and bent at the elbows on a ninety-degree angle, and his fists were clinched. He brought both arms back down in on motion and yelled out "CHA CHING."

Tucker sat there looking at Ryan. He was not amused. Tucker then looked over at the two guards who were still standing, watching the show.

He motioned for them and said, "Please escort Mr. Tyler and Mr. Roberts off my ship."

I noticed Tucker didn't use sir when he addressed us that time.

Tucker looked at me, knowing Ryan wasn't listening.

"Come back tomorrow morning at nine and see Captain Nichols." Tucker said, calmly. "He will make the arrangements for your cruise. Now then gentlemen, goodnight."

I followed Ryan as he headed to the door, followed by the two guards. He didn't say anything else or make any additional gestures. He just walked away as if he were strolling down the street.

When we got to the T in the dock, the guards stopped while Ryan and I continued walking toward shore. Once we got to the shore and were in an open parking lot, Ryan went into a whooping hollering dance for a few minutes, allowing his emotions and the adrenaline to flow out of his body. I stood there and smiled while shaking my head. My friend was some sort of character, and I couldn't help but clap and laugh as he did his victory dance.

Chapter 23

  Ryan and I met Captain Nichols at the yacht at nine in the morning. The captain was pleasant and congratulated Ryan on his victory the night before. He said it was quite a thriller and that the game will be talked about in many circles for a long time.

  Captain Nichols handed Ryan a credit card and told him to go into town and get what he needed for the trip ahead. Ryan and I had not talked about the cruise yet, last night he was too emotional about the game he and Tucker played. I wasn't interested in going on the cruise. I just had to find the right moment to tell him.

  All I wanted was to get on a plane and go home, start a new life, maybe become a hermit and live back in the mountains away from people. I had enough money to buy a small farm and get away from everyone. People are hard to love, and people don't give much love. I'd had enough of the drama and poker games. I loved my friend dearly but it was time for me to go away and live the simple life I desired.

The captain instructed Ryan and I to buy some warm clothing because we would be in winter weather for a bit. He also suggested we buy summer clothing for the trip through the Panama Canal, and on to Hawaii. Mr. Tucker was paying for it all. Tucker had been such a butt last night, and so had Ryan. At least Tucker was holding true to his word, paying for all our expenses.

Before we left the yacht to go on a shopping spree, Nichols had us write down all our favorite foods. He explained that the ships pantry was going to be stocked today. If we wanted something special to eat, or any other special needs, he needed to know now. He also told us the ship would set sail tomorrow at noon. We needed to be there for loading at ten o'clock in the morning.

Ryan and I talked quite a bit after we left Nichols. I explained that I didn't want to go on the cruise. Ryan appeared to be hurt, he said he put on the show last night for me, and betted the millions so we could take this trip, and it would be fun.

"No, Ryan, you didn't do that for me. You didn't ask me, you didn't consult me. You did that for you. It was a display of who is the best man? Who has the most power? Who's going to win? You and I could go on a cruise anytime and anywhere we want. You aren't going to lay a guilt trip on me with the 'I did it for you' line, it won't work."

"Alright, Jake, you're right. I was a total jerk last night. In some way, I did do it for you though. You talked about a cruise, and you'd been in jail for so long. I thought, dang, if this super yacht is sailing for Hawaii, how nice it would be if Jake and I were to go along for the ride. What an adventure!"

Ryan knew how to talk to me, how to make me think things over. There I was having a guilt trip, even though I'd just said I wasn't going to allow him to do it to me.

"Come on, Jake, it'll take a few weeks tops. We'll get to see the Panama Canal, and Hawaii. Heck, once we get to Hawaii, we can stay there for a while, what better place to be. Let's give it whirl. What else do you have to do anyway? After the cruise you can go to the bank, get your money, and spend the rest of your life living anywhere you want."

Ryan had a point. Dang it! Seems he always made sense, even when I didn't want him to. I really didn't have anything to do, and it would be nice sailing on the big yacht with a few people versus a large cruise ship with a thousand or more.

"Alright, I give in but if we get to the Panama Canal and I'm not happy that's where I depart, no questions asked, okay?

"It's going to be a blast, Jake. Come on. Let's go spend some of Tucker's money."

§

The following morning at ten sharp, Ryan and I were at the dock with our luggage, ready to board the ship. The day before we had gone from store to store swiping Tucker's credit card, buying coats, shorts, pants, hats, and lots of each. We had five suitcases each to load onto the yacht.

Captain Nichols was at the ramp and helped us get our bags onto the deck of the yacht. We were almost finished when Mrs. Tucker showed up with a dozen people toting bags for her and her sons. They had six large heavy-duty carts loaded to the top. The men had straps tied to the luggage to keep the load from falling off the carts.

Mr. Tucker was a pussycat compared to Mrs. Tucker. She was loud and demanding, and we could hear her jabbering long before she got close. Her voice was shrill and she had a strong English accent. It was like listening to fingernails raked down a chalkboard when she spoke.

"Get the hell off the ramp," she demanded. "Can't you see I've got bags needing to be loaded aboard?"

She was huffy and had no patience. Ryan and I had two more bags each to haul up the ramp and we were done. It wasn't going to take more than a minute.

Mrs. Tucker stood there at the bottom of the ramp with her arms crossed as we toted the last of our luggage up the ramp and onto the deck.

When we finished, we looked back at her. She had her nose turned up and her hands on her hips.

"The ship leaves in two hours. Wars have been fought and won in the time it's taking you two to throw a few bags aboard."

Once we got our luggage on board, we still had to get it all to our cabins, one deck below the superstructure. Ryan turned around and looked down at Mrs. Tucker, still standing there with a scowl on her face.

"Your majesty, can we assist you now?" Ryan said.

"You two must be the Neanderthal's Scotty told me about, ugh," she replied. "Don't screw with me. I'm not a pushover like him. I'll throw both your asses overboard if you cross me even once. Now move on or I'll start now with you, Shorty!"

Captain Nichols chuckled.

"Come on lads, I'll show you where your cabins are located."

The cabins were spacious. Mine had a queen size bed and a large bathroom. All the furniture pieces were cherry wood. The place spoke high class. I was curious about the rest of the yacht and wanted to see it all.

The captain had told us to be in the stateroom at 11:30 for a meeting of the crew and guests. After I put my things away, I went and knocked on Ryan's door and we went upstairs together. After everyone had wandered in, Captain Nichols rang a little brass bell to get everyone's attention. He then gave a short speech about the voyage and stated that we would be at sea for some time and we needed to get to know one another and enjoy the trip.

The captain spoke about Viscount Tucker and gave a lot of background on the man. Tucker had descended from a long line of members of the royal court. His family had served with kings and queens over the centuries. The Tuckers went from wine tasters to wine producers. Later they went into the liquor business, and became very successful at it. He wasn't going to be on the trip, he had to be in India overseeing the new distillery that was under construction. I was grateful of that. I knew he and Ryan would come to blows if they were together again.

The captain introduced everyone. He started with Ryan and me, which didn't take long. He never mentioned the poker game two days prior, nor how it was we ended up on that trip. I'm glad he didn't. I quickly discovered Captain Nichols had a lot of class. He was someone I wanted to get to know. I knew nothing about the ocean and wanted to hear his stories and learn about sailing the seas.

The captain spent a considerable amount of time talking about Mrs. Gertrude Tucker. It was apparent to me she had been born with a silver spoon in her mouth and had never worked a day in her life. She grew up with the royal family. Nichols didn't indicate that she was a blood relative in any way, so my guess was she wasn't. Her two grown sons were with her, Joseph and Preston. Both men looked to be in their early forties. They were dressed for the yacht club and clung to Mrs. Tucker's side. It was very

214

odd. They didn't appear to be retarded or anything, just mama's boys. I was curious about them, expecting I'd find out more as the trip got underway.

There was a nice looking woman standing behind Mrs. Tucker, and I had been anxiously waiting for Captain Nichols to get to her introduction. She looked to be early twenties, tall slender build, long dark curly hair, and a smile that made my heart beat faster. I noticed her as soon as she came into the room. She was a nice looking woman and carried herself in a lady-like fashion. She seemed and a bit on the shy side, and it added to my attraction to her.

Captain Nichols introduced her as Marie Whitney. She was Mrs. Tucker's personal maid, tending to all her needs. He didn't say anything else about her. I made a mental note to ask the captain about her as soon as the opportunity presented itself.

Jordan Riddle was the next person introduced. He was Mrs. Tucker's personal chef, and would be preparing all our meals. Ryan was the gambler here not me, but if I was going to make a wager, it would be that Mrs. Tucker wasn't a beans and potato person like me. I hoped I'd be able to eat the food. I didn't think I was going to be on this cruise, so I didn't put anything down on the food list that Captain Nichols had presented to us yesterday.

The final two people the captain introduced were Modan Hogan the chief mate/engineer, and Ronald Golden, the second mate.

To end the meeting, the captain went over a few rules of do's and don'ts. He explained that the ship had twelve guest rooms for up to twenty-four people, but this voyage only had five guests. The captain also said that if the ship had been fully booked a staff of twenty-four would be required to attend to the guests needs. For our trip, he said Mr. Tucker had denied his request for additional crew. It was a cost cutting measure, since it would be the final voyage as his yacht. Therefore, being short of staff, he said that he may at times need our help.

"Yeah, the penny pincher won millions of dollars in a poker game, so he has to cut staff on the yacht, go figure," Ryan said to me.

"From the looks of the amount of luggage Mrs. Tucker brought on board and her personal maid and chef, it doesn't look as if her pennies were cut off," I replied.

"Yeah, and I can tell she is royalty alright, a true, real life, Drama Queen!" Ryan stated. We both had a good chuckle then went back to our cabins to finish unpacking.

Chapter 24

For the first hour after setting sail, I was on the main deck looking at the other boats and ships going by. I enjoyed viewing the variety of docks and houses along the shoreline. It was January sixth and cold outside. I had a down filled coat on. Still, standing along the railing with the yacht moving swiftly through the water, made it much too cold to stand outside for very long.

Ryan stayed out with me for a few minutes, but decided it was too cold, so he went to the game room. He knew what was up with me, he knew I was afraid of getting seasick and was trying to keep fresh air moving through my lungs. After playing a few video games, he came back out to stand with me along the railing.

"Settle down," he said. "You won't get seasick unless we hit a storm or something."

"I know, Ryan, I know. If I can watch what I eat for a few days, I should be ok. First, I must get to get used to the movement beneath my feet. This is worse than that swinging bridge we use to play on."

We were expecting to be at sea for three days before stopping for a day on Sao Miguel Island. I didn't know there were any islands out in the Atlantic before reaching America. I talked to Captain Nichols about it. He informed me there were nine islands making up the Portuguese archipelago of the Azores, and Sao Miguel was the largest of the islands.

"Why are we stopping there?" I asked.

"Mrs. Tucker wants to visit a well-known coffee shop in Ponta Delgada. She claims they had the best cream filled pastries of anywhere in the world."

"Captain, I'm going to get a real education on this trip. I'm far from being refined, worldly, or proper. So this is the life of royalty, aye!"

"Well mate, enjoy it while it lasts. One thing though, we need to work on your accent. The way you pronounce words is quite unusual," he said, laughing.

"I'm a southerner Captain. I don't think you've got much to work with here, I'll just have to be myself and not compete with you folks from the old country."

"Fair enough, sir, I'll try to be more patient as I learn your language," the captain said, still laughing.

Captain Nichols appeared to be open minded about things. He was easy to talk with.

In the open waters, I got bored looking out at the endless sea and I was chilled to the bone, so I began exploring the ship. I nearly ran over Marie as she was entering the gym and I was leaving. Mrs. Tucker had gone to her cabin for a nap before dinner, which allowed Marie time to exercise.

"Oh, excuse me," she said.

"I'm Jake," I said, holding my hand out to shake.

"Yes, I know, I noticed you at the briefing, I'm Marie."

"Yes, I know, I noticed you as well, I mean, you being Marie.

We both giggled as I nervously fumbled over my words. She seemed to be a little shy but interested in talking. I could tell my face was red from blushing. I was never good with talking to girls, and I needed much more practice.

"I understand you recently broke out of prison," she said.

My face felt flushed as I started to explain to her that wasn't true.

Marie smiled and looked at me with her big brown eyes, then started laughing.

"I'm sorry," she said. "I know your story, I just couldn't help myself."

"So you're a brat, I like that." We both laughed.

Marie asked if I'd like to sit for a bit in the stateroom. She said she was going to exercise but had a few minutes to spare. I agreed, then followed her to the bar area.

We started getting to know each other a bit and I was already finding myself attracted to her. She was pretty, but more than that, she was kind and sweet. Her words were soothing to my ears and I liked the sound of her voice.

"You don't have a British accent," I said.

"No, I don't. I was born in Corning, New York."

"Oh really, that's interesting. So how did you end up here?"

"My parents were both from the suburbs of London. They moved to New York in the late 1950s but my grandmother stayed in London. When I was fifteen she became ill and my parents moved back to take care of her."

"She didn't want to come to the states?"

"No, she was too elderly to travel."

"That must have been a culture shock to you."

"It was, but I adjusted quickly. People are pretty much the same anywhere you go."

"How did you end up with Mrs. Tucker?"

"I have an aunt who worked for the Tucker family for years. She retired just as I was getting out of high school. She convinced Mrs. Tucker to give me a try as her maid, and I've been with her ever since."

"Do you like that? I'm trying to be nice here, but she seems hard to get along with."

"She is indeed," Marie said while laughing. "But it pays well, and I get to travel a lot. I also have the best of everything at my disposal. Not too many people have that you know."

About that time, Ryan entered the room and came to sit with us. After a few minutes, Marie said she needed to get downstairs and lend the chef a hand with dinner.

"I apologize for keeping you so long, and causing you to miss your exercise session," I said.

"It was worth it," she said, winking.

"Will I see you again?" I blurted out.

"If you don't jump overboard you will," Marie replied while leaving, laughing at what I'd said to her.

Ryan started laughing. "Do you know what you said?"

It hit me then and I started laughing too.

"I need some lessons on how to talk to women without being nervous and saying stupid stuff," I said.

At dinner that evening, Mrs. Tucker sat at the head of the large table. Preston Tucker sat to her left and Joseph Tucker sat to her right. The captain sat at the other end with Ryan and me on either side of him. Mrs. Tucker said the remaining people could sit where they wished, except Marie. Mrs. Tucker had her sit beside of Joseph. Mrs. Tucker announced that would be the arrangement throughout the cruise.

I was trying to find ways to like Mrs. Tucker, but she made it more difficult with each passing breath. Why did it matter where anyone sat at the table? I wanted to sit near Marie. In Mrs. Tucker's eyes, Ryan and I were nothing more than trespassers. This was her ship, but that didn't mean she had to be rude all the time. It made me wonder if she had the same bloodline as Momma. Imagine, me related to Mrs. Tucker!

After dinner, Chef Riddle cleared the dishes and then served dessert. It was some kind of chocolate cake with swirls of vanilla inside, covered with a layer of minty chocolate. I'm not much of a mint person, but I had to admit it was good.

While everyone was eating dessert, Mrs. Tucker went to the piano and began to play while Preston sang. I didn't have enough knowledge to identify the style of music she was playing, but whatever it was, I couldn't deny that she played excellently and made the piano keys sing. Additionally, Preston had a great singing voice. When the song was over, Ryan and I both clapped. For the first time since our voyage began, I detected a semi-smile from Mrs. Tucker and sensed she felt a slight degree of pleasure for our gesture of appreciation.

I was hoping to talk with Marie after dinner, but part of her job was helping the chef clean up, and wash dishes. I sat with Ryan in the theatre as we watched a movie on the big screen and each smoked one of the Viscount's expensive cigars.

When we arrived at Sao Miguel Island, the temperature was 68 degrees. I'd never experienced such a nice temperature in January before and thought it was wonderful. Mrs. Tucker was all excited about shopping in Ponta Delgada and visiting the cafe.

The first mate lowered the tender into the water and we all climbed aboard to go ashore for the afternoon. Mrs. Tucker was wearing a straw hat. She wore a lime green dress. There was a bright red silk scarf of some sort wrapped around her neck and shoulders, and hooped earrings big enough to shoot a basketball through them. The Tucker brothers were dressed in white dress shirts, white pants, white shoes, and white beanie caps. They looked like little twin sailors. Ryan and I tried to stay our distance from those three. They didn't want to be associated with us and we felt likewise!

Ryan wanted to check out an area where pool halls and pubs were located. I wasn't interested and decided to do my own thing. After making Ryan promise he'd stay out of trouble, we went in different directions. Marie didn't have to accompany Mrs. Tucker, so I asked her if she wanted to do some sight-seeing with me, and she accepted.

We checked out a few shops and as we strolled down one of the streets, I reached out and took her hand. She didn't object. The soft smooth skin of her hand felt good in mine. Having her companionship was great. I was now glad that Ryan had talked me into going on the cruise. She was nice, and didn't put me down or talk ugly to me. I was hoping she liked me and would want to spend more time with me as the cruise continued.

We stopped at a little café to eat lunch. We were sitting at a window booth. As we were finishing our lunch, we saw Ryan running past the cafe window and on down the street. I slumped back in my chair, knowing something was up. A minute after Ryan ran past us, two men came running by.

"I knew he couldn't keep out of trouble," I said.

The men hesitated briefly to peer through the café window then kept going. I knew they were looking for Ryan.

"Come on, let's go, we've got to make sure they don't catch him," I said to Marie.

We hurried along in the direction Ryan had gone but didn't see him or the two men again. After half an hour, we decided to head back to the tender. When we got there, Ryan was sitting on the boat, kicked back in a chair, and drinking a bottle of beer.

"Did you have a little trouble in town?" I said.

"Two big men in jeans and flowered shirts, did you see them?"

"Yes, we saw them. I thought you were going to stay out of trouble, Ryan."

"Oh, give me a break Jake, trouble seems to just find me sometimes. Where was my bodyguard when I needed him most?" Ryan was smiling.

"I don't know how you do it, Ryan Tyler, but I can't even get mad at you. You're such a charmer."

"He's a con man and you're a wimp," Marie said. "And all this time I thought you were a hardened criminal!" Then she kissed me on the cheek. "Lucky for me, I'm attracted to wimps and jailbirds," she said, then climbed into the boat.

As soon as we were aboard the tender, the Tuckers arrived, each carrying several shopping bags. They came aboard and we headed back to the yacht. At dinner that evening, the captain announced it would take us nine days to reach the Panama Canal. We would stop there for a day, refuel, go through the locks reaching the Pacific Ocean, then on to Hawaii.

Two days into that leg of the trip, we hit some rough seas. I had avoided being seasick up until that point then I lost the battle. I was sick for two full days. The nausea was almost unbearable at times. I seemed to fare better when out on the main deck in the open air. Thankfully, we were heading into a warmer climate. That should at least make it tolerable to stay outside.

During my sickness, Marie would come and be with me as much as time would allow. I was discovering that my life was much better with her around, even while being sick. I promised myself that if I lived, I was going to spend every moment with her I could. Presently though, I was so seasick I could barely hold my head up.

I finally began feeling better and was able to start eating again. Ryan and Marie played a big part in nursing me back to health.

Chapter 25

We were about nine-hundred miles from the
Panama Canal when the captain got a call from one of his
sailing friends whom he spoke with daily on ham radio.
There was something big going on in Panama. Ryan and I
were sitting by the forward pool on the main deck when the
captain came by in a rush.

"Is anything wrong?" Ryan asked.

"Come and let's see, lads."

We followed the captain to the stateroom where the
big screen television was. He had to hook up a satellite
link then go through a few programming procedures before
he was able to bring up a station on the screen. He tuned

into one of the major news programs and immediately we started putting together pieces of news and finding out what was going on in Panama.

The captain flipped through a few more channels and locked into the BBC. We were able to see some live footage from the canal. There was a tower of smoke in the background as a news reporter stood in the foreground. Then the screen returned to the newsroom where a female newscaster gave us the story.

"Two hours ago a large cargo ship flying an Egyptian flag was traveling east through the Mira Flores Locks in Panama. A series of explosions ripped through the hull of the ship and it sank almost immediately inside the lock, blocking all eastbound travel. Minutes later, while authorities were attempting to clear traffic in the westbound lock, a fully loaded Iranian oil tanker midway through that lock also exploded, sending fireballs hundreds of feet in all directions. Reporters at the scene are saying that ship also sank, blocking all traffic through the Panama Canal. This is clearly a sophisticated organized terrorist attack. Thus far, no group has stepped forward claiming responsibility for the attacks."

We sat watching the screen and were speechless. The captain sat motionless, and all of us were trying to absorb what we had just heard.

"It doesn't look as if we are going to Hawaii after all, does it?" I said.

An hour later, all the stories coming in from the news confirmed what we had first heard. The Panama Canal was closed to all traffic. It was going to take months to clear the two sunken ships from the locks. It could take even longer if the locks were damaged by the blasts.

The captain was able to get into contact with Viscount Tucker. They had several conversations that afternoon regarding the canal and our destiny. Mrs. Tucker and her boys were with the captain during those calls as

226

well. Since we'd started out on the cruise, I had never seen either of those forty-year old men leave their momma's side.

Just before dinner that evening, the captain called for everyone to gather in the theatre. Marie got there before Mrs. Tucker, so the two of us were able to chat some before the meeting. One thing about Marie, she was extremely loyal to the Tuckers. Business came before pleasure. She was one hundred percent dedicated to her job and took care of anything Mrs. Tucker desired, no questions asked. I wanted to ask her about Preston and Joseph, but there never seemed to be enough time. I didn't want to spend our short stints of time together talking about the Tuckers.

After everyone was in the theatre, the captain spoke.

"As you know the Panama Canal has been hit hard by terrorist attacks and is now closed. My suggestions to Viscount Tucker were to either port in the United States until travel through the locks is possible, or return to England. After extensive discussions with Viscount Tucker, I'm about to tell you his decision.

The yacht's new owner awaits our arrival in Hawaii. When Mr. Tucker signed the contract, he agreed to a delivery date of no later than February, fifteenth. This being January, ninth, there is little more than a month to get the ship into the new owner's hands. Every day past February, fifteenth without delivery will cost Viscount Tucker a penalty of one hundred thousand dollars. You don't need a calculator to determine that will quickly add up to an absorbent amount of money in penalty. Viscount Tucker has been in contact with the new owner who says he will exercise the contract in full, no exceptions, or excuses."

I'd been spending a lot of time with Captain Nichols in the wheelhouse during our cruise and he had educated me on map reading. I knew we were getting close to the British Virgin Islands and was thinking perhaps Ryan and I could get off there and fly home, or fly to Hawaii. I was also hoping I could convince Marie to come with me.

Captain Nichols continued. "Viscount Tucker wants us to continue our trek by changing course. We will stop in Recife, Brazil to refuel and resupply, then stop again in the Falklands to do the same before rounding the tip of South America and on to Hawaii."

"Alright, our adventure continues," Ryan, said.

"Heck no, Ryan, I'm getting off this boat. That's many more weeks at sea and besides I've heard too many horror stories about storms along the tip of South America putting even big ships on the sea floor. They can drop me off in the Caribbean! My sailing days are over. I've had enough of this and I'm going home."

"Calm down, Jake, don't be irrational, let's mull this over before jumping ship, pun intended."

As soon as everyone got up to disperse, I approached Marie and asked if she could talk with me for a few minutes. She could tell I was upset.

"What's wrong, Sweetie?" She asked.

She had never called me Sweetie before. I was blushing.

"Marie, let's get off the ship. We can go back to the states. I've got over a million dollars waiting for me in a bank in Virginia and a good job there as well if I want to work. I want you to be with me. I can't stay on this ship any longer. I need to be on land."

Marie looked at me, smiled, and gently kissed me on the lips. It was also the first time she had kissed me on the lips. I wanted to kiss her back, but I needed to get these matters cleared up first.

"Jake, I want to be with you, I think you're a good man and we could make a wonderful life together; but first I've got to see Mrs. Tucker to Hawaii. I'm obligated to her. I took an oath to serve her needs long ago and I feel

228

like I need to continue until we get to Hawaii, then I'll go with you anywhere you choose. Besides, you and I need time to get to know one another, it could turn out that you don't like me."

Now I was in a dilemma. Do I get off the ship and wait weeks on end to be with Marie? My other option was to stay there on the yacht and endure more of the Tuckers and the open seas. I was sick of saltwater surrounding me and still a little queasy from when I was seasick. I needed to be on land where I belonged, but I needed Marie to be in my life.

Marie could see the wheels turning in my head. She kissed me again, only this time it was a deep passionate kiss. The closeness of her body next to me, the smell of her hair, the sensation of her lips pressed against mine, all of those things had my senses reeling.

"I've got to go. Mrs. Tucker is expecting me. I'll see you at dinner. We can talk more then." Then she left.

I left the theatre and went straight to the wheelhouse to talk to Captain Nichols. I had gained a lot of respect for the captain and valued his opinion. I asked him if we could talk and he told me yes, as long as I didn't mind him working while we spoke. He was pulling maps from a map file cabinet and laying them on the map table.

I figured they were maps of the areas we were sailing toward now. The captain told me he had changed course before the meeting down in the theatre and we were well on our way to Recife, Brazil.

"I was banking on us sailing past the British Virgin Islands, Captain. I was hoping I could get off the yacht there."

The captain took his attention from the maps and looked up at me.

"I knew ye sailors legs were weak mate, but I's a bit surprised. You fancy the young lady downstairs, as she does you. Will she be going with you lad?"

229

"No sir, she's dedicated to Mrs. Tucker until at least Hawaii, otherwise I'd steal your tender, and we'd leave now."

"Ah, ye always give me a good chuckle, lad, I like that." He replied. "Yes, Miss Marie is a good one, lad, very dedicated indeed. She'd make ye a good wife one day if ye could find the patience to wait a bit."

"Well, Captain, it looks as if I've got more time now to decide what to do. It appears I can't get off the boat until we reach Brazil. Not unless I can talk you into turning the boat around."

"She's a yacht, mate. She's a super yacht, not a boat."

I'd forgotten. The captain didn't have many pet peeves but his ship was the dearest thing to his heart and it was far from being a boat."

"I'm sorry, Captain, I meant no disrespect. Wanting to get off the ship has nothing to do with you. You've shown me nothing but kindness and it's been great getting to know you. I'm just not a seaman. I'm a hillbilly, a mountain man, and I need dirt under my shoes."

"It'll be fine, ole lad. I'll make me ship sail as smoothly as possible for ya. Give er some thought lad about staying with us. 'Tis a great adventure and perhaps I can persuade Mrs. Tucker to let the young lady spend more time with ya."

"Captain, how long will it take us to get to Hawaii?"

"Well mate, I'll have to do some calculating."

"Just a rough estimate will do."

"Hmmm, well, from here to Recife will take about four days, then from Recife to Stanley in the Falklands will take another eight to nine days. Once we leave Stanley, travel will be somewhat slower until we round the tip of South America. I'm guessing from Stanley to Honolulu will be another eighteen days, totaling thirty-one days, give or take a couple of days one way or the other. For sure mate, we'll have to top our tanks off good in Stanley, and still we'll hit Honolulu running on fumes."

"Thirty-one more days!"

"Yes, mate, but that means taking little or no time ashore during our two stops we've planned. Viscount Tucker will have me walking the plank if I's don't deliver his ship on time."

I did some calculating in my head, if I got off in Recife, it still would be a month before I'd see Marie again. The kiss she gave me in the theatre was still fresh on my mind. I wanted to be close to her, hold her, and kiss her more. I was having a difficult time, both my head and my heart were trying to do the thinking, and they were pulling me in opposite directions.

Ryan was sunning in a lounge chair by the pool. I sat down beside him to talk about what I was thinking. I really needed to be on dry land, but I wanted to be close to Marie as well. I asked Ryan if he wasn't feeling the need to get off the ship also, play some poker or something. He laughed and said he felt like the excitement of playing poker had run its course.

After his show with Tucker, he didn't feel like he could top that and anything else would now be boring. Ryan said he was in it for the thrill and excitement, and that was petering out. Now he was looking for something else exciting to do. Besides, he'd been spending a lot of time playing poker with Chief Mate Hogan down in the engine room. Ryan said Modan Hogan was a fierce competitor and he enjoyed playing with him.

"The man couldn't have much money to lose, Ryan. I hope you haven't bankrupted him."

"Heck no, man, we don't even play for money. The loser has to do sit ups or chin ups."

"That explains why Hogan is bulking up then!"

Ryan laughed so hard his spilled his drink on his chest then cursed me, saying it was my fault.

"So tell me, Ryan, do you want to stay on the ship?"

"I think I do, Jake. It's a heck of a long ride but I've enjoyed it so far, minus the Queen of Drama and her two tit sucking wimps. I'm a bit excited about seeing the Falkland Islands, and sailing around the tip of South America. Not too many people can say they've done that before. I might want to write a book about my adventures one day."

"A book! Dang it, Ryan, neither of us have ever been able to sit for more than five minutes our entire life without getting bored. So how the heck are you going to write a book?"

Ryan punched me in the arm and that started it, we wrestled for a minute before I got him in a headlock. He pinched the back of my left leg hard, I jerked, and that threw our momentum backward and we fell into the pool. We pulled ourselves out of the water and sat on the side of the pool for a few minutes laughing, at, and with each other. It was like old times.

"I needed that bath, Ryan. I needed to spend that energy and clear my head."

"Yeah, me too, ole buddy - me too."

"I think I'm going to stay with the ship. I don't know for sure, but I think I'm falling in love."

I needed to stay with my best friend and needed to pursue a relationship with Marie. What else did I have to do, go back to Virginia and deliver packages for the Newtons, taking a chance on having a run in with the law again? At least out on the open seas I didn't have cops chasing after me.

At dinner that evening, Mrs. Tucker was in rare form. I don't know what got her panties in a wad but she was meaner and nastier than usual. She looked down the table sneering at Ryan and me.

"Well, rumor has it you two cockroaches may be getting off my yacht in Recife. Is there anything I can do to help?"

I suppose word travels faster on a ship than on land. How did she know what I had been contemplating? She'd be happy if Ryan and I both jumped overboard that night. I didn't want to reply to her remark, giving her the satisfaction of knowing she'd gotten to me.

I knew it. I just knew it. Ryan had to fire back, with both barrels blazing.

"Well, I'm glad you asked about our plans Mrs. TRUCKER! Sure, you can help. You can take your tits out of your boys' mouths for a minute and come down here to kiss my rosy red ass!"

Everyone stopped eating and sat straight up. Mrs. Tucker bolted upwards from her seat, leaned forward toward Ryan. She had fire in her eyes.

"Well, I have never!"

"I don't doubt that," Ryan said, "And I doubt you will tonight either!"

I stood up. As I rose, Mrs. Tucker sat down.

"Ladies, gentlemen, let's be civilized here." I said. "Ryan and I are going to continue with you to Hawaii, and we will be on our best behavior. If everyone can just try to get along with one another, it will be a fun and pleasant trip. I'm sorry for what just took place, now please, let's eat this fine meal that's been prepared for us and enjoy the evening." Then I sat down.

Mrs. Tucker stood up again. She was so irate now she was shaking. "Interesting you used the word 'CIVILIZED'! The likes of you two are anything BUT!" She screamed out. "Come along, Preston, Joseph, and Marie, I need you in the salon."

They all started walking toward the door.

Ryan couldn't quit, it just wasn't his nature to give up on a battle without being on top and getting the last word in. "The only way that salon is going to help your looks is if the chair you sit in is electric!"

I placed my elbows on the table and placed my head between my hands as I looked at Ryan across the table.

"Oh dear lord, this is going to be a long trip," I said.

The next few days were quiet. At mealtime, all you could hear was silverware hitting the china as no one said a word to anyone else. The tension was high, as Mrs. Tucker remained angry. She purposely was finding things for Marie to do so she wouldn't have any free time to spend with me.

Ryan was mouthy and in private kept making jokes about Mrs. Tucker and the twins, as he called them. I didn't say much about Mrs. Tucker, I was trying to distract Ryan so he'd lighten up. I did tell him though, if I had a chance, I was going to throw her overboard into the shark-infested waters. Ryan's comeback to that was, "what do you have against sharks?"

We only stayed in Recife for four hours. It was just long enough to restock our food supply and take on fuel. Mrs. Tucker went off shopping with her sons and had Marie with her. Ryan and I went on a breakneck pace shopping spree of our own. Ryan bought a new camera and I purchased a nice Bowie knife with a leather sheath. We still had Mr. Tucker's credit card and used it for everything we bought.

As we were heading back to the ship, we passed by a jewelry store. I convinced Ryan to stop long enough for me to buy something for Marie. He didn't want to go in, so he waited for me outside. I found a pendant with a bright diamond surrounded by intricately woven gold ropes, hanging from a beautiful gold chain. I used my own money to purchase the necklace. I didn't want to present her with a gift I'd bought using Tucker's funds.

We hurried back to the ship and arrived just before the Tuckers and Marie.

It so happened Mrs. Tucker had a headache that evening and missed dinner. She had Chef Riddle bring her a snack to her cabin. The Tucker boys were at dinner and it was shocking to see them not by their mother's side. They ate quickly, excused themselves, and headed to her cabin. The air at dinner was lighter that evening and everyone loosened up and enjoyed a meal with conversations flowing back and forth.

After dinner, Marie and I were able to walk around the main deck. It was a gorgeous evening, with temperatures somewhere in the mid-eighties. The breeze generated by the ship's movement and the sun setting as a bright red ball in the western sky made it a perfectly romantic evening. As Marie and I stood at far end of the bow against the railing, I reached into my pocket and took out the box containing the necklace.

"I bought you something today."

"You took time out to think of me, how sweet of you."

She opened the box and was speechless.

Finally she spoke, "Goodness, I, I love it Jake, I love it."

I placed it around her neck, fastening the clasp, and kissed her gently on the lips. She hugged me continuously for five minutes while tears of joy ran down her face and onto my back. We didn't say a lot more that evening - we didn't have to. We had been falling in love with each other and every time we were together, it grew deeper. That night few words were necessary. We just held each other close and stood there at the bow basking in the moment.

The remainder of the trip to Stanley was uneventful. Ryan and I avoided the Tucker trio as much as possible. I saw Marie every chance I could, which wasn't often enough. It was mid-January but the weather was pleasant. We were south of the equator and it was summer there.

We pulled into port at the town of Stanley in the Falkland Islands on January-twentieth. Everyone wanted to get off the yacht and spend a day on land. We still had twenty-six days to get to Honolulu before Tucker would have to start paying the $100,000 a day penalty.

The captain figured he could spare one full day for everyone to go ashore. He said we couldn't take any more time than that. The distance from Stanley to Hawaii would require conserving fuel, meaning going a few knots under cruising speed.

Chapter 26

       I was expecting the temperature in Stanley to be nice since it was summer, but found out the daily average for that time of year was only sixty-two degrees. The Falkland Islands are classified as having a tundra climate. I grabbed a jacket to take ashore with me, just in case I needed it.

       I enjoyed the day in Stanley. It is a town of only twenty-two hundred residents and easy to get around. I never was a big city person, so Stanley suited me perfectly. The Tuckers were together doing whatever it is they do. Marie was free so she and I were off to explore the town. Ryan didn't want to join us, said he was going to visit the cathedral and whalebone arch, then check out the war memorials and shipwrecks in the harbor.

Marie and I went to the cathedral as well, had lunch in a fish and chip restaurant, and enjoyed ourselves just strolling about town going in and out of shops. It felt good to walk on solid ground and not have to think about balance. What felt best was being with Marie. I liked watching her and learning about her. I was love stuck and knew it. We both were.

We stocked the yacht well with food and any supplies we might need for the longest leg of our journey. The captain had the diesel tanks topped off and some routine maintenance performed by certified mechanics in Stanley Harbor.

I was dreading the rest of the trip. It was many days at sea, but then it would be over. My biggest dread was going around the tip of South America. The captain had already reassured me that the weather for the next few days was going to be crystal-clear. He said that we would be long gone from that area before the weather changed. I still had an uneasy feeling about it all. I would be happy when we hit the Pacific, started sailing north, and put that part of the trip behind us.

Marie and I had talked about going to Maui for a week once we got to Hawaii. We wanted to have lots of time alone to explore the island and spend time together, not having to worry about anyone else. It would be just the two of us spending long days together.

As we rounded the tip of South America, the weather was cold and frigid. The sea air stung my cheeks and nose. I couldn't endure staying outside for more than a few minutes at a time. We were two hundred miles off shore in normal shipping lanes but didn't see another ship. I liked walking around on the main deck at night but it wasn't tolerable there. I enjoyed looking in the distance for lights from passing ships, wondering who the people were and what their lives were like. I liked the mystery of it all.

We sailed around the tip of South America then into the Pacific without even the slightest of rough seas, just at Captain Nichols had promised. Then we headed north-northwest, and I knew that every passing day would bring us warmer weather as we got closer to Hawaii. I was thankful we had brought along both summer and winter clothing. We had been through a wide range of temperatures during the trip. I was looking forward to soon being able to ditch the winter gear for good.

I entered the wheelhouse the third morning after we'd rounded South America and headed out into the Pacific Ocean. I found Second Mate Goldman was still on duty and in charge. We exchanged greetings and made small talk for a few minutes until Captain Nichols entered from his quarters. Second Mate Goldman was finishing his twelve-hour shift. Captain Nichols chatted with Goldman for a few minutes about positioning and how he had charted the course throughout the night. The Captain then relieved him of duty for the day.

It was routine for Goldman to be in control of the wheelhouse from 6 p.m. until 6 a.m., then Captain Nichols would split the remaining twelve hours with Chief Mate Hogan. It wasn't uncommon though for Captain Nichols to come in during the evening and give Goldman a break for an hour or two.

On this trip, having a short crew, Chief Mate Hogan was also the Chief Engineer. That required him to spend a lot of his day doing routine maintenance down in the engine room. All together Captain Nichols himself spent fourteen or more hours each day in the wheelhouse, steering the ship.

Captain Nichols was old school and charted our course with maps and a compass. He even had a sextant mounted on the control panel in front of the big wheelhouse window. I'd seen him use it the evening before but didn't know if he was playing, or actually taking star shots to use in determining where we were. We had the newfangled GPS equipment, along with radar, but the captain didn't trust it as much as using old-fashioned methods. He knew that those were tried and true.

Captain Nichols was a pleasant man to be around, always cheerful and polite. He wasn't just like that to me, but the other guests and crew as well. He didn't seem to mind me coming into the wheelhouse. He actually welcomed me in the wheelhouse since I showed a keen interest in his knowledge about ships and being at sea. Besides, I enjoyed his company.

I got bored after a while, watching the water in front, behind, and to either side of us. I went to eat breakfast and afterward went to the gym and walked on a treadmill, lifted a few weights, and rode a stationary bike. I was trying to rid myself of built up energy. In another day or two, the pool should be pleasant to swim in again. It was a heated pool but I didn't like my head freezing while the rest of my body stayed submerged in the nice warm water, so I'd wait a few days until the air temperature was higher.

I spent time later that day with Marie, helping her in the laundry room with her daily washing. Mrs. Tucker was still finding ways to take up all of Marie's free time so she couldn't spend it with me. If Mrs. Tucker knew our plans once we arrived in Hawaii she'd really have been upset. I was certain Marie had not spoken to her about that.

Marie was such a good person and a dedicated employee. Not once did she ever say anything negative about Mrs. Tucker. Marie was a good influence on me, and I don't think she even realized it. I'd for the most part only experienced the negative side of people throughout my life. Marie was a positive person and was always seeing the good in people.

I had spent the late afternoon that day with Ryan in the game room. I had found a couple of things I could beat him at, pinball, and pool. We played several games of both that day. Ryan loved to win, but he didn't want me to let him win. He was finding pinball to be the most challenging. I normally beat him by a large margin. When I got tired and left him that afternoon, he stayed for a few more hours practicing. He said he'd challenge me to another game later in the evening.

Chapter 27

The next morning, like most others on the horribly long cruise, I got up, showered, and put on fresh clothing. I then went to the top deck for some fresh air before climbing up to the wheelhouse for an hour of conversation with Captain Nichols.

I'd had about all the sailing of the seas I could stand and I was longing to have my feet planted again on dry land. Spending so much time at sea gave me a deep respect for those sailors who could stay out on the ocean for months on end.

I knew soon this journey would end and I could get back to my normal life, whatever that was. I just had to hang in there for a while longer.

I went down to the main deck and stood at the bow, watching the waters ahead. Ryan spotted me and came over to talk. I told him that when we got to Hawaii, I wanted to spend time there vacationing with Marie.

"Vacation? You're on vacation now!" He said, in a joking manner.

I grabbed him and quickly had him in a headlock and rubbed his head with my fist. All the while, he was laughing. Ryan seemed to be doing well. He liked the sailing the seven seas stuff much more than I did.

I was hoping Ryan's gambling days were over and that he'd move on to something else. I had noticed a change in him on this trip. He seemed to have matured. Well, except when he was around Mrs. Tucker.

The morning was always the calmest part of the day, before everyone else began to stir. The captain and I could just sit and chat without interruption. I had gotten to where I looked forward to our daily morning visit. I liked going to the wheelhouse to observe the ships operations and talk to the captain about his voyages.

I thought a lot about the trip so far and how I'd made new friends. Prior to going to London, Ryan was my only friend. Now, I had both the captain and Marie I could call friends. Aside from the agony of being on the ship so long, a lot of good had happened on the cruise

I climbed the stairs as normal then went inside the wheelhouse. I sat down in one of the three leather chairs that pointed to the large front glass, giving a bird's eye view of the ocean ahead. The captain had the ship on cruise control and was at the chart table with his maps plotting where we had come from the day before.

"Where are we, Captain?" A question I asked every morning.

"We're approximately 800 nautical miles west of Punta Arenas, Chile," he said.

243

I had been studying the maps with the captain for weeks now and had a relatively good picture in my mind where we were. Since rounding the tip of South America, we were heading northwest toward Hawaii while at the same time getting further and further out to sea. There were thousands of miles of ocean around us. Even with the Panama Canal shut down, we hadn't spotted another ship in days. I thought that was odd. With the canal closed, I thought shipping lanes in this part of the world should be a lot more crowded.

"Do we have enough fuel to get us to Hawaii without running out of gas?" I asked.

"I's hope so mate, at least to get us close enough to call for a tow truck."

I laughed at his joke. I liked the captain's sense of humor.

"Someday I might have my own yacht Captain, but two things will be different."

"And what's that mate?"

"It will be much smaller of course. It will never go out to where I can't see land. And, it will have a queen aboard, but it won't be Drama Queen Tucker."

The captain's chuckle turned into a long laugh.

"That sounded like three things mate, instead of two."

"Oh yeah, I guess you're right." I laughed also.

"Will that queen be Miss Marie Whitney?" He asked.

"Ah yes, that would be a dreamboat for sure!" I replied.

"I know you fancy her. Me can tell mate. She feels likewise I's a thinkin."

"Yes, Miss Whitney, if only I could pull her away from having to wipe the Drama Queen's butt for a while."

The captain laughed loudly.

"Soon you will lad, soon you will."

I got out of the chair to walk over and view the map the captain was looking at. While doing so, I looked out the window toward the stern of the yacht. The eastern horizon had a thin black line across it. I didn't notice it when I came up on the deck just minutes before. It looked exactly like someone had taken a thin black magic marker and drawn a line across the skyline where it meets the ocean.

"Captain," I said, "What do you make of that?"

He looked up then studied the sky for a moment.

"That's strange, lad, I didn't see anything on radar this morning about a storm to the east, and she looks to be a bad one, good thing we're moving away from her. I'd expect about this time tomorrow or the day after, the coast of Chile will be in for some bad weather."

The captain and I chatted for a few more minutes then I told him I was heading to the galley. Chef Riddle was going to make me one of those delicious Spanish omelets for breakfast. I asked the captain if I could bring him anything from below.

"I've got me a container of hot tea for now lad. I'll be fine for the time being."

When I got to the galley, Chef Riddle already had the place smelling like breakfast. Marie was there, setting the tables with fresh linen and silverware. She was always helping someone even when it wasn't her job, such a good work ethic and such a sweet lady. I helped her finish getting the tables ready then we sat for a few minutes and drank a cup of hot tea together.

Chef Riddle served Marie and me each a steaming hot, Spanish omelet, hash browns, and a cup of diced peaches. We ate, then sat and enjoyed a second cup of tea while talking about our upcoming time on Maui. No one else was in the galley, so it was nice, just the two of us talking.

Marie looked at her watch and told me she had to get below to the laundry room. Mrs. Tucker required fresh linens on the beds daily. With that, plus towels and clothing, it was a continuous job trying to keep things washed and dried. Marie headed out and I finished my last sip of tea.

I headed to the exercise center to put a few miles in on the treadmill. I had decided to change my routine starting that morning, since I wasn't getting much exercise on the yacht. I wanted to start getting in a few extra miles of walking each morning before getting on with my day. After the walk, I headed to my cabin for a shower and change of clothes, then up to the wheelhouse again to sit for a while. I figured by now the Tuckers were stirring and I wanted to avoid them. There wasn't any use in ruining a perfectly good morning.

When I climbed the stairs to the main deck, the first thing I noticed was the eastern sky. The black line I'd seen just two hours ago had grown. It was much higher in the sky. The storm seemed to be growing stronger by the minute. The skyline there was black as pitch. The sight of it spooked me. The captain had told me it would move east toward Chile, not toward us.

I climbed the stairs on the port side of the superstructure and entered the wheelhouse. The captain had the helm locked on cruise still. Various charts were lying out on the table. The captain was on the radio, franticly trying to reach someone. He turned to look at me and I could see panic and anxiety on his face. That spooked me further and made my stomach start churning.

"We're in trouble, aren't we?" I blurted out.

The captain's voice was much lower than I'd ever heard him speak.

"Aye yes, lad, yer a smart one, no use in me lying to ya. I've been trying to reach someone on the radio and can't get a soul. The radar seems to be malfunctioning. Ye have already seen the storm behind us. I'm going to send out an SOS call."

"How can it be moving our way?" I asked, with a voice of fear.

"I don't know, me's never seen such an eerie sight," he replied. "I've had me ship going maximum speed for over an hour now, hoping to put some distance between us and the storm, but she's gaining on us lad. In all me years at sea, I've never seen a storm move so quickly, nor skies so black, I suppose it'll be upon us in a few hours or so. I better notify the others."

The captain moved back to the table to view the charts and was in deep thought. I took a deep breath and let out a sigh. The thing I feared the most, was that we would encounter a bad storm and rough seas. It looked as if we were about to get both. My worries had subsided after we cleared the tip of South America, but now days later, we were about to encounter a major storm.

"Is there an island nearby, Captain, where we can pull into a harbor and take shelter?"

The captain could tell I was quickly becoming terrified. He looked up from the maps.

"Don't fear, my lad, she's a good ship with a strong hull and firm backbone. I've weathered many a storm, and we shall weather this one as well."

The captain's words didn't give me much comfort.

"I'm going to call below lad. I'll tell everyone to meet in the galley in thirty minutes, to talk about the storm heading for us this morning. I need you to prepare to batten down the hatches and make sure nothing is on the main deck that would easily blow away."

The words had no sooner left Captain Nichols mouth when suddenly the bow of the yacht raised upward nearly two feet and the stern went down, then the stern jumped upward as the bow went down. We were both holding on to keep from bouncing around inside the wheelhouse. I looked toward the bow and could see a large wave moving forward away from us.

The captain yelled out in a voice filled with fear.

"There must have been an earthquake at sea, that was the beginning of what will be a tidal wave thousands of miles from here, she's gonna get bigger as she goes, good thing we weren't further out."

I looked back toward the stern and what I saw caused me to freeze in place.

"Captain!" I cried out.

Captain Nichols looked back.

"Sweet Mother of Mercy, help us all!"

A thousand yards behind us, the sky and sea were as black as the darkest night anyone could ever imagine. Along the front edge of the storm, heat lighting was pulsating outward in all directions while at the same time swirling in a counter-clockwise direction. The lightning pulses came through the clouds as purple with a tinge of red and gray.

The captain immediately went to the wheel and took the ship off cruise control.

"Quick lad, go batten down the hatches!" The captain screamed out.

At the same time, he was reaching for the microphone to warn the others. I darted out the wheelhouse and nearly flew down the stairs. I zoomed around the superstructure looking to ensure that the portholes were closed. At the same time, I was hitting the "emergency door close" switch on both the forward and aft stairways leading to the decks below. My heart was beating out of my chest. I returned to the stairway leading to the wheelhouse. I ran up the stairs and into the wheelhouse cabin while latching the door behind me.

I was out of my senses and didn't know what to do next, or why I had even returned to the wheelhouse. It must have been my instincts. My brain was telling me to go to the highest ground possible, as if it would do me any good.

The captain was standing at the wheel, hands at ten and two o'clock, feet shoulder width apart and legs stiff as if bracing for an impact. In the few minutes it had taken me to run around the deck then back to the wheelhouse, the yacht had already began to rock back and forth gently.

Another minute went by. The big yacht began pitching forward then backward, as well as from side to side. I looked out the window. The waves, which mere seconds ago were only a few inches high, were now splashing onto and over the main deck. The captain had grossly miscalculated the speed at which this storm was coming. It was already upon us.

I grabbed a handrail to keep from sliding across the room toward the large map table. In the next instant everything inside and outside the wheelhouse became a light show of red, purple and gray flashes spaced no more than three or four seconds apart.

Each flash looked like an x-ray with dull shades of purple and red. Less than a minute after the light flashes began, they were gone, and the cabin filled with a blackness so thick it seemed to penetrate right through me. The ship was rocking violently in all directions and the sound from the wind was deafening. My ears popped loudly from the pressure difference brought about from the storm. Then the wind striking the yacht created a sound that pierced my ears to the point I feared my eardrums would burst at any moment.

I wanted so badly to put my hands over my ears. I had enough wits about me though to know I had to keep holding to the railing. If I let go I would surely be tossed about the cabin like a rubber ball. I was saying a prayer with every breath I took, fearing that none of us were going to get out of this alive.

I couldn't tell where the captain was or if he was even in the wheelhouse. The super yacht was rocking like a toy boat in a bathtub. My ears were hurting so bad from the sounds of the wind, I couldn't think or concentrate on anything but the pain. My feet were slipping from under me as the ship rolled back and forth. At times, I'd have footing and the next second I'd be holding myself in place only by the death grip my hands had on the railing.

My face and all other parts of my body were being hit by small objects from inside the cabin. Everything loose was now a projectile, flying about aimlessly. Maps were flying about and would catch on my body or arms, then fly off as suddenly as they had attached themselves to me. I felt the ship was going to rip apart but I couldn't see or hear any of it, all I could do was hang on and keep praying.

I expected that at any moment, I'd be swimming in the ocean. The darkness, horrid winds, and waves continued for hours. My hands blistered as I continued my death grip to the railing. Then the blisters burst, leaving the raw skin to burn fiercely as I continued to grip the handrail.

I received injuries from the flying debris but couldn't tell how badly I was hurt. My body ached and cramped, but I couldn't tend to my wounds. All I could do was continue holding on. I knew if I let go I'd be thrown from the wheelhouse into the sea.

At some point, all my strength was gone and I let go of the railing. I slid forward on the floor and hit the front console, then started sliding back in the same direction I'd come from. The ship suddenly rolled and I was thrown against one of the pilot chairs.

With all the strength left in me, I reached up and grabbed the armrest. I pulled myself up into the chair. I quickly found the seatbelt and latched myself in. I could tell there were shards of glass and other debris in the chair but it didn't matter, I had used all my energy. It was unthinkable to unbuckle to clean the seat off. Although there wasn't a large amount of water in the cabin, there was enough to make everything wet. The taste of seawater was in my mouth and burning my eyes.

My mind was going in a multitude of directions at the same time. I knew we were all going to die there as the ship tore apart. Marie, Ryan, where were they? Were they safe? Maybe things were better below than here in the wheelhouse. I wished I could get to them. I needed conformation that they weren't hurt.

Shortly after I'd buckled into the pilot chair, I was no longer able to hear anything at all. I felt like I was dead, being carried away by some strange force. I was powerless to do anything.

Suddenly, instead of hearing nothing, I began to hear ringing in my ears. After a short time, I could hear wind again and knew the storm must have moved forward past us. The barometric pressure must have pulsated between an incredible high and low. I wondered how that could that happen in such a short time span?

My head was still hurting from the ringing in my ears, but not as bad as before. The ship was still rolling back and forth, but not as severely. It was still pitch black everywhere. Holding my right hand in front of my face, I could only feel the presence of my fingers. I couldn't see a thing.

I suddenly realized t that the wind gusts for some time had been hitting me directly in the face, indicating the windshield had blown out. The wind was cold and heavily laden with moisture. I felt chilled to the bone and the cold air added to my misery.

A few minutes later the darkness started going away. I couldn't see objects, just a dim gray light everywhere.

Another hour passed and the winds were down to just a loud roar. The rocking of the boat, although still violent, was nothing like the last few hours had been. I knew the yacht had to be taking on water and perhaps would soon sink. I was helpless. I had to stay strapped in until I could see clearly.

In the hour that followed, the sustained wind was around ten to fifteen knots. The large gusts of twenty to thirty knots were coming about two minutes apart. The darkness was slowly abating and I began to see the outline of the cabin walls and objects inside the wheelhouse. The ocean swells were dying down. The yacht was bobbing in the water, instead of thrashing about violently in all directions.

I began to move my arms and legs. I was stiff and everything hurt. The illumination in the cabin was getting lighter by the minute and the winds were now down to perhaps five knots with only occasional gust. I could see the main deck below now and for a short distance out over the water. The waves appeared to be a few feet high at best. The ship's wheel was only a few feet to my left. I could see it turning back and forth by itself.

Captain Nichols was nowhere in sight. I feared he had been thrown overboard and was somewhere out in the open sea. I unbuckled the seatbelt and moved forward, not knowing if my legs would hold me when they touched the floor. The glass and other debris in the seat beneath me were digging into my pants. I winced in pain as I slid forward. I didn't want to use my hands because they were raw and bleeding, but I had to, in order to get out of the chair without falling.

The yacht was positioned to where the waves were hitting the port side at a forty-five degree angle. I moved over to the wheel. Using my palms more than my fingers, I steadied the wheel and then turned the ship left toward the waves. It worked, the waves were now hitting against the bow instead of the side of the yacht.

I was amazed the wheel reacted because the engines weren't running. I then remembered Captain Nichols telling me how the rudder system was set up with mechanical linkages. That meant the steering would work even if the ship's engines or generators weren't working.

I was able to think again. The shrill sounds that had been piercing my ears earlier were now gone. I knew we had somehow survived the worst of the storm. I was concerned about Marie and Ryan, fearing they were hurt. I was also fearful the ships damage would cause it to sink.

The light was still getting brighter. I could see a hundred yards off the bow. There was the same degree of light everywhere in all directions, just a dull grayish to yellow glow. It was like being in a large meeting room with only a single forty-watt light bulb glowing.

Another fifteen to twenty minutes went by. The yacht was going in and out of one to two foot waves. It was easy to manage the wheel and keep the ship on course by following the direction the waves were going. Then it hit me. How strange! The ocean waves weren't normal. All the waves were flowing in the same direction. It was as if we were riding a set of rapids on a river. The ship had no power yet we were moving along at ten to fifteen knots, bobbing up and down in the water. We were flowing along in the same direction as the waves.

The ringing in my ears had all but gone away and I started hearing normal sounds again. Until then, I couldn't tell anything about the ships condition. Suddenly, I could hear creaking and groaning as the big yacht moved back and forth. It grunted deeply, as if it were a wounded animal - trying to use its remaining strength to escape from the hunter.

I heard a moan and looked toward the back of the wheelhouse cabin, on the portside of the big map table. Captain Nichols was laying in the corner. He was covered in wet paper, maps, and broken glass, all of which were sloshing around in two to three inches of water in the cabin floor. I was elated he was still in the cabin and alive, but now worried that he was seriously injured.

"Captain, are you alright?" I yelled out.

The captain moaned. I looked and saw him moving, trying to raise himself up. His pant legs were torn and I could see blood oozing down his left leg. The light was still dim, so I couldn't tell anything else about his condition.

I turned back to the bow, to ensure I still had the ship steering us parallel to the waves. I turned back again, to observe the captain. He sat up with his back against the wall in the corner. I called to him, telling him to watch the broken window above his head. It was fractured and swinging back and forth from the frame. Only a thread was preventing it from crashing to the floor.

The captain scooted forward toward me, pushing a pile of wet trash and glass with his feet that grew rapidly as he moved in my direction. He reached with his right hand and grabbed the handrail that ran along the edge of the map table, in an effort to pull himself up. I was still looking forward to check our direction then back again to check on the captain. All the time, I wanted to let go of the wheel to assist him but unable to. I was fearful that the ship would turn to one side or the other and capsize.

The captain managed to pull himself up. He gingerly scooted forward until he was able to thrust himself into the portside pilot chair and buckle himself in. I could see him more clearly now. He didn't appear to be badly injured, but was certainly shaken. Like me, he was bruised and battered. His left hand was holding his stomach as he made a grunting sound. After a few more minutes, he seemed to regain his orientation.

"Me got hit by something in the belly lad, and it threw me away from the wheel."

He and I both were moaning and wincing with nearly every breath and certainly with every move of our extremities.

I took a good look around, trying to access the damage within my line of vision. I couldn't tell much about the main deck below or anything else outside of the wheelhouse cabin. The large front window of the cabin was shattered and had caved in. It was intact as one giant piece and folded over the long console. The instrument panel didn't appear damaged but nothing was illuminated. The big compass setting on the console held the windshield slightly elevated. I looked at the compass and saw it wasn't working.

I spotted the microphone hanging from the dash, bouncing up and down from the cord like a yoyo. I grabbed it and pressed the call button, hoping it worked so I could make contact with everyone below. I was hoping to hear news that everyone was ok. The microphone however was dead. All the power was off.

All the windows on the port side were gone except for the one remaining piece still swinging back and forth by a thread. The cabin had a massive amount of debris strewn about and everything was soaked with seawater. The cabin ceiling had partially caved in on the port side with a big swag present near the mid-point of the cabin.

Captain Nichols was slowly regaining his faculties. He leaned forward, with a peculiar look as he stared out the open windshield toward the sea ahead of us. You could easily tell the ship was pitching, toward the bow, at about a fifteen to twenty degree angle. We were speeding through the water, despite not having engine power.

"What do ye make of this, lad?" He said, with a voice indicating he was confused.

"I was hoping you could tell me, Captain."

"We're going down river," he said, "We're going down a bloody river."

"Captain, I'm weak inside and out. I can't stand here much longer." He told me to release the lever to the left side of the helm and let the wheel slide back to the middle pilot chair. I did so, buckled into the pilot chair, and resumed steering the vessel. It took a lot of effort just doing that small task, but it felt good to sit again.

A short time later, we entered a deep fog bank. The sea air was cold, all my muscles were aching, and I still felt chilled to the bone. The ship's movement slowed, as if we'd been running our engines and they suddenly stopped. The captain was still holding his mid-section and moaning. Still, through that distraction, he also noticed the ship slowing. He said something about checking a displacement gauge, which would indicate if we were taking on water. All the instruments were out. There was no power to run anything, so it wasn't possible to check any of the gauges.

The swells had dissipated and the ocean was once again calm. The water was merely lapping against the ship's sides. Suddenly I felt the bottom of the ship scraping against something and scooting along. A few seconds later, the captain and I were both thrown forward in our chairs. We heard a deep thud and the ship came to a sudden stop. The big yacht then listed to the port side about five degrees. Our seatbelts kept us from being thrown from the pilot chairs, but the sudden jerk cut into our midsections sharply. We both cried out in pain.

"We've run aground!" The captain cried out.

Burning Rock

Act Three

Chapter **28**

The captain and I unbuckled our seat belts and slid out of the chairs. We were both moving gingerly, everything hurt. We still hadn't assessed our wounds but it was certain neither of us had life threatening injuries. I hurt everywhere. My fingers and the palms of my hands hurt the worst. It was going to take a few weeks for the broken blisters and torn skin to heal over.

For the first time in eight or more hours, things were calm. During that time, the only thing I could do was hold on, trying to survive. There had been little time to think of the others below, but now all my thoughts were

about them. *Ryan and Marie, are they okay?* I told
Captain Nichols I needed to get below and find the others.
He said he'd come also but as he tried getting out of the
chair he sighed loudly, then sat back down.

"Lad, I'll be there soon as me can, but first I've got
to get me strength back."

I knew what he meant, I was moving purely on
adrenaline. I had no energy. The small refrigerator just
inside the cabin door was still intact. I opened it and took
out two bottles of water. I handed one to the captain and
drank the other myself. The water was refreshing and
soothing to my dry throat. I drank the entire bottle in one
gulp.

The starboard side door of the wheelhouse was
jammed so I had to push it hard with my shoulder. It took
strength I didn't think I had in order to force it open. The
door was warped and would only open about twelve inches.
I pushed hard against it once more, but it wasn't going to
open any further. I squeezed through the opening and
started down the steps.

The fog was lifting but I still couldn't see any
further than a few yards off the side of the ship. The
stairway leading to the wheelhouse had pulled loose at the
bottom. It bounced up and down as I went down the steps.
I moved toward the stern, in order to get to the main
stairway leading to the decks below the superstructure.

The slight list of the ship made it difficult to walk. I
had to brace myself against the walls with my hands, which
burned each time my skin touched the metal. I got to the
entrance leading to the decks below. I was worried the
hatch doors would jammed. That worried soon vanished. I
saw that both doors were missing.

I started down the stairs from the main deck to the
first deck below. There was a strong smell of diesel fuel. I
knew a supply line or one of the fuel tanks had ruptured. I
didn't hear any sound except the slight moaning of the

yacht as the water lapped against its side from the now small waves.

The thirty-two foot tender was missing from its docking bay. From the looks of the surroundings, it didn't leave peacefully. Much of the roof above the docking bay was shredded, and the side support beams were bent, twisted, or both. The empty docking bay now provided the only source for light into the corridor of the first deck below.

"Is anybody here? I cried out. "Is anybody hurt?"

There was no answer. I fumbled around and felt my way along the wall on the starboard side as I continued deeper into the ship, reaching the first cabin door. The hallway, like the wheelhouse cabin, was littered with a variety of objects in a pool of water a few inches deep. As I extended my hand to touch the cabin door, I realized it was open. I held myself against the doorway and yelled inside.

"Is anybody here?" As before, there was no answer.

I knew there were glass enclosed emergency supply cabinets in the corridor, located between every other cabin. They contained a section of fire hose, an axe, first-aid kit, and a flashlight. I slid down the wall until I felt the doorframe of the cabinet. It didn't open on my first try. I pulled hard and it flung open. I placed my hand inside and felt my way around until I detected the shape of the long cylindrical flashlight, and then unsnapped the retaining ring.

I was envisioning in my mind the layout of the hallway. I tried to think about how the cabins were spaced. When I turned on the flashlight, I wasn't ready for the reality of what was present. Several of the ceiling tiles were missing. Several more hung down from the framing overhead, ready to fall. The listing of the ship made the hallway look narrow and twisted. Most of the debris floating in the water was bits and pieces of the ceiling tile. That was a good sign. I could travel further down the hall with little obstruction.

Suddenly I heard movement further down. I moved quickly toward the area from where the sound was coming. I got to the next cabin on the starboard side. The door to that cabin was also open. I shone the light all around but didn't see anyone. I heard more noises and headed down to the next door. The sound was coming from a cabin on the port side. When I got to where the sound was coming from the cabin door was closed. I turned the knob and pushed. The door swung open, but only after applying quite a bit of pressure.

"Oh, thank God." I heard someone say. My hearing wasn't back to normal yet and I couldn't make out the voices. I didn't know if it was male or female voices I was hearing.

"Who's there?" I cried out.

"It's Joseph, and Mother."

It was Joseph and Mrs. Tucker. They were in the bathroom. The furniture in the room was scattered about. I crawled and climbed over and around the bed, and opened the bathroom door. The two of them were huddled together in the corner. Mrs. Tucker was crying softly as she lay in Joseph's arms.

"Are either of you hurt?" I said.

"Not seriously," Joseph replied.

I asked if they could walk and Joseph said he thought they could.

"I'll help you with your mother, Joseph. I'll help get both of you to the top deck."

I extended my hand and Joseph grabbed hold so I could assist him getting up from the floor. I could feel pain in my back, but nothing like the pain in my hands. I gritted my teeth and held on. Joseph stood up, still holding his mother. I threw her right arm around my neck while

Joseph had her other arm around his. I held the flashlight in my free hand, and the three of us moved along and around obstacles, making our way out of the room and into the corridor.

As we exited the room, Captain Nichols was coming down the stairs ahead. I yelled out, asking if he would be able to help get Joseph and Mrs. Tucker to the main deck. The captain scooted along the wall until he met us, then took Mrs. Tucker's arm from around my neck and assisted her and Joseph back toward the stairway.

I went to the next cabin on the portside and looked inside. It appeared to be empty so I moved across the hall to the cabin on the starboard side of the ship. I yelled asking if anybody was there and received no reply. I shone the light around the cabin, just to make sure it was empty.

I was ready to move on when I caught a slight movement out of the corner of my eye. It was inside the large closet to the right of the bed. The accordion doors of the closet were slightly open and inside I could see a figure of someone lying on the floor. I hurried over to the closet and saw it was Preston Tucker. He was curled up in a ball and holding tight to what looked to be an old worn out baby blanket. He was whimpering and had the corner of the blanket in his mouth. I placed my hand on his shoulder and shook him gently.

"Are you okay?" I said.

"I…I.., I think so," he stuttered, after pulling the blanket from his mouth. I pulled his right arm back slightly hoping he would assist me in pulling him to his feet. He pulled back, raising the blanket up over his face.

"Gosh dang it Preston, if you're okay, then get up, your mother and brother are up on the main deck and I'm sure they are worried about you!"

He pulled the blanket off his face and looked me over, then slowly with my assistance stood up.

"Are you sure you're okay?" I repeated.

"Ya…Yes," he whimpered. I lead Preston, still holding his blanket, out the door and into the hallway. The captain had returned to the bottom of the steps and was standing there looking in my direction. I yelled to him that I had another one, and led Preston over to the captain. He took Preston from me, and led him up the stairs. I was exhausted and sat down for a minute amid the water and bits of ceiling tile floating about.

Captain Nichols had led Mrs. Tucker and Joseph to the stateroom on the superstructure main deck. He then took Preston there as well. He returned to the corridor of the first deck below, and found me sitting in the water at the bottom of the stairwell.

The captain had brought a flashlight from the stateroom. I slowly rose to my feet then we headed back down the corridor. The captain's pace was steady but he was moving slower than I was. I looked back to make sure he was okay.

"Keep moving lad," he said, "We have to find the others. There will be time to rest later."

The captain sped up and went ahead of me, leading the way. I could hear a banging noise on the bulkhead door that leads to the second deck below as we reached the midway point of the corridor. Then I heard a voice. It was Marie screaming, "Help me!" I hurried around the captain to reach the door, sloshing through water and negotiating the slight angle of the listing ship.

"Marie," I screamed out. "Are you hurt?"

"No, I'm ok," she reported. "The door is jammed and I can't get out."

I had tried to open that door earlier, just before finding Preston, and found it was indeed tightly jammed shut. The captain caught up to me. We were both talking to Marie through the bulkhead door. I moved back to the end of the corridor and removed the fire axe from the emergency supply cabinet. I came back to the door, ready to attempt forcing the door open or cut off the hinges. The captain put out a hand to stop me.

"It's no use," he said. "You'll never cut through a bulkhead door with that."

"Is it possible for you to make it to the bow end of that deck, Marie?" The captain shouted out.

"I don't know," she replied.

"I need for you to try lass. If you can, we'll meet you at the bulkhead door on that end."

I quickly moved along the wall to the bow end of the corridor. I lifted the latch on the bulkhead door that led to the stairway. It opened with ease. Just as the door opened, I saw Marie coming up the stairway holding a flashlight. She dropped the light, rushed into my arms, and embraced me tightly. I was so happy to see her and to find that she wasn't hurt. I let out a deep grunt when she hugged me, which caused her to back away slightly.

"Oh my sweet baby, are you hurt?"

I told her I was banged up somewhat, but would be fine. I was trying to be macho and manly, but I couldn't hide the pain. I was going to be sore for a while. We hugged again, and I kissed both of her cheeks as tears streamed down her face.

I told Marie that we had found the Tuckers, and they were all fine. The captain once again caught up with me and told Marie that the Tuckers were up in the stateroom. I then asked Marie if she was up to helping us search for the others. I'd not found Ryan and was concerned.

Marie reported she'd not seen anyone. She'd been in the laundry room since the storm first hit. There was a hammock hanging in the laundry room. She would often lie in the hammock and read a book while the clothes were washing and drying. She'd jumped into the hammock when the ship began to rock back and forth and had ridden out the entire storm there. I was thankful she had done that, it turned out to be the safest place she could have been.

Marie said she wanted to help search for the others, but first she needed to get a breath of fresh air. She said the diesel fumes had all but overtaken her, and she was extremely nauseated. I told her to go ahead, get some air, check on the Tuckers, and then find us later.
I had only been below the main deck a short time span, but already I too was becoming sick from the smell of diesel fuel.

Marie headed to the main deck while the captain and I searched the remaining rooms on the first deck below. We went from cabin to cabin and then checked the theatre, but found no one. We returned to the forward bulkhead door where we had met Marie, ready to proceed down the stairway to the second deck below. As we arrived back at the bulkhead door, I saw Marie was coming down the corridor with a flashlight in her hand.

The three of us made our way down to the second deck to continue the search. We skipped the laundry area since Marie had been there alone. After searching all the staff cabins, and the machine shop, we still had not found a soul. All the while, we were yelling out for Ryan and the others. I was starting to panic. Ryan should have been in his room on the first deck. Where could he be?

After searching the second deck, we moved quickly to the bulkhead door near the bow, which led to the third and bottom deck. The door opened easily. The stench of diesel fuel was strong there, causing us all to cough.

At the bottom of the stairs, Marie and I headed into the engine room while the captain went toward the fuel tanks and generators. There was a layered cloud of steam in the air, hovering at eye level and extending to the ceiling. We had to stoop down in order to get a clear view of what lay in front of us.

We were wading in over a foot of seawater mixed with a large amount of diesel fuel. As our lights shone on the water, a colorful array of shimmering rainbows appeared, coming from the water and fuel mixture. Marie was a few steps to my right.

I was squinting and looking around all the pipes and hoses trying to see the back of the compartment. I could see the giant diesel engines still connected to the transmissions, followed by the drive shafts that extended through the hull. As I moved toward the stern, the depth of the water increased. It was now up to my knees. My skin was stinging as the rising water made contact with cuts and scrapes along my legs and my knees.

I heard Marie gasp. I looked back and saw her standing stiffly with no movement; her hands clasped against her face. I waded over to her side in the knee-deep water. Five feet in front of her was Chief Mate Hogan, lying face down in the water. His arms stretched out on both sides. He was partly floating in the mixture of water and fuel. I waded past Marie until I had reached Hogan, and grabbed his shoulders. While going down to my knees, I flipped him over onto my lap. There was no use checking for a pulse or trying to perform CPR, he was dead.

I held his limp body for a few seconds. I hung my head, fighting an overwhelming desire to cry. I could hear Marie behind me sobbing uncontrollably. I turned and pulled her to me. I held her slender body close to me, and wiped the tears away as they streamed down her face. A large lump was in my throat, and it was hard to swallow. I held Marie until her sobs subsided.

I felt helpless and didn't know what to do next. For countless hours on end, we'd been through a living hell and instead of easing up; it was getting worse by the minute.

I regained my composure. There were still others missing, and I'd still not found Ryan. We couldn't do anything more for Hogan. Still, I didn't want to leave him in the water. I wrapped my arms around him then dragged him toward the starboard side of the engine room, where the water was most shallow, and propped him up against the wall.

I went back to Marie. I put my arms around her and slowly led her back toward the bulkhead door. There was a metal chair mounted to the floor to the right of the door. Marie sat down, saying she was feeling dizzy and weak. As I was assisting Marie, I heard Captain Nichols yelling for me to come quickly.

I didn't have the strength to move fast. I shuffled my feet along the floor toward Captain Nichols. He was about thirty feet away, near the generators and fuel tanks. I could see that one of the generators had torn away from its mounts and was sitting at a forty-five degree angle between the ships wall and the number three diesel fuel tank.

I had to duck beneath some pipes and wiring that had fallen in order to reach the captain. As I stooped to go beneath the entanglement of wires, pipe, and metal bracing, I saw Captain Nichols down on his knees. Ryan laid stretched out on the floor. The captain was holding his head.

I hunched over to miss the overhanging maze of low hanging material and sloshed forward through the water. Almost instantly, I was kneeling down on the floor beside Ryan and the captain.

"He's alive but we have to get him out of here and fast," the captain said.

Ryan was unconscious. Both of his arms and everything from his waist down were covered in blood. A tourniquet made from Ryan's belt was wrapped around his left leg just above the knee. I saw what remained of his left leg caught between the generator and a large metal table. The skin of his leg had somehow wrapped over his wound, hiding the gruesome scene. The slab of skin was all that held his lower left leg to his body.

The captain told me to hold Ryan's head, so I quickly moved to where we could exchange positions. The captain moved close to Ryan's leg, reached into his pocket and took out his folding knife. He severed the hanging skin, allowing Ryan's lower leg to fall away.

"You do as I say lad, else your friend will die here. We got to get him up on the main deck where we can treat him properly."

The captain grabbed Ryan's good leg with one hand and put his other around Ryan's waist. I cupped my arms beneath Ryan's armpits, and we lifted him. We shouted to Marie to come get our lights, so we could see. She ran over to us. I could see she was shaking all over. Still, she grabbed the flashlights and shone a light ahead of us, leading us up to the stairs.

We struggled with Ryan's weight as we went through the corridors, then up each flight of stairs, until reaching the top deck. The ship was listing only a few degrees at most. However, it threw our balance off, and we nearly dropped Ryan several times. There was no way we could be easy with Ryan. We did the best we could, especially considering both the captain and I had already spent any energy we had. At that point, we were functioning merely on adrenaline and human spirit.

As we climbed the stairway and made it to the landing of the top deck the cold fresh-air hit us in the face. It was exhilarating to our lungs to take in fresh air free of diesel fumes. I was wet from head to toe and sweating profusely. The cold air felt good to my body, but I knew we needed to continue forward. We had to get Ryan, as well as ourselves, inside the stateroom and out of the elements.

The stateroom was the most logical place to be at that time. It was closest to the decks below, contained a lot of space, and was free of the diesel smell. We took Ryan there and laid him on the carpeted floor in the direction the ship was listing, placing his head at the lower elevation. I sent Marie up the superstructure to the captain's quarters to get blankets and a pillow.

Mrs. Tucker, Joseph, and Preston were sitting on the floor with their backs against the bar. They were drinking scotch, complaining about the ship being wrecked, and the terrible ordeal they had just gone through.

I told Preston and Joseph that I needed them to go below and search for Chef Riddle and Second Mate Goldman. They sat there ignoring me, while Mrs. Tucker mumbled something about suing Captain Nichols for wrecking the yacht. I got angry. It was no time for them to act like spoiled brats, and I had no patience for their nonsense.

"If I have to tell you again, I'll hurt the both of you!" I said. "Go now!"

Both Preston and Joseph jumped to their feet and scurried toward the door. Mrs. Tucker looked at me with as evil a look as I'd ever seen on her face.

"You heartless bastard, they were giving me comfort!" She screamed at me.

I ignored her, thinking I would deal with her later. She'd been shaken up from the storm but wasn't badly hurt. Right then, there were more pressing issues than her comfort.

I turned my attention back to Ryan. The captain had sat down and slumped over from exhaustion. He had some wounds that needed cleaning himself, hadn't eaten all day, and I was worried about him. Still, Ryan was the critical one, needing the most attention.

Marie arrived with blankets and a pillow.

"I can't stand the sight of blood Jake," she said.

"It's ok, Baby. I don't like seeing it either, but I've got to try to help Ryan."

Her eyes welled up with tears, and she started sobbing,

"I'm afraid he might die!" She blurted out.

I was scared too. I didn't have any experience with treating wounds, and most certainly not anything as serious as what had just happened to Ryan.

Marie came over and put her hands on my back. While kneeling beside me, she placed her head against me. She was still crying. She knew as little as I did about first aid, so all she could do was be there for moral support. Somehow the knowledge of her being there, and knowing she would not leave me, gave me strength to continue.

I put the pillow under Ryan's head. He groaned in pain and was semi-conscious. He was trying to speak but couldn't form any words. Finally, I ascertained that he was asking for water. Marie leaped up and went around the bar, returning in an instant with a bottle of water.

She held Ryan's head as I poured a small amount into his mouth. He coughed slightly, but drank perhaps an ounce before closing his lips tightly shut. His eyes were closed the entire time. Marie lowered his head onto the pillow, and we covered him with the blankets.

Marie looked down at Ryan's leg. She started into a state of shock. I didn't have time to think about it, or it would have caused me to do the same. I told her not to look, so she turned away. I needed her now and had to keep her focused. I told her to go to the EMT kit in the owner's office to get some alcohol and large gauze bandages.

I wasn't certain about anything I was doing, but I knew Ryan had lost a considerable amount of blood. I had to try to cover the wound and keep dirt out. I decided that if I could sew the flap of skin over the wound, it would act somehow to seal things off. The tissue was most likely already dead, but I couldn't think of anything else to try. Ryan's leg was still bleeding, but it was oozing and not flowing. The tourniquet was still in place. I determined that for now; it needed to remain there.

Marie came back with the first-aid supplies. She also had a bottle of water for each of us. She told me to drink the water to keep from getting dehydrated. We both drank, and it was very refreshing, but it caused my empty stomach to cramp.

I turned my attention once again to Ryan. I asked Marie where we could get a needle and some heavy thread. She said that the captain kept a sewing kit in his cabin, and that she would get it. She had brought some peroxide when she had gotten the first-aid supplies. I used the peroxide instead of the alcohol. While Marie was gone for the sewing supplies, I soaked gauze in peroxide and cleaned around the wound. The peroxide foamed profusely, and Ryan jerked a few times. I was hoping I wasn't making things worse.

I felt so helpless and wished someone could be there to tell me the right thing to do. The captain would be of help later, but for now, he was too exhausted. He was now slumped over and sleeping. He had done all he could for the time being.

Marie came back, holding a needle, and a spool of thread used for sewing fabric. I asked her to thread the needle for me. My hands were too raw and stinging to attempt it. She was able to thread the needle quickly. I started sewing the skin flap over Ryan's open wound. Marie looked away. The wound appeared to be clotting. I put the stitches in without having to wipe away fluids. After I was done, I took a roll of gauze and wrapped the leg as best as I could.

After wrapping Ryan's leg, I went outside for a breath of fresh air. I was shaking, knowing it was because of mental, as well as physical exhaustion.

The fog lifted with patches still lingering about. What small amount of light there had been earlier was now dimming. I knew that wasn't because of the storm, it was

271

nightfall. There was an eerie feeling about the place. I didn't know if we were on the mainland or an island.

I remember the captain saying there weren't any islands for a thousand miles around us. Perhaps we had been pushed back toward South America, but then I thought of how the storm had been coming from the east and heading west. I didn't see lights anywhere. It was quiet outside except for a small breeze whistling as it struck the ship. I was out of strength, and my mind was a buzz saw of emotions and thoughts.

I didn't know if the captain had sent up a signal flare, he never said. I headed up to the wheelhouse, got a signal flare, and shot it into the air from the now open windshield. The flare burst way up into the sky and slowly floated down. It provided enough light that I could see the water, which was now as calm as if it were sitting in a glass. I could also make out the outline of land with high hills and a beach area, but no lights. There didn't appear to be a soul around.

I heard crying and ran back down the steps to the main deck. I turned the corner and saw Joseph and Preston coming up from the stairway. I ran over to meet them.

"We couldn't find Golden, but we found the Chef; he's dead!" Preston cried out.

My heart sank again. How could the nightmare go on? When would it stop?

"Where is he?" I said.

"He's in the galley, lying face down on the floor."

How could that be? We already searched the galley and saw no sign of Chef Riddle. I couldn't think anymore, couldn't function. I went back inside the stateroom. Marie had gone back to the cabins below and gotten more blankets for the captain, herself, and me. She covered the captain, who was stretched out on the floor and snoring.

I got a light and went down to the galley to see for myself. Sure enough, Chef Riddle was dead. I went and got a bed covering and placed it over his body. It seemed like I should have done more, but I didn't know what else to do. I got dizzy and had to sit down for a moment to keep from passing out. I sat there on the wet floor and tried to rest briefly. I also needed to clear my mind.

I returned to the stateroom, where I collapsed on the floor beside Ryan and Marie. As I lay down, she curled up behind me and covered us with a blanket. I thought about how comforting that felt. In the next moment, I was asleep.

Chapter 29

When I woke the next morning, the captain and Marie were gone. A small amount of light filled the stateroom. The sun was rising and trying to burn off the heavy fog that now enveloped the ship. I reached over and felt Ryan's forehead. He was warm but not hot. He had survived the night, and I had gotten some rest. Perhaps now I could take better care of him. I found my flashlight, turned it on, and looked at his leg. Amazingly, most of the gauze was still white and not soaked in blood, but his leg was very red and severely swollen.

I heard the door open just as Marie and the captain came in. They had gone to the galley to look for food. We all needed to eat and get our strength back. The three of us sat on the floor near the bar eating bread with cold cuts and had bottled water to drink. All three of the Tuckers were at the opposite end of the bar all huddled together and sleeping. From the looks of the empty scotch bottles, I would guess they'd all passed out sometime last night. I'm sure they would wake up soon, have hangovers, and expect Marie to take care of them.

We all were wretched looking. It was easy to tell we'd all been through quite an ordeal.

The simple food tasted wonderful. I hadn't realized how hungry I was until the food touched my lips. I had a million questions for the captain as we sat there.

"Where do you think we are?" I asked

"I don't have a clue mate, not an inkling of a clue. When I got up this morning, I went to the wheelhouse and looked at the compasses. Neither the magnetic nor the gyroscopic are working, which is strange," replied the captain.

"Just before the storm hit you had told me we were about 800 miles off the coast of Chile, and that there weren't any islands anywhere."

"That's right Sonny, and I figure we were in that storm for ten hours or better as she carried us westward at a speed of at least twenty knots."

"So do you think we are on an island that no one knows about?"

"Oh I doubt that me friend, these oceans are well traveled, plus we now have satellites and such looking down upon us, so there are no longer undiscovered islands. I surmise we've run aground on the mainland."

"What mainland, Captain? You aren't making sense to me."

"I don't know, mate. Me head's just rattled and not thinking straight. I suppose we'll find help today for sure. As soon as this fog lifts, we need to get ashore and look for folks, but in the meantime, we need to search the ship for me missing crew member."

"What about the radios, Captain? Is there some way we can hook a battery up and get them running, so we can call for help?"

"I tried that this morning, lad, but nothing on the radio. I put out a distress signal though, it's supposed to work somehow even without power. Someone's bound to receive that."

"I still have lots of questions Captain, like what kind of storm was that? How did it move that fast? Why was it as if we were on a river going downstream through rapids?"

"I don't have answers right now, lad, but in time. Now let's get a plan together. We've got to find help for your friend, he's critically injured."

It was still getting lighter outside. Visibility now was better than any time since the storm. I gave the captain and Marie both a hug. I knew I had to be strong, be a leader. There would be time for tears later. For the first time in my life, I felt that people really needed me and looked to me for leadership. I felt so incompetent though, not knowing what to do next. Most of my life I'd listened to Ryan and let him lead. Now, I was the one who had to step up to the plate and try to make the right calls, not only for him, but for the rest of us as well.

I went back over to Ryan and wiped his face and arms with a damp cloth in order to remove the dried blood. The temperature in the cabin felt like it was around sixty degrees, so I knew he wasn't going to overheat or get too cold. Right then, there were two things pressing, finding Second Mate Golden, who was still missing, and getting Ryan to a hospital as soon as possible.

Captain Nichols handed me a flashlight and told me we needed to search the cabins again. Marie said she would sit with Ryan. As we came out of the stateroom onto the main deck, I looked out beyond the yacht and could see the shoreline. We were perhaps a hundred yards offshore in a horseshoe-shaped bay.

There was a small beach area, then a cliff perhaps a hundred feet high. On top of the cliff, it looked like the land consisted of gently sloping hills. To the right of the beach area, about another hundred yards down the shoreline, I could see a small stream flowing into the bay.

Beyond the bay, the stream quickly disappeared into a thick tree line back into a cove. Far in the back of that cove, I could see a waterfall. It was perhaps twenty feet wide, coming down from the cliffs, likely forming the stream that was flowing into the bay. It was hard to make out much detail due to the fog. At any other time, I would have thought, what a paradise, but at that moment, it seemed cold and desolate.

"I don't see any signs of life, Captain."

"I'm sure once we get beyond the bay here, or atop those cliffs, we'll find someone who can help us."

We turned our flashlights on and headed down to the first deck below. With light now coming through the porthole windows, we had a better view. Somehow, most of the furniture and other things bolted down held during the storm. The smell of diesel wasn't as strong but still penetrated my nostrils, giving me a slight headache. Only a small amount of water remained in the corridor. Already a mildew smell was detectable. Even with the diesel fumes, that distinguishable smell couldn't be masked.

We diligently searched all twelve of the guest rooms, the theatre, the tender bay, food storage, and galley, but no sign of Second Mate Golden anywhere. The captain and I wrapped Chef Riddle in the bed covering I'd placed over him the night before. His body was beneath the large butcher-block table, sitting in the middle of the kitchen.

Numerous pots, pans, kitchen linens, and other debris were scattered about the floor. So much litter in fact, it explained why in my hurried search last night I'd missed seeing Riddle. As we covered the chef, no words were spoken. At that moment, nothing could have been said which would have given any comfort.

We made our way down to the second deck below and again performed a diligent search. We found no sign of Second Mate Golden, so we continued down to the bottom deck. The diesel fumes were worse there, but still not as bad as last night, or perhaps I had gotten accustomed to the smell. It didn't appear the water had risen any during the night.

We searched the entire deck and there was still no sign of Golden. The captain said he feared that Golden had been swept overboard during the storm. I didn't like even entertaining that thought. Still, I knew the Captain was probably right because there wasn't a sign of him anywhere on the ship.

We didn't want to leave Chief Mate Hogan in the engine room, so we dragged him up to the deck above. We placed him in the hallway then the captain got a blanket to cover his body.

We went back to the bottom deck again briefly to assess the damage. It appeared the bow had cracked open when we went aground, letting the seawater in. The engines were still intact, and didn't appear to be damaged.

We looked at the generator where we had found Ryan. It had broken loose and slid into the large built-in tool chest and workbench sitting directly to its right. Many of the tool cabinet drawers had opened up, spilling the contents.

The massive generator had slammed into Ryan's leg when the mounts broke. I was still wondering what the reason was for Ryan's presence in the bottom deck? I had a lifetime of unanswered questions about what had taken place in the last twenty-four hours.

The captain checked the fuel tanks. They were all nearly empty. I asked if there was some sort of dump valve that Hogan would have activated during the storm to release the fuel, but he said there wasn't.

One tank was slightly crushed inward near the bottom corner. That appeared to be where the diesel fuel was leaking from inside the ship. Still, that didn't account for the thousands of gallons of fuel missing from the tanks. All the tanks were welded against the ship's hull. There was no way to see if the hull had cracked in the bottom or the side, releasing the fuel into the ocean, but that was what we expected had happened.

We had spent enough time there so we headed back to the second deck. We carried Hogan into his own cabin. After making sure he was properly covered, we headed back to the main deck.

When we reached the main deck, the first thing I noticed was that the fog was completely gone and there was a cloudless sky above. The sun was fully visible. I estimated the temperature was in the lower fifties. The Captain and I both went to the railing and looked over the port side of the yacht on the bow end. The water along the edge of the yacht had a rainbow of colors, giving support to our theory of the diesel tanks being ruptured and leaking outside the yacht. What little was left in the tanks was still leaking into the ocean.

The water in the bay was calm and had a mirror finish. Just past the area where the diesel fuel polluted the water, I could see the sand in the bottom of the bay. The ship wasn't in more than three feet of water, four at most. I saw lots of fish swimming, along with a few small sharks. Although the sharks were small, I knew if there were small ones, then larger ones were nearby.

My attention turned to the shoreline. The trees in the cove just past the beach, were absent of leaves, but budding. They appeared to be mostly birch and willow trees. I looked above the cliffs and saw the hills were covered in a thick forest of deciduous trees, all of which appeared to have blooms and buds on them also.

"Captain, wherever we are, it appears to be springtime. We certainly aren't in a tropical area," I said.

The Captain was scratching his head. I could tell he was in deep thought, just as I was, wondering about our surroundings.

"I'm as confused as you are lad. We are in the southern hemisphere. It's almost February. It should be autumn and heading into winter, but the trees indicate its spring."

We went back inside the stateroom, where I saw Marie catering to the Tuckers. The poker table was set up with folded paper beneath the legs, in order to make it level. Chairs were surrounding the table, three of which were occupied with the Tuckers. Marie was taking a wet cloth and wiping the face of Mrs. Tucker. There was food on the table, which I assumed was gathered by Marie. Ryan was still and seemed to be sleeping comfortably.

'How is Ryan?" I asked.

"He woke up a little while ago. I gave him some water," Marie said. "Did you find Mr. Hogan?"

"No," I said. "We've searched the entire ship."

Joseph and Preston were sitting at the table with their heads hung low. Mrs. Tucker was finishing a hard roll and clearing her throat as Marie and I were talking. She indeed looked like someone who had been shipwrecked. Her hair was all tangled, and makeup was running off her face, exposing a multitude of deep wrinkles. She looked directly toward the captain and me with a scowl on her face.

"You sorry wretched excuse of a captain, what have you done to my ship? Where are we? What have you done to get us help? I'll have your ass thrown into prison for this neglect. I demand you go immediately and get me a helicopter. I need to get to a hospital. Can't you see I need medical treatment? You worthless---"

"Hold on Mrs. Tucker," I said, cutting her off. "Right now isn't the time or place to be fussing and fuming at anyone. We have a crisis here, and if we don't work together it will only get worse."

Her eyes were squinted and her forehead wrinkled, as she pointed her finger at me.

"If you think for one minute I'm going to sit here and be lectured by some half brain part human----"

"Mrs. Tucker, where are you hurt? We need to know so we can help you." I said, as I approached the table.

She waved her left arm, shooing me off then looked down and picked up another roll and took a bite. The captain didn't say a word. I know he was deeply hurt by her statements. I felt certain he had worked for that family many years, and had been loyal to them, giving his best at all times. It was clear to see he felt responsible for the shipwreck and thought there must have been something more he could have done.

There was nothing but silence for more than a minute as everyone watched Mrs. Tucker. We were all expecting her to continue fuming, but she didn't. The captain sat down on the floor. He was still exhausted, and his old body couldn't keep up at the pace that we'd been going. He was both mentally and physically exhausted, and Mrs. Tucker's remarks didn't help matters.

"Preston and Joseph, we've got to get ashore and try to find help, will you men help me do that?" I said.

They both looked up at Mrs. Tucker, as if they were seeking approval to go play. Mrs. Tucker ignored everyone and kept eating. The men looked at each other. Preston gave a nod of approval.

"The three of you go get help," Marie said. I'll get the captain up to his quarters and put him into bed for a while, then get Mrs. Tucker and myself cleaned up and into some fresh clothes. I'll also tend to Ryan while you're gone."

"Thank you Marie, thank you so much!"

She smiled then came over and hugged me tightly.

"It will be okay," I said. Then I kissed her gently on the lips and looked into her brown eyes. I wanted to tell her how much I loved her, but it wasn't the right place. Still, she knew. I smiled and kissed her again, this time on the forehead.

I turned back to Preston and Joseph, still sitting at the table with Mrs. Tucker.

"Gentlemen, let's go to our cabins and change our clothing. Get something to put some snacks and water in, then meet me at the port side of the life boat in about twenty minutes."

"Why snacks and water, we're barely off the beach?" Preston asked.

"I've looked the beach over, Preston. It's empty. We're going to have to go down the beach until we find someone. If we don't find anyone, we will have to find a way to get on top of those cliffs in order to find someone to help us. I'm glad you asked the question though it made me think. We're going to need to take some rope also, in case we have to scale the cliff."

Preston and Joseph got frightened looks on their faces when I mentioned scaling the cliff.

Chapter 30

It felt good to get out of my wet stinky clothes and put on fresh ones. Before heading back to the main deck, I grabbed a baseball cap, sunglasses, a jacket, and backpack. I also went to the galley and searched for food to take on the hike.

I looked in the refrigerators. The food inside was cool. I knew it would start to spoil soon. I grabbed some cheese and a jar of pickles, then placed them in my pack. I went to the dry storage and grabbed some crackers and a few power bars, two bottles of power drink, and two bottles of water. If we had to walk into a village or a town, it could take a few hours.

I had gotten some rest the night before, but it was going to be a while before I got any real strength back. As I was heading out, I stopped at the first-aid compartment located in the hallway. I took out two aspirins and swallowed them down. I also put some first-aid cream on my hands and wrapped gauze over and around my hands and fingers. I then placed a pair of cloth gloves on my hands, hoping it would afford them some protection.

The sting of my hands and the soreness of my ribs and shoulders reminded me of the horrifying storm which we had gone through. It was only hours ago but felt like weeks since the yacht had run aground on the sandbar, cracking the hull, and removing any hope the ship would sail again.

Preston and Joseph were at the lifeboat when I got there. The ship initially had three lifeboats. A quick assessment earlier revealed that only two were now aboard. The third lifeboat must have been blown off the ship during the storm. We removed the boat from the tie downs and used the manual crane wench overhead to lower it into the water.

The water was cold, so I didn't want to jump in and swim ashore. Besides, sharks and other creatures could be in the water waiting for a meal to swim by. The Tucker boys, who'd likely spent most of their lives in and around the ocean, weren't attempting to jump in the water either, so the lifeboat was the best plan.

In less than two minutes, we were on the beach and climbing out of the lifeboat. Although it was a foreign place to me, it felt good to be there. I had my feet on land, and it felt good having the earth beneath me. I was hoping there would be an airport there. If so, I could leave by air. I didn't want to get aboard another ship, for as long as I lived.

Preston and Joseph didn't want to split up, so I told them to go to the right, and I would go left. We agreed that whether we found someone or not, we'd be back at that spot in no more than four hours. We looked at our watches, but I had forgotten mine had stopped. Joseph and Preston both noticed theirs had stopped also. It was so strange. The storm must have contained some sort of high-density magnetic activity or something, which destroyed the movement in our watches. Aside from the flashlights, nothing electrical was working.

I jogged down the beach. The distance from the water's edge to the base of the cliff varied from only a few feet in spots to about fifty feet in the widest areas. The sand was a light-brown color and packed hard. I kept hoping to see footprints in the sand that someone had left behind but found none.

It didn't take me long to reach the far end of the horseshoe-shaped bay. It came to a sharp point then the beach waned away. I was able to hug close to the cliff and reach the tip of the point without getting my feet wet. I looked around the point and viewed what laid beyond. I had hopes of seeing people walking along a shoreline with houses and hotels sitting in the background. I figured the people there spoke Spanish or Portuguese. I knew neither, but was sure I could communicate to them that we were shipwrecked.

My heart sank as I looked around the edge of the cliff beyond the bay. There was nothing but the blue ocean splashing against a tall rocky cliff as far as I could see. There weren't any hotels, people, not even a beach. The water along the cliff past the bay was a deep blue, indicating the water was very deep. The landscape at the edge of the water looked cold and empty. Above the cliffs were hills, covered in a variety of hardwood trees starting to blossom, just as the ones above the cliff in the bay area.

I turned to look back. I could see the yacht sitting in the bay, as if we had pulled in to visit and would soon be back at sea on our merry way. I thought of Ryan, wondering if he was going to live. I began to panic. I had to get help for Ryan. He needed to be in a hospital, under a doctor's care. He can't die on me, he just can't! I've depended on him for so long, now he needs me. I can't let him down. I must do everything I can to save him.

I ran back down to the beach where the lifeboat sat, continued past it and into the dense trees of the cove, where the stream ran. I was following a path, but it wasn't one made by man. It was an animal path. The path led to the stream and ran beside it toward the waterfall that I'd seen from the ship. I yelled for Preston and Joseph. I could hear the water rushing from above, as I got closer to the falls.

"We're over here," I heard Preston say. I just knew they had found someone. As I got closer, that thought vanished. I realized the two men were alone.

As I approached the bottom of the waterfall, I could see Preston and Joseph. They were sitting there on a large rock, drinking some of the water they'd brought. The waterfall was gorgeous, falling from a hundred feet or more above into a large pool of water about half an acre in size.

There wasn't any doubt the water coming off the waterfall was freshwater. It was surrounded by large boulders, which had broken loose from the cliffs over time. The water gently flowed out of the pool into the streambed. It then flowed to the ocean where it mixed with the salt water.

"I take it that you didn't find anyone!" I screamed at the Tuckers, throwing my arms up in frustration. I quickly realized that it wasn't their fault, and I apologized for my outburst.

"We haven't seen anyone," Preston said. "We went past here to the point of the bay, where the beach ended. Past that, it's just cliffs and no beach."

"The same thing on the other end, just cliffs and water" I stated, as I hung my head.

I looked up at the water flowing from the top of the cliff above.

"We've got to find a way up there," I said.

The path I had followed to the rock ended where I was standing, but a few yards behind me another path went to the left around the rocks. I walked on the path for about thirty yards until it led me to the base of the cliff. The cliff had a "V" shaped trench there, creating a parting in the cliff at that point. The path continued up the narrow steep slope of the trench to the cliff top. The trench was covered in loose material, likely a result of wildlife digging their hooves or paws into the ground in order to gain traction. Although the trench was steep, it looked to be climbable.

I went back and got the Tuckers. I told them to follow me. I'd found a way to the top of the cliff. When we got to the base of the path where it started up the steep incline, Joseph spoke for the first time since we'd left the boat.

"I can't climb that," he said.

"I can't either," Preston said. "I'm terrified of heights."

I looked the two of them over.

"Guys, we're in trouble here, and we've got to find help. Now I know you two play tennis, polo, and all sorts of other sports all the time, so surely you can climb this hill!"

"We just can't," Preston said. "We'll wait for you here."

I shook my head at them. It would be wasted energy for me to continue trying to coax them forward. I looked up the path. I figured that if I got to the top and lost my balance, the worst I'd do is slide back to the bottom.

I started up the path without them. I had to lean forward and dug into the dirt with the toes of my shoes, and used my hands to balance myself. The climbing wasn't that bad. It didn't take long before I had reached the top. I looked back to the bottom and saw Preston and Joseph clapping. I moved forward a few steps. I was disgusted with them and wanted them out of my sight.

I didn't see any houses or sign of human activity. The land consisted of gentle slopes to rolling foothills. There was a large variety of trees, all in bloom. Beneath the trees were a host of flowers and other plants sprouting forth, also indicating that it was springtime.

The path at the top of the cliff forked three ways, left, right, and another straight ahead. I took the path to the right, toward the top of the waterfall. The path was about fifty feet back from the top of the cliff. As I walked through the dense trees, I could not only hear the water as it spilled over the cliff, I could feel its mist in the air. There was a gentle spring wind blowing, which carried the mist of the falls inland.

Before I reached the top of the waterfall, the tree line suddenly ended. It gave way to thick tall grass and a field of cattails. The ground was soft, but I didn't sink in. The path continued through that area, but it ran beneath the tall grass, so I had to brush the growth back as I forged forward toward the edge of the water.

I stopped as I cleared the edge of the grass. I stood looking at a breathtaking view of a beautiful lake formed between the gently sloping hills. I guessed the size of the lake to be around seventy acres. It was supplied by several small streams coming out of the hills. The lake was shaped like a 'Y', with a couple of small coves branching off the main lake body.

From my vantage point at the water's edge, I could see a variety of fish swimming in the lake. I stepped closer to the waterline. A number of large turtles swam off into deeper water for protection. On the far side of the lake, I could see several ducks sitting in the water. A few more were in a meadow area just to their left.

I was in awe of the beauty of the lake and the land surrounding it, but disappointed that there was no sign of human activity. I walked along the left side of the lake until I ran across a brook flowing out of what appeared to be a deep flat hollow. It was a meandering stream, indicating flatter land.

I could have taken a running start and jumped across the stream at that point, but I needed to save all the strength I could. I walked a short distance upstream until I found a log that had fallen across both banks. It provided an excellent bridge for me to cross the stream.

I walked along until I reached the far end of the lake away from the waterfall. There, another slow-moving brook dumped water into the lake. There were plenty of rocks in that shallow stream, making it an easy walk across to the other side. I continued on, until I was where the ducks had been swimming. I looked and saw they were all in the water now, swimming near the other side of the lake where I began.

I wondered if the ducks were used to seeing people, or if this was the first time they had ever encountered a human. It concerned me that such great surroundings wouldn't have any signs of human. I was fearful that the entire area was uninhabited.

I walked through the beautiful meadow and found another animal path on the far end. As I approached the tree line, several deer jumped up and took off running in different directions. I wasn't prepared for the action. My heart nearly jumped out of my chest.

I got down on one knee, recovering from the scare, and decided it was time for a drink of water. I stayed there for a few minutes eating some cheese and crackers, all the while listening to the noises surrounding me. There was something strange and wrong with the land, but I couldn't put my finger on it.

All I could hear was the ducks making noise on the far end of the lake. There was also a slight wind. It gently whistled through the new growth of leaves sprouting forth on the trees. It was calm and peaceful, reminding me of the years past. I'd spent many days like that in the glens of Big Reedy.

Although peaceful, it was at the same time depressing. I began to wonder if I would find people. Would I find help for Ryan? Would we be rescued? There must be people around. The land seemed to have an abundance of everything needed to sustain life. If we were on an island, then it was a big one. *There must be people somewhere around here, there must be.*

I felt panic creeping in as I start up the path beyond the meadow. I quickened my pace through the trees, noticing I was slightly gaining elevation. To my left and right were foothills that gently sloped upward a few hundred feet. I estimated the distance from the left ridge to the right ridge to be a half-mile or more. It wouldn't be hard to climb up to the top of either side, but I decided to continue up the valley.

I plunged forward another thirty minutes. The valley floor ended, and a steep hillside began. The low angled hills ran parallel with the stream. At the valley head the hill jutted upward at a sharp angle for several hundred feet before coming to a peak. It wasn't long before I could tell the two ridges I'd been walking between met at a point directly in front of me.

As I arrived at the top of the ridge, I looked out beyond and saw the ocean, nothing but water all the way to the horizon. Water in front, water to the left, water to the right. It made me start thinking again there was no human life there, aside from those of us who had been shipwrecked.

The sun was going down. I figured I'd been gone much longer than I realized. I wished I'd had a watch. I thought about how simple a device a watch was, yet so powerful a tool.

I headed back down the hill and followed the path back to the lake. I encountered deer again as I got close to the meadow. It was the same result. My heart nearly jumped out of my chest after their sudden start. I made a mental note about the deer population there, just in case we weren't rescued soon and were forced to hunt for food.

I wanted to take one of the paths to the left of the lake. The land looked as if it widened there and went further, but I didn't have time to go there. I needed to get back to the yacht to check on Ryan. I also needed to meet with everyone and make a plan for what we were going to do next.

All the signs I'd seen led me to believe we were on an island, but I couldn't be sure. Perhaps we were on a peninsula and the paths to the left would lead us to a town along the coast. No matter, further exploration would have to wait. I was hoping that during my absence, a patrol boat might have come by the yacht. I thought that perhaps everyone was awaiting my return so we could leave. I was hoping that, at the very least, the captain had been able to make radio contact with someone. If so, a rescue boat would be on its way to us.

When I got back to the steep path leading to the bottom of the cliff, it was starting to get dark. The cove area where the waterfall was located was nicely protected from storms. It was blocked from the evening sun, so it got dark there much quicker than the area on top of the cliffs. I exited the tree line and walked across the beach. The lifeboat was gone. The Tuckers hadn't waited on me.

Chapter 31

The tide was low, so I walked on the sand to within fifty yards of the ship. I saw the lifeboat sitting in the water, tied to the back of the yacht at the tender bay. I yelled out but no one answered me, which made me more upset. I was tired, hungry, worried, totally exhausted, and I was about to lose my cool with the Tucker family.

I studied the water for a moment and didn't see any big fish swimming around. I waded through the water until reaching the bow of the yacht. The water was a little less than knee deep, and I was thankful for the tide being out.

I banged on the side of the yacht with my fist, hoping it would scare away anything wanting to bite my legs. My fist against the hull only produced a thud. I had no choice but to continue toward the back of the yacht. My choices were to move forward or return to the beach. The cold water became waist deep as I forged forward, reaching the stern. I was barely able to reach into the bay area where the tender once sat. Standing on my toes, I was able to grab hold of a tie-down point. Then I pulled myself out of the water and onto the yacht.

I climbed up through the four feet of the bay area damaged by the tender's escape, before reaching the first deck below. I laid there on the deck for a few minutes, letting myself recover. That little feat of coming from shore to the yacht, took more energy than the trek from the beach to the lake and back.

I was no longer just angry. I was now wet, cold, and angry! I stormed up to the main deck and into the stateroom. Marie was there with Ryan. He was partly sitting. She had made some sort of broth and was feeding him. I smiled as I knelt down and greeted the two of them, happy to see them both. I was pleased to see Ryan was alert and eating.

"You're dripping wet, and look exhausted," Marie said.

"I'm okay, how is Ryan?"

She sensed that I wasn't okay. She knew I was angry, but she didn't question me about it.

"He's considerably better than yesterday," she said.

Ryan's voice was weak, but I could tell he was doing better by the remark he made. "I'm ready to run a marathon," he said.

Marie patted him on the head. "Get some rest," she said.

Ryan gave me a sort of weak thumbs-up then closed his eyes.

"I searched the cabins and found some antibiotics in the main medicine cabinet down in the galley area," Marie said. "It's a full bottle and has Chef Riddle's name on the label. I think Ryan needs something for the infection in his leg, so I got him to take one earlier. He's been awake off and on. I've been making him drink water and some broth as well."

"That's great, and a good idea with the pills. They will help fight against infection. Somehow, we must also get that swelling down. The ice is all gone. I wish we had a way to make more."

Marie's face suddenly hardened.

"Did you find anyone, Jake?"

"No, not a soul," I said, shaking my head. "I'm assuming the captain never got ahold of anyone by radio either. Otherwise, you would have already said so."

Marie let out a low sigh, "It's going to be okay. I'm sure someone's searching for us."

"Where is the captain?" I asked.

"He's down below. I think he's in the galley sorting out the food, trying to save all he can. He's been back in the wheelhouse looking at maps all afternoon, trying to figure out where we are, I suppose."

"What about the Tuckers?" I could feel my body stiffening and my voice getting harsh.

"They took some booze and food back to Mrs. Tucker's suite. She's been crying all afternoon. I don't know what to do for her."

"Did the two wimpy brats say why they left me and came back to the ship?"

"They only said you cursed them and then left them to fend for themselves. They didn't know if they could ever find their way back after you abandoned them."

"That's all a pack of lies, Marie. I've walked for miles trying to find help. They didn't go any further than the base of that waterfall!"

Ryan had gone back to sleep while Marie and I were talking.

"I'll be back later," I said, then got up and headed out the door. My anger had just escalated into a frenzied fury.

I burst through the door into Mrs. Tucker's suite. She and her two sons were sitting at a small table, covered with shot glasses, a bottle of Scotch, and a variety of snacks.

"How dare you come barging into my private suite? You barbarian bastard!" Mrs. Tucker said.

She was standing as I approached the table. I backhanded her, knocking her onto her bed. My left leg was up without even thinking as I kicked Preston in the face, sending him flying into the wall. On the way down, he upset the table, causing the Scotch bottle, glasses, and food to scatter in every direction. In the next instant, my right fist came in an uppercut fashion and caught Joseph under the chin, raising him several inches out of his chair then crashing onto the floor. I stood there with arms extended by my side with fists clenched in rage. I felt like a ninja warrior ready to take on all three of them at once, begging them to make the next move.

Mrs. Tucker climbed upon her bed and scurried all the way to the headboard. Then she turned to look back at me. I saw blood dripping from her lip, and she was wiping it away with her hand. Preston was lying in the floor not moving and Joseph was now on his hands and knees with his head to the floor groaning from the pain I had just inflicted upon him. I pointed my left index finger at Mrs. Tucker.

"I'm now in charge of this ship, so hear me clearly, because I'm only going to say it once. There will be no more leaving someone behind, no more trash talking to Ryan, the captain, or me. No more private drinking parties, and no more Marie having to wipe your ugly ass. There are two dead men on this ship and another missing. Have you even taken a second to think about them? Until rescued, you will take care of yourself, work where needed, and do exactly as you are told. If I say jump, you dang well better be prepared to jump high! Do the three of you hear me? Do you?"

I looked at Mrs. Tucker. She was nodding yes. I turned to Preston and Joseph. They weren't looking at me, but both were nodding yes. I picked the Scotch bottle up off the floor, pulled the cork out, and took a long deep swig before throwing the bottle down. All three of the Tuckers were staring at me.

"And if a word of any of this little meeting is told to Marie, I'll catch you sleeping and thrust a knife deep into your hardened hearts."

I then stormed out of the room as quickly as I had arrived. My throat was burning from the Scotch, and I wondered how they could drink such horrid stuff.

I didn't want Marie to see me in such a rage. I was embarrassed that my temper had flared so brutally, but I was at the end of my rope. I knew if I didn't do something now, the action of the Tuckers would continue, and perhaps get worse.

I headed to my cabin to get the wet clothes off. How nice it would be to take a shower. I thought of the waterfall. At that moment, I would like to have be standing beneath it, even though the water would be icy cold.

After changing clothes, I laid down on the bed for a few minutes, just wanting to close my eyes briefly, rest, and get my heart to stop beating so hard.

The next thing I knew Marie, was knocking at my door. I told her to come in. She opened the door and peered in. She said I had been gone for three hours. I must have fallen asleep.

"I've got some food prepared up in the state room," she said. "Why don't you come up and eat something with me?"

My stomach was empty and I was in need of some nourishment.

"Sounds great, I'll be right up," I replied.

As I left my cabin and entered the hallway, I got a sniff of the diesel fuel, but now it was only a slight odor in the air. I thought about the engines below and if they would work. Even if we could get them working, the fuel was gone, and besides the ship's hull was damaged and leaking. If only the tender hadn't been lost. If nothing else, we could have made a makeshift sail for it, and set out to sea. A thirty-two-foot boat would make an excellent life raft.

My mind was going over the few hours I had been ashore. I couldn't help but think somewhere along that shoreline humans were present. It was just too big and had too many resources available. People had to be there.

I used my flashlight to get down the hallway to the stairs. I wondered how long the flashlights would last before the batteries would be drained. I made a mental note to talk with everyone about conservation of the lights.

It was dark when I arrived on the main deck. The day seemed short and little had been accomplished. Every hour Ryan went without medical treatment increased the danger of him not surviving. I was hoping to hear some good news from the captain. Perhaps he had heard something on the emergency radio.

As I entered the stateroom, I saw the big table was set up with candles, drinks, and food. Ryan was sitting up and alert, so I went straight to his side.

"How are you feeling, buddy?"

As soon as the words left my lips, I thought about how stupid the question was. Here was someone who'd just lost their leg, and I was asking how they felt. Does Ryan even know his leg is gone?

Ryan spoke, but his voice was low and weak.

"Jake, good to see you man. My body hurts all over, and I hurt my leg."

I couldn't tell him about his leg right then, I was afraid he would go into shock or something. It would have to wait until he was stronger. Maybe he knew though, he had to. He had to have been the one who applied the tourniquet.

"We're shipwrecked, Ryan. I think we may be on an island. We've not found help yet, but we should soon. Hang in there. You and I have lots of money to spend when we get back home."

Ryan tried to grin. I could tell it hurt too much. He put his head back down and closed his eyes. Marie came over with some broth she'd heated over candles in the galley. She said it was time to get another dose of the antibiotic in him. We were able to get Ryan alert again, long enough to get the pill in him and a few spoons of broth. Afterwards, he closed his eyes and was soon asleep.

"Let's go over to the table and eat, Jake," Marie said.

We got up and went over to the table where the food was sitting out. Marie told me the Tuckers had been up earlier and ate, then retreated to Mrs. Tucker's suite. She also said the captain was in the wheelhouse and should be back soon and wanted to talk to the both of us.

I asked about the food. Marie and the captain had gotten some lasagna from one of the refrigerators in the galley. It was already prepared and had been placed there to be cooked for our evening meal on the day the storm hit. It was going to spoil so they cooked it on the propane grill out by the aft pool.

The lasagna tasted good to me. It wasn't as good as it would have been baked in an oven, but it was very tasty. I hadn't had anything hot to eat in a few days. I ate several large portions before stopping. Marie giggled and said I must have really been hungry.

After I finished eating, Marie and I sat and talked for a while. She was so lovely to look at. She was dressed in a light red flannel shirt and had a red bandana tied around her dark curly hair.

"You look beautiful," I said.

"Oh stop it, Jake," she said as she took her hand and gently stroked my face. Tears were in her eyes.

"Thank you," she said. "Thank you for helping us."

I felt guilty about what I'd done. I confessed to her about my moment of rage earlier. I also told her about what I had done to the Tuckers. I told her I was sorry for losing my cool. Even though the events of the last few days have been horrid, I had no right to lash out and physically hurt someone.

"I knew you were angry when you got out of the water and came inside," she said. "I would be also. I don't like that you lost your temper Jake, but I have to admit; Mrs. Tucker has been calmer this evening than at any time since we left South Hampton!"

The captain entered the stateroom just then and was carrying a map roll. We cleared the table, and he unrolled the maps and placed shot glasses on the corners for paperweights. The captain placed an X on the map, indicating our position when the storm hit. He had also taken a compass and drawn three circles from that point, which indicated distances we could have traveled once the storm hit. The largest circle indicated a six-hundred-mile radius from the X.

"Let me explain this to ye, mates," the captain said. "I figure we were in that storm the better part of six to eight hours. Storms don't push a ship very fast mates. Twenty knots would be a very fast pace with a sail, and we have no sail. I remember that the engines stopped as soon as the storm hit us, so all our movement was made by the storm pushing us.

"I don't follow you, Captain," Marie said.

"I'll explain her to ya lass. Even if we had been in the storm for twelve hours, we'd had to average a speed of nearly fifty knots to reach the six-hundred-mile circle, which is impossible. The closest island from where we were when the storm hit, is near the Chile coast line, some eight-hundred miles to the east, and we were moving toward the northwest."

"So you don't know where we are?" I said.

"That's right, lad. We've got to be on an island. One that doesn't exist!"

"But it does exist, Captain. I was on it today. It's big, and has a beautiful freshwater lake fed by several steams. There's lots of wildlife, and a large hardwood forest on this island that doesn't exist."

"That may be true, lad, but these maps are computer generated from satellite information, and I'm telling you, it doesn't exist! Do you recall how we went through rapids for a few hours before we grounded here, and how we were traveling pitched downstream? This is the ocean my friend, and the ocean doesn't flow like a river."

"So what are you saying, Captain? That we came through some sort of wormhole or time warp or something? That we aren't in the real world anymore."

"You two are making me nervous," Marie pitched in.

"A wormhole," said the captain. "I don't know about a wormhole, but I do know nothing is normal about anything we've been through. Did you notice the sun today mate? It came up behind the yacht, but didn't cross the sky over us. It made an arc, coming up on the right of the stern, and set over the same horizon, to the left of the stern."

"I didn't notice that," I said, alarmed. "I did think the day was short though." I felt chills on my arms as we were having the discussion. Right out of the blue, something dawned on me.

"Captain," I said loudly. "Oh my goodness, it just hit me. I was on the island and loved the beauty of the place but knew something was wrong. I don't know why I hadn't figured it out earlier. Many of the trees only had branches on the same side of the tree where the sun was shining.

"My word lad, your observation confirms it. The sun must not cross the sky here. It comes up in the east, arcs upward, then sets in the east as well."

"That's impossible," I said. "We're all just tired and not thinking logically."

It was too much to take in at that time. It was too much after everything we had been through to think of something weird like that. Marie looked puzzled and frightened. I'm certain if I had a mirror to look into, my face would have the same expression.

"What else have you thought of, Captain?" I said.

"Those trees ye spoke of on the island, they be blooming, but it's fall here in the southern hemisphere mate. The leaves should be falling off. If me didn't know better, I'd guess we were north of the equator, and quite a bit north at that."

The captain was right. We had discussed that briefly earlier today, and I was thinking about it as I had explored the island. I was totally confused about everything and started to fear we were lost somewhere, never to be found.

"Is your watch working, Captain?" I asked. "She's not mate, and neither are any others aboard. None of me compasses are working either, not even the gyroscopic one. I've tried me emergency radio, but it doesn't work. Nothing electric or magnetic works!"

"Our flashlights work," I said.

"I can't explain everything mate, but I'm telling ye, I don't think we are in the real world as we know it!"

The room was silent as the three of us sat looking at each other. My thoughts were going in a million and one different directions. The captain was correct. Nothing about this whole situation was right. The island, if that's what it was, was huge, a mile wide and several miles long. How could it not be discovered, inhabited, shown on a satellite map? My body was tired, and I couldn't think clearly. All these odd things only added more weight to our burden.

"Let's change the subject," Marie said. "We need to plan on not being found for a week or more so let's concentrate on what we need to do."

"Captain," I said. "You're the oldest, wisest, and more experienced in matters like this, what do you suggest?"

"Older perhaps mates, but experienced in these matters, I'm not. Marie is right we need to plan. We need to ration our food supply. We should keep the freezers closed and not open them. The food is thawing, but it will last a few more days. Eat what will spoil the fastest. In the meantime, we need to see what freshwater supplies we have, because that will dwindle down quickly."

The captain hesitated. Then in a lower and sad voice, he continued.

"We need to get our two dear friends to shore and bury them. They've already begun to deteriorate."

"I agree with you, Captain," I said. "First thing tomorrow morning we can load Chief Mate Hogan and Chef Riddle into a lifeboat. We'll take them ashore and bury them near the stream leading to the waterfalls. Its sandy soil, so it should be easy to dig there."

I looked away so the captain and Marie couldn't see the tears in my eyes. The captain stood up and said he was going to go to his quarters. He said he would see us in the morning at first light. After he left, Marie and I sat there for a long time, not saying anything. I just starred at the flickering light put off by the candles. I was thinking about our lives and what had taken place to change everything in only a short time. I thought about how we never made it to Hawaii. Marie and I would have spent time together there, and perhaps Ryan would have been with us, enjoying life to its fullest.

Marie broke the silence finally.

"Let's see if we can move a bed from below up here to put Ryan in."

I took hold of her hand, "You're always thinking of others. What a wonderful person you are."

She smiled back at me as we got up to go retrieve the bed. Before we left the stateroom, Marie stopped, remembering there was a day bed in one of the closets in the owner's office. We discussed moving Ryan to the owner's office, but decided not to chance moving him too soon and start the bleeding again.

We got the bed from the owner's office and set it up in the stateroom. We carefully lifted Ryan, trying to keep his swollen leg from hitting anything. Ryan groaned loudly as we picked him up, but soon afterward, he was alert for a bit and thanked us, saying the bed felt good.

We said a prayer for Ryan by his bedside then Marie went to check on the Tuckers and then change clothes. I made a bed on the floor beside of Ryan and lay down. I don't remember Marie coming back and laying down beside me to sleep, but there she was the next morning when I woke up.

Chapter 32

The captain got up early and went to the galley to gather some of the food needing to be eaten first. He brought a smorgasbord of food up to the stateroom and placed it on the table for everyone to eat when they got out of bed. He also made coffee on the propane grill. I'm not a coffee drinker, but the nice aroma aroused me. Anything warm would be welcomed by my insides at that point.

The Tuckers came up to eat and sat silently at the table. Surprisingly, they didn't get up and leave when I sat down with them. I told them about our plans to bury our friends. I was nice when I asked Preston and Joseph if they would get the lifeboat ready after breakfast. I informed them that the captain and I would bring the bodies up to the main deck, wrapped in blankets so no one would have to view the corpses. Preston told me they would have the lifeboat ready.

The captain and I got ready to go below while Marie cleaned up after breakfast. I was shocked when Mrs. Tucker said she'd help Marie. Ryan was the gambler. I would bet however, that Mrs. Tucker would put on three or more sets of gloves before handling a plate someone else had touched. Even Preston and Joseph were taken aback when she announced that she'd help.

Even though we'd gotten some needed rest, it was still a struggle to get the corpses to the top deck. Preston helped us put the two dead men in the lifeboat, but Joseph backed away. I didn't press him to help us. I felt it was more a mental issue, not just him just being lazy.

I'd found two tools from the engine room that were suitable for digging. One had a spade-shaped metal tip connected to a long metal rod. The other was a six-foot long metal rod with a four-inch flat plate welded on the end. I didn't know the intended purpose of the tools, but they were the closest things I could find that was suited for digging. We put the tools in the boat then all the men went ashore to dig the graves.

The water was calm that morning, just as the day before. We didn't make it to shore before the boat bottomed out from all the weight. I got out and pulled the boat onto the sandy beach using a rope. No one had thought about how hard it would be to carry the bodies along the beach and into the wooded area.

I sent Joseph back to the yacht to get one of the fire axes. We would cut poles and make a crude sled to pull the bodies on. While he was gone, the captain and I went a short distance into the woods along the path by the stream and found a suitable spot for the graves. We decided it would be easiest to dig one large hole instead of two.

Preston stayed at the beach until Joseph came back with the axe.

The digging was easy, but a lot of dirt had to be removed. It took a lot of square footage to be large enough to place two adult men into the grave. We wanted to get the hole at least three feet deep but hit water just a little more than two feet down.

I was pleased to see that Preston and Joseph pitched in and helped with the digging. Before the hole was finished, they were covered from head to toe in a muddy mixture of sand and dirt. They complained to each other a lot about their condition but didn't utter a word of complaint to the captain or me.

There was only enough room for two people at a time to dig, so while the Tucker boys were in the hole, I cut poles and used saplings to create a crude sled. We used it to drag the bodies along the beach and into the woods, until reaching the gravesite.

We placed the two dead men, still covered in blankets, into the hole. The plan was to go back to the ship and clean up as best we could. Then everyone would come ashore for a funeral service. It only seemed right to send the two men off with a service of some sort.

When we got back, Mrs. Tucker insisted on her two sons taking a long nap and rest before the funeral service. She went on about how dreadful a morning it had been for her boys, and suggested we have an evening service. I didn't want to argue with her. We all had suffered traumatic events over the last few days. From what I'd witnessed watching her two sons, I felt certain they indeed had never faced anything like they were now. We decided to have the service just before sunset, to end the day saying goodbye to our friends.

I stood along the railing on the main deck observing the sun. The captain was right. The sun had risen behind the yacht but wasn't coming overhead. Instead, it was moving in an arc across the eastern horizon. My thoughts turned back to the mornings events. The hole we dug for the graves had gone smoothly and quickly since all four of us had helped.

Even with the sun not setting as normal, we still had at least five or six hours before the funeral service and time shouldn't be wasted. I asked Marie and Captain Nichols if they wanted to go ashore with me and hike up to the lake. They could look things over from up there, and it would give me an opportunity to head down the ridgeline to the left of the waterfall in search of people. They agreed.

We packed some food and water in separate knapsacks and informed Mrs. Tucker of our plan. She was a bit vocal about Marie going, stating her suite needed to be cleaned. I said she could take care of that herself, and reminded her of what I'd said the evening before. She apologized then and said she'd take care of it herself. I thought those were strange words coming from her. I knew my little outrage talk hadn't really changed her.

We checked on Ryan before leaving him again. His leg was still fire red but it appeared some of the swelling was going down. For the first time, I was beginning to think he was going to be okay. The medicine Marie found may be saving his life. He was now able to hold a bottle of water himself.

After talking to Ryan about our plan, he asked us to leave him some water and crackers by his side. Seeing he was thinking logically again and was showing some signs of hunger made me feel better about leaving him for a short time. He was a bit more alert today although he didn't stay awake long before dozing back off again.

We got into one of the lifeboats and went ashore. We walked to the base of the pathway leading to the top of the cliffs. I was surprised how quickly both Marie and the captain could climb to the top. They actually went up the slope faster than I did.

We worked our way through the cattails and grass to the lake. The ducks were in the water near us as we came through the grass, but they quickly swam away as we approached. Both Marie and the captain were pleasantly surprised by the beauty of the place. The pristine landscape looked as if a painter had dreamed up a perfect lake, teeming with life, and a mountainous backdrop with budding trees of numerous species.

Marie wanted to go around the lake to the meadow as I had done yesterday. The captain stated he would like to go as well. I told them I would travel up the path directly to my left and travel as fast and far as I could in about two hours. If I hadn't found anyone by then I'd come back and meet up with them. If I did find someone, I'd have them fire a shot or something, giving a signal that I'd found help.

I followed the worn animal path along the streambed. It made multiple twists and turns along meadows and small rock outcrops. Along the way, smaller tributaries branched off from the main stream both left and right, coming from shallow hollows. The ridgeline on both sides rolled up and down anywhere from a hundred to three hundred feet in height.

I traveled at a fast pace for what seemed like over an hour. The sun was directly in front of me at that location, making a low arc across the sky. If I was indeed going east, and the sun was in my face, then it meant the island or peninsula was shaped like a boomerang. By looking from ridge-top to ridge-top, I guessed that the island was close to two miles across at the widest point.

I had traveled at least three miles up the path, and the land appeared continued that far again in front of me. I decided to climb to the ridge-tops on both sides of me to see what I could view. I had carried along a yellow slicker, just in case I encountered rain. There were no clouds in the sky when I left, but nothing was normal here, and I didn't want to chance on getting wet. I hung the jacket in a small tree near the path I was following. I could use it as a marker to find my way back to the same spot.

I hiked to the top of the ridge on the left. As I topped the ridge, I looked down below and saw the ocean. As far as I could see, there was nothing but blue water and white capped waves. There was no sign of people. The birds were singing loudly in the trees overhead, but I could still hear the waves crashing below, indicating there were more cliffs and no beach. It was a breathtaking view from up there, but that wasn't what I was looking for. I would had much rather have seen a dirty run down village with filthy living conditions.

I ran back down the hillside until I got back to the jacket. I rested for a few minutes then crossed the stream and went toward the right-side ridgeline. It was at least a half-mile from the stream to where the hill got steeper and shot upward to the ridgeline. As I got near the ridge, I was breathing heavily and had to stop and catch my breath. After a few minutes, I climbed the last few hundred feet to the summit.

The ridge was covered in large rhododendron bushes and laurel so thick I couldn't see more than thirty feet in any direction. I walked along the flat ridge for a few hundred yards then the ground turned up steeply. I could see a rock outcrop ahead so I climbed through the jungle of rhododendrons until I reached the rock formation. I climbed atop the chimney shaped rock, which perched me well above the treetops. It was a crystal-clear day. I could see for miles around in all directions.

Looking behind me, I was quite sure I could see the end of the land near the lake where Marie and the captain were. The opposite side of the hill from where I had come seemed to flatten a bit before meeting the ocean. Ahead, all I could see was more rolling hills covered in the budding trees of springtime. It was more of what I had witnessed so far, just trees, hills, and water. The trees there had more growth on the side away from the sun than the ones near the lake.

I noticed the top of the rock I was on had a thick bed of moss. Growing out of the moss was what appeared to be edible mushrooms. That too, seemed out of place. Down in the valley to my left there was a small area where the morning fog had not burned off. I thought that was strange as well, but then many things there were strange. The land was beautiful and mysterious, but terribly lonely.

As I looked far ahead to where I'd not yet traveled, it appeared the land narrowed to a point like an arrowhead then met the water. I was certain then we were on an island. We were on a single island. There were no other islands in sight, just one big island in the middle of the ocean.

I was disappointed and the lonely feeling I'd had the day before returned. There was no sign of human life anywhere. I knew my sightline out over the horizon had to be thirty miles or more, and nothing else was in sight. I felt horribly alone and lost. I slowly climbed back down the rock and headed down the hillside toward the stream below.

I knew my travel along the ridgeline had placed me upstream quite some distance from my jacket. I decided that instead of backtracking, I'd go straight from the ridge to the brook. Then I'd walk downstream to where my jacket was before heading back to the lake.

When I got near the valley floor, I discovered a large butte. It peaked out higher than the tree tops, sixty to eighty feet above the ground, and covered an area of four to five acres in circumference.

The walls of the butte didn't appear to have any ledges or areas of broken rock. It would be impossible to climb to the top without some good rock climbing gear. The entire structure was an oval shape. It looked similar to a huge cylinder that had sprouted up from the ground. I studied it for a minute and wondered how it could have ever been formed. The butte had a dull but mirror type finish. I stood there pondering on the structure. I wondered how it could have such perfectly slick sides and exist over the centuries without heavy erosion taking place?

I couldn't see the top of the rock structure. A thin cloud layer was hanging near the top. I thought that was odd. I realized that was the fog area I'd seen from up on the ridge.

I walked around the back of the butte toward the upstream side. The rock formation butted against the stream there. The brook at that location was too wide to jump across, so I backtracked around the butte to what I called the north. A few feet from the stream, there was a large opening at the base of the rock. It was a cave or cavern. The opening was at least eight feet high and twenty feet across.

My heart started pounding. I feared panthers or bears had a den inside. I made my way downstream from the opening, trying to be quiet and not disturb whatever may be inside the cave. When I got a few hundred feet away, I stopped and peered back to ensure nothing was coming after me. I then decided to ease toward the cave opening again, all the while the hair on the back of my neck felt as if it was standing straight out.

I was afraid to get too close. I had no weapon to protect myself, but I wanted to see inside of the cave. I got within a hundred feet and dared not go any further. I could see the cave opening clearly from that vantage point. The opening appeared to go deep into the rock structure. I didn't see any signs of animal life, but just in case, I wasn't going to hang around any longer. I then took off in a run down the path along the streambed.

When I got to the yellow slicker I slowed down, but only long enough to retrieve the jacket from the small tree I had draped it around. I then continued running back in the direction of the lake. I had to stop twice and catch my breath, bending over placing my hands on my knees, while looking back up the path, expecting to see some wild animal coming at me.

When I got to the lake, Marie and the captain were sitting on the fallen log I had crossed the day before, waiting for me to arrive. I sat on the log with them for a few minutes as we talked about what we'd seen and found. I told them about the island and what I'd seen looking out from the chimney rock atop the ridge. The captain told us he feared that would be the news, feeling all along that we were alone.

We started back to the yacht. As we passed by the graves, we were all silent. I didn't look at the bodies lying there covered in blankets. I felt ashamed we had left them there uncovered all day. We would cover them as soon as the graveside service was over. We continued back to the yacht, to get prepared for the ceremony. The funeral was yet another unpleasant task I wanted to get behind us.

We exited the trees and headed across the beach. The captain spotted it first and pointed it out to Marie and me. The lifeboat was gone from the beach.

I was instantly filled with rage. We had the lifeboat pulled well upon the shore, so there was no way the gentle waves lapping against the sand could have pulled it away.

"I'll kill all three of them," I cried out.

"Let's keep calm until we find out what happened," Marie said.

I didn't say another word, I was as mad as a hornet after someone had torn its nest apart. The tide was out again so the three of us waded through the water, which was up to our knees by the time we reached the bow. I was in the lead, and stormed on through the water toward the stern and climbed up into the yacht. In my rage, I'd completely forgotten about Marie and the captain and didn't take time to assist them getting on board.

"Hey, remember those of us who love you!" Marie said.

Her words caused me to slow down for a minute and get some sense about me. I stopped and reached down to help her and the captain back aboard the ship.

"I still don't see the lifeboat," the captain said.

I remembered then; the lifeboat should have been docked there at the stern where we were. Maybe I had jumped to conclusions. Perhaps a wave had come in and pulled the lifeboat back out to sea. I wheeled around and walked hurriedly into the stateroom. Ryan was lying in the bed sleeping. No one else was around. I quickly went to him, got on my knees, and placed my hands on his cheeks. They were cool to the touch, so I knew his fever had left and had not returned. I pulled the blanket back to look at his leg. It was still very red but seemed to be less swollen than it was earlier.

I got back on my feet and was getting ready to head down to Mrs. Tucker's suite, expecting them to all be in a half-drunken state. Before I took the first step, I heard the captain crying out to me,

"Both lifeboats are missing!" He said.

"What?" I exclaimed.

"Both boats are missing!" He repeated. "The one on the starboard side is gone as well."

I raced out of the stateroom and down the stairs toward the cabins below. I burst into Mrs. Tucker's cabin in the same manner as yesterday, only today I was more ill than the day before. I feared that I was so out of control that I might inflict serious harm to her and her sons. The room looked as if a hurricane had blown through, but the Tucker's weren't there. I yelled out for them but got no reply.

I went to Joseph's cabin, opened the door, and walked inside. Clothes were scattered about. Drawers were opened, as if a thief had come in during our absence and ransacked the place. No one was there either. I met the captain as I was leaving the cabin and headed toward Preston's room. He told me he had been to the galley, and it had been ransacked. He also said that a large portion of the food supplies were gone. We both realized then that the Tuckers had loaded both lifeboats and headed out to sea, leaving us behind.

We returned to the stateroom and told Marie about our dilemma. She was devastated that Mrs. Tucker would do such a thing, leaving us all behind. The news hit her hard. She sat down with her back against the bar and began crying. The captain went and sat beside her. He was shaken as well. We were on an uninhabited island that didn't exist, and our only chance of escape had just left with the majority of our supplies. I knew Marie needed me at that moment, but I had too much rage built up inside to be any comfort to her.

I ran up the stairs and into the wheelhouse. I grabbed the captain's binoculars then used them to scan the ocean, looking for the Tuckers. They were nowhere in sight. What would I have done, even if I had of spotted them? I had no way to get to them. It's good I didn't find them. I was so full of rage I would have swam out there and caused them serious harm.

I walked back to the stern and jumped into the water, then waded around the yacht and back ashore. I went to the gravesite, picked up the spaded tool and furiously began covering the bodies. We would have a ceremony for our fallen friends later, but not tonight.

As I threw the last of the dirt, sand, and mud on the graves, I collapsed onto the pile of muck, crying profusely. Crying because of my lost friends I'd just buried, crying because we were shipwrecked, crying because we were stuck there, and crying because the most logical means of escape, the lifeboats, were now gone. It was the lowest point in my life, and I felt there was no hope.

Chapter 33

The next morning Ryan was more alert than the previous days, and his voice was getting stronger. His leg still looked horrible, red, blue, black, and swollen. Still, it was much better than a few days ago. I thought he had a chance of survival, but unless we got him to a hospital soon I knew that chance was ever so slight. Marie was a fine nurse, and was doing everything she could think of that might help. We just needed someone with real medical experience. There were still a few days of antibiotics left, and I was hopeful by then any sign of infection would be gone.

"How are you feeling this morning, Ryan?" I asked.

"I'm hungry and thirsty."

I asked Ryan about the Tuckers, and if he had seen them yesterday as they loaded the lifeboats. He had not. He must have slept the entire time. I was still very angry, and wished I could have gotten my hands on the Tuckers.

Marie heard us talking. She was already up preparing food that Ryan could eat and keep down. The captain wasn't in the stateroom. I needed to find him and discuss our new dilemma. I wanted to hear his, as well as Marie's, suggestions on what we needed to do since the lifeboats were gone.

I wasn't sure using the lifeboats to leave the island and seek rescue in the ocean would even have been a good idea, but it would have been an option. It would have been an option for all of us, not a select few. I still couldn't believe the Tuckers would do such an underhanded thing. Now we didn't even have transportation to and from shore.

Since seeing the small sharks in the water a few days ago, I'd not seen any since. The sharks were only one problem the water was also cold. Getting wet up to our chest, going to and from the yacht also put us in danger of getting sick, and we had no medical supplies.

Marie arrived with some warm, thin oatmeal and started feeding Ryan small spoons of his breakfast. I looked at her and could see the worry on her face. She didn't have to tell me why, I knew. She was shipwrecked on an island that appeared to have never been inhabited or even visited by humans. Everything that meant security to her was now gone, and the woman she trusted as her employer left her, and the rest of us, for dead.

Ryan ate nearly a full bowl of oatmeal and then sipped some orange drink Marie had brought to him. I reached over and stroked Marie's hair, then took the back of my hand and gently stroked her cheek.

"Thank you for your kindness and help," I said.

317

Marie looked up and gave me a gentle smile then laid her head onto my chest and began to weep. She was trying to maintain her composure. She couldn't hold back any longer though, she was at the end of her wits.

"I need you," she said.

I pulled her closer to me and kissed the top of her head.

"We all need each other right now," I replied.

Ryan looked at us, and comically said in his best sarcastic voice "Do you two need a blanket?"

I was still holding Marie as the two of us looked at him and let out a small chuckle. "Well, he's getting better. He's getting that smart mouth back," I said.

We all three chuckled. "Oh lord, it hurts when I laugh," Ryan said.

Marie took the bowl and glass and headed toward the bar. I asked Ryan if he was up to talking. He told me if I was talking about his leg, he knew it wasn't good, but he felt like everything was going to work out okay. His attitude was good despite our circumstances. It encouraged me to go on, to see that we all survived and got off the island. Ryan wanted to know what all had happened. I didn't hold anything back. He had the right to know. We discussed everything, beginning with the storm.

"I only have one question right now, Ryan," I said. "We found you on the bottom deck, what in the devil were you doing down there?"

"I was in my cabin when the first wave hit," he said. "I immediately started getting a strong smell of diesel fumes through the air vent. I figured one of the tanks had been damaged and quickly headed down to the engine room to turn the fuel tanks off. I had spent a lot of time with Chief Mate Hogan down there. He'd shown me about anything there was to know about the engines and generators.

Anyway, I had just shut off the main valve when the ship rolled. I was thrown across the floor. At the same time, the No.2 generator broke loose and slammed into my leg. I got numb and couldn't feel anything below my waist. When I saw my leg just hanging I grabbed my belt and made a tourniquet, I knew it was bad. After that, I got sick at my stomach and threw up. I don't remember a thing after that."

The captain entered the stateroom and asked if he could talk to Marie and me. I propped some pillows behind Ryan's head and elevated his leg then walked over to the bar where the captain had sat down. Marie went to the backside of the bar and pulled up a stool to sit on.

As I was walking over to the bar, I asked the captain what he thought the chances were of the Tuckers being rescued, and being able to describe where this island is.

"It's a toss-up," he replied. "Regardless, we have to sit down and regroup, and plan a new course of action."

The captain's voice was stern, and he didn't appear to be himself. His kind gentle nature was missing. He was worried. I knew too, just like Marie, that he was hurt deeply by the action of the Tuckers. The captain, had also worked for that family for years and had been loyal and served in any way possible, only to be deserted.

"I've been in the galley," the Captain said. "Some of the food in the refrigerators has spoiled. Only a few items in the freezers are still salvageable. The Tuckers took most of the remaining bottled water and canned drinks. They also took a large part of the dry goods, and destroyed a lot more in their rush to get things loaded and get away. Me spirit is broken. I've had all me old body and mind can stand. I'm spent."

Marie was sitting on the stool leaning forward toward the captain. She looked up him with her eyes squinted, and her lips pursed. It was a look I'd not seen from her before.

319

"Do I need to take charge here? Do I need to whip some butt and take names?" She said.

In a demanding voice, she continued talking. "The two of you listen to me. We are going to spend this entire day cleaning up the stateroom, which is now our living quarters, and we are going to clean up the galley and take inventory of what we have left. We will determine what needs to be eaten first and what can be stored, and we will ration everything as needed. I want the two of you to figure out how you can fish and hunt to get food. You also have to figure out how we are going to cook that food, because we're about out of propane. Ryan needs you. I need you, and we all need each other, so throw your whiney attitudes to the side. If you want to cry, cry at night, but when the sun rises I expect you to be up and working. Now, is there any part of that you need repeated?"

I laughed loud, and replied, "No ma'am. You got my attention!"

Marie shook her head from side to side then smiled. She got up from the stool, reached across the bar and kissed the captain on the nose, then did the same to me.

The captain shook his head and grinned. "I've been put in me place," he said. "Thank you for bringing me back, lass."

I walked outside for a breath of fresh morning air and saw that the fog had already burned off. I stood at the railing looking inland at the island. The island, at least for now, was going to be our home and provide the food we needed to sustain ourselves.

Every day since we'd been there, the forest had become more alive. Even from this distance, I could hear birds on the island singing. The trees and flowers were showing a dazzling array of spring colors and filling the air with pleasant fragrances. The sun's strength was getting stronger each day. It was hard not to admire the beauty of the place despite our circumstances.

Marie came out to join me and laid her head on my shoulder. "How long, realistically, do you think we will be here?" She said.

I turned to face her then pulled her close to me, burying her head in my chest. I began to stroke her long curly locks of hair. Her presence and warmth gave me a sense of comfort I'd never known. I knew that without her here, it would be much worse. It would likely be that Ryan would have died, leaving the captain and I here alone.

"I think we need to plan long term," I said.

The captain came and stood beside us along the railing. I could see he too was admiring the beauty of the island. Marie asked him the same question she had presented to me.

"We need to plan for the worst," the captain replied. "We could be here for weeks, months, or God forbid, years."

"What do you base that on?" Marie asked.

The captain didn't hesitate before answering. "Me still thinks we are in a different time frame than the rest of the world, although me can't explain it exactly lass. A wormhole, a time warp, me don't have a name for it mates. I've sailed these oceans nearly all me life and spent many a day listening to others who've done the same. Nothing I've ever heard, nor anything I've ever witnessed, could compare to that storm we went through, or explain where we've ended up.

The captain was looking out beyond the ship with his head held high, and in deep thought as he continued. "And look at this place mates. No people, no sign of people, no old wrecked ships, no garbage from passing ocean vessels, no huts or lodges from hunters who have been on the island, and nothing on me maps to prove this place exists. She's a big island with a lot to offer, and has never been discovered, not even in these days of satellites in space looking down upon us. The sun rises and sets in a peculiar manner and seems to think for itself and change course at will."

The captain dropped his head, "And our only viable means of escape left yesterday."

I changed the subject. "Captain," I said. "Why don't you go disassemble your bed and bring it to the state room, then after I get done helping Marie in the galley, we'll sit down and figure out how to make a fireplace? Won't it feel good to have a nice fireplace in the state room to warm us and provide a nice place to sit and talk?" I knew I needed to keep the captain busy, and his mind occupied. Otherwise, he'd continue slipping toward a state of depression.

"Sounds like a nice idea, mate," he said. Then he turned to go toward the wheelhouse. As he was walking away, another idea hit me.

"Oh, wait a minute captain. Be thinking of a good way for us to make a raft to ride ashore on. We don't want to be plunging into those cold waters every time you and I go hunting. The raft also needs to be big enough to haul firewood back to the yacht"

The captain turned to look at me while scratching his chin. I could tell he was already thinking about the raft.

"You've a good mind for thinking, mate. Indeed, I'll make up some plans for a nice vessel to carry us ashore."

After the captain left, I stood there for a few more minutes holding Marie. I looked out to sea. It looked like a storm was developing along the eastern horizon, but it didn't appear to be heading inland. Seeing the dark clouds made me nervous, even though they didn't have the appearance of the ones I saw when we were at sea.

I wondered if the Tuckers were okay. As mad as I was at them, I hoped they were safe. None of them had any skills, aside from party arranging, and tennis playing. I wondered if they'd taken any of the tarps off the yacht to cover themselves as a shelter from the sun and rain. Perhaps they had already been rescued by a passing ship and were in a dining room drinking hot tea and having a nice breakfast. If that were true, I hoped they wouldn't forget to mention that the four of us were here.

Marie and I spent many hours cleaning the galley and food storage room. For every box or carton the Tuckers pulled from the storage shelves, they spilled or destroyed several more. The floor was covered in damaged containers of food, which we would have to eat right away, or they would spoil. As we worked, it made us both angry. If the Tuckers were going to leave, they could have done so without destroying what food we had left.

During our working time in the galley, we'd taken a few breaks to check on Ryan. In my mind, I kept thinking of a good way to build a fireplace in the stateroom. I was also wondering how we'd gather wood to fuel it. Although it was spring, and summer would soon be here, the warmth of a fireplace would be the farthest thing from our minds. Still, we had to cook, and we'd have to boil water for drinking.

It would be hard to carry water from the brook on the island to the yacht, but aside from distilling seawater, of which we had no means, I saw no other way to provide fresh water. We were already at the point where we needed to ration what bottled water we had left. We needed to figure out a way to catch rainwater also.

As we were finishing the work in the galley, Marie and I were getting concerned about Captain Nichols. We'd not seen him since that morning. I was hopeful that he had been disassembling his bed and perhaps drawing out some plans for the fireplace.

I remembered seeing a set of acetylene and oxygen torches in the engine room. Those would come in handy for cutting metal. There was a welding machine also, but we had no way of running it without electricity. Perhaps we could capture enough diesel fuel from the bottom of the storage tanks to run one of the generators for a short time and operate the welder. That way, we could construct a metal fireplace with a cooktop. I told Marie I was going to go check on the captain as she finished sweeping the galley.

As I entered the main deck, a cold rain hit me in the face. The storm I'd seen earlier had moved ashore. I didn't think the storm was going to move toward us when I'd seen it earlier. It was just another reminder to me that I was in a strange land I needed to be on guard to expect the unexpected.

I checked on Ryan. He was awake and had raised himself to a sitting position on his own. His strength was coming back. He still looked pale, and he'd lost quite a bit of weight. I didn't know if I could have survived what he had gone through. The pain had to be excruciating.

Ryan asked for something sweet to eat. I agreed to get him something if he'd eat it in small bites, I was still afraid he wouldn't be able to keep solid foods down. As we were talking, Marie came in with an arm full of fruit, which needed to be eaten. Ryan decided that would be better for him. The three of us sat together eating grapes, berries, and peaches.

I was about to get up and go look for Captain Nichols when he entered the stateroom. He came in out of the rain wearing a yellow hooded slicker. He took the slicker off and hung it on the hall tree by the main entrance door.

One of the double entrance doors lost its glass during the storm. The captain had taped a piece of cardboard over the opening. The cardboard was soaked from the rain and sagging a bit. I made a mental note to find something more substantial to replace the cardboard.

The beautiful pristine yacht we set sail on in England now looked like something you'd find in a salvage yard.

The captain had a worried look on his face. I'd seen this look far too many times lately and knew something was wrong. I didn't have to ask him what it was. Marie beat me to that.

"Are you okay Captain? You look worried!" Marie said.

"Me got more bad news mates," he said. He pulled up a chair and turned it backwards, then sat in it directly in front of Ryan's bed. My heart was beating fast again. I wish people who had bad news would just spit it out. I hated hesitation. It made my heart beat fast and made me anxious.

Finally, the captain spoke. "Me put some markers in the water by the ship a few days ago. I didn't say anything yesterday, but the ship had moved a few inches. She's moved another four to six inches today. The anchor cable was broken during the storm, and the anchor was lost at sea. I've scratched me head on this one and can't think of another way we can anchor the ship. I'm afraid I'm losing me ship for good, mates. She's slipping back out to sea, and with no means to anchor her down. We can't stop her. The sandbar we be on ends not too far out. When the ship reaches that point it's all she wrote."

My head was spinning. Ryan spoke up, asking the captain to explain this further.

"Me thinks that we've got two weeks, three at the very most. The ship will slide down the sandbar a bit at a time. When it reaches a point where more of her is in deep water than what lies on the sandbar she'll slip away quickly. The water level in the engine room will rise as we slide into deeper water. If not for the cracked hull, I'd be happy with this situation, for soon we'd be afloat again, but that's not the case. The ship is going to sink!"

Chapter 34

The captain's news changed everything again. I was so tired; we all were. For days on end, it had been mental and physical anguish. My hands were healing but still tender. The back of my head was also tender from the bumps I took during the storm. My ribs were sore. I ached all over from using muscles in ways I wasn't used to. The physical part though was nothing compared to the mental stress.

Being lost was not a good feeling, being lost somewhere on a deserted island was worse. Could the Captain's theory was right? Could it be that we were in some sort of time warp or wormhole? I wanted to quit, lie down on the beach, and just die, but deep down, I hoped a rescue would be coming soon.

Surely, there were search planes looking within a grid for signs of the yacht. Viscount Tucker might even have the Royal Navy out looking for us. I just had to keep moving forward and dealing with the blows as they came until they found us.

The following day the captain informed us of the ship's continuous movement. He'd checked the marker again. We were another four inches out toward the open sea. We sat together in the stateroom and made yet another new game plan. We had to get everything we possibly could onto the island before the ship slid into the deeper waters and sank.

Looking from the stern of the yacht, a color distinction could be seen in the water about forty feet out. It indicated the sandbar we were sitting on ended. Beyond that, the water was much deeper. For now, the ship had leveled off somewhat and was practically sitting upright again. Nonetheless, we all knew as it slid out to sea it could easily tilt over or capsize. We also knew we couldn't do a thing about it.

Using a hacksaw from the engine room, the captain helped me cut four aluminum support posts from the bottom deck. We cut the posts from the stern end. We knew the metal fuel storage tanks that ran from the floor to the ceiling would still provide enough support to prevent the deck above from collapsing. The posts were eight inches in diameter, hollow aluminum pipe, twelve feet in length, and perfect for pontoons. We were going to build a raft.

We sealed the ends of each post by using cans of expandable foam and caulking. We spaced the posts on the main deck two feet apart and cut sections from the aluminum railing and laid it across the pipes forming an open deck. Next, eight feet by four feet wall panels torn from the cabin walls were used for the main decking. With plastic tie straps, metal wire, and rope, we were able to tie everything tightly together. The raft wasn't sea worthy but it should hold for what we needed.

Marie helped as the captain and I removed all the tools and supplies we could from the bottom deck. The water in the engine room on the stern end was now waist deep. If an item in the engine room could be torn loose, unbolted, cut apart, or peeled loose, we did so, and moved everything to the deck above or to the main deck.

Building the raft and removing things from the bottom deck took a full day, and we still weren't able to recover everything we wanted. We needed to erect a temporary shelter on the island, so the hand tools and other items salvaged from the engine room would come in handy.

During the night, it rained again, but stopped around daybreak. It was going to be a beautiful spring day. I looked toward the island and saw that the trees were getting greener. The smell of spring was strong. The fragrant aroma of plants blooming could be inhaled even from out in the bay. I thought about how different this was from what I'd always seen in movies, where people always were shipwrecked on tropical islands with palm trees and coconuts. Not here; wherever we were, it was evident there were four seasons.

Using rope we'd gathered from various places on the yacht, we formed a tight tagline from the bow of the yacht to the beach. I drove a bed rail deep into the sand on the beach to tie the rope too. We would use the rope and long poles to pull and push the raft to and from the yacht.

Everyone worked at a steady pace, taking few breaks. We had to load the raft as heavily as possible to make every trip count. The food, clothing, and bedding were the first things taken ashore. That took us three days.

We built a tent shelter, in the cove beyond the beach. Using a fire axe, I cut long poles and placed them between trees, forming a framework. Plastic sheeting and canvas were placed over the poles, making a large tent. That gave us at least a temporary shelter to protect things from getting wet. By the end of each day, everyone was exhausted, and no one had a problem falling asleep at night.

Ryan continued to get stronger and wanted to help. His attitude in spite of his horrific injury was remarkable. The swelling in his leg continued to go away, but his entire leg up into his left hip, was black as coal.

Ryan tied some ropes for us and did a few other small tasks. He was far from being able to get out of bed so there wasn't much more he could do. Still, we wanted him to feel useful, so we gave him plenty of tasks to keep him busy.

I knew we'd soon have to move Ryan to the island. We had purposely waited to do that, as long as the yacht remained steady. Each day brought a slight degree of healing to his leg, but we didn't want to rush moving him.

The captain measured the yacht's movement several times each day. Since he first informed us the ship was moving, it had slipped three and a half more feet toward the open sea. We all feared at some point the yacht would break free and suddenly shoot out to deeper waters, capsize, and sink. Wanting to remain on the yacht as long as possible, we were gambling with our lives each day and night by remaining onboard.

Over the next four days, we moved more tools, cooking utensils, small personal items, furniture, and anything we could carry, over to the island. We even salvaged screws and hinges from the doors, walls, and cabinets. We had to think long term. If something had a potential use, large or small, we moved it ashore. Once the ship slipped away into deeper waters, we'd have no way to recover anything left behind.

It had reached the point where we decided it was too risky to keep sleeping on board the yacht. If the ship were to slide out into deeper waters at night and suddenly capsize, we'd most likely perish. The captain expected the yacht would soon go from gradual movement to a break-over point and quickly slip away into the deep water.

The following morning, we packed our beds onto the raft and took them to the beach. On the next trip, we moved Ryan to the island. He was apprehensive about being moved from his bed for the first time, and being placed on a homemade raft added to those fears. He knew that if he were dumped overboard it would be, at best, difficult for him to swim.

Marie and I got in the water and swam alongside the raft in order to give Ryan the assurance that if he did fall off, we would be nearby to help him. The captain stood on the deck of the raft and used a pole to push it toward the beach. The water at the stern of the ship was over our heads at that time. When the yacht was first grounded, it was only slightly above our knees.

The captain and I returned to the yacht once Ryan was ashore. We placed him in a bed beneath an additional shelter we had erected just for living space. Marie stayed ashore also, to help Ryan, and arrange items as we brought them over from the yacht.

The captain didn't say it, but I knew he wanted to be the last one to abandon ship. He alone remained onboard, removing additional items, as I pulled and pushed the raft ashore with the cargo.

Two or three times a day during the last three days, we had to add slack to the tagline in order to keep it from pulling the bed rail out of the sand. The captain had been very accurate in his prediction of how the ship would react as it slid out to sea. We were all exhausted from our labors. We were also on edge knowing that soon the ship could sink.

The evening after getting Ryan on shore, we had a seafood feast of sorts. We boiled shrimp that Marie had caught in a pool of water just off the edge of the cliff to the left of the beach.

She had gathered flour and cornmeal from the floor of the galley, which the Tuckers had spilled. She used it to make some sort of pasty substance and form it into balls, to be used for bait. It worked like magic. The shrimp flocked to the bait. Using her skillful abilities, she used a net to cast out and gather them in.

We were all very appreciative of her talent and feasted on the fresh shrimp. Marie's beautiful face got slightly redder each time we bragged on her talent throughout the evening. We found ourselves laughing a bit that evening for the first time in many days. The laughter lifted everyone's spirit.

The next morning we were eating breakfast as soon as daylight broke. We were talking about taking the raft back to the yacht for another day's work. Our intent was to remove more of the padded wall sections from the cabins and hallways.

We were nearly finished eating when we heard a loud snap. Marie and I ran from the trees onto the beach and over to the raft, which we had pulled ashore the night before. It was then we noticed that the tagline, going from the bedrail to the yacht had broken. Captain Nichols was a few paces behind us, but caught up as we stopped at the raft.

A thin layer of fog was hovering just above the water in the small bay. The water was calm and had a mirrored surface. The bay was somehow well protected. I'd only seen waves in the area a few times since being there. Most of the time only small movements of water could be detected. Often it was no movement at all, as was the case that morning.

"She's about to go," the captain said in a low voice.

We looked out and could see the bow of the ship was elevated a few feet. I could hear the super yacht creaking and moaning. A few minutes later, the big yacht jerked backwards, moving quite a bit further out of the bay area. The bow made a large splash as it came crashing down to meet the water again. The ship moved back another fifty to seventy-five feet quickly then slowed to a near stop. The yacht was level and still after that, as if it were ready to be boarded and sail out to sea.

Over the next hour, it moved backward perhaps thirty to fifty more feet, toward the open ocean. Then it began to list slightly toward the starboard side. Even with the fog sitting on top of the water, we could see bubbles boiling up from around the yacht's cracked hull. No one moved. We stood there the entire time watching. Even though this event was expected, I wasn't prepared to see it happening.

All we could do was stand and watch as the magnificent yacht made the journey to Davy Jones' locker. In the next fifteen minutes, we witnessed the ship move further out and continue to list heavily then suddenly it capsized. As the bottom of the yacht was revealed, I could see a split in the hull about twenty feet long. We continued watching, as that exquisite multimillion-dollar vessel which had safely carried us for thousands of miles, sank out of sight.

When the last part of the yacht went under, an immense loneliness, coupled with despair, came over me. Marie was still standing beside of me, holding my hand and silently weeping. Even if I could have found the words to express my feelings at that moment, I could not have spoken them.

I hadn't noticed that the captain was on his knees in the sand. He was passively staring out to where the mighty ship had sunk out of sight. Although he had predicted its death himself, he too wasn't prepare for that moment.

Another chapter of our lives had just passed, and although a new day had dawned, it only brought about more uncertainty. The four of us were stranded with no way to get help of any kind. We were at the mercy of others to find and rescue us. We had no choice but to remain there for the time being and somehow survive with the resources available on the island. Although we lost the yacht, we were fortunate to have been able to salvage so much material before it sank.

Chapter 35

It was two days after the yacht sank before we made a decision about what to do next. We spent those two days organizing the things we had taken from the yacht. During that time, we also rested and mourned for those we had lost and for the loss of the yacht.

Everything was discussed at great length. We all agreed it would be best to move everything possible up to the lake. We could build a more suitable shelter there. The lake was an excellent freshwater source, and the forest would be at hand to provide firewood and food. Since it was higher ground, we could also make a large signal fire. The fire could be lit if a plane were to fly over, or if a ship was spotted out at sea.

It took weeks to build a crude cabin and move the things we needed from the cliffs below up to the lake area. We used pulleys and rope to transport things up the ravine to the top of the cliff. Although that was difficult, the pulley system made the job much easier, especially with the larger heavier items. I noticed each day how our body fat was disappearing. Our arms and legs were becoming toned and muscular. Captain Nichols wasn't able to keep up with Marie and me. He was many years older, but could still do a good days work. He mostly stayed up at the lake area and worked from there.

After another week had passed, we erected a temporary shelter by the lake for sleeping quarters. It was a daunting task getting Ryan up the steep ravine without injuring him further. It took the three of us working for several hours to do so. He was happy to be off the beach, and was amazed at the beauty of the lake and surrounding woodlands.

Ryan wanted to help in any way possible. He assisted the captain in performing small tasks. He would scoot along with his one leg. His leg continued to heal, and he slowly regained his strength. The scar was ugly and the wound area was tender, but Ryan seldom complained. He realized, as we all did, how fortunate he was to have survived such a serious injury without medical treatment.

We were all pleasantly surprised at the captain's carpentry skills. Removing all the materials we could from the yacht proved to be a blessing. Considering the tools we had to work with, the captain, with our help, was able to erect a rather sturdy cabin. It was still a crude structure, but it provided protection from the elements. We worked daily to improve our living quarters. Soon it felt like more than just a shelter it was our home.

As we were sitting around the fire talking one night, the captain went off by himself for a few minutes. When he returned, he presented Ryan with a hand-carved wooden peg leg he'd been working on. It had a leather piece attached for strapping to his stub. You would have thought Ryan had won the lottery again as he began stumbling around trying to use the peg leg, whooping and hollering all the while.

It took him a few weeks, but Ryan adapted to hobbling along rather well with the wooden leg. He was thrilled to be moving about, and he was very useful in what had now become our daily chores, gathering edible plants and berries, fishing, and improving our crude cabin.

At the end of each day, we sat at a clearing atop the cliff near the waterfall, overlooking the ocean. We sat there each evening as we watched the sun set. It became the captain's favorite place. Each day he charted how the sun set in a slightly different location, trying to figure out its movement and make sense of the pattern.

The captain also liked looking out over the water, reminiscing about days of old, sailing the seas, and taking about all the ports he'd been to. He watched in hopes of spotting a ship. We all worked together erecting a large pile of wood there to be lit as a signal fire. The captain also made notes on the ocean currents, saying that if we weren't rescued, he'd know the best season for us to prepare a sturdy raft and set sail to the east. One thing that greatly concerned us was we didn't have any degree of certainty that where the sun came up was east.

Living there wasn't bad other than the fact we had no way of getting new supplies. Once we ran out of something or something broke, that was it. There were no replacements. We limited the spices we had from the yacht, and kept trying to find herbs on the island that we could use for seasoning our food.

One thing we found out quickly, to survive we had to hunt for food daily. Marie and I both developed hunting skills, and then honed those skills until we became proficient hunters. I was happy that I had purchased the bowie knife during our trip. The knife was a tool I depended on every day now. I quickly learned that there's a big difference between hunting wild animals for sport, versus hunting game for survival.

The fish and turtles from the lake were plentiful, as well as rabbits, squirrels and deer in the forest. We occasionally spotted a fox or a bobcat, which seemed to be the only predators on the island. Insects weren't too much of a problem, and I'd not seen a snake in the entire time we'd been there.

Until we arrived, the only thing the deer had to worry about was over-population. It soon became apparent that the animals on the island we had to fear were skunks. There must have been hundreds of them. We had to be certain we didn't leave any fish or other food scraps lying out or a host of skunks would invade our homestead. They were especially active at night.

The cabin we built was near the lake at the edge of the meadow. We planted a large garden in the meadow using seed from peppers, corn, tomatoes, and potatoes brought from the yacht. The rabbits and deer liked our garden too, so we had to erect cages and a fence around the crops to keep the animals from eating them.

It wasn't a tropical island. I knew that as summer waned, autumn, and then winter would follow. I was as hopeful as everyone else we'd be rescued long before winter, but if we weren't, we'd better be prepared. Not having a good shelter and food supply we'd soon run into major trouble when cold weather came.

We shared our clothing. The captain and Marie we're thankful that Ryan and I had shopped a lot with Viscount Tucker's credit card. The extra summer and winter clothing we'd brought along would prove beneficial as the seasons changed.

In late May, Marie was down at the ocean fishing for shrimp or anything else she could gather into her net.

As she approached the beach area at the far end of the bay, she discovered a large assortment of items had washed ashore. She was excited beyond measure, knowing that at least occasionally a ship passed by.

Once she notified us, the captain and I quickly went to look for ourselves. We soon realized it was debris from the lifeboats. Mrs. Tuckers straw hat she always wore in the sun was among the debris. Her name was on the custom label inside the brim. A piece of an oar, clothing, water bottles, and a host of other items appeared on the beach over the next few days. We knew then the Tuckers had not made it. Something had happened and whatever it may have been; we feared they were all dead.

That brought about a time of sadness again for all of us. The Tuckers didn't make it, nor were others notified we were here. It didn't give us much hope of trying to build a raft for escape. The lifeboats were much more sea worthy than any raft we could ever dream of building. If the lifeboats couldn't hold up in this ocean, nothing we constructed could either.

As the days passed, we continued to look for a plane overhead, or a ship passing by, but never was one spotted. Although our hopes for a rescue remained, our lives slowly turned to learning to live on that unclaimed land and make the best of what we had. Each day we added a little extra something to the cabin. Be it a homemade curtain or a set of steps, everything helped to make it feel like home.

Our lives were busy during the day doing chores and gathering food. The evenings were a time to sit, relax, and talk. In the beginning, the talk was about our past lives, missing family, and our homeland. Over time, the conversation changed. We began to talk more about the events of that day, and what we were going to do tomorrow.

We started spending our evenings on the small front porch of our crude cabin, telling wild tales and playing silly games. One of our favorite games was trying to make each other hungry by taking turns talking about foods we missed, like hot fresh doughnuts, or the taste of a chocolate milkshake.

I mentioned once about missing the new pick-up truck I bought once out of prison. After wanting it for years, I'd finally gotten it. Then I'd only gotten to drive it a couple of times before flying to London. Everyone teased me for weeks, making sounds like a truck and honking a horn.

Once we were talking about sounds that we missed. I had just said I missed the sound of a motorcycle taking off and running through its gears. Marie's turn was next, and she said she missed the sound of her neighbor's dog barking. Ryan and I thought that was hilarious and laughed until Marie got a homemade broom and began beating us both over our heads with it.

We named the place Antipode Island, which meant people living at opposite ends of the globe. We felt Antipodes Island was appropriate, since we were living on the opposite end of the earth from everyone else.

The captain never joined us on the porch until after dark. He still liked to go to the cliff and watch the sunset. He never talked about it, but I could tell his heart was broken. I didn't know if it was from the Tuckers actions, or some lost love he left behind in England. Perhaps it was something entirely different. It may have been a combination of many things. He mentioned once about a son and a grandson. Regardless, the evenings brought about an air of sadness in him, and he liked being alone.

As summer lingered, we gathered corn and beans from our garden, and in the fall, we dug potatoes. We didn't have a place to store the food, and although we could dry the beans, the other crops would rot quickly unless eaten. It was looking as if we would have to spend the winter there and would need plenty of food to survive.

I got brave one fall day, lit a torch, and explored the cave I'd found when we first arrived. I had a handmade spear in one hand and the torch in the other as I went back into the cavern. As it turned out there were no bears, or any other animals inside.

The cave was seven to eight feet in height, and as much as twenty feet wide in a few spots. Fifty feet into the cave, it split off into three tunnels. One tunnel went left for another fifty feet. It was caved in past that point. The middle tunnel went a little further, perhaps seventy-five feet, and ended. It was also very narrow.

The third tunnel went right several hundred feet. There were several twist and bends then it ended in a large room about forty feet in diameter. The ceiling in the room was forty to fifty feet high, and dome shaped. I thought it was odd that the outside of the butte had slick firm walls, unworn over the ages, unlike the inside of the cave, which was hollowed out with tunnels, and contained a large cavity.

Just before reaching the large room, there was a ledge on the left about four feet off the floor. The top of the ledge was about four feet wide and eight to nine feet in length. I climbed up and found a stone lying there that looked like a spearhead. A long dust trail ran from the end of the stone. I thought it might have been a wooden rod, which had long since rotted away. I wasn't sure about the stone, so I placed it in my pocket to take back for the others to see. If I was right, that meant that at some time in history, humans had been there.

For several days after finding the stone, we all debated about whether or not it may have been a spearhead, or just a piece of rock naturally shaped to a point. I stuck to the spearhead theory because the roof over the ledge in the cave was smooth, and no rock appeared to have fallen out.

I didn't find anything else in the cave. I discovered, however, that even on a hot day it was very cool inside. It was cool enough that we could store food there to preserve it longer. Outside the cave, I noticed near the top of the rock formation that the mist remained even on clear cloudless days, just like the first time I was there. I wanted to know what was on top, and what would cause the fog or mist to be present?

The rich soil in the meadow had never been farmed before and was full of nutrients, just right for crop growing. Our plants produced more yield than we ever could have imagined. I knew the cave was a long way from our garden, but it would provide the perfect spot for storage of potatoes, onions, and corn. We began storing our vegetables and our meat as well. The constant cool temperature inside the cave acted like a refrigeration unit, and the meat would keep much longer.

There was no evidence that animals had ever used the cave, which we all thought was strange. Nonetheless, we thought with meat stored inside it would be a temptation to all the critters, and they would wander in. We built a fire-pit at the mouth of the cave and concluded that animals would be less tempted to venture inside if the rock walls were sooty and had the smell of fire. We never knew for sure if that was what worked, but no animals ever entered. Even the skunks steered away from the cave.

We carried a few chairs and some other items to the cave for use when we were hunting that area and needed shelter. Ryan had even ventured as far as the cave a few times and liked the way the area looked. We talked about how much it reminded us of the mountains back home where we used to play as kids.

We tried to figure out a way to climb the butte and see what was on top, and what would cause the foggy mist to hang in the air at all times. We all four scratched our heads a lot trying to engineer a way to climb the sheer walls, but never came up with anything that was workable. I climbed every tree surrounding the butte, trying to get a view of what might be on top of the rock formation. I could never see through the fog layer and finally gave up trying.

Ryan put on a comedy act for us at the entrance of the cave one day. He performed some sort of funny ritual. Then he declared there was a holy burial ground up on top the butte, which he said was protected by the fog god. He was quickly becoming a comedian. Ryan never ceased to amaze and amuse us with his weird comedy.

Chapter 36

During one of our many late-night conversations, the captain told us he was licensed as a minister of marriage. He stated that he had married several couples aboard various ships over the years. Marie and I looked at each other with a gleam in our eyes. The next day, I asked her to marry me.

The captain performed a ceremony on the clearing by the cliffs the following evening. Ryan gave her away and then the captain and Ryan both tried to sing a love song. That part was a disaster in itself, but we all enjoyed it and laughed the entire evening long.

Our honeymoon was two days alone at the cabin while the captain and Ryan stayed at the cave on a hunting trip. We missed them so much we went to the cave each day to visit with them. We stayed until dusk, giving us just enough time to get back to the cabin before dark.

Living without luxuries such as prepared foods, hot showers, and a washing machine, was difficult. Still, even despite our circumstances, it was the happiest time of my life. For the first time since I was old enough to remember, I felt loved, cared for, and needed. I had a happy family, the thing I'd always wanted.

There was a tight bond between the four of us. Although I would have welcomed the sight of a helicopter flying in to take us back to civilization, I could never be as happy as where I was at that time.

The fire axes salvaged from the yacht, proved to be a blessing. Using them, we cut many cords of firewood to burn, keeping us warm, and providing a means to cook food. The fireplace I had conjured in my head to be placed on the yacht was never built. With no way to cut, shape, and weld metal, we had to build our fireplace in the cabin from fieldstone. Using clay mixed with sand, the mortar we made was nearly as good as anything you could buy in a store.

Once we found out how good the mortar was, we used it to seal cracks between the logs in the cabin. The fireplace sat in the middle of the largest room of our three-room cabin, with a rock chimney that extended through the roof. The light and warmth emitted by the fire gave our home a cozy feeling. In winter, our beds closely surrounded the fireplace as we tried to stay warm on the bitter cold nights. The winter was long with lots of snow and cold temperatures that followed each snowfall. We all got cabin fever long before the spring weather allowed us to spend much time outside again.

The lake froze over early in the winter, and we were able to skate across it without fear of falling in. Marie got the idea to cut blocks of ice from the lake and store it in the cave. She expected it would last into late spring, maybe summer, and we'd have ice. With nothing more to do on those cold winter days, we did just that. We built a crude sled, which we used to transport the ice blocks from the lake to the cave. We could only make one trip each day but over a few weeks, we had what we thought to be a good supply of ice for our experiment. We constructed a makeshift freezer from the insulated panels gathered from the yacht, which worked out well.

§

A year passed, as did another, and another. It was a summer evening of our third year on the island. It had been a hard day of working in the garden, cleaning the cabin, and stacking firewood. Marie, Ryan, and I sat on the porch as usual playing games we'd made up and laughing at each other's answers. When it got dark, the captain had not returned from sitting at the cliff's edge watching the sunset. As more time passed, the captain still didn't show, and we all became worried.

I got a torch and lit it, then headed around the lake to go look for him. As I approached the clearing by the cliff, I saw the captain sitting there in a lounge chair from the yacht. The chair was now discolored from the sun of summer and cold of winter. I spoke as I approached the captain, but he didn't reply. When I got beside him, I noticed his head slumped slightly to the right and figured he was sleeping.

"Wake up old man, time for bed," I said.

I often joked with the captain calling him an old man. He would snap a response back about still being able to take me down.

The captain still didn't answer. I laid my hand on his shoulder and he didn't move. His shoulder was cold. I placed my hand on his cheek and it too was cold. I began to panic. I dropped to my knees and shook the captain, only to find his body stiff, cold, and unresponsive. I checked for a pulse and found none. He was dead.

"NO!" I cried out loudly into the night, "NO!"

All my strength left me as I slumped over Captain Nichols and began to cry. This man was the father I never had, my mentor, my friend. It couldn't be real, how could he be dead?

We buried Captain Nichols at that same spot. We placed his feet pointing toward the sun. With the sun rising and setting in an arc, over the same horizon, the captain would be able to see both sunrise and sunset from where he lay. The digging was hard in the ground on top of the cliff so the grave was a bit shallow. We carried dirt and rocks, and made a mound over the grave and made a large wooden cross, which we placed on top.

For weeks, none of us had much to say, and we could eat very little. We mourned for our dear friend, and our thoughts were of him every moment of each passing day.

Chapter 37

I was twenty-three years old when we landed on the island. After that, another sixteen years passed by. I'd then lived nearly as long on the island as I had in the world where other people resided. In all those years, we'd never seen a ship sail by or a plane fly overhead. Several times, I thought I saw a streak in the sky from a jetliner or the silhouette of a ship at the edge of the horizon, but it was always just my mind playing tricks on me.

Over the years, the bond between Ryan, Marie, and me grew even stronger. We were closer than any family could ever imagine being. Each day required a lot of hard work for our survival, and everyone did their share of the work. I can only think of one time when there was even a crossword. It was something small and insignificant between Ryan and me. Shortly afterwards I couldn't even remember what the dispute was even about.

Marie got pregnant once. It was three years after we buried the captain. We were excited about an addition to our family. We made a cradle and other things for the baby over the next several months. When Marie delivered, the baby was stillborn. It did something to us all but more so to Marie. She was a long time getting over losing the baby. It was a boy. We named him Nicholas, after our dear lost friend Captain Nichols. We buried him beside the captain, so they could be close together and keep one another company.

The skills I'd learned as a youth playing in those West Virginia hills became invaluable, as we had to live off the land. We all learned a lot about farming, when to hunt, and how not to kill too much of the wildlife for food, thus depleting the population to the point of possible extinction. Marie and I became experts at spear fishing. Ryan devised an assortment of fish traps over time, which often provided us with a supply of fresh food.

We tested plants carefully, in order to determine what was edible and what wasn't. We also discovered many plants that could be dried or ground up for use as spices.

Marie and I laughed at Ryan a lot. The accident on the ship changed his outlook on life completely. He turned into a kind man, always wanted to help Marie and me anyway possible. Instead of the need to get ahead, win tons of money, and be famous, he was now a giver and a helper.

Ryan also continued his comedy, keeping us entertained. Once, the three of us were sitting on the small dock we'd constructed to extend out into the lake, in front of the cabin. Ryan pulled one of his fish traps out of the water, and it contained a three to five-pound catfish. It was during one of the few lean times when we'd not caught much to eat and had been rationing food.

Ryan removed the fish from the trap, held it close to his face, and told the fish "I'm gonna eat you!" Then he started singing a song to the fish, making up the words as he went. Marie and I were sitting on the porch watching his comedy show and holding our sides while laughing.

There was nothing complicated about life on our island. The work we had to do daily was hard, but no one ever complained, unless it was about a backache. Aside from missing our loved ones, we were very content and happy.

Chapter 38

It was mid-July. We left early in the morning to travel up the streambed to the cave. As in winters past, we'd cut large ice blocks from the frozen lake and carried them by sled to the cave. Over the years, we'd perfected our ice storage methods. Normally, we could have ice until the middle of August. It was a treat to go there on a hot summer day, and chip off pieces of the ice to put in a glass of herbal tea.

That day we were sluggish as we made the trip to the cave. It was hot and muggy, with a temperature that must have been in the high nineties. We were all dreaming about how soothing it would be to have a piece of ice to melting in our mouth.

On the way to the cave, we stopped at the cliff overlooking, where Nicholas and Captain Nichols were buried. We placed a few wild flowers on the graves. It was something we did quite often and always a short prayer was spoken by one of us.

As we were at the overlook, I saw some clouds that startled me and made me uneasy. Out over the horizon where the ocean meets the sky, a thin black line was present. It reminded me of that dreadful day many years past. Ryan and Marie saw it too. Even the slightest storm still made us all nervous and put us on edge.

We decided if we were at the cave and a storm rolled in, we'd spend the night there. It had been a few weeks since we'd made camp there, and we were overdue to spend the night. We often agreed that going to the cave was like going on vacation, and we all looked forward to the hike. Ryan, even with one leg, had become a good hiker.

We made the long hike to the cave. I went inside to chip some ice while Marie and Ryan placed wood in the fire pit we'd made just inside the mouth of the cave. We were going to brew some tea, and once it cooled, put the ice in and have a nice cold drink on a hot summer day.

Ryan would do his usual comedy routine afterward to keep us entertained. He liked to take a stick, and draw pictures in the soot on the rock ceiling over the fire pit and tell some wild tale while he drew. We'd sometimes fall out of our chairs laughing so hard, which encouraged Ryan to continue.

Ryan used to make jokes about his leg but Marie and I never laughed at those. It just didn't seem like the right thing to do. We asked him not to make sport of a bad situation where we'd come so close to losing him.

A hot fire on a hot summer day doesn't sound like good logic, but it was the only way for us to cook and to brew tea. The cool air exiting the cave gave us the same feeling as having an air conditioner, so the heat from the fire didn't cause us any discomfort. The tea was Marie's development, a blend of several different herbs that only she could mix correctly. I'd tried making the mixture several times and it wasn't drinkable, but she could make it and it was as good as anything I've ever drank.

As we sat there drinking our tea and chewing on some deer jerky, it started raining. At first, it was a light rain but soon became a downpour, producing so much noise we had to talk loudly to hear each other. The wind picked up. It blew the rain far enough into the cave to douse our fire.

We pulled our chairs back and sat for a long time watching the rain come down. The once small stream down to the right of the rock formation swelled quickly, and became a swollen river. We knew that even after the rain stopped it would be a long time before we could use our well-worn path by the stream again. We'd have to go back to the cabin in a different direction.

After a couple of hours, the rain hadn't let up. We got bored, and decided it was time for a real meal instead of just a piece of jerky to chew on. Marie and I went back into the deepest section of the cave to get some of the few potatoes left over from last fall's harvest and some dried rabbit, which together makes a wonderful stew. Ryan was going to start a new fire a little farther back in the cave with some wood we had stored there.

Just as we were reaching the back of the tunnel, our torches all at once got very dim, nearly going out. Then the ground started shaking. At first, I thought I was having vertigo or something. Marie turned to look at me. I could see her face from the glow of the torch as it rekindled. She was shaking also, and terrified. The ground began shaking violently, and simultaneously we fell to the floor of the cave. It was an earthquake!

I'd never been in an earthquake but there was no mistake; this was one, and a big one at that! I could hear rocks falling but couldn't determine from where the sound was coming. I was able to grab hold of Marie as we both fell. We clung as close to the wall as possible. It wasn't much protection, but it kept us from being in the center where rocks were more likely to drop.

Within less than a minute from when the ground started shaking, it stopped. I asked Marie if she was okay. She nodded yes. I stood up then helped her to her feet. My torch had gone out when we were shaken to the ground but thankfully, Marie's was still lit. I grabbed my torch and held it against hers until it once again caught fire.

Ryan! Was he okay? Marie and I quickly made our way back through the cave. A few rocks had fallen from the roof. They were small, and there weren't as many as I had imagined. As we approached the mouth of the cave, we found that the roof had collapsed some distance from the entrance. We were completely sealed inside. I instantly became weak, feeling like all the blood had drained from my body.

I yelled for Ryan and could hear a faint moan. Oh lord, oh no, it can't be! Ryan was buried in the rubble. Marie and I both screamed for him then listened. Faintly I heard Ryan. "I'm hurt Jake. I'm cold. I'm pinned between-"

We never heard another word from Ryan. Only silence followed. "Ryan," I kept screaming his name as I tried to move some of the rocks. Marie was crying and frantically trying to assist me. We were only able to move some of the smaller rocks. Most of the rocks on the ground were boulders, and the edge of the cave-in where we were was still ten feet or more from the cave entrance.

After hours of trying to dig ourselves out and find Ryan, we gave out. We had no tools to dig with and Marie and I both had spent all our energy. We slumped down by a large boulder and cried in each other's arms. I was in disbelief that I had lost my lifelong friend. It couldn't be true. It just couldn't! Marie and I both went from crying and uncontrollable sobs, to loud cries of grief and despair as we sat there holding one another. I wanted it to be me lying under that pile of rubble, not Ryan. Up until that time, our concern was about trying to dig through the rubble and find Ryan. It hadn't sunk in that we were entombed.

The torches got dim again and Marie said, "Oh no." The words had just left her lips when the ground began shaking. We quickly rose to our feet and ran further into the cave as rocks started falling all around us. We headed back toward the cavern in the tunnel on the right. The intersection where the cave split into the three tunnels caved in behind us mere seconds after we passed by. If we had any doubt before it was clear now, Marie and I were buried alive.

Just as the earthquake stopped, we could hear something else, a noise like rushing water. Then it quickly grew louder. The torch gave us no visual warning as a wave of water, coming from the large room deeper inside the tunnel, swept by our feet. It rose to our knees within seconds. We couldn't go back because the cave roof had collapsed behind us. Our only choice was to work our way back, against the current, and try to reach the rock ledge. It was a struggle going against the current of the rapidly moving water and trying to keep our balance.

Marie was in front of me and fell into the water. The hydraulic force of the water quickly swept her into me then I fell also. I was able to grab her and pull us both up, but I lost my torch in the process. We were able to salvage Marie's torch, but it was doused out by the water, and we had no means to relight it. Only a few more feet and we would be at the ledge. I grabbed ahold of the cave wall. We struggled through the water until I could feel the ledge.

354

I pushed Marie onto the ledge, and then I climbed up. The water was now about a foot below the ledge and seemed to be leveling off.

From the top of the ledge to the top of the cave was less than four feet, so we couldn't stand up. The ledge was narrow but long, so we both were able to stretch out easily. We were freezing from the cold air of the cave. Both of us were soaked. As we shivered in the eerie darkness, I felt toward the far end of the ledge and found a plastic crate we had stored there. The crate contained a few yellow onions, stored there from last fall, and two small bags of pecans.

We normally used the ledge for storage of many other food items. During the spring and early summer, however, those supplies had been depleted. I knew there was nothing more in that crate, but still I was hoping a blanket or a jacket would have been there. We used to leave a jacket or long-sleeve shirt on the ledge and wear it as we worked in the cold cave, but as time passed our clothing wore out and we had little to spare.

Marie and I lay on the ledge shivering and crying. Only once had I ever experienced such thick darkness. It was while we were in the storm that brought us to the island. We both knew this was the end. We had been through so much over these many years, all the heartaches, disappointments, and solitude on the island.

We'd had more than our share of life's trouble, then to end it with even more torture. The only comfort I had was that I was with the love of my life. I wandered hopelessly for years, feeling unloved and uncared for. Then I met Marie. I could never dream of living without her.

Periodically, I would reach my arm down from the ledge until I felt the water, giving me assurance it wasn't getting deeper. Marie and I both wished several times that the cave would fall in upon us and end this misery. There weren't any more aftershocks, but the water wasn't abating.

We had no clue where the water had come from, keeping us from moving through the cave. Even if the water dried up completely though, we were trapped with no means of escape. It was going to be a slow death.

Selfishly I was hoping it would be me to die first, but at the same time, I couldn't bear the thought of Marie being there in the cold wet darkness all alone.

After more hours of crying and lashing out at the world, we shed our wet clothes and wrung them out, then waved them in the air for as long as we could, hoping to air dry them. The rock ledge was cold, so we sat on the plastic crate as we waved our clothes in the thick, penetrating darkness. The movement helped warm our bodies, but as soon as we stopped, the cold returned.

After more hours had passed, our clothes felt dry, so we put them back on. We then laid down and tried to sleep. It was restless sleep and when we could no longer lay, we sat on the crate. Each of us ate an onion and a few of the pecans. I had no idea if the running water was clean, but we drank it to quench our thirst.

The water had to be coming from the far end of the cave, out of the large room. I wondered where the water could have originated from? Could the stream have swollen to the point it was high enough to filter through cracks in the rock wall? That wasn't likely because, the river now flowing through the cave tunnel was too large, too much volume. The cave walls weren't cracked, unless the earthquake caused them to be. Several thousands of gallons per minute were flowing past the ledge. Like so many other things about this land, it didn't make sense.

More time passed and it was the same, darkness, running water, and a bone-chilling cold. Marie and I took turns rubbing our hands across one another, trying to keep our blood circulating and gain some warmth. As time passed, we became weaker. Our hand movement slowed as we tired. Our strength, like our hope, had left us.

We slept off and on, but never was it peaceful sleep. We would take turns holding each other to apply any warmth we could. Then the onions and nuts being eaten without any other food upset our stomachs. Several times, we had to ease off the ledge into the cold water and relieve ourselves. It was misery on top of misery.

My best estimate was that three or four days had passed since we'd perched ourselves onto the ledge. Then another earthquake came, not as strong as the first or second, but still violent. All we could do was curl up to one another, praying it would cause a large rock to fall on us and end our lives. Two smaller aftershocks quickly followed the initial quake.

We had been on the island for sixteen years and not even a tremor, so why this, why now? Why not some other time? Why take the life of my dear friend? Ryan. Oh my dear friend Ryan. My heart ached so badly over the loss of my dear friend. I was near the point of diving into the water and letting it sweep me away.

Some time had passed since the last aftershock. I reached my arm down from the ledge to touch the water. It appeared the water level had subsided a few inches. I told Marie, but she didn't respond. I knew she had given up. We both were extremely weak, and I knew we wouldn't last much longer.

I didn't feel as cold anymore. Was it numbness, was I dying? I curled up beside Marie and held her close until we both fell asleep.

Cramping in my stomach woke me. I took off my pants, in order to keep them dry. I then slid off the ledge to relieve myself. I expected to feel the cold water as I eased down. My feet hit the cave floor only to find a few inches of water present.

The inflowing water had subsided. After relieving myself, I climbed back onto the ledge and pulled my pants back on. I shook Marie to wake her up then told her about the water situation, but she hardly responded. I was wondering if the water may have somehow cleared the cave and that's why it ran out. It wasn't logical thinking but nothing about the island had ever seemed logical.

I told Marie I was going to feel my way through the cave. She didn't want me to go, but I had to find out. Although I was prepared to die there, I was going to give it my last-ditch effort before I climbed back on the ledge and closed my eyes for the last time.

I placed both hands against the wall of the tunnel, feeling my way as I walked along. Using my memory, I tried to envision the features of the wall, which I had passed by so many times with the aid of a torch. It was different than I remembered. My weakened state, plus the thick black darkness, made it confusing to judge distance as well as dimensions.

It didn't take but a few minutes until I came to the end. Tons of loose rock and mud blocked the way, and I could go no further. It was exactly what I expected deep down, but my mind wanted me to think the water had cleared all the debris from the cave, and we could free ourselves.

I worked my way back. When I got back near the ledge, something caught my eye. I could swear there was a dim light of some sort deeper into the cave. I was talking to Marie as I approached the ledge, but didn't want to say anything about what I was seeing, knowing it was likely my mind playing more tricks on me. Then I heard Marie in a muffled voice say, "Jake, is that a light?'

"Oh my goodness, Marie, I thought it was just me. I'm going to go that way and see!"

I quickly felt my way along the ledge and went a little further into the cave. Marie was talking, but my mind wasn't able to comprehend her words. All my attention was on what lay ahead. I could hear water, mud, and small rocks falling, then there was more light. Although it wasn't much light, it was blinding. I had to put my hand over my eyes until I was able to adjust to the brightness.

"Marie," I cried out, "It's really a light!"

Marie yelled out with joy as she eased off the ledge and felt her way to my location. We inched our way closer to the light source. It was coming from up above. The ceiling of the large domed room had fallen. The material that had fallen out was heaped up on the floor of the cave. The fallen rock and mud was cone shaped as if it had fallen through an hourglass.

Water and mud were still dripping from up above. As the material fell away, it had broken through to the ground above, letting light shine in. The hole was getting a bit larger as the mud slid through the opening. Fresh warm air was blowing in from the ground above. It invigorated us and gave us hope. We took in deep breaths of the fresh air. We were both overwhelmed with joy, in the hope that we could dig our way out of the cave and live. Yes, live to see another day - another sunrise and sunset.

We remained in the same spot for several hours as material continually dripped from the hole above. We didn't want to climb up the rubble pile as long as rock and mud was still falling. We were afraid a large rock would fall out and hit us. We could also easily cause a catastrophic failure of the ground above, and be buried in rock and mud.

Finally, the rocks and mud stopped falling. I climbed on top of the mound of rubble beneath the hole and peered up. I could see tree roots higher up protruding out of the ground around the perimeter of the hole. The opening to the ground above was about ten to twelve feet higher than the top of the mound of rubble lying on the cave floor.

The soil that had fallen from the hole, along with water, had formed a soupy mud. I kept sliding off from the mound and sinking into the muddy mire. Marie and I gathered rocks surrounding the bottom of the mound and piled them together in one place, so we could climb up into the hole. That task took several hours and I don't know where we found the strength to do the work.

Standing on top of the pile of rubble, I lifted Marie onto my shoulders and pushed her up into the small opening. As I held my hands over my head, supporting her feet, she was able to grab the roots and climb up. It took all the strength I had left to lift her. I was about to collapse, and drop her. Suddenly, I felt her weight being lifted off my hands. Clumps of mud and water continued to fall down hitting me in the head. Finally, Marie reached the top and climbed through the opening onto the ground above. Her voice was muffled coming down through the hole in the ground, but I could hear her rejoicing as she lay on the ground, totally exhausted, but having escaped from the hell below.

Once she caught her breath, she looked back down into the hole as I looked up to her. Her hair was matted and full of mud and twigs, and her face looked hollow from the days we had spent in the cold cave with no food, but to me, she was more beautiful at that moment than ever before. She laughed, and the sweetness of her voice was back. I knew we were going to survive this tragedy.

She told me a large tree had fallen. The trunk must have dislodged the root system to create the hole out of which she had just climbed. I didn't remember ever seeing trees on top of the rock formation. Of course, there was always a fog there to conceal them. If that were the case though, trees would have extended higher than the fog bank. That too didn't make sense to me.

I started thinking about how we'd get off the cliff top once we cleared the hole. We were going to be on top of the slick walled butte, with no way to get down. We'd come too far though not to figure that out. I had to get out of the cave first. Then we'd worry about getting back down to the ground.

I asked Marie to find a vine or something she could lower into the hole, so I could climb up. It was several feet up to where the roots were sticking out of the ground, and I couldn't reach them. She found a substantial tree limb that had broken off the fallen tree. She stripped the smaller branches off and lowered the long limb into the hole. The limb wasn't long enough to reach from the mound of rubble to the top of the hole, but it was long enough to get me up to the roots hanging above.

Climbing up the limb was difficult, and I fell off twice before reaching the roots on my third attempt. My body was weak and aching. I had to rest before continuing. Finally, I was able to get both arms on the ground outside the hole and pull upward as I wiggled through the opening.

As my head cleared the top, I could immediately tell the air had a different smell, but then I'd been in the damp air of the cave for more than three days. As I cleared the hole, I rolled over onto my back trying to catch my breath from the hard climb.

Marie was on the other side of the uprooted tree as I cleared the hole. She was trying to say something as she rushed over to me. She was talking too fast, and I didn't understand what she was trying to say. She looked at me and realized I didn't understand what she had spoken, so she repeated herself, only slower that time. "Someone has been here before!" she exclaimed.

I thought she must be confused, forgetting we were on top of the butte now.

"What do you mean?" I asked, with a puzzled look on my face.

"The tree that fell has writing on it, a carving. It's hard to make out the letters, but I think it says, "Welcome to Burning Rock."

My heart was pounding as I listened to her words.
Suddenly, I heard something I'd not heard in many years -
In the distance, a train whistle blew.

The End

ABOUT THE AUTHOR

Mingo Twain spent his childhood growing up in the wild and wonderful mountains of Southern West Virginia. Fortunately, for him, he has a caring family that stands by each other. He has a wonderful mother, unlike the one in Burning Rock.

He currently resides on a small lake in McCalla, Alabama, where he enjoys sitting in the evenings on his deck. With notebook in hand, he overlooks the calm peaceful water as he pens wild tales for your reading pleasure.

He enjoys the lighter side of things. When asked why he likes to write he responds, "I can't dance, and it's too wet to plow."

Thank you for taking time to read my work. I hope you enjoyed this book and the ones to follow.

Mingo Twain.